Storm Coming

PRAISE FOR *STORM COMING*

"*Storm Coming* is a first-rate historical novel, well researched and delightfully perceptive. Jack Lewis has crafted an artful account of the early action in 'Western' Virginia—one of the most compelling and overlooked chapters of the Civil War."
—W. Hunter Lesser, author of *Rebels at the Gate*

"...a wonderfully detailed book that comes at the twisted, confusing history of western Virginia as a story teller would, following key historic characters, both Union and Confederate, as they negotiate the political and military realities of this civil war within the Civil War."
—Matthew A. D. Borders, historian and Certified Battlefield Guide for Antietam National Battlefield

"Lewis's heroes all have heart and are sympathetic even in their flaws. The writing covers complicated scenarios with clear, strong wording... And although the subject matter is at times bleak, the darkness is undercut with a dry but hearty sense of humor that even a humble layman such as myself can appreciate. I would recommend it to anyone who is curious about the history of our area, or anyone who's simply looking for a good yarn."
—*New Castle Record*

"*Storm Coming* is one of the best historical novels I have read this year. The story was very well handled by Jack W. Lewis; the character development was wonderfully crafted. Alexander's journey was poignant and very believable, mainly because it is based on a true story and because Mr. Lewis brought the character to life with his sharp words and supreme handle on the story. This novel was truly tremendous."
—Rabia Tanveer for *Readers' Favorite*

A READERS' FAVORITE FIVE-STAR NOVEL

Storm Coming

A novel of the Civil War in western Virginia

JACK W. LEWIS

and

CAROL S. LEWIS
CONTRIBUTING EDITOR

SURBER PRESS

This is a work of historical fiction. Most characters are real and most events actually happened on the dates indicated. Conversations between characters are fictional and solely the product of the imagination of the author. Any resemblance to current events or locale, or to living persons, is entirely coincidental.

Published by Surber Press, Eagle Rock, Virginia
www.surberpress.com

ISBN: 978-0-9897139-2-4

Cover design by Jack W. Lewis
The image of the cavalryman on the cover is from a painting by Edwin Forbes in 1864 titled *Cavalry Orderly, Rappahannock Station, Va.* Forbes was commissioned by the Federal government to sketch and paint live scenes during the Civil War. This painting once belonged to J.P. Morgan. He gifted his collection in 1919 to the Library of Congress.

Printed in the United States of America   2 3 4 5 6 7 8 9 10

This book is dedicated to the memory of

Alexander J. Swaney
and
Harrison H. Hagans

Smithfield, Pennsylvania cavalrymen
who fought to save the Union
and
the citizens of western Virginia.

Thank you.

ACKNOWLEDGMENTS

This book would simply not exist without my wife, Carol Lewis. She is an avid reader of novels, an author, a professional editor, and once ran her own book publishing business. Ever mindful of keeping me busy so my brain doesn't atrophy, she suggested we take a course together in writing a novel. An engineer writing a novel? It just didn't seem to fit with the technical books I write. But I like challenges and gave it a try. I got hooked and started writing about a subject I've always loved, the American Civil War. Thank you, Carol!

And many thanks to those who helped by reviewing the manuscript and offering suggestions. My Coast Guard Academy classmate and former roommate, Richard Zins, was a big help. Not only did he find typos and misspellings, he offered many valuable suggestions. I think he has suffered through three drafts and as I write, he is laboring though the final chapter. Thank you, Dick!

Other friends and family have helped with edits and suggestions. Lynne Friedmann, Jim Surber, Frank DeBord, Jr., Eric Surber, Paul Russell (also a Coast Guard Academy classmate), and Matt Shears were very helpful. Matt is working on his doctorate of divinity and was kind enough to review the sermons I wrote for Harrison Hagans, the Methodist Episcopal minister who joins the same cavalry company as my protagonist. Thanks to all of you for your help!

I am also indebted to the folks at the West Virginia Archives who created a detailed website of the day-to-day birth of the "Child of the Rebellion." They preserved an inspiring story that I think all Americans should read and understand. They freely make historic images and photos available and several are theme images used in the first page of each chapter.

I am also grateful to the authors of the books listed in the bibliography at the back of this book. They provided reams of valuable information and insights.

And a big "thank you" to my readers. I hope you enjoy the book. Please write if you have any suggestions or comments.

TO THE READER

This is essentially a story of the creation of the state of West Virginia, told from the viewpoint of a young farmer living in Smithfield, Pennsylvania, and from viewpoints of the many men who fought in the western Virginia mountains or debated in the meeting halls of Wheeling and Richmond.

The firing on Fort Sumter on April 12, 1861 by the state of South Carolina changed the lives of everyone in the United States. The people who lived in western Virginia and bordering counties in Pennsylvania and Ohio were particularly affected, because a convention of state delegates in Richmond was in session trying to decide if Virginia would secede from the Union and join the already formed Confederacy, or stay in the Union. The fate of Virginia hung in the balance.

This little-known story is told as a novel so readers can hear the characters, know what they are thinking, and feel their emotions. I did not simply imagine characters and events. Most of the events are historically accurate in time and place and the principal characters all lived during those times.

In my research, I found many different versions of the battles and events. I list the literature consulted at the end of the book. I tried to avoid historical "opinions" by going back to the words of the people involved, their letters, their testimonies and the words of responsible newspaper editors and other documents. I did not intentionally change any facts. I condensed battle scenes, convention sessions, town meetings, proclamations, and eliminated many minor characters. When I had to choose between conflicting viewpoints, I depended most heavily on words written as close to the time of the event as possible. The interpretation of characters, and the dialogue between them, where not supported by historical documents, is entirely my own creation.

As there are a lot of characters in the book from both sides of the war, military ranks and terms can become confusing. In the back of the book a section titled MILITARY RANKS AND TERMINOLOGY, and a table listing ranks of key officers and their attributes, provide further information. If you are unfamiliar with military ranks of the Civil War or the differences between such terms as *unionist, secessionist, militia,* and *regulars,* please read this section before beginning the novel. I assume the reader knows the difference between North and South, and that northern solders were called "yankees" or "yanks" or sometimes "bluebellies" and southern solders were called "rebels" or "rebs," or sometimes "secesh" or "sesh."

JACK W. LEWIS

CHAPTER ONE

All God's Children

June 30, 1863, April 14–15, 1861

South Carolina Artillery Firing on Fort Sumter April 12, 1861

TUESDAY, JUNE 30, 1863, 12 NOON
CEMETERY HILL, GETTYSBURG, PENNSYLVANIA

Damnable heat! The noonday sun beat down on the men and their horses. Private Alexander J. Swaney—AJ to those who knew him well—sweated, soaking through his shirt and navy shell jacket. Even his trousers were damp with perspiration. His horse, Shiloh, had to be even hotter, carrying all of his gear, a heavy blanket, saddle and rider for days as they had kept watch over Lee's army, now invading Pennsylvania. AJ wanted to dismount, let his horse graze on the lush grass growing up around the granite headstones in front of them, but now wasn't the time. Next to him sat his commander, General John Buford, erect and tanned and also sweating, astride his horse, Grey Eagle. Buford peered through his field glasses at the grey-clad soldiers in the distance marching toward a red-brick building with a white cupola.

Brigade commander Bill Gamble also watched. Lowering his field glasses he said, loud enough so Buford and all of his staff could hear, "That's infantry, General, not a scouting party… looks about the size of a brigade to me."

"I don't see any cavalry," Buford replied. "Do you, Bill?"

"No, that's odd. Infantry marching alone in enemy territory without a cavalry screen."

AJ gazed at the distant soldiers, the pastoral countryside, and the town. They sat next to a cemetery on good high ground and everyone on Buford's staff—dedicated, dependable and experienced fighters—recognized that fact. These were men AJ knew well. Like him, most of them had been with General Buford for numerous engagements and trusted his judgment and courage. They knew he wouldn't turn away from a fight, but he always looked out for the welfare of his men. AJ counted himself lucky to have been assigned as an orderly to such a man in these dangerous times.

Captains Keogh and O'Keefe, Buford's "Irish Twins," were soldiers of fortune who had been acquainted with AJ's ancestral family back in Ireland. He knew them, along with Captains Gaskell, Wadsworth and Morrow, to be gallant, tough, hard-riding fighters. They were also here with their general. All of these warriors understood the importance of the high ground they were on—from here their army could halt Lee's invasion of Pennsylvania... *if only we can hold them off long enough*, AJ thought.

"General, if we're looking for a place to fight the rebels, this sure looks like wonderful ground," said Gamble.

Buford nodded. "And I suspect those rebels down there are looking at us, saying the same thing. We have only two brigades and Reynolds with his 1st Infantry corps is a day's march away."

"Look!" Gamble pointed down, raising his glasses again. "The rebels are turning around, heading back where they came from. Surely they're not running from us?"

"I suspect they're under orders not to engage us until their armies are massed. Lee may be turning his men away from Harrisburg and heading here to Gettysburg. If he does, he will be here in force tomorrow morning, trying to grab this high ground," Buford said. AJ admired Buford's almost uncanny ability to assess military situations, forecast the reactions of other leaders, and develop successful strategies to cope with them. He was willing to bet the general would turn out to be right in his predictions.

"General, do we dare try to hold this place until Reynold's corps arrives?" asked Gamble.

"We need to ride down there and take a look at those hills. I owe Reynolds a dispatch but I want to send him all the information we can gather, so he can decide what to do. If we try to hold back a rebel infantry corps, they could destroy our two cavalry brigades before Reynolds reaches us… Private Swaney, ride down this hill and tell Colonel Devin to bring up his brigade and meet us in the town."

AJ was familiar to everyone in Buford's 1st Cavalry division as one of the General's most trusted orderlies, and one who shared Buford's exceptional love of horses. They knew him as a modest man, an excellent rider and marksman, with a reputation for speaking "horse lingo," of being able to get a horse to do just about anything. The horses under his care stayed well and sound.

As he approached Colonel Devin's brigade with his orders, AJ prepared himself to be the butt of yet another of the colonel's jokes. Devin was a likable leader, a ruddyfaced Irishman who enjoyed light, often bawdy, banter with the men. Especially the quieter, shyer men like AJ, who were easy to embarrass with his style of humor.

Saluting, AJ said, "Colonel Devin, sir, General Buford sends his regards and wishes you to move your brigade up and meet him near the Seminary, that red-brick building with the white cupola. Rebel infantry up ahead, but they're retiring down the Cashtown Road."

"Thank you, acknowledged, Private Swaney," Devin replied. "Say, I've been meaning to ask you—how d'you keep that fine-looking animal so shiny and clean?"

Sensing that one of Devin's jibes was coming, AJ chose to parry, keeping a straight face. "It's simple, Colonel. I taught my horse how to wash himself like a cat."

Devin and his staff roared, as AJ turned his horse to ride away. He wasn't fast enough. Devin called, "Hold on there, Swaney! Ride with me a moment. I've got a story for you. Did you hear the one about the General's wife and the parrot?" Grimacing, AJ fell in with the colonel, steeling himself for another ribald bar joke of the sort Devin favored. AJ had come to understand that this crude levity was one of the common defenses some men had against the ever-present fear of death.

He listened, laughed, and made his escape from Devin, riding back to Buford and hovering nearby in case he was needed. AJ knew he wouldn't get much sleep that night. General Buford would be up till the early hours of the morning, riding about the moonlit countryside to get the lay of the land, sending more dispatches and gathering intelligence. AJ thought of the battle to come. Cavalrymen would be killed or wounded tomorrow morning. Another full-scale slaughter would begin, here in this peaceful little town.

He spent a few moments thinking about the pretty face of the girl he loved and hoped to wed when all this was over. Then he prayed for success on the battlefield and safety for General Buford and his staff.

He thought of the promises he'd made to his family and his sweetheart, not to take any "unnecessary risks." He wondered what determined whether a risk on the battlefield could be considered "necessary." At this point, two years into the War of the Rebellion, he had risked his life many times, and he knew tomorrow would be no exception.

He hummed the old hymn "How Firm a Foundation," a hymn of fortitude, of courage. It took him back to the early days of April in 1861, when he first heard about the firing on Fort Sumter, the event that had forever changed his life.

SUNDAY APRIL 14, 1861 9:30 AM
SMITHFIELD, FAYETTE COUNTY, PENNSYLVANIA
UNION METHODIST EPISCOPAL CHURCH

"Has a war really started? I can't believe this is happening to our country!"

AJ mumbled to himself as he hunched along on the muddy road to church, barely noticing the gusts of wind and scattered raindrops pelting him. News of South Carolina firing on Fort Sumter two days past had spread like wildfire, reaching his small village of Smithfield in Fayette County, Pennsylvania yesterday evening. Now there were rumors that

Virginia might secede from the Union and join the Southern Confederacy, formed in February by the cotton states of South Carolina, Mississippi, Alabama, Florida and Louisiana. "A new country? And if Virginia joins it'll be just a few miles away from us. It's hard to believe!"

His mind churned. He thought of himself as a simple man, with a simple life and simple desires. He wanted nothing more than to work his family's farm, get the planting and harvesting done on time, care for their stock, and eventually marry the girl he loved. Sophia. The thought of her took his mind away momentarily from impending war, to a vision of her frank blue eyes, the same blue as the distant mountains.

Sophia's family owned the farm adjacent to the Swaney place, and AJ had known her for most of her life. Until now, she had been the focus of his thoughts about the future. But these bewildering events in South Carolina had added a new and very unpleasant complication to his formerly uncomplicated life. *What if Virginia does secede? Morgantown, Virginia, is just a half day's ride from Smithfield, and Wheeling not all that far away.*

"This could be a disaster. Our county borders Virginia," AJ mumbled. "Will their armies attack us? Will our armies attack them?"

"Alexander Swaney!" His mother tugged at his sleeve. "What are you *muttering* about? Do you even know you're talking to yourself? Can't you be a little more sociable this Sabbath morning?"

"Sorry, Ma." AJ blinked and looked down at his mother, a tiny woman but always a force to be reckoned with. She only called him by his full name when she was irritated. He took her arm and tucked it under his and tried to smile at her. The rest of his family, and several neighbors who had joined them along the way, hurried together toward the white frame church ahead, to escape the cold spring rain, coming down even harder now. Everyone was quieter than usual, AJ noticed. And it wasn't just because of the rain. *Probably lost in their own worries about war, just like me,* he figured.

Other churchgoers joined them at the door, nodding and greeting each other as they wiped their feet, shook the rain from their capes, hats and jackets, and entered the vestibule. The pastor, Harrison Hagans, greeted AJ with a big smile and AJ smiled back. His spirits were always lifted by the man, who had become universally liked and admired in Smithfield as an inspiring preacher and a good neighbor since he had arrived to take over the little church a year ago. The young pastor's services were well-attended, as folks came from all around, even from other denominations, to hear his thoughtful sermons. He spoke like he was talking to friends, AJ thought. He could tell Harry always told the truth as he believed it to be. Most people called Hagans "Reverend," but AJ knew him simply as Harry and thought of him almost as an older, wiser brother.

AJ felt a hand on his shoulder and turned around to see his cousin William Swaney, known to all as "Tip." "Cousin AJ! You're looking a little waterlogged," he said with a smirk.

"I'm surprised to see you at church, Tip," AJ responded, none too warmly. Tip ignored the comment, looking past AJ to scan the crowd. AJ figured he was looking for Sophia and the thought riled him. The cousins had been competitors all their lives and recently Tip had decided to compete with AJ for the affections of Sophia.

"She ain't coming to church today," AJ said, a little smug in his inside knowledge, told to him by his sister Cynthia, Sophia's best friend.

Tip's head whipped around. "What? Who?"

"Sophia. That's who you're looking for, ain't it? Her grandma ain't doing so good and she and her ma rode out to see about her this morning."

AJ could see that he had hit the mark, as Tip appeared crestfallen. AJ almost felt sorry for him. He knew his cousin would never have come all the way to Smithfield to go to church in the rain, if not for the chance to "make time" with the girl that AJ considered his own. Tip glanced toward the front of the sanctuary, eyeing the Reverend. AJ figured he was looking to see whether he could yet make an escape before Harry spotted him. He knew his cousin well.

"Now, Tip, you ain't going to try to give the Lord the slip, are you?" AJ grabbed him by the arm. "He ain't some little girl you can run out on, like you always do."

AJ had to admit he was deeply concerned about Tip's new interest in Sophia, but he wasn't going to give his cousin the satisfaction of letting him know it. He and Tip were almost the same age—AJ would turn 21 in a few days and Tip in just four months. They had played together and fought together all their lives, competing to see who was the strongest, the fastest, the toughest, the best rider, the best shot. AJ came out ahead on strength, riding and hunting, but Tip could beat him in a footrace. And since Tip had learned to fiddle, he'd become a real lady's man, which AJ had never been. AJ was quiet, sturdy and dark where Tip was boisterous, lanky and blonde, and Tip had about 2 inches on him, which rankled. The females seemed to like Tip's joshing, smooth talk and his fiddling, singing and dancing. He had women sweet on him all over the county.

But AJ was different. He had his eye on just one woman. Sophia. AJ's sister Cynthia was the same age as Sophia and the two girls had rambled the two farms together almost as soon as they could walk, holding hands, sharing secrets, always underfoot. Sophia was sprightly and fun-loving as a girl, and made him laugh. He couldn't remember when he noticed that she had turned from a gangly tomboy into a curvaceous, fresh-faced young woman. After that he had kept his eye on her for a long while before getting up his courage to pay her a compliment, let her know that he *had* noticed. She had laughed at him then, but she obviously enjoyed the attention and began to bat her eyes at AJ from time to time. After her sixteenth birthday last year, she had often let AJ walk her home from church and last fall she'd agreed to accompany him to a frolic at the Barnhill place on the other side of Smithfield. She was easy to be with, and didn't make him anxious and worried like most other girls did, as he tried to think of something witty or smart to say to them. Sophia talked a lot herself, so he didn't have to say much. His regard for her had grown steadily.

Sophia turned 17 last month, and since then AJ had been working up the gumption to talk to her about marriage. He had done nothing more than hold her hand occasionally, and that only to help her over a fence or through a gate during their rambles, but AJ dreamed that she wanted just what he wanted—to stay there in Smithfield, live on the farm and raise a family together.

Tip had only recently become an obstacle in these plans. AJ hadn't seen much of him the last couple of years since he had started courting so heavily and playing his fiddle at dances and barn raisings and weddings. He was much in demand. Rumors floated that Tip had gotten a girl in the family way and AJ believed it. AJ always knew he had Tip beat in the morals department.

But a few weeks ago, a cloud had descended. Sophia had agreed to go with AJ to a barn dance between Smithfield and Fairchance, the first frolic in the neighborhood after the long winter. He had washed the little buggy and groomed his horse Shiloh till he shone. AJ had thought perhaps this was the night when he would find the nerve to talk about marriage. It turned out that Tip was playing the fiddle at the dance. Sophia had spotted him right off. "Ain't that your cousin, Tip?" she'd asked. AJ had to admit that Tip did look extra good that night. He wore a flashy silk bow tie, and he laughed and sang and played his fiddle the best AJ had ever heard him play. At a break in the music, Sophia had said, "Let's go over and speak to him," and grabbed AJ's hand and pulled him over to where Tip stood, mopping his forehead with a big red bandanna. AJ saw Tip look her up and down and then grin at her, like AJ wasn't even standing there. Sophia had dropped AJ's hand like a hot potato and grinned back at Tip. AJ could feel his rejected fingers curling into a fist, ready to punch that grin right off his cousin's face.

"Well, well," said Tip with a leer. "How grown-up you are now, Miss Sophie. Let's you and me get us a drink and catch up."

"It's Sophia," she replied, laughing, but she had let Tip take her arm and lead her over to a table in the corner holding a bucket and a gourd dipper. AJ could feel his face go hot as he trailed behind them awkwardly. He could read on Sophia's face that she was enjoying Tip's flirtatious banter—the kind of thing AJ wasn't good at, he knew. She looked even prettier than usual and Tip couldn't take his eyes off her. AJ had a sick, sour feeling in his gut. *Tip's only doing this because he knows I like her...*

Fortunately the dancers soon grew restless and Tip was called back to fiddle duty. Sophia wanted to dance. AJ hung back—dancing was something else he wasn't much good at—but she persisted and showed him the steps, laughing at his clumsy efforts. He sunk deeper into gloom as the night went on and made an excuse to leave early. On the buggy ride home, Sophia had asked him question after question about Tip. He replied with vague, one-word answers. "What's the matter? Cat got your tongue?" She tried to tease him out of his black mood, but AJ was hurt, confused and thoroughly angry at Tip. It certainly hadn't been a night to bring up marriage.

To make matters worse, his sister had told him that Tip had called on Sophia at home last Tuesday. *And now here he is at church, of all places, looking for her again!*

* * *

AJ tightened his grip on Tip's arm and, putting an artificial smile on his face, he maneuvered them both toward an empty pew near the back. "Come on, *Cousin* Tip," he said. "The service is about to start. And me and you need to do some talkin' afterwards." He gave Tip's arm a final squeeze, noticing with satisfaction that his cousin winced, and then let him go. They took their seats on the wooden pew. AJ resolved to focus on the worship instead of his jealousy of Tip. He did look forward to hearing Harry's sermon today, especially in light of the recent political storm. The young pastor's messages frequently interpreted important current events, and AJ was hoping he would address the matter of South Carolina firing on Fort Sumter in today's sermon. *If anyone can make sense of all this, Harry can,* he thought.

As the minister stepped up into the pulpit, he motioned to the woman playing hymns on a small pump organ at the front of the church. She stopped the music and Harry paused while the congregation grew quiet. Then, in a booming voice that reverberated from the walls of the church and seemed to echo in AJ's chest, he spoke. "These are the times that try men's souls." He paused for at least a minute in the dead silence that followed, allowing the words from Thomas Paine to fill the minds of the listeners. AJ wondered if those were tears he could see glistening in Harry's eyes. Then the Reverend, speaking in a somewhat softer voice, seemed to AJ to be aiming his words directly at him.

"I know from searching my own heart that you all must be gravely concerned for the welfare of your family and your livelihood. The firing on Fort Sumter by the State of South Carolina is an act of *war*. An act, I fear, that will bring forth a decisive reaction by our new President.

"Nearby are Virginians who have always been our friends. As most of you know, I came here from Virginia and my family still lives there. I've spoken with folks in Morgantown, Wheeling, and Parkersburg and know that they have felt estranged for many years from Richmond and eastern Virginia. Yet, they are truly Virginians and their Governor Letcher has called a convention, now in session in Richmond, to study whether or not Virginia should vote to secede from our great country. Almost unthinkable! All counties in Virginia, including the western counties, are represented at this convention. The delegates to the convention voted just ten days ago *not* to secede. That was good news indeed.

"But now I understand the delegates are planning to vote *again* three days from now. We know not how the Virginia delegates will vote this time, so we can only wait and see, and pray that they will vote again to keep the great state of Virginia in these United States. But what if the delegates approve an Ordinance of Secession, as many now fear they will? The slave-holding counties of eastern Virginia are powerful and have profitable businesses built on the backs of their slaves. The Virginia counties west of the Alleghenies have few slaves. These Virginians, like us here in Fayette County, depend on their livelihood from farming, trade among themselves, and trade with the bordering states of Pennsylvania, Ohio, and Kentucky.

"I ask you to take a moment now and close your eyes. Put yourself in the shoes of our Virginia friends living in the northwestern part of Virginia, just south of us. Ask yourself if you feel safe in Morgantown, or Wheeling, or Parkersburg, or any of the towns and villages near those cities. Think about that 250-mile-long border with the State of Ohio, separated only by the Ohio River, and the 150-mile-long border with Pennsylvania, separated only by an imaginary line in the dirt. Do you fear the possibility of an invasion from Federal armies coming from those two states?" He paused and looked at the faces in front of him. "Most likely you do. So, you see, as we may fear the possibility of invasion from a Confederate Virginia, if she does secede from our Union, northwestern Virginians surely fear an invasion from us who live in Pennsylvania and Ohio.

"So let us not be hasty in our judgments of those Virginians living in northwestern Virginia. Let us instead go back to our homes and gather our families and loved ones around us. Discuss all your thoughts and fears and, above all, let's stay calm. If you have friends or family in Virginia, pray for them, and write to them and openly discuss your concerns. Invite them to discuss theirs with you. I will speak again next Sunday about the events of this coming week and any other developments that may come to pass.

"Above all, do not let fear dominate you for God has not given us a spirit of fear. Remember what David wrote in Psalm 46: 'God is our refuge and strength, a very present help in trouble.'"

Conflicting thoughts swirled through AJ's mind during the rest of Harry's sermon, and the singing and prayers that followed. *Harry thinks Virginia may secede. If that happens, we will certainly be at war with our neighbors. But Harry said folks in the northwestern Virginia counties have not been getting along with folks east of the Alleghenies for a long time. Does that mean the northwestern counties in Virginia won't secede? How could that happen?*

At the end of the service he glanced at Tip sitting next to him, his head tilted backwards, eyes almost closed. He had seen his cousin nod and doze several times during the sermon. AJ poked him in the arm and said, "Come on, Tip. Outside." AJ wasn't sure what he would say or do—this was the Sabbath and he was at church after all—but he fully intended to speak his piece about Sophia.

The two young men both stood, stretched, grabbed their hats, and walked toward the door at the rear of the church. Harry was already there, shaking hands with his flock as he did after every service. Tip slipped through the crowd ahead of AJ, avoiding the pastor's eye. Harry laid a hand on AJ's arm as he moved past to follow Tip and said, "Could you wait for me just a moment outside, AJ? I'd like a word with you."

AJ nodded his agreement and called to his mother to go ahead without him, that he would catch up shortly. The rain had finally stopped. He looked around and spotted Tip at the edge of the churchyard, wiping the moisture from his buggy seat and untying his mare. AJ's long strides carried him to the buggy quickly. "Just hold on a minute there," he said. "I've got a bone to pick with you."

Tip turned and faced him. "And what would that be, Cousin? Are you going to pick a fight here in the churchyard? What would our dear Lord think of that?" He laughed maliciously.

AJ's hand curled again into a fist but he succeeded in maintaining control. "Miss Mosier and I are seein' each other, which you well know. What do you mean by calling on her this past week, and why were you lookin' for her today?"

Tip laughed again. "As far as I know, she's a free woman, and a mighty purty one too. Fair game. Unless she's engaged herself to the likes of you since I last spoke with her? No, I didn't think so. Didn't think she'd be that foolish." He raised his bushy brows and stared AJ down.

AJ looked daggers at Tip for a moment, gritting his teeth, then averted his eyes and turned to walk away.

Tip jumped into the buggy and clucked to his mare. "Let the better man win!" he called over his shoulder.

AJ turned back, a sudden thought entering his head. "Tip, what about that Martin girl over in Haydentown? Ain't you going to marry her? Do the right thing?"

He could hear his cousin laughing heartily as he headed the buggy down the road toward Haydentown.

AJ clenched both fists and yelled toward the departing buggy, "If you hurt Sophia, so help me I'll…"

"AJ!"

He spun around to see the pastor standing behind him, frowning. "Is there something you'd like to talk about, my friend?" he asked.

AJ shook his head and tried to slow his breathing. "Not right now, Harry," he said, taking a deep breath. "Maybe later. What did you want to see me about?"

Harry hesitated a moment before answering, and AJ began to feel uneasy under the pastor's steady gaze. Then Harry said, "I'm doing my rounds tomorrow to the shut-ins and the elderly, and I was wondering if you might be able to ride with me."

AJ scratched his head, thinking of the chores awaiting him, then replied, "Yes… I would surely like that. I think it'll be all right with Pa. It'll be too wet for plowing tomorrow anyhow. I'll just have to feed the stock and milk the cows at first light, before we leave. What time?"

"About 8 AM."

"I'll have Shiloh saddled and be ready to go. Meet up at our place?"

"Yes. By the way, AJ, I've been meaning to ask, have you been making wedding plans with Sophia Mosier?"

The younger man was shocked and flustered. *Can he read my mind? Has Sophia been talking with the pastor?* he wondered. AJ swallowed hard and stammered, "Well… not exactly. But I'm surely thinking about it." He looked down the road where Tip's buggy could still be seen in the distance, and then turned back to Harry. "Has *she* said somethin' to you?" he asked, hopeful.

"No, no," Harry answered, "but I can see it in *your* eyes when you look at her. She's grown into quite a lovely young woman."

Suddenly AJ's mind was gripped by a shocking thought: "*You* ain't interested in marryin' her, are you?"

Harry laughed out loud. "That's one thing you *don't* have to worry about, AJ!"

"She just turned 17, you know," AJ said, sheepish at being laughed at but relieved that he didn't have another potential competitor. "I been thinking real hard about asking Mr. Mosier for her hand, but I'm just not sure getting engaged or marryin' is such a good idea right now. These rebels firin' on Fort Sumter has got me real worked up, Harry." *And that ain't the only thing that's got me worked up.* He thought about Tip's laughter and imagined punching him in the nose.

"I understand, believe me." Harry gripped AJ's shoulder firmly. "If I can be of help, let me know. And don't underestimate the power of prayer, my friend. By the way, AJ, please keep in mind that calling the South Carolinians 'rebels' is a little demeaning. After all, folks in Charleston were the first to treat the British to a tea party in their own harbor, even before the Boston party. I suspect they believe they have the right to secede from the Union they helped to create, even though I would argue with them that secession will only create more problems, not solve them. This whole issue of slavery, I think, will end up tearing our country apart. It's an evil that will test our Constitution and our moral fiber. After all, our founding fathers did agree that *all* men are created equal, didn't they?"

AJ stared at the pastor, slack-jawed. He often felt when talking with Harry that his brain lagged so far behind that he had no chance of ever catching up. AJ blinked and said, "Well…"

Harry laughed. "Just a thought. Sometimes I get carried away. See you tomorrow at 8 sharp."

AJ waved farewell and quickly caught up to his family on the road to home, about a mile from the church. The rain had started again but was now just a light mist. They all walked gingerly, skirting the mud puddles, discussing the Reverend's sermon, and passing greetings to their neighbors.

SUNDAY APRIL 14, 1861 6:00 PM

SWANEY FARM, SMITHFIELD, PENNSYLVANIA

After supper that evening, AJ's mother and sisters cleared the table. His father James announced, "Like the Reverend said, I think we should all be gatherin' in the parlor and talking about this war that might be comin'."

James and AJ pulled in chairs and stools from the kitchen to seat everyone. The small room felt crowded when they all gathered in it. AJ's parents had six children and four still lived at home. Their two oldest daughters, Elizabeth, 22, and Mary Jane, 18, were both married now and lived with their husbands. Alexander James, AJ, was their oldest son, their mainstay. Cynthia Ann, 16, worked hard helping her mother with the endless house and farm chores, even more so since her sisters had left home to start their own households. She was a tease and a constant promoter of romance between AJ and her bosom friend Sophia. AJ, in turn, liked to tease Cynthia, because he thought she was in love with Harry Hagans, although she would never admit it to him.

AJ's youngest sister Earsela, aged 13, was a quiet, self-contained girl, like AJ, although unlike AJ she spent most of her free time reading books when not doing her chores. She did well in school when the farm work allowed her to attend. Her ambition was to go to one of the new normal schools and become a teacher. The youngest, John Thomas, aged 12, was an earnest, talkative boy who worshiped AJ. He followed him like a puppy if permitted. Like Earsela, John still attended school when the farm work allowed it.

After everyone was seated, AJ's father poked up the fire and took his seat to start the family discussion: "I'm not so sure I believe this Fort Sumter thing will lead us to war. Even if it do come to that, the folks this side of the mountains, includin' them living in the west of Virginia, will most likely be left alone, because they don't own no slaves. Or not many anyway."

AJ's pa, James Swaney, was 45 and the son of Irish immigrants. He took great pride in his family, particularly his oldest boy, with his thrifty, hardworking ways, and he counted on AJ to take over the family farm someday. Other than Cynthia, James was the main promoter in the household of AJ's hopes of marrying Sophia. He already loved the neighbor girl like a daughter and believed she and AJ were well-suited for each other. And he made sure AJ knew it.

AJ's mother Ruth cleared her throat. Three years older than her husband, she made it a habit to let her husband speak first, but AJ knew it was her practical ideas that almost always held sway in family decisions.

Her forehead was still smooth and her hair, most always parted in the center and pulled into a knot at the back of her head, was thick and dark, with streaks of gray. Although a small-boned woman, she had knobby rough hands from the farm work and hid them in her apron. She rubbed grease on them and often lamented her thick knuckles.

She spoke up now. "I don't think it's going to be that simple, Jim. That's wishful thinkin' on your part, I believe. Those people in Richmond are rich slaveholders and if war does start, they'll come lookin' for soldiers out here in the western counties of Virginia, to fight that war for them. Then what're we goin' to do? We're just up the road from Morgantown. Why, they could come up here and force you and AJ to go off fightin' for them, for all we know."

AJ felt a hot, bright explosion in his chest. He jumped to his feet and shook his fist in the air. "Well, that ain't *never* gonna happen, Ma!" AJ shouted. "I'll *shoot* any rebel that tries to take me or Pa, or any of us, away from this farm!" AJ stood, shaking after his outburst, his arm in the air and his face turning scarlet. He tried to say more, but words didn't come. It seemed that his throat had seized up. He gasped for breath. Earsela and John burst into frightened tears. Cynthia stared at him, open-mouthed. They had never seen AJ so angry.

"Now, no more o' that, AJ! You're scare'n the chil'ren," his father commanded. "What's come over ye? I know ye mean well and everyone knows ye're a good shot with your rifle. But don't be talkin' of killin' people just yet. You all just calm down now and stop yer cryin'. Let's just put our heads together like, and think about gettin' ready for hardship, if it does come our way. Should we be hidin' extra food in places only we know about? Should we be lookin' for a place to hide our livestock? That kind of thing…"

After a long pause, during which the only sound was the two younger children snuffling, Cynthia spoke up. "Well, Pa, we could do more canning this fall, and maybe we could dig a hole in the ground out back and store some extra food, so only we know where it is."

John wiped his red eyes and sheepishly suggested, "Maybe AJ and I can look for some places to keep the animals up in the mountains, where no one could find them."

"That's the spirit," said their father, "and do ye have anything to add, Earsela, me lass?"

The girl's eyes were also red. She looked down at her lap for a moment, but then responded, "Yes, Pa. I think we need some way to alert us, and all our neighbors too, when enemy soldiers might be coming. I've read that horse soldiers can ride fast and make surprise raids. Maybe you and AJ could set up an alarm, with shotguns or some other sort of noise, that could warn everyone if enemy soldiers are coming our way. It might give us time to hide our animals in the woods, and hide our food."

AJ and his father stared at Earsela, and both nodded. James replied, "Earsela, me darlin', a stroke of genius! Me and AJ will see to settin' up somethin' like that. Now you all go up and get ready for bed. AJ, stay here a bit and talk with me."

While his mother and the children headed off to bed, AJ, sheepish, said, "Sorry for flyin' off the handle, Pa. I got a lot on my mind. Somethin' just snapped."

"Never mind that, son," his father replied, "apologies accepted. The Reverend mentioned to me today about ye ridin' out with him in the mornin'. Are ye goin'?"

"Yes, Pa, but I'll take care of all the morning chores so you don't have to get up so early. We plan to leave at 8 and I'll be back in time to do the evening feeding and milking."

"That's all right, son, I can take care of that if ye don't get back. I'm hopin' maybe you and the Reverend can talk some more 'bout this war comin' down on us. Maybe Ruth is right—I'm guilty of too much wishful thinkin'. I trust the two of ye to decide what's best for us all."

AJ nodded. "We're all confused right now—none of us knows just what might happen, Pa."

"Remember your Grandpa James came to this country years ago from Ireland, to git away from the fightin' between the Irish lads and the Johnny Bull English. He told me before he died that livin' here was the first time in his life he'd felt free. He said he sat down and cried the first time he saw slaves here, it scared him so, thinkin' that the Irish might somehow be made slaves too."

"Pa," AJ exclaimed, "that won't *ever* happen in America!"

"I sure hope not, son, but the stories yur Grandpa used to tell me scared me pretty good and they still stick inside me head. He used to call it 'comin' a storm' when those Johnny Bull soldiers came lookin' for our Irish lads. They would come to a house and tear it up and drag away anybody they thought was harborin' our lads. They th'owed old men and women in jail and leaved them there, whether they was guilty or not. They would give away the people's very homes. They did those crimes and got away with it all. My boy, is it any wonder the Irish are known to be fighters? Why, I think it's in our very blood. Look at you tonight, when you got all het up. And the way you and your cousin Tip used t' fight. Sometimes I thought you and him would kill each other!"

"Me and Tip were just kids then. But I might have to fight him again, Pa. Did you see him at church today? You know, he was only there because he wanted to see Sophia!" AJ felt his fists clench again, as though they had a life of their own. "I don't want to see her mixed up with him, Pa! Even if she don't choose me, I just couldn't *stand* to see her with him. He wouldn't treat her right."

"Well, son, you better be gettin' Sophia wed, like I told you before."

AJ sighed and collapsed onto a stool. He felt helpless. "I know, Pa. I was plannin' to ask her to marry me this fall, after harvest, but now this war talk has got me all confused. You talked about Grandpa and his 'storm a'coming'—well, that's how I feel. A bad storm is comin' our way, and there's no place for us to hide from it. I don't know what to do!"

MONDAY APRIL 15, 1861, 8:00 AM
AJ'S RIDE WITH HARRY, SMITHFIELD, PENNSYLVANIA

The Swaney farm was about a mile from the main road that Harry traveled when making his weekly visits. This main road was an old road that ran south to and through Morgantown and other towns in Virginia, and as far as Cumberland, Kentucky. To the north, the main road intersected the National Pike—providing easy access to the larger towns of Uniontown and Monroe—and ran as far north as the eastern side of Pittsburgh. The land over which these roads ran was rich farming land. In some places dark coal, mined in the area for fuel and coke production, could be harvested right from the surface of the ground and burned in fireplaces to provide heat for warmth and cooking.

Today AJ and Harry would travel the main road north to Uniontown, get on the National Pike to go east to Monroe, and then move south on a less-traveled mountain road from Monroe to Fairchance. From there it was an easy ride back to Smithfield. All together it was a round trip of about nine miles and would take up most of the day.

AJ awakened at 4:30 AM and listened for sounds of rain on the roof. Hearing nothing, he slid out of bed and put on his riding pants and a light woolen jacket. Downstairs he slipped into his boots and went out to the barn to feed the animals and milk the cows. He threw some corn to Buck and Sally, the stocky plow horses, and to Shiloh, his riding horse. After the chores were finished, he moved Shiloh out into the aisle of the barn, asking him to stand while he mucked out his stall.

Shiloh was a dark bay Morgan gelding that his father had bought him two years ago as a yearling. AJ had learned about Morgan horses from an older neighbor who owned one, and he had long wanted a Morgan that he could train himself. He knew they were descended from a stallion named Figure born in West Springfield, Massachusetts in 1789. Figure was owned by a man named Justin Morgan, from whom the breed got its name, and the horse had been legendary in his day—he could outwalk, outtrot, outpull and outrun all the other horses in the vicinity, and he was able to pass his superlatives on to his progeny. AJ was first attracted to Morgan horses because they were handsome and well behaved. They were a hearty breed with an impressive head and arched neck.

Shiloh was a fine example of the breed, he thought. The horse was now three years old, 15 hands and still growing, intelligent, muscled and sleek from AJ's nearly daily riding and frequent careful grooming. The gelding's smooth gaits were easy to sit and lately he had become an obedient and willing jumper of fences and small streams. AJ had spent hours training his horse, who now readily obeyed his soft voice commands. AJ had also broken him to harness and he had become a flashy buggy horse in addition to a riding mount. *This horse can do anything*, he thought with satisfaction.

This morning, after a thorough brushing to remove a few last vestiges of Shiloh's long winter coat, AJ searched everywhere on the body of the horse for cuts and bruises. He paid special attention to the hooves, making sure there were no cracks and that the shoes were on tightly. After grooming, AJ walked Shiloh outside the barn and then trotted him in a circle to make sure he was sound on all four legs. The horse stood obediently when AJ placed a blanket on his back, then the saddle. He willingly opened his mouth for the bit and AJ slipped the bridle headstock over his ears.

The sun was up now. Shiloh soon pricked his ears and turned his head to face down the road. "What do you see, boy? Is that Harry and Betsy coming up the lane?" AJ whispered. "I don't see anyone yet, but I know you do."

As he waited for Harry to appear, AJ thought about their friendship. Harry also loved to ride, although he always said AJ was twice the rider he was. The two occasionally rode out together through the countryside, but this was the first time for AJ to accompany Harry on his regular church rounds. The young pastor would visit with elder members of his flock who were no longer able to attend the Sunday church meetings, or with anyone else who needed help or counseling.

AJ often wished he were more like Harry. The two of them were different in so many ways. AJ was six feet tall—he had been a late grower, but now was taller than his pa by over an inch. He was sturdy, with ropy muscles and an unruly mat of straight black hair and brown eyes so dark the pupils weren't visible. People said AJ got his dark looks from the "black Irish." AJ wondered what "black Irish" meant and he wondered whether there was a trace of Indian blood on one side of the family or the other. In the summer his skin turned dark cinnamon. Harry was five years older than AJ and was a little shorter and stouter, with grey eyes and wavy, red-blond hair that grew lighter in the summer. His fair skin freckled and turned red in the sun.

The personalities of the two men were different too. AJ was naturally shy, "a bit backward," as his mother and sisters termed it, especially around the fair sex. Harry, on the other hand, was gregarious, warm and talkative. He laughed easily and loudly, and he loved to read, study and learn new things. He was drawn to words like AJ was drawn to horses. Hagans was a man who never talked down to anyone and treated all men, women and children with respect. "They are all God's children," he once told AJ, "and it is my job—and my privilege—to look after them."

A minute or so after Shiloh had heard their approach, Harry appeared on his mare. The two horses called to one another and Harry bellowed, "How are you, my dear friend, on this beautiful morning that God has made just for the four of us?"

AJ was used to Harry's loud voice and flowery speech. He smiled and said, "I feel all right today. The rain has stopped and Shiloh's rarin' to go."

"Well, perhaps we can jump a few fences and ford a few streams on our ride today. You ready?" Harry asked.

"Yep. I didn't eat too much this morning, since I know every stop we make, the lady of the house gives the preacher and his friend somethin' extra good to taste."

Harry laughed and they trotted together down the lane and onto the main road leading toward Uniontown. In between their stops to visit the shut-ins and elderly parishioners, AJ hoped to get a chance to talk seriously.

"AJ, what are your thoughts about my message yesterday?" Harry asked.

"Well, Pa took your advice and had us all talk last evening, about what we might do should there be a war." AJ looked down for a moment, pondering how much to tell Harry. Then he admitted, "I sorta made a fool of myself."

"Oh? In what way?"

"Ma said somethin' about the Virginians maybe coming up here to our farm and hauling me and Pa off to war to fight for them. I lost my head. I jumped up and said I would shoot anyone who tried to do that. I figure I hollered pretty loud, because Earsela and John busted out crying. Pa had to step in and calm us all down." He shook his head. "I need to learn how to hold my temper, Harry. It don't flare too often, but when it does, seems like I lose control of myself. And seems like it's happenin' more lately."

"Well, pray about it, AJ. The Lord can surely help you with self-control. And you might want to try my method. When I find myself getting mad, I slowly count to ten before I say anything at all. It gives me time to think before speaking. By the way, talking about shooting, have you ever shot anyone, AJ?"

"Aaah... no, but I've killed a lot of small animals and plenty of deer." For some reason AJ thought of the tiny bluebird he had killed with his slingshot as a young boy. He shuddered at the memory.

"God said in the Ten Commandments, 'Thou shalt not kill.'" Harry sighed and frowned. "It's a thorny question, my friend. Like you, I've never killed anyone, but I think there might be times when I could take someone's life. Perhaps I'll write a sermon soon on war and killing—I'm sure it's on many people's minds."

"I hope you do, Harry. It's somethin' that really bothers me. I could hardly believe it last night when I said I would shoot anybody that tried to force me and Pa to fight for them. By the way, last night Pa said I ought to talk with you some more about the war, and what we should do to get ready for it. He thought you might have some ideas. He's worried too."

Harry nodded, and began to tell AJ about what he had heard from some of his western Virginia pastor friends and their reactions to the Fort Sumter action.

"Is it all about slavery, Harry?" AJ asked.

"Slavery's a big part of it, but the South has other grievances."

"Pa also told me last night that his father once said to him that the first time he saw slaves, it made him cry. It seems Grandpa thought the Irish who live here might be turned into slaves too. I guess he had some real bad memories of the wars with the English and how our people were persecuted back in Ireland."

"I can't see anything like that ever happening here with the Irish, although I do hear about them being mistreated from time to time. Some men seem to find excuses to hate all folks that are different from themselves. However, tell your father I do share those feelings about slavery, as you already know."

Harry stood in his stirrups and pointed at the path ahead of them. "Can you jump over that gate up ahead, AJ? If so, I'll fall in behind you."

AJ turned Shiloh toward the gate. It was an intimidatingly high and solid log gate, but AJ knew his horse was up to it. He asked Shiloh to jump it with a barely noticeable squeeze of his left leg. Shiloh responded to AJ by pricking his ears and gathering his hind legs under him in a slow canter; he stared steadily at the gate, sizing it up. As they approached the jump and AJ felt Shiloh's front legs starting to leave the ground, he raised himself off the saddle, leaned forward, fed the reins slightly forward, and placed all his weight on the stirrups. Shiloh tucked his front legs well under him and sprung, clearing the gate by a good foot. Then AJ leaned back to take his weight off Shiloh's front legs as they touched the ground. As Shiloh's back feet landed, AJ sat back in the saddle and signaled his horse to drop back to a trot and then to a walk. Shiloh snorted and tossed his head but otherwise was unfazed. AJ was proud of him—it was the largest jump he'd taken so far.

AJ looked back to see how Harry was doing. His friend was on the ground, holding Betsy's reins as he opened the gate. "A graceful and dazzling performance, AJ," he yelled and with a wink he added, "Betsy and I decided to forgo that one."

MONDAY APRIL 15, 1861, 8:00 AM
CYNTHIA AND SOPHIA, SMITHFIELD, PENNSYLVANIA

Cynthia awoke when she heard Harry's booming call to AJ. She peeked through the window curtain to catch a glimpse of the freckled preacher and watched the two men ride off. She thought of AJ's outburst last night and could hardly wait to tell her friend Sophia how AJ had behaved. Her mother was already up and busy in the kitchen as Cynthia came down the narrow stairs.

"Have Earsala and John gone to school today, Ma?" Cynthia asked hopefully.

"Yes, I fixed them a lunch and they had griddlecakes with maple syrup before they left."

"Can I have some too, Ma?"

"Girl, when you come down here at this hour you can make your own breakfast. I've already washed the pan. The day's half gone!"

Shamefaced, Cynthia made a plate of cold leftover mush and bacon and ate it quickly. Then she asked, "Can I run over and talk to Sophia for just a little bit, Ma? I know it's late, but they wasn't… weren't at church yesterday and I'm worried about her grandma."

Her mother, redfaced from sweeping, sighed, used to Cynthia's ways of avoiding Monday wash chores. "Yes, I suppose, but don't stay long. Remember, it's washing day and we don't have Earsela to help. Tell Mrs. Mosier I said hello and I'm praying for her mother."

"Cynthia, don't forget…!" Her mother hollered after her but Cynthia had already grabbed her bonnet and was headed out the door. She ran all the way down the lane to the Mosier's stone house and arrived out of breath. Her friend ran out to hug her. Then they walked to the barn, arms around each other's waists, and climbed into the hayloft, their favorite spot for sharing secrets.

"How is your grandma?" Cynthia asked.

"She's not doing so well and the rain seemed to get her down. But I think she'll be all right. She's eating and sleeping a little better. But tell me quickly, what happened yesterday? Did you make eyes at Preacher Harry?"

Cynthia flushed pink. "Oh, Sophia, I tried, but he pays me no mind. I suppose he thinks I'm too young for him… and not smart enough. And please, please, do *not* tell AJ about my plans to get Harrison to notice me. AJ teases me about him all the time anyway. I just try to ignore it."

"And how's AJ? He seems not quite himself lately."

Cynthia nodded. "All the men seem to think, or maybe seem to be hoping, war is coming. Ma said something last night about rebels maybe coming to take Pa and AJ away to fight. Suddenly, AJ jumped up and hollered that he was going to *kill* the rebels! He was shaking all over, Sophia! He looked so scary he made Earsala and Johnny cry. Pa got mad and told him not to talk like that in front of the children. Can you imagine, Sophia?"

Sophia's forehead wrinkled. "That's not like AJ," she said thoughtfully. "He must be really bothered about all this war talk."

Cynthia studied her friend's face closely. "You're worried about him, ain't… aren't you? I think you *do* love AJ, no matter what you say."

Sophia giggled and covered her mouth. "Oh, Cynthia, I like AJ just fine, but lots of times he seems more like a brother than a beau. He is awful sweet though. I think he got jealous when I flirted with Tip at the dance." She smirked at the memory.

"Oh, I forgot to tell you—Tip came to church yesterday and I'm sure he only came to see you. AJ didn't look too happy to see him. I almost thought they'd get into a fight in the churchyard!" They laughed at the thought.

"Tip and AJ have always been rivals, you know," said Cynthia.

"Well, Tip is handsome, and he's very funny. He makes me laugh. And I do like it that he's paying attention to me. But I hear lots of stories about him and other girls…"

Cynthia nodded. "You just be careful around him, Sophia." She sighed. "Oh, you know I've always hoped you and AJ will marry someday. Then you'll be my real family instead of my pretend sister."

Sophia's face turned serious. "I know I'm old enough to marry, Cynthia, but I'm not sure I'm ready. I'm just not sure *what* I want yet. And besides, AJ has never mentioned a word to me about marriage."

"Then he's a big lummox!" said Cynthia, stamping her foot. "I've told and told him that he better ask you soon or somebody else will sweep you up. I would hate that!"

Sophia laughed. "We'll see. But you know, if a war does come, it could change everything."

Cynthia nodded. "I guess we're just going to have to wait and see what those folks in Richmond are going to do about joining the Confederacy. It's all so frightening… and exciting at the same time. Well, you have at least two men after you now, and I have no one. Please keep praying that Harry will finally notice me."

They climbed down from the hayloft and Cynthia said she had to go home and start the chores. As she was leaving, Cynthia remembered the last words her mother had said. "Oh, please tell your ma that my ma said hello, and she's prayin' for your grandma," she called over her shoulder as she ran toward home.

Monday April 15, 1861, 6:00 pm
AJ with Harry, Smithfield, Pennsylvania

Harry had finished his pastoral visits and he and AJ were on the last leg of their ride, still talking about war concerns. They passed near Haydentown and Harry asked, "Doesn't your cousin Tip live near here? I was surprised to see him at church yesterday."

AJ frowned. "Yep. So was I. I suspect he was only there because he thought he'd see Sophia."

"Ohhh," Harry responded, nodding. "So that's it. A rival for your affections…"

AJ nodded. "Please don't joke about it, Harry. I'm awful worried. Not just for myself, but for Sophia. I know he's my cousin, but I don't trust him with women. And Sophia's still so young."

"I've heard some rumors about his lady friends," Harry responded.

"As I told Pa last night, I don't know what to do, especially with war coming our way. Should I ask her to marry me, or wait to see what's goin' to happen? What if we have to go off and fight, Harry?"

"AJ, it's a difficult situation, I'll grant you. If this war does come, it will likely change our lives in ways that we can't foresee. But if you love Sophia and want her to be your wife, then I think you must speak with her about it. Do you have any idea how she feels about you?"

AJ bit his lip and considered for a moment. "If you'd asked me that a month or two ago, I would've said I thought so, but now... I don't know."

They heard hoofbeats on the road and both looked up to see a horse and rider coming toward them at a full gallop. His horse was sweating heavily—white foam hung from its mouth.

"Have - you - heard?" the rider gasped.

"Whoa, buddy! Heard what?" AJ said, grabbing the reins of the rider's heaving horse, which looked ready to collapse.

The rider cried out, "Lincoln is calling for 75,000 soldiers to put down the rebellion!"

"Take it easy, man," Harry said, "Where did you hear that?"

"I was in Morgantown waiting for a package to come in on the train. The stagecoach passengers from Grafton Station arrived and were all excited, talking about war. This means *war* for sure, I tell you!"

"Easy, sir," AJ said, "looks like your horse might die on you unless you get off him *now* and walk him."

AJ convinced the man to let them help save his horse. It was clear that he had run the animal hard—had perhaps run him all the way from Morgantown. This news from Washington was terrible, but not worth killing a horse over, in AJ's opinion.

As the man finally calmed down and walked off with his horse, Harry and AJ looked at each other, shook their heads sadly and started again for home. "This means Virginia will secede for sure—right, Harry?"

"Well, let's wait and see how the vote goes in Richmond. If they vote to secede this time, I think there *will* be war. I'm almost sure of that. Washington can't let *Virginia* secede from the country."

"What do you think your Virginia friends down in Morgantown and over in Wheeling will do?" AJ asked.

Harry shook his head. "I don't know. These are unsettled times."

The two friends waved as AJ and Shiloh turned up the lane to the farmhouse. AJ went through the motions of caring for his horse, feeding the other animals, and milking with a heavy heart. His thoughts jumped from the gathering war clouds to Tip chasing after Sophia. He wondered, could I kill an enemy soldier? If I did, would I ever be the same? *Maybe I can practice on Tip,* he thought. He realized that in the last two days he had become so angry that he had thought of killing. *This coming storm is changing me already.*

Jack W. Lewis

CHAPTER TWO

Now Is the Time for Us to Act

April 16–April 21, 1861

The Powhatan House Hotel on Broad Street, Richmond, Virginia

Tuesday, April 16, 1861, 6:00 am
Virginia State Convention, Richmond, Virginia

General John Jay Jackson of Wood County, Virginia awakened and stared out the window at a hangman's noose placed there during the night. Hooligans, he assumed. He knew the noose had been placed there on the roof of the Powhatan House Hotel by one of the many extreme secessionists roaming the streets, and the noose was meant to frighten him into voting for secession.

"At 61, nothing frightens me," he mumbled. "If I get my hands on one of those hooligans, I'll hang him upside down by his feet using his own noose and let him dangle there for a day or two. After all, I *am* a brigadier-general in the Virginia militia and I will not be bullied!"

When he was much younger, Jackson had been an apt pupil, and at thirteen years was admitted to Washington College, Pennsylvania, where he remained for a year, before being appointed by President James Monroe as a cadet to West Point. He entered that institution in 1815 and graduated in 1818, in his nineteenth year. He had fought in Florida in the Seminole War under Andrew Jackson, had served six terms in the Virginia House of Delegates, and had attended all sessions of the current Convention. He had watched the predominantly unionist delegation, who had voted 45 to 95 against secession on April 4, become more and more sympathetic to the Confederacy after the firing on Fort Sumter and Lincoln's call for 75,000 militia to put down the uprising. *Now*, he thought, *the vote tomorrow might well swing to the secessionist side.*

"This will be my last chance to appeal to all the delegates to stick with the Union," he said to the man who brought in his breakfast.

"Yessir, Mr. General, I surely hope your speech goes well. Is there anything I can get for you?"

34

"Yes, there is. You can get someone to take down that damn fool noose hanging outside my window!"

"Yessir, Mr. General, we got somebody up on the roof takin' care o' that right now. We sorry 'bout that, Mr. General. Seem like a lot of folks around here have gone crazy."

Over breakfast Jackson reviewed his speech. He was unsure if it would do any good, the way things were going. He recalled how staunch unionist Jubal A. Early from Franklin County nearly got into a fight with that hot-headed secessionist, John Goode, and how John Baldwin of Staunton, a lawyer and a slave owner, challenged anyone to deny that the national government had always supported Southern property rights, including slaves. And those were the days before Fort Sumter and Lincoln's call-up of the militia. Jackson particularly remembered how impressed he was when Waitman Willey, a Morgantown lawyer he knew well, had the guts to raise the unresolved issues of the disparity in political power between the eastern and western sections of Virginia. These were the same issues that had been a focus of the Virginia Constitutional Convention of 1850–1851. At issue was the preferential taxation rates the easterners had on their slave property. Few voters in western counties owned slaves and the tax dispute threatened not only to divide this convention further, but also gave notice that western counties would not take kindly to Virginia seceding from the Union.

The person who bothered Jackson the most was the ex-governor, Henry A. Wise. He had gradually won the confidence of the radical secessionists and had become their champion. Jackson believed he was secretly plotting to start a war with the Union behind the backs of the delegates and the newly elected Governor Letcher. Why, he acts like *he's* still the governor, Jackson thought.

Having finished his breakfast and the review of his speech, Jackson walked to the Convention and took his place. When the Convention came to order, he rose to be recognized and commenced his speech.

"I stand here an old man," he started, and reminded the delegates of his love for his country and for Virginia, and his 35 years of service to the Commonwealth. The delegates all applauded and John paused for a moment before continuing. "I stand here today having taken the oath to support the Constitution of the United States twenty-seven times." Jackson paused for effect.

"Was that an unmeaning ceremony?" he continued. "Was it of no consequence that I called the eternal God to witness that I would be true to the Constitution of Virginia, as well as the Constitution of the United States? Is it there registered for nothing?"

He paused again and saw many delegates fidgeting in their seats, as he had reminded them that they were contemplating breaking promises made before God. It appeared to be a hard pill for many of the delegates to swallow. The number of delegates applauding was much smaller.

He continued eloquently in the same vein, stating that the consequences of secession would be the "final ruin of the country," in his belief. The old general paused again to let his words sink in. Then he spoke his final words: "That God may grant you sufficient light and wisdom to do what is best, is my earnest prayer."

The room was quiet as Jackson sat down. Then a mixture of hisses, boos, and applause arose from the delegates. His heart was full and he knew he had done his best. He wondered whether he had converted any secessionist to vote to stay in the Union. Or had things just gone too far? He would talk over strategies tonight with other western county delegates he knew to be unionist and they would decide what to do next if the vote was for secession… as he feared it would be.

TUESDAY APRIL 16, 1861, 6:30 PM
MOSIER FARM, SMITHFIELD, PENNSYLVANIA

AJ walked slowly along the road leading to the Mosier farm as the sun disappeared behind the hill. He intended to call on Sophia this evening and talk about their future together and had chosen to walk the short distance to the Mosier farm instead of riding Shiloh, to give him more time to think. His thoughts were in a turmoil and he still had not made up his mind whether to propose. *Besides, she might not even want me*, he thought. But Harry had urged him to talk to Sophia, so he had resolved to try. He was determined to at least warn her about Tip and urge her to stay away from him.

Confused and frustrated, AJ wondered, *How can I possibly explain to Sophia all that is going through my mind? That I love her, and at the same time I'm in a stew about maybe having to go off and fight? What if I'm killed or wounded? She's still so young—would she still love me when I'm gone from her? Or if I come back missing an arm or a leg? Or does she even love me now?*

He walked up the porch steps and knocked on the door, not sure what he was going to say. He could hear shuffling of feet inside. The door sprang open and there stood Sophia, a big smile on her face. She smelled like a fresh-picked rose. Her pink cheeks matched the pink ribboned hairnet holding back her curls. He stared at her, feeling his heart throbbing like a spring of water, wanting nothing more than to put his arms around her.

"Oh, it's you. Well, don't just stand there with your mouth open," she said, holding out her hand to him. When he took it, he felt a jolt like a bolt of lightning hit him. She led him inside. "I thought you was somebody else," she said. "I wasn't expecting you tonight. But I'm glad to see you anyhow."

His heart suddenly stopped its throbbing. "Who *were* you expectin'?" he asked.

She avoided his eyes. "Oh, just your cousin, Tip. He came by here last Tuesday and said he'd try to come up again tonight."

So the fancy ribbon and pinkened cheeks were for Tip. AJ began to get riled.

As he followed Sophia into the parlor, hat in hand, he saw her parents were there, her father reading a newspaper and her mother darning a basket of socks. Both looked up and greeted him while Sophia motioned for him to sit.

"How's your mother doin', Mrs. Mosier?" he asked. He listened for several minutes while Sophia's mother, a talkative woman, went on about the hardships of illness and aging. All the while a cloud descended on his heart. *So she's waiting for Tip,* was all he could think about. *Have I lost this battle already?* He felt like giving up and going home. Then he remembered his cousin's reputation and the other poor females left in his wake. Even if she didn't choose him, he couldn't leave Sophia to Tip.

Desperate, he turned to her and asked, "I've got a powerful thirst. Walk to the spring with me, just for a minute?"

"It's getting dark, AJ," she replied.

AJ stood up anyway and reached his hand toward her. "We've got a while before the last light. Besides, there's a bright moon coming up. That is, if it's all right with your ma and pa?" He looked at Sophia's parents and they both nodded. "Go on, Sophia, we trust you with AJ," her mother said.

Sophia sighed, but stood and followed him out onto the porch, grabbing a shawl from a hook near the door. The spring was a short walk down a grassy path.

"I really just wanted a chance to talk to you," AJ said. "Especially before Tip gets here... if he's really comin'."

"Why wouldn't he come?" she asked, sounding a little irked.

"Well, he's not real reliable. That's what I wanted to talk to you about." AJ steeled himself and went on, determined to get it out. "Sophia, do... do you have *feelings* for him?"

She looked away, obviously uncomfortable. "I don't really know what you mean. I like him all right. He's tells a lot of jokey stories and he's fun to be around."

AJ grabbed her arm. "Listen, Sophia, he's not what he seems. I don't think you should see him anymore!"

"Oww, you're hurting me, AJ. What's come over you? You ain't yourself lately! And what's the harm in meeting a feller once in a while and talking to him? I talk to you."

"That's different!"

"Why?"

"Because we've known each other so long, and... I look out for you."

Sophia looked him full in the eye. "Yes. Just like you do for Cynthia, right, AJ? Just like I'm another little sister you have to watch out for?"

"No, I didn't mean that, Sophia, not exactly."

Sophia grabbed the drinking gourd from the nail and thrust it at AJ. "Well, here's the spring, and here's the gourd—do you want a drink or not? I'm ready to go back."

It wasn't going well. AJ dipped a gourd of water from the burbling, stone-lined spring and brought it to his lips. Sophia studied him, a frown making furrows in her forehead. "You know what I think? You're just jealous of Tip!" she exclaimed.

AJ hung the gourd carefully back on the nail and counted to ten.

He took a breath. "If that's what you want to think, young lady, you go right ahead. I'm being serious—I'm worried about you gettin' hurt."

"You sound just like my folks, AJ. At least Tip likes to josh and not act so serious all the time."

AJ felt the sting of her barbs. Just like her parents. Not as much fun as Tip. He swallowed hard and stood up straight. "Well, don't never say I didn't warn you, Sophia. If you ain't enjoying my company, I guess I'll move along home now and let you get ready for the company you really want to keep tonight. *If* he shows up."

39

He tipped his hat and turned to leave.

"Oh, AJ, don't be such a… lummox!"

He stomped down the path toward home, leaving Sophia to toss her head and make her own way back to her porch. *Lummox, am I?* He wasn't sure exactly what that was. As he walked, stewing, he could hear the sound of creaky buggy wheels approaching on the road and then Tip's raspy singing voice: "Froggy went a'courtin' and he did ride, uh huh…"

WEDNESDAY, APRIL 17, 1861
VIRGINIA STATE CONVENTION, RICHMOND, VIRGINIA

The secessionist faction in Richmond, led by former Governor Henry Wise, had been busy last night, and many nights before, secretly plotting to start a war. Wise had made up his mind. Regardless of how the Convention voted today, Virginia *would* join the Confederacy. Wise did not like the incumbent governor Letcher, who he considered to be a unionist. Wise wanted to seize the Federal arsenal at Harper's Ferry and grab all the arms before Lincoln found out about the result of the vote for Virginia secession, which he was sure would take place today. To make last night's raid he chose a young bold cavalry officer who had been present during the John Brown raid and knew the Harper's Ferry area. "Can you capture the Federal arsenal at Harper's Ferry early tomorrow and bring back all the arms stored there?" he had asked Turner Ashby.

"Do you have the approval of our new Governor Letcher?" Turner had bluntly asked him.

"Leave that to me, Turner. I've waited too long for this Convention to act. I know the delegates will vote tomorrow *for* the Ordinance of Secession. We must strike before the Federals hear the results, so we can capture the arms we're going to need to defend our rights against the northern aggression," Wise had replied.

"Well, sir... you have *been* the governor, so I will take orders from you, as if you were *now* governor," Ashby had replied.

"Then off you go, my young cavalier! Strike a blow for the Old Dominion that will make us all proud," Wise had said.

After sending off Ashby last night, Wise made a "courtesy" call on Governor Letcher, seeking his approval for the orders he had just given Ashby. Letcher did not agree with Wise's plan of action. Letcher had told Wise he thought it would not be honorable to act in advance of the convention vote today and he wanted nothing to do with it. Wise thought differently and was not about to chase after Ashby to stop him.

So this morning, before the Convention opened, Wise notified Letcher that the Harper's Ferry raid was already in motion. Governor Letcher shook his head. He knew there was no time to stop the attack.

As the Convention opened, Wise rose in his seat to be recognized. Wanting to be dramatic, he produced a large horse pistol and laid it on his desk. Then he announced, "I know that Virginia armed forces are now moving upon Harper's Ferry to capture, for the public defense, the arms there in the arsenal. There will be a fight or a foot race between our Virginia militia and Federal troops before the sun sets this day!"

Most of the delegates were aghast at this bold move, as it was clear to all that Wise had usurped the power of Governor Letcher. Many cheered the news. A few, not intimidated by Wise's pistols, loudly objected.

After the roar of the delegates died down, Allen T. Caperton of Monroe County rose to be recognized. He was one of the few secessionists from the western counties. "I appeal to gentlemen. I implore them to come now and put their hands to the work, and aid if possible, if not in averting this war, in maintaining it. This is all I have to say. I have troubled this Convention but little since its commencement. I have not engaged in those discussions which have occupied our time for months. But, sir, now is the time for action. I could not suppress the inclination I felt to make one appeal, at least to my Western friends, to come up and aid us in accomplishing what we are now about to engage in. War is upon us, and we are compelled to make the best of it. Let our Western friends, by all means, assist us in so doing."

A vote was taken immediately and this time the delegates passed the Ordinance of Secession by a vote of 88 to 55. The vote of the citizens of Virginia to ratify, or not, the Ordinance was set for May 23. Most delegates assumed that vote would be just a rubber stamp on their vote today.

As they had agreed upon the night before with General John Jackson, seven western Virginia delegates, "western friends" as Caperton mistakenly called them, left Richmond on the first Richmond, Fredericksburg and Potomac passenger train for Washington. The passenger coach they boarded had two rows of seats that could be folded back, so they grabbed four seats on each side and folded back the two front seats so they could converse among themselves.

As the train pulled out of the Richmond station, John Carlile of Harrison County spoke first. "That convention turned into a sham. As I said at its start, it was illegal since it was convened by the General Assembly and not by a referendum of the people. So I consider the Ordinance of Secession that was just voted for to be null and void."

"Then we have the outrageous performance of Henry Wise today," said Marshall Denton of Monongalia County. "The man is a madman and a traitor. I could see it in Letcher's eyes that Wise ordered the attack on Harper's Ferry without his knowledge."

"A madman he is, Marshall," Chester Hubbard of Ohio County chimed in. "Here with us sits Sherrad Clemens in great pain, wounded by Wise's mad son in a duel, because Sherrad dared to criticize his father. And this mad son of a mad father is the editor of the *Richmond Enquirer!* Have they *all* gone mad in Richmond?"

John Carlile spoke again. "As soon as Virginia joins the Southern Confederacy, which I know will be soon, I think it will then be time, gentlemen, that we lead our western counties out of this Confederate State. As Waitman Willey reminded everyone at the convention, we all know that a division of the state into West and East Virginia has been on the table for a long time due to the well-known taxation inequities. Now is the time for us to act."

"Here, here," said the others enthusiastically, nodding and shaking their fists.

"It will take a while to create a new state," resumed Carlile, "and I'm certain the Confederate State of Virginia will try to stop us by force. However, I know we will have our Federal government, and at least the states of Ohio and Pennsylvania, on our side. History might call it the State of Virginia's Civil War. But, whatever history calls it, we cannot fight our neighbors in Ohio, Pennsylvania, and Kentucky, to say nothing of trying to fight all the other northern and western states. Our constituents would never let that happen. As General Jackson said last night, I fear that the state we are leaving on this train tonight, the homeland of the father of our country, will witness its land, farms, buildings and economy destroyed by the coming war. Now look at Sherrad, how he suffers. Let us leave the man to nurture his wounds in peace and not add to his misery. Let's try to get some sleep now and think on what needs to be done. God willing, we will go our separate ways home once we reach Washington."

SUNDAY, APRIL 21, 1861, 9:45 AM
UNION METHODIST EPISCOPAL CHURCH
SMITHFIELD, PENNSYLVANIA

It was full springtime in the mountains. The air carried a faint perfume of fruit tree blossoms. Tiny new leaves danced in the breezes, which still carried a slight chill. The sun's rays warmed the people walking the road to church. If this had been normal times, everyone's spirits would have been lifted by the glorious springtime Sabbath. Instead, dark war clouds laced with disturbing rumors filled the minds of the worshippers as they entered the church. They came hoping to hear truthful, and maybe a few encouraging, words from Reverend Hagans, and to pray that there would be no war.

Reverend Hagans stood erect in the pulpit, wondering if there would be enough room for all the folks to fit into his church this morning. As the rows of benches quickly filled, Hagans announced in his booming voice, "There is standing room along the windows." As people continued to file in, he saw there was still not enough room. Many men gave up their seats to the women and stood just outside the church door.

Hagans thought about why his church was so full: *they've heard all the rumors of the mania sweeping the streets of Richmond and they're afraid war is coming to Smithfield.* Most folks in the congregation knew Hagans had traveled to the Morgantown courthouse on Wednesday to sit in on a meeting of Virginia men who believed in preserving the Union, and had stayed over to find out the results of the Richmond Convention vote on the Ordinance of Secession. *Now they want to hear the facts, not rumors, and they know I will tell them the truth*, he thought.

The pastor decided to set the mood for this service by calling for all seven verses of the hymn "How Firm a Foundation." His own bright tenor rang out as he led the congregational singing. This he followed by asking the congregation to recite together Psalm 23. He could hear their voices were strong and full of emotion as they recited: "Yea, though I walk through the valley of the shadow of death, I will fear no evil: for thou art with me; thy rod and thy staff they comfort me." Then, stepping behind the pulpit he began his sermon.

"I know you have fears; so do I. I deal with my fears by seeking the Lord and seeking the facts, and I believe that is why you are here today, to seek the Lord, and to get those facts as I know them to be. This past Wednesday I traveled to Morgantown to attend a meeting of people who believe the State of Virginia should stay in this Union we call the United States of America. There were many men at the meeting who hold high places in the Morgantown area and who have thought long and hard about the problems facing their state. I can tell you they think as we do. They don't want war and they don't want the State of Virginia to secede from the Union.

"I don't have time here today to repeat every word that was said at that meeting, so I will speak only of the high points. If you can get a copy of the *Morgantown Star* newspaper, I understand a summary of the meeting is in yesterday's edition." The pastor paused and looked around the church, making eye contact with several of his church members, including AJ.

"The Morgantown leaders framed the results of the meeting in the Whereas-therefore-Resolution format used in contracts. I'll read the 'Whereas' part first and then the resolutions. Please stop me if you don't understand some of the words they use, as I want you to understand every resolution.

"Whereas, An alarming crisis now exists in this country imminently threatening the existence of the American Union, and all the blessings of that civil and religious liberty, to secure which our Revolutionary fathers waged and endured all the hardships and privations of a seven years' war. And whereas, the present deplorable condition of our public affairs has arisen from the indiscreet and useless agitation of the slavery question in our national legislature by demagogues and selfish politicians North and South. And whereas, the time has come when it behooves every *true* friend of the Union and his country to rally under the flag and to maintain the same with an unwavering hand and under the most adverse and trying circumstances."

Hagans paused again. "Any questions on that long Whereas?"

There being no questions, he continued.

45

"Therefore be it Resolved, That we the people of Monongalia county, without distinction of party, deprecate and hereby enter our solemn protest against the secession of Virginia in the present exigency as unwise and inexpedient and fatal to her best interests and the interests of our whole country; believing as we do, that amongst its legitimate and immediate results, will be the utter ruin and bankruptcy and desolation of our hitherto proud and powerful Old Commonwealth."

Hagans paused again and looked up. "Any questions on that resolution?"

A man in the back yelled out, "What does deprecate mean? Ain't that what we do in the privy?"

Many in the congregation roared with laughter, but Hagans only smiled and calmly replied, "No, that means to express disapproval. It simply means this group of people disapproves of Virginia seceding from our Union. I think the word you are confused with is *defecate*."

"Thank you, Reverend," the red-faced man mumbled, as a few folks laughed again.

Hagans nodded. He was glad the brief humor had lightened the mood in the room. He continued with the reading of the resolutions while the congregation listened closely. Finally, he read the last resolution.

"Resolved, That in case an ordinance of secession is passed by our State Convention, that our Delegates be requested to propose a division of the State, by some line that will sever us from all future connection with Eastern secessionists."

"Oh, my!" one woman near the front of the congregation exclaimed. "Those folks in Morgantown mean to secede from Virginia!"

"Yes, Maggie, it does appear that way," Hagans replied. "I guess they believe if Virginia can secede from the Union, then their county can secede from Virginia. This last resolution seems to spell it out more clearly."

"Did the folks in Morgantown know how the Richmond Convention voted before they wrote that last resolution?" another man asked.

"No, they didn't," Hagans replied. "Apparently some Virginia militia attacked the armory at Harper's Ferry and cut the telegraph lines. So word of the convention vote results didn't arrive until a few of the western delegates got back home."

"Do you know the final results of the vote?" the man asked.

"Yes," Hagans replied solemnly. "It was 85 to 55... in favor of secession."

A great sigh and whispered comments arose from the crowd and then silence fell. The pastor saw many of them shake their heads and frown, and some women pressed handkerchiefs to their eyes. *Lord, please guide me,* he prayed silently, *and help me to guide them, through this trouble to come.* The man who asked about the vote called out, "What do you think is going to happen now, Reverend?"

Hagans paused to think, examining his heart. *Should I tell them what I really think will happen?* Finally he responded, "I think many folks in the western counties of Virginia agree with the people in Morgantown, and especially on that last resolution. I've already heard that the returning delegates are planning a meeting in Wheeling to discuss how they can separate from Virginia. The Richmond folks will not take kindly to this." Harry looked from face to face, to see how they were reacting to this news. He saw shock on some faces. He pushed on.

"They will likely try to *force* the western counties to stay loyal to the Confederate State of Virginia. I think there is going to be a fight over this and men from western Virginia will wage war against men in eastern Virginia. The western Virginians will likely reach out to our Federal government, and to the people of Ohio and Pennsylvania through their state governments, for help in the form of arms and men. Mind you, I don't know if this will all come to pass, but I suspect it will."

The same man asked Reverend Hagans, "What would *you* do if the western Virginians asked you to come and help them fight, Reverend? After all, even though you were born here in Pennsylvania, you lived in Virginia for most of your life. I know you're a man of God, but you're also a strong young man."

Harry paused again to think over his response. "Matthew, I can't at this time answer your question because I haven't given the subject enough thought. But, I can tell you this: I think slavery is a great evil in our land and God wants us to abolish this evil. Some of us have seen runaway slaves passing through here, seeking freedom. Some of the runaways ask us for food, water, and other help. Many of us, like the good Samaritan of Jesus' parable, see to their needs. When I look into the eyes of these men and woman, I do not see slaves, I see people like us who just have a different skin color. I believe that the evil of slavery is splitting our country apart and that we all bear the responsibility for it. We must go through some difficult times as a nation, in order to cast off this evil. I asked you to sing this old hymn with me today for a reason. The third verse of the hymn tells us:

Fear not, I am with thee, O be not dismayed,
For I am thy God and will still give thee aid;
I'll strengthen and help thee, and cause thee to stand
Upheld by My righteous, omnipotent hand.

"Remember the righteous God we serve stands with us through troubled times," he urged them. "Have courage and stay the course. I pray you will ponder these things in the coming weeks.

"Now please join with me in asking the Lord's guidance in the days to come. Let us end this service by reciting together our Lord's Prayer."

As Reverend Hagans greeted the Swaney family at the door after the service, he again asked AJ to stay for a moment until everyone had left the church and asked whether he could ride again with him on his rounds the following day.

AJ said he was willing and had some things he wanted to talk over with Harry when they rode together. Harry noticed that AJ looked rather pale and downcast. *Probably just worried sick about the coming conflict*, he thought.

CHAPTER THREE

Never Break Your Word

April 22–April 23, 1861

Sketch of Camp Floyd, Utah Territory c. 1860

MONDAY, APRIL 22, 1861
CAMP FLOYD, UTAH TERRITORY

"Whatever the future has in store for me, I will live and die under the flag of the Union!" shouted Captain John Buford, United States Army, Second Dragoons. He wadded up the two letters he had just read and flung them onto the floor. Second Lieutenant Wesley Merritt came rushing into the room with pistol in hand, obviously expecting to see his commander under attack.

"What's wrong, sir?" Merritt yelled.

"Oh, put that damn thing away, Wesley. Those letters just sent me over the edge." He pointed to the crumpled papers at his feet.

Merritt, still breathing hard, holstered his pistol. He eyed the letters curiously. "Mind if I look at them, sir?"

"Go ahead. They're worth a good laugh." Buford shook his head as he watched the young lieutenant retrieve the wrinkled letters and peruse them. The first was from Kentucky's Governor Beriah Magoffin, offering Buford a command in the Kentucky state militia. *Magoffin thinks he can entice me to come back to Kentucky. Well, I'm in the U.S. Cavalry and damn proud of it. And here I'll stay, come hell or high water.*

The second letter was from the provisional Confederate government offering Buford a commission as a general. *That's the one that really got my goat,* Buford thought. He had little patience with his fellow Southern officers talking about resigning their commissions to join the military forces of their home states in the South. *We all signed an oath, dammit! It's treasonous!* He could feel his dander rising again. He paced the small room, scowling.

Merritt was not accustomed to seeing his normally quiet and unassuming superior officer so irate. He nervously slipped the two letters back onto Buford's desk and said, "Yes, sir, I see what you mean, those letters *are*... hilarious, sir."

Buford allowed a slight smile to play on his lips, amused at Merritt's attempt at diplomacy. Although Merritt was new to his post, Buford was already impressed with his deportment and his fine horsemanship. He was a quick learner and clearly understood what was going on around him here at Camp Floyd. Buford mentally corrected himself: *Now re-named Camp Crittenden, now that Floyd himself has joined the ranks of the traitors!*

In 1858, believing Mormons were rebelling against the laws of the United States, President James Buchanan had dispatched 3,500 troops, nearly one-third of the entire U.S. Army, to suppress the rumored rebellion in the Utah Territory. There the Army constructed Camp Floyd, named in honor of then Secretary of War John Floyd. No rebellion or war ever took place in Utah, but the army stayed on to monitor the Mormons, explore the western frontier, and provide safety for immigrants moving west to California, Oregon, and Washington.

And now Floyd has resigned and gone back to Virginia, probably to work on getting Virginia to secede from the Union, Buford thought, his scowl returning. The Camp's commanding officer, Colonel Cooke, himself Virginia-born but loyal to the Union, had promptly and angrily changed the name of the camp, to honor the famous compromising senator from Kentucky, John Crittenden.

Buford recalled his recent conversation with Beverly Robertson, also a graduate of West Point in the class behind him, and a good cavalry officer. Robertson had told Buford he would resign and join the military forces of Virginia if his native state seceded. Buford had shouted, "By God, Beverly, that is treason! When you received your commission, you took the same oath that I did to defend the Constitution of the United States against all enemies, foreign and domestic. You swore this freely and before God. Soldiers can, and should, be hanged for treason!"

Robertson had stood, redfaced and speechless, and then turned on his heel and walked away, saying, "Sorry you feel that way, *sir*."

How could I feel otherwise? How could you feel otherwise, Beverly, after all we've been through on the frontier? You're a dragoon too. How could you even contemplate disloyalty to the Army that has trained and fostered us all these years? Such were the thoughts that went through Buford's mind, but he had held his peace after that episode. *Strange times are upon us, when brother opposes brother.*

Both Buford and the junior officer Merritt had excelled in the equitation course at West Point. A cadet learned to ride bareback and was drilled in how to ride in a group with his full equipment. A cadet also learned how to feed and care for a horse, how to train the horse to perform various gaits, obey leg commands, and perform a variety of maneuvers while the cadet directed saber blows at dummies.

Upon graduation, Buford had applied for and was commissioned a brevet second lieutenant in the First United States Dragoons. While in that regiment, Buford had learned the arts of a true dragoon, a special kind of cavalryman armed with expensive weapons and skilled in both mounted and unmounted operations. Dragoons carried sabers and single-shot pistols or 44-caliber Colt revolvers for mounted operations and a breech-loading carbine for dismounted operations. Both rider and horse needed a great deal of training. It was common knowledge to most commanding officers that it took at least two years to become a true dragoon as well as a true cavalier. Buford had honed his skills in a bloody frontier campaign against the Sioux. Merritt had come to Camp Crittenden to learn from a master, and Buford was that master. And proud of it.

MONDAY, APRIL 22, 1861, 9:00 AM
SMITHFIELD, PENNSYLVANIA

"Harry, from what you said in church yesterday, I'm figurin' the state of Virginia is headin' for its own civil war," AJ said as they turned onto the road toward Uniontown.

"Yes, I think so. You know, AJ, this disagreement between the eastern and western counties of Virginia has been going on for a long time. Even as far back as when Virginia adopted its state constitution in 1776, when this country got started. Virginia's constitution at that time gave voting rights only to white men owning at least 25 acres of improved land or 50 acres of unimproved land. Many folks trying to settle the western counties could not even vote because their land didn't meet those conditions. The easterners with their large plantations held all the power."

"But that's not the way it is now, is it?"

"Not exactly. State conventions were held in the early years of this century and they produced some improvements for the western counties. But the slavery issue always ended up putting the political power of the state in the hands of slave owners in the eastern counties. Another convention was held later in Richmond to develop a new state constitution, but it left out a lot of the important reform issues. The new constitution was passed anyway by a fairly large margin, but in the western counties, it was voted down in a landslide."

"So then what happened?"

"Calls for the western counties to secede from the State of Virginia started up right after that, led by newspapers like the *Kanawha Republican*."

"So the western counties wanted to form their own state even before I was born?"

"That's right, AJ. Over the next twenty or so years, the Virginia General Assembly tried different things to ease the tension between the two sides of the state. Almost twenty new western counties were created, which helped to relieve the imbalance in voting power. And the state also spent some money to help the westerners. For example, the Staunton-Parkersburg Turnpike and the Northwestern Turnpike were built to improve west-east transportation and communications."

"That don't seem like it would have been much help in solvin' the real problems, Harry. I heard somethin' about a Virginia convention in 1850, when I was about 10 years old. Did that one help any?"

"It did help a little. One important change was that all white males over the age of 21 were given the right to vote, whether or not they owned property. Unfortunately, the property taxes on slaves were still a big issue. While the delegates agreed to allow other property to be taxed at its total value, the slave property was valued at far less than its true worth. That meant that the westerners, who usually didn't own any slaves, or very few, were carrying more of the state tax burden than the easterners."

AJ squinted as he tried to grasp all that Harry had just relayed to him. "How do you know so much about these problems in Virginia?"

"Well, you know I lived near Morgantown for a long time, and my father has a store there. He keeps me informed. I also do a lot of reading and talking, and try to attend important meetings when I can. I believe it's important to keep my flock informed of the facts that affect their lives. That way they have more time to spend on their spiritual life and happiness, instead of wasting time on hearsay, gossip and worrying about things they can't control."

"Harry, I surely do admire you. I'm just surprised you spend so much time with a know-nothin' like me..." AJ sighed.

Harry shook his head. "You know much more than you think you do. You're a good man. And I want to make sure you stay on the straight and narrow."

Harry and AJ visited several more homes and farms along their route to Uniontown and Monroe. They learned from a friend of Harry's in Uniontown that a large meeting of unionists would be held that day in Clarksburg, Virginia. His friend thought they would announce a convention in Wheeling sometime in May to discuss the formation of a new state from the counties of western Virginia. His friend also told them that Virginia militia had seized the arsenal at Harper's Ferry and the Gosport

Navy Yard at Norfolk over the weekend. The two young men were disturbed, but not much surprised, at the news. It only served to confirm their own suspicions of what was coming.

As they left Monroe and trotted along the road to Fairchance, AJ's thoughts turned from war to Sophia. He felt the now-familiar ache in his chest return.

"Harry, can I ask your advice about somethin'?" AJ asked.

"Of course. About Sophia?"

AJ nodded. "You said I should talk to her, tell her how I feel about her, sort of feel her out about getting married. I hiked over to her place Tuesday after supper to try to have that talk." He paused, trying to find the words to describe what had taken place.

"I surmise from the haunted look in your eye that it didn't go well."

"Well, it turned out she was waitin' for a visit from Tip and didn't seem any too glad to see *me*. We had some words—I tried to warn her about Tip and how he is with the ladies. Seemed like she took offense. She told me I'm too serious, and I act just like her parents."

"Well, it sounds like your talk got a little off track. What exactly did you tell her?"

"I told her to stay away from Tip—that he's no good for her."

"Hmm. Did you happen to mention your feelings for her anywhere in that conversation?"

AJ hung his head and sighed. "No... Didn't seem like the time was right."

"So? Are you two not speaking to each other any more? I noticed that you weren't together at church yesterday."

"Well, how can I talk to her, now I know she thinks of me like a parent, or a big brother? I was wantin' to marry her, Harry, not be a brother to her! She don't understand me one bit. And she's avoidin' me now. She barely nodded to me yesterday at church. I've give up hope, Harry. I don't have a gift for talkin' to females, like ol' Tip has. Women make me nervous and I don't get my words straight, and the next thing you know we're both mad."

"Well, my friend, I don't have a lot of experience with females myself, at least in a romantic sense, so I may not be the best adviser. But I'd say give it more time. Anyway, you weren't sure you wanted to marry right now, with all the uncertainty about war. You're both young. Don't retreat after just one skirmish, AJ. You might win the battle yet."

AJ frowned. He didn't share Harry's optimism. "Maybe," he answered. "But I think I'm going to give up on love, and just try to get myself ready for whatever might be coming at us. By the way, Harry, talking about you and females reminds me of my sis. I think Cynthia might have her cap set for *you*. I tease her a lot, but I can see the way she looks at you."

Harry's mouth set in a grim line. "Yes, I know," he said.

After a long and uncomfortable silence, AJ realized that he should change the subject altogether. "Harry, if what your friend was tellin' us about Harper's Ferry and Norfolk is true, then I figure the President is going to look on both of those as acts of war."

"Yes, I think President Lincoln is going to treat those attacks as acts of war. I'm not sure what Governor Letcher and his advisers are thinking, but it seems they are going to have a war on at least two fronts, one with the northern states and one with the people of the western counties of their own state. I pity Virginia, AJ. I fear it will become one of the biggest battlegrounds of the coming war and that beautiful state, the one that has fathered so many of our presidents, including our beloved George Washington, will be laid to ruin. And I fear for my family there."

Both men shook their heads as they contemplated the debacle to come.

MONDAY, APRIL 22, 1861, 8:00 PM
SWANEY FARM, SMITHFIELD, PENNSYLVANIA

"Pa, are you still awake?" AJ called, as he opened the door to the kitchen.

"I am." His father was sitting at the rough-hewn table, reading the Bible. He rubbed his eyes and then added, "And how was yer ride? Did the Reverend get his visitin' done?"

"We had a good ride. Shiloh did well, lots of spunk. We talked with one of Harry's friends that lives in Uniontown. He passed on some bad news, Pa. The Virginia militia attacked Harper's Ferry—the arsenal there—*and* the Navy shipyard in Norfolk."

James shook his head. "I can't hardly believe what's happenin' to our country, son. Seems like those folks in Virginia surely mean to start a war."

"That's just what Harry and I were sayin'. Harry thinks the Virginia folks living in the counties west of the Alleghenies are going to secede from Virginia. Those folks are mostly loyal to the United States, just like we are. Harry says there was a big meetin' in Clarksburg today and he heard they were planning a convention in Wheeling sometime in May to talk about forming a new state. Can you believe *that*, Pa?"

"I'm glad to hear it. Makes me feel a tad safer living here so close to those Virginians. Though I bet ye the Richmond politicians will try their dangest to stop them startin' up a new state."

"Yes, Pa. But I'll also bet you those loyal western Virginians are planning right now to gather together some men and arms, to defend their right to do it."

"We'll see, son. I been meaning to ask ye, how's things goin' with Sophia? Any wedding bells in our future?" he said with a big smile.

AJ frowned. His father had obviously not even noticed that he and Sophia were currently not seeing, or even speaking to, each other. James had a habit of ignoring or denying anything he didn't want to see or hear. "No, no time soon, Pa. Things aren't going real smooth right now."

James's face fell. "Oh. I'm right sorry to hear that, me boy. You know I think an awful lot of that young lass."

"Yes, I know, Pa. I did talk to Reverend Harry about it and he said I shouldn't give up hope."

"Good Lord, no, me boy! Don't give up at the first hint of trouble. A woman can be… how d'ye say?… complicated. Be patient."

AJ fidgeted. *Be patient. Easy to say, but not so easy to do.* "I don't know, Pa, right now I think I should just forget about females and think about what we can do to protect ourselves. All these war signs has made a mighty big difference in how I'm lookin' at everything."

"Ye're right, me lad, it's hard for me to be in your shoes. But I really like your sweetheart Sophia and would hate to see her endin' up with somebody else. I for one would lean toward ye marryin' her soon and settlin' down right here. After all, if war does come, it's likely to be a short one. Or we might not have to go to war at all, if those blamed secessionists would just calm theirselves and see reason."

James closed the Bible and placed it on the table. He stood and stretched his arms and yawned. "Past my bedtime. Son, I said my piece, but it's up to you to make up yer own mind. I'll abide by whatever ye decide. I won't try to push ye into anything, and I won't hold ye back none neither."

AJ nodded. He stood silently, feeling awkward. Then he patted his father softly on the back and said, "Well, good night, Pa."

TUESDAY APRIL 23, 1861
LEE'S OFFICE, RICHMOND, VIRGINIA

Robert E. Lee sat tall and straight in the chair of his new office, reading the order he had just received from Virginia Governor John Letcher:

EXECUTIVE DEPARTMENT, RICHMOND, VA
April 23, 1861

Major-General Lee having reported to the Governor, he will at once assume the

*commander-in-chief of all the military
and naval forces of the State and take
charge of the military defenses of the state.*
JOHN LETCHER

Lee turned over in his mind the pivotal conversation he'd had a few days ago with his mentor, General Winfield Scott, and that with Governor Letcher the day before.

He had asked to speak with General Scott, the top general in the U.S. Army and also a proud Virginian, in his office at 1600 hours. At exactly 4 PM, Lee, in his best uniform with all his ribbons bright and in exactly the right order and place, knocked on the door, entered the room at the General's command, stood at rigid attention, and saluted. The General stood up, returned the salute and motioned for Lee to sit down in the chair opposite the General's desk. Lee noticed immediately that the man he had always revered had grown old. This famous general, a national hero after the Mexican War, had taken so much pride in how he looked in his uniforms. He now weighed almost 300 pounds and his uniform hardly fit him. Still, at 6 feet 5 inches he was a commanding, almost intimidating, man.

"Colonel Lee, you are the finest soldier I've ever seen," General Scott began with great authority. "You served me well as a member of my staff during the war with Mexico. Three times I promoted you for your gallantry. I asked the President to promote you to your present rank of colonel. I understand that the President has now proposed to promote you to general and place you in command of all military forces in our country. What is it that you want to say to me?"

Lee had replied, "I am honored, General, and thankful for all that you have done for me. I received a telegram from Governor Letcher informing me that the Virginia Convention has just voted for secession. I fear that the command the President is offering me might place me in a position of taking up arms against my home State, my family and friends.

I wanted to ask you whether there is any possibility of a position for me that would keep me out of the war?"

Scott had leaned forward, looked Lee in the eye, and pounded his fist on the desk. "My God, Colonel, you were just offered by the President the highest military position in our country. Your duty is to your *country*. Have you forgotten the oath you took on becoming an officer? As for me, I have no place in my army for equivocal men. If you cannot fulfill the oath you took when you accepted your commission as a colonel in the United States Army, then for your sake turn in your resignation now, before you're hanged for treason."

Lee was not especially shocked by the harsh reply, though he was un-accustomed to feeling the wrath of this much-admired superior officer. Up to now they had almost always seen eye to eye. He knew the General was a man of action who expected immediate obedience to his orders and who looked after the welfare of his men. In his own way, the General was looking after Colonel Lee now, by giving him an out. Lee bowed his head slightly and replied, "Then I will resign immediately, General, and please accept my apologies. It is my allegiance to Virginia that places me in this quandary."

Scott replied, "Colonel Lee, I too was born in Virginia *and* I hold sacred my duty to my country. You are excused."

Lee had returned to his family home, Arlington, in Washington City to read the Bible and pray over the matter. He told his family of his decision to resign and drafted a letter of resignation to General Scott, handing it to a slave to deliver to the War Office. His wife Mary, a loyal unionist like most of his family members, was shocked, but she promised to stand by him.

Yesterday, Lee had sat in Governor Letcher's office, telling him what had happened when he was called into Scott's office.

"Well, what can you expect from someone who's outlived his useful-ness?" Letcher replied. "He was once called 'Old Fuss and Feathers.' Now I understand he's called 'Old Fat and Feeble.' He's an old man, probably an abolitionist, and doesn't understand that states have the absolute right to secede from the Union. Forget him! I now offer you command of all military and naval forces in Virginia and will get you promoted to Major General today. Do you accept my offer?"

Lee still held General Scott in high esteem and didn't like Letcher's remarks. But he was now committed to the path he had chosen, come what may. Lee had simply replied, "I accept your offer, Governor Letcher."

Lee turned his attention back to Letcher's letter in his hand. He took out a piece of writing paper and wrote the following order in a neat hand:

HEADQUARTERS, RICHMOND, Virginia,
April 23, 1861
GENERAL ORDER NO. 1

In obedience to orders from his Excellency,
John Letcher, Governor of Virginia, Maj.
Gen'l Robert E. Lee assumes command of
the military and naval forces of Virginia.
R. E. LEE, Major-General

CHAPTER FOUR

Perhaps Your Letter Was Premature

April 27–May 6, 1861

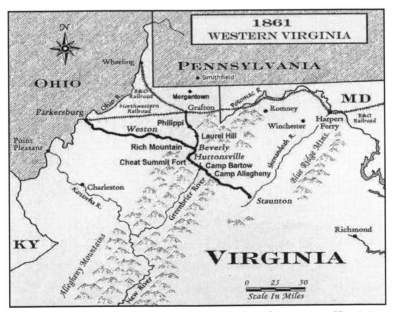

Location of towns, villages and B&O Railroad in western Virginia

SATURDAY, APRIL 27, 1861
SWANEY FARM, SMITHFIELD, PENNSYLVANIA

"John, wake up," AJ whispered in his young brother's ear and shook him lightly by the shoulder.

Opening his eyes and yawning, John said, "I'm awake. AJ, are we goin' to shoot the long rifle today?"

"Yes, we both need practice. Who knows what's going to happen, with Lincoln calling up the militia? We need to be ready for anything, John boy. Get on your clothes and come down for breakfast. Ma's making griddle cakes and bacon for us."

The two gobbled the stack of fried cornmeal cakes topped with molasses and butter that their mother sat in front of them. They thanked their mother and hurried outside. The sky was beginning to lighten.

As they entered the cavernous barn, Shiloh called out from his stall. Man and boy could tell the horse was eager to go, the same as them. AJ had been up for a couple of hours and had already fed the animals, milked the cows and saddled Shiloh. Lately he had been filling up his time—what there was left over after all the farm work—with drilling, shooting and training Shiloh. It helped him to keep busy. Like his ma had told him, if you sweated enough, sometimes it could heal you.

He slung his haversack over his shoulder, grabbed his rifle and walked Shiloh out of the barn, John by his side. He could see the boy's eyes shining bright with excitement and smiled. AJ mounted first, then grabbed John's hand and swung him onto the back of the saddle. They had done this many times before and Shiloh stood quietly while John settled himself behind his brother.

"Off we go, John. Grab hold of me. We'll head on over to my 'shootin' range'." With just a click of AJ's tongue, Shiloh trotted down the path to AJ's makeshift firing range. AJ could feel John's grip tighten around his waist.

"Are you ready for a rifle quiz, little brother?" AJ asked.

He enjoyed testing John. It wasn't easy to trip him up. He knew John took his shooting and hunting skills very seriously, just like AJ.

"Yes, I'm ready! I already know your rifle is called a muzzleloading long rifle. It shoots round lead bullets by burning black powder. Grandpa gave it to you and he got it a long time ago, from the Swiss-Germans who lived near Philadelphia. They invented the long rifle and built it by hand. See, I told you I could remember!"

"Very good. And why's it called a rifle?"

"Oh… well, it's called a *long* rifle because it has a long barrel, with grooves inside that make the lead ball spin. That's called the rifling, so it's a rifle. And that's what makes it shoot so good, right?"

"John, you're a good student, all right. You know, if you studied your schoolbooks as much as you study shootin' the rifle, you'd be the star pupil."

They arrived at the long clearing, away from the farm buildings and corrals, where AJ had set up targets. They dismounted and John tied Shiloh to the hitching post. AJ handed the rifle to John. "Show me how to load it, little brother."

"That's the fun part!" John slowly and carefully took the lid off the powder horn and put the right amount of powder into the barrel. Then he placed a small wad of paper over the muzzle, placed the lead ball on the paper, and pushed it into the muzzle with his fingers. Then he removed the ram and jammed the ball and wad of paper into the barrel, until it was seated at the bottom of the barrel. AJ watched him closely and was satisfied that the boy knew what he was doing.

"Good. How much powder did you use?"

"About 100 grains."

"How much does a grain of powder weigh, John?"

"The same as a grain of wheat."

AJ smiled. His student had done his homework. "You do have a good memory. Remember, the more you practice, the easier it gets to choose the right weight of powder you need to hit a target."

They moved into position and AJ sighted down the barrel at one of the man-sized, straw-stuffed targets he had built and painted, about 150 yards away.

"I'll shoot for awhile, then I'll let you fire the rifle. First we have to plug our ears," AJ said as he pulled out several small, clean cloth squares from his jacket pocket.

"Here, John, ball these up and put them in your ears. It will keep you from losin' your hearing. You want to be able to hear those rebels creepin' up on us."

John smiled as he watched AJ load the pan with powder, pull the frizzen back in place, leaving the hammer in the half-lock position.

"John, did you remember how to prime the rifle?"

"Yes, but I like to watch you do the primin'."

AJ then pulled the hammer back to its full cocked position, took aim at the target and pulled the trigger, releasing the hammer so the flint struck the frizzen, which made sparks to light the powder in the pan, which then lit the powder in the bore, which launched the lead ball on its track to the target. *It's so complicated, it's amazing it works almost every time!* he thought. Flame came out of the pan a split second before the rifle discharged the ball. The explosion was loud but was muffled by the cloth in his ears. He hit the target, but thought he could do better.

"Now it's your turn, John."

John loaded the rifle correctly and readied it to fire. The rifle was heavy and the weight caused John to shake when he held his aim too long.

"Little brother, I suggest you take less time to aim. That way, you won't have time to shake and it'll improve your shot."

John listened, took aim quickly and hit the edge of the target.

"Good job. Keep on loadin' and shootin'."

AJ let his brother fire several more times. On his last shot, John hit inside the bullseye of the target. AJ noticed that the boy stood up straighter. *He's proud of himself, and he should be,* AJ thought. *I'm proud he's learning to shoot, and sure enough he might have to defend our farm if I'm away fighting... but I hope not.*

Before leaving the range, AJ showed John a trick he'd been working on with Shiloh. "Let me show you how I use Shiloh to help me steady the rifle so I can hit a far-away target. See that farthest target yonder? It's about 250 yards from where we're standin'. I'll reload with more powder this time and you go bring Shiloh over here."

AJ loaded the rifle with near maximum powder load. As John led Shiloh over, the horse raised his head and perked his ears. AJ positioned the horse so he could place his rifle over the saddle and see the target. Then he spoke in a gentle voice: "Steady, stand, shootin'." The horse flicked one ear back toward AJ and obeyed. AJ took aim and slowly pulled the trigger until it fired. Shiloh twitched his tail and flicked both ears back, but did not flinch. John retied Shiloh to the hitching post and he and AJ walked out to the target to see how close the ball came to the bullseye. AJ's shot was inside a 5-inch circle around the center of the target.

AJ was proud of the shot. John shook his head and said, "The target was so far, how could you even see it?"

"It takes a lot of practice and learnin' how the ball's path changes with the powder load, the raisin' of the barrel, and the crosswinds. There's a lot more to learn, but I can teach you."

On the ride back to the house, AJ told John stories of the roles that long rifles played during the Revolutionary War battles of Saratoga and the Cowpens. He told him how Morgan's sharpshooters, with their rifles, helped win those battles. The British learned to fear the American long rifle soldiers dressed in buckskin. General Washington sometimes took advantage of this and dressed some of his infantry in buckskin, even though they only carried plain muskets. His little brother seemed to revel in the stories. "I wish I could shoot in a real war!" he said.

AJ frowned and shook his head. "No, you don't, little brother. I hope to God you never have to."

SUNDAY, APRIL 28, 1861, 10:00 AM
SMITHFIELD, FAYETTE COUNTY, PENNSYLVANIA
UNION METHODIST EPISCOPAL CHURCH

After starting his service with a hymn, prayer, and scripture reading, Harry began his sermon. "There is more news about the turmoil taking place to the south of us. A large convening of about 1,200 citizens was held this past Monday in Clarksburg, Virginia, regarding the situation in that state. The convention adopted a Preamble and resolutions condemning the actions of the current governor and others in Virginia who have already demonstrated hostility toward the United States government, all without waiting for the final vote of the people on secession, which won't take place until May 23. Most of the resolutions from the Clarksburg meeting were included in the Thursday edition of the *Wheeling Intelligencer*. I'm going to summarize only the most important parts of that meeting for you.

"Without approval of the people of Virginia, their governor has taken it upon himself to call up Virginia volunteer militia and has allowed acts of war to be committed against the Federal government by seizing its ships and obstructing the channel at the mouth of the Elizabeth River, by taking from Federal officers at Norfolk and Richmond the custom houses, by tearing from the nation's property the nation's flag and putting in its place the emblem of rebellion, and by marching on the National Armory at Harper's Ferry.

"Northwestern Virginia, separated as it is by the mountains from the rest of the state, feels itself to be in a dangerous position and demands that its citizens provide for its own safety. The convention resolved that all of the northwestern Virginia counties should appoint delegates to a convention to be held in Wheeling on May 13, to determine what action should be taken in this emergency.

"The people at the Clarksburg meeting also appointed delegates from their county to represent them at the Wheeling Convention. One of the delegates, John S. Carlile, I know for a fact is intent on having the loyal northwestern counties form a new state, to remain in the Union.

"Does anyone have questions?"

A man in the back rose from his seat and asked, "Reverend, does one state have the lawful right to create another state out of its own territory?"

"There is a provision in the Constitution of the United States that allows a state to create another state out of its own territories. The division must first be agreed to by the General Assembly of that state, and the division must then be approved by both houses of the United States Congress."

"Then how does Mr. Carlile plan to form this new state, Reverend?"

"That's a good question, to which I don't have an answer right now. Again, we will just have to be patient and wait to see what happens."

There being no further questions, Harry opened his Bible and said, "Turn this morning to Luke, chapter 11, verse 17: 'But he, knowing their thoughts, said unto them: Every kingdom divided against itself is brought to desolation, and a house divided against itself falleth.'"

MONDAY, APRIL 29, 1861
LEE'S OFFICE, RICHMOND, VIRGINIA

"General Lee, what have you done to prepare military defenses in the western counties of Virginia?" Governor Letcher asked as he entered Lee's office.

"I have not done anything yet, Governor, as I'm awaiting the results of the people's vote on the Ordinance of Secession on May 23."

"What does that have to do with preparing for the defense of our state?" Letcher growled.

"Defense against what, Governor? We have not seceded from the Union until the people vote on the ordinance and I understand that the people in our western counties are preparing to vote against that ordinance."

"We are going to have a problem with those westerners, General, and I need you to recognize this and prepare for it. When the Ordinance was passed on the 17th, I wrote a letter to Andrew Sweeney, Mayor of Wheeling, informing him the Ordinance of Secession was passed and ordered him to seize at once the custom house of that city, the post office, and all public buildings and documents in the name of the sovereign State of Virginia. Do you know what he wrote back to me?"

"I can only guess, Governor. Since we are not a sovereign state unless the people vote *for* the Ordinance, I suspect he said he wouldn't do it."

Letcher replied, "More than that, General Lee. He wrote back 'I have seized upon the custom house, the post office and all public buildings and documents in the name of Abraham Lincoln, President of the United States, whose property they are.'"

"Perhaps your letter was premature, Governor. Were you not asking the mayor to do something that the people of our state have not yet voted their approval of?"

"Look, Lee, we are past all of this. The people *will* vote their approval and after our attack on Harper's Ferry and the U.S. Naval Shipyard in Norfolk, the die has been cast with the Federal government. I need you to take action now to defend our state, not question my orders."

"I will obey your orders, Governor, but it is my duty to inform you of what I see are the consequences of these orders. I can write orders to heads of our militia units in the western counties, but I fear they will be interpreted by many there as a usurpation of their rights as citizens of our state. I believe that will increase their animosity and distrust of our state government."

"Just write the orders, General Lee, and let me worry about the westerners."

"Yes, sir, I will write orders today to Major Loring in Wheeling, Lt. Colonel McCausland in the Kanawha Valley, and Major Boykin in Weston. You will have a copy of these orders on your desk tomorrow."

FRIDAY, MAY 3, 1861, 8:00 AM
KELLEY'S OFFICE, PHILADELPHIA, PENNSYLVANIA

For almost 10 years Benjamin F. Kelley, a 54-year-old man with deep-set eyes and a military bearing, had been a freight agent for the B&O Railroad. He had moved with his family from Wheeling to Philadelphia in 1851, to be near his ailing wife, who had been placed in the Pennsylvania Insane Asylum after suffering from a disease contracted in 1846 that attacked her brain. They had married in 1835 and had six children together before she fell ill. Last year his beloved wife died and after her funeral his children had moved back to Wheeling.

Kelley was a proven salesman and had been promoted several times since joining the B&O. His job now was to divert freight traffic from the Pennsylvania Central Railroad to the B&O Railroad. As he briskly walked to his office, he thought back on the day he interviewed for the position.

"Are you the man for this job?" John W. Garrett, President of the B&O, had asked.

"Yes, I am," he replied.

Then he went on to tell Garrett about the rigorous physical training and liberal education he had received at the American Literacy, Scientific, and Military Academy—often called the Partridge Military Academy—located in Norwich, Vermont. It prepared him physically and mentally to take on any job and do it well. Garrett had hired him and they had since become close friends.

As he walked into his office, his secretary greeted him, "Good morning, Mr. Kelley."

"And a very good morning to you," he replied, glancing down at the telegram on his desk.

"That just came for you, Mr. Kelley," his secretary announced and then added, as an afterthought, "I think it came from Wheeling."

Kelley picked it up, opened it and quickly read. Andrew Sweeney, mayor of Wheeling, wanted him to come back and form a regiment of soldiers loyal to the Union. The mayor said it was an emergency brought on by the Richmond Secession Convention's vote to secede from the Union. The B&O Railroad needed to be protected and he could think of no person more qualified than Kelley to organize and command the regiment. The mayor offered him a commission as a colonel.

Kelley thought hard for several minutes. He had liked living in Wheeling and felt a strong loyalty to the area. He had moved there after graduation and become a successful businessman, joining the Guards Military of Wheeling and becoming the commander of the Fourth Virginia Regiment, a uniformed militia unit. This telegram stirred intense patriotic feelings and pride. It also put him in a quandary. He loved his country and was loyal to the state of Virginia, in spite of the poor way the dominant easterners in the state had treated the westerners over so many years. He did not approve of secession and felt it would harm both his state and his country.

He was proud of his business achievements and enjoyed his new job in Philadelphia. But he had to admit he felt some remorse in leaving the Wheeling area, where he still had four sons, two of which were now at an age when they were likely itching to get in on any military action that might fall out of this secession. A part of him wished the telegram had not come, as it complicated his life. Yet he felt duty calling him. *I'll write to President Garrett and ask for his advice,* he thought, *since this job will likely involve protecting the B&O. Taking command of a regiment might be the most important job I could do right now, for myself, my family, my country, and the B&O Railroad.*

FRIDAY, MAY 3, 1861, 6:00 PM
COURTHOUSE, CLARKSBURG, HARRISON COUNTY, VIRGINIA

The day for the mass meeting dawned gloomily and when it was time for the meeting, rain poured down in torrents. Francis Pierpont, a lawyer for the county and an outspoken opponent of Virginia's secession, wondered whether anyone would brave the weather to attend. But shortly, through the rain and mud, on horseback and in wagons, people packed into the courthouse until it was overflowing. It looked to him that at least 1,000 people had come, from all over the county, to hear the speakers talk about the Richmond Convention, which had voted to take their state out of the country, and decide what to do about it.

When the starting time grew near, the crowd began to chant for their favorite speaker, John Carlile. When he didn't appear, they began chanting for another favorite, Waitman Willey, who was also scheduled to speak. Sensing the growing frustration, Pierpont came out and greeted the crowd, apologizing for the lateness of Carlile and Willey.

"Gentlemen, we have all gathered here this evening because we know our liberties are threatened. Your very presence is evidence enough to tell me that you want something done about it. If you will allow me, I will examine this act of secession that the convention in Richmond has approved and point out a few of its weaknesses and fallacies."

The crowd roared with approval and many cried out, "Hear, hear!"

Pierpont was stirred to the very depths of his soul. For about two and a half hours, he delivered what he thought was perhaps the greatest speech of his career. He denounced the "infamous usurpation" at Richmond, and every point he made against the traitors was cheered. He reminded the crowd that every officer of the State of Virginia, on assuming their office, had taken an oath to support the Constitution of the United States, had sworn allegiance to the United States Government, and that the Constitution expressly declared that levying war against the United

States, or giving aid and comfort to its enemies, was treason and merited punishment.

At the end of the meeting, Pierpont said, "If the ordinance of secession is passed on May 23 by the people of our State, it will place our state of Virginia in direct hostility to the Federal government and transfer the war from South Carolina to our own doors. Western Virginia has patiently submitted to and borne up under the oppression of Eastern Virginia for half a century. If secession is the only remedy offered by her for all her wrongs, the day is near when Western Virginia will rise in the majesty of her strength and patriotism, and repudiate her oppressors, remain firmly under the Stars and Stripes—the glorious emblem of our nationality and greatness."

He surveyed the cheering crowd with elation. *These are stern men,* he thought, *ready to fight if necessary to maintain their liberties!*

SATURDAY, MAY 4, 1861
HARPER'S FERRY, VIRGINIA

Colonel Porterfield gazed at the train wending its way around Maryland Heights and entering the great covered bridge—a thousand feet long, they say—that crossed the mighty Potomac. The train slowly made its way up the river on the Virginia side toward Wheeling and the Ohio River. The chugging sounds of the engine, hissing steam and puffing smoke, echoed from the surrounding mountains and mixed with the roar of the rapids from the Shenandoah River, coming in from the south, and the Potomac River, coming in from the north. Here at this spot, beside this small lovely village, these two fabled rivers joined forces and ground their way through the mountains.

It was a sight to behold and Porterfield had thought he would get to spend many days here viewing the countryside while inspecting the troops under the command of his friend, Colonel Thomas J. Jackson, who had been sent here to take command of the area and the mustered-in troops for the Virginia militia.

But all of this had changed suddenly when he received the telegram that he still clutched in his hand. It was from Major-General Robert E. Lee and it read: *Colonel George A. Porterfield: You are directed to repair to Grafton, Taylor County...*

As he mulled over the contents of the telegram, his friend Jackson came up to him on the porch where he was standing, holding one arm in the air, a strange habit of Jackson's that Porterfield did not understand. Something to do with circulation, he thought. Jackson had sweat running down his face from the warm day and the climb up the steep steps. Tom, as Porterfield knew him from their Mexican War days, had been hard at work trying to salvage weapons from the Federal Arsenal that the Union soldiers had burned, just before Turner Ashby showed up with his Virginia cavalry to seize the arsenal and its weapons. Porterfield and Jackson had heard that Ashby's raid had been perpetrated by ex-Governor Wise without the knowledge of Governor Letcher. Both agreed that Ashby was brash and foolish. Nevertheless, Governor Letcher had just issued a proclamation calling for 50,000 volunteers and it was probably that proclamation which resulted in the change of Porterfield's orders to go to Grafton, and Tom's new order to form a brigade of infantry.

"Tom, you used to live near Clarksburg. As I recall that's near to Grafton, isn't it? What do you think my chances are of forming up several companies to protect the B&O Railroad out there?"

"Well, if my sister is any indication, you're going to have your hands full. She is a unionist through and through. When she heard about the vote for secession, and that I'd been appointed a colonel in the Virginia militia, she wrote and said she *never* wanted to see me again!"

Porterfield was surprised to hear this. He knew the northwesterners in the state were not exactly happy about Virginia seceding from the Union, but he fully expected them to eventually fall in with the rest of Virginia and do their duty. He grimaced.

Jackson was curious. "What's going on, George? I thought you came here as an inspector."

"I did, but I just received a telegram from General Lee ordering me to take up residence in Grafton. Lee wants me to form up companies to protect both branches of the railroad. Just wondering what I might encounter out there."

"Well, I understand many of the western county delegates left the Convention right after the delegates voted for secession. Now they're stirring up the people out there with their unionist speeches. I don't envy you this new assignment."

"Lee apparently contacted Major Loring at Wheeling and directed forces under him to give protection at the railroad terminus there. Lee has ordered me to protect the terminus at Parkersburg, placing there a suitable officer in command. Lee says Major F. M. Boykin, Jr. will be under my orders. Lee also mentioned that he has sent 200 muskets to Major Boykin to be distributed by me."

"I don't know those two majors and I surely don't know anything about 200 muskets being sent," replied Jackson. "But I'm sure you'll contact both of these officers and get their understanding of the situation."

"Yes, Tom, I was planning to do just that. I'm sorry to hear about your sister's reaction to your promotion."

Porterfield watched Jackson depart, his arm still in the air. Porterfield went inside and pulled out a map. He could see that Grafton was a strategic town on the B&O Railroad, located at the junction of the B&O branch serving Wheeling and the Northwestern Virginia Railroad serving Parkersburg. On a stagecoach road leading south from Grafton was the small town of Philippi, and further south was the town of Beverly, located on the Staunton-Parkersburg Turnpike. *Might be a supply line and an escape route should I ever run into an overwhelming force.*

Sunday, May 5, 1861, 10:00 am
Smithfield, Fayette County, Pennsylvania
Union Methodist Episcopal Church

In his Sunday service Reverend Hagans told the congregation what he knew about the Clarksburg meeting on Friday night and the news about Lincoln's latest call for volunteers. He spoke with the last family to leave the church and then turned to AJ. "Have you heard about the President's new call for 40,000 volunteers to enlist for three-year service?" he asked.

"Three years! It's a lot longer than I was thinking," AJ replied.

"Yes, but at least Lincoln did add, 'unless sooner discharged.'"

"I know, but didn't we hear he also asked for 25,000 volunteers for *five*-year service? How long could this war last?"

"Well, AJ, this is one of those mysteries that God keeps from us, to see how we're going to handle it. Think about what George Washington faced. Each year part of his army left him because their enlistment was up. No one ever thought that war would last seven years."

Seven years... The thought of it almost made him cry. AJ couldn't bear to think of having to fight for that long. *Why, I'd be almost thirty, an old man.*

"Are we riding tomorrow, Harry?" Accompanying Harry on his Monday pastoral rounds was an activity AJ looked forward to nowadays. He could share his concerns and ideas with his close friend, and it provided an opportunity to condition Shiloh for future long marches.

"Yes, we can talk about all this tomorrow. Go home and get some rest. I'm worried about you, AJ. You don't seem like your usual self."

"I'll be ready."

AJ knew he wasn't himself. A big Sophia-shaped hole had been cut out of his heart. He tried to keep busy, as a cure for his heartsickness, but it didn't seem to be working. AJ glanced across the churchyard at Cynthia and Sophia in their colorful Sunday best, talking and laughing. Not so long ago, in happier days, he would have been standing and laughing with them, asking to walk Sophia home, enjoying her light banter. He stared at her profile, memorizing it, and she suddenly turned and saw him looking at her. She colored and raised her hand as if to wave, but then turned her head away. AJ turned his head too and pretended that he had merely been looking down the road and not at her.

MONDAY, MAY 6, 1861, 8:00 AM
MAJOR-GENERAL McCLELLAN, HQ, CAMP DENNISON,
CINCINNATI, OHIO

Now it's official, he thought. The latest telegram from Washington made him a Major General in the regular U.S. army. He read it aloud: *Commander Department of Ohio, General Order No. 14, Adjutant General's Office, Washington, D.C., May 3, 1861.* He liked the sound of this new title.

The title was even bigger than it sounded. The new department was responsible for the defense not only of the state of Ohio, but also of the states of Indiana and Illinois. Some of his aides said they heard it would soon include western Pennsylvania and western Virginia—the latter being included because all indications pointed to western Virginia's intent to remain loyal to the United States. The storm clouds of war were gathering and now George Brinton McClellan would finally have the opportunity to show what he was made of!

His self-congratulations were justified. McClellan had been specially accepted at the age of 15 into West Point and graduated second highest in the Class of 1846. He was twice brevetted for gallantry in the Mexican War—he went in as a second lieutenant and came out a brevet captain. In civilian life he became chief engineer and vice president of the Illinois Central Railroad and, later, the president of the Ohio and Mississippi Railroad—a position he had just resigned to reenter the military service. The governors of Ohio, Pennsylvania, and New York, the three largest states in the Union, wanted him to command their state militias. Governor William Dennison of Ohio had been the most aggressive pursuer and offered him a commission as Major General of Volunteers. Most importantly, he had won the hand of his charming wife, Mary Ellen Marcy, who had a total of nine marriage proposals to choose from—now his Nelly. And he was just 34 years old!

An aide popped his head in the door and announced, "General, it's almost time for the review." George snapped out of his reverie. He had to process thousands of men who were volunteering for service and he had to supervise setting up training camps. This had been going on since he accepted his commission on April 23. It was going to be another long day.

MONDAY, MAY 6, 1861, 8:00 AM
SWANEY FARM, SMITHFIELD, PENNSYLVANIA

"Good morning, AJ," Harry said with his usual warm smile. "Did you rest well?"

"Tossed and turned," AJ said. "Just too much on my mind, I guess."

"Sorry to hear that, my friend."

"When I left you yesterday I couldn't get the enlistment out of my head. So as soon as I got home I asked Pa if he would be disappointed in me if I volunteered to enlist in the army for three years. Pa said I should do what I think is best for the country. He said he could handle the farm till I got home. We talked about finding a boy to help him, somebody too young to join up."

Harry nodded. They rode on in silence for several minutes, each lost in his own thoughts. Finally, Harry broke the long silence. "Have you ever been to Wheeling, AJ?"

"No, I've only been as far as Morgantown. Why?"

"Well, I've been thinking about going to Wheeling and sitting in on some of the convention sessions that are supposed to start next Monday. I want to hear what they're planning and maybe meet some of the delegates. Also, I've been thinking about enlisting for three years too, and maybe I can find out what western Virginia is planning. I prefer to be in a cavalry unit but I haven't heard anything yet about enlisting as a horse soldier. The way you ride and handle a rifle, you would probably make a good horse soldier, AJ. You certainly have one of the best trained mounts I've seen in these parts."

"I'd like to go with you to Wheeling, but I'll need to talk to Pa about the plantin'. Don't want to get too far behind. I'd like to get into a cavalry unit too. Maybe we can enlist at the same time. Do you think they let you bring your own horse?"

"Not sure about that, but I'll ask around. It would please me very much if we could join the same outfit. I need to stop at this next house. You want to come in? Mr. Sutton isn't doing so well. I'm afraid he's not long for this world."

"Yes, I'll come in with you. Pa told me Ol' Man Sutton was a good friend of my grandfather's."

Harry and AJ let Betsy and Shiloh drink from the nearby watering trough and then tied their horses to a hitching post. Harry reminded AJ that Mr. Sutton used to live in Smithfield, but after his wife died he had moved in with his daughter and husband. Both of them had since died and Mr. Sutton, now 89 years old, got his meals from a kind neighbor. His doctor visited him every few months and Harry visited about once a week. Mr. Sutton was hard of hearing and his eyesight was dim, but seemed to have a good memory.

Harry knocked hard, opened the door, and loudly announced, "Mr. Sutton, it's Preacher Hagans. Can I come in?"

The old man was sitting by the fire in a cane chair, his head on his chest. He jerked awake at the noise and blinked. "Who? Yes, yes, come in. Of course you can come in. Sit down, Preacher. Is that James Swaney with you?"

"No, Mr. Sutton, that's his son Alexander."

"Who? No, no, I don't believe it is. James's son is just a tot about 4 or 5 years old. How are you, James? It's been a long while since I saw you last. How's your Pa?"

Deciding it best not to try to explain, AJ bellowed, "Doing very well. And how are you?"

"Not worth much, James, I can't hear too good anymore and my eyes are bad. Can't say much for my mind either. Heh heh."

At this point, Harry took over and talked with the old man about his health, God, and the regular visits Harry made to his wife's gravesite in Smithfield. Mr. Sutton thanked him, reminding him that he wanted to be buried by her side. "Miz Smith next door has been right good to me and feeds me. I want her to have anything that's left after I kick the bucket, Preacher." Harry nodded and then helped the old man to his feet so he could slowly walk out to the gate, to pet the horses.

"Yessir, I cain't see 'em too good, but I can smell 'em," Mr. Sutton said, taking a deep, wheezing breath. "I allus liked that horse smell. Fine animals!"

Mrs. Smith came over to chat with them for a while, and then AJ and Harry helped Mr. Sutton back inside. AJ watched the old man's weak, tottering steps and thought about what it must be like to grow old. *I hope I at least get a chance to find out,* he thought.

As he and Harry turned to leave, Mr. Sutton lifted a frail hand in their direction. "James, farewell. Thank you for comin'. I sure hope your Pa is well."

AJ eyes filled as he hollered back, "It was good seeing you again, Mr. Sutton!"

As Harry and AJ mounted, AJ said, "I don't know how you do this, Harry. It's sad seeing a man that old and frail, with so few friends and no family left. It scares me to think of dyin' alone."

"He has the hope of Heaven, AJ. That makes a difference."

MONDAY, MAY 6, 1861
MOSIER FARM, SMITHFIELD, PENNSYLVANIA

Sophia didn't sleep well and awoke tired and foggy-brained. She kept seeing AJ Swaney's dark eyes glancing over at her after church. It was strange not to be speaking to him. Things were so awkward between them now, after that night by the spring. It had never been like this before. She still felt a flash of anger whenever she thought about how AJ tried to tell her what to do. *Just like he was my father.*

Still, she had to admit she missed talking to him, missed seeing that special look in his eye. When he had looked at her that way, she felt like a grown-up woman. But why couldn't he just tell her how he felt? Cynthia thinks AJ cares for me like a woman, but why can't *he* tell me so? Do I really want a man that can't say what's on his mind?

The grinning face of Tip Swaney intruded into her thoughts. He was an attractive tease, lively where AJ was quiet. She liked having a man around that joked and laughed and paid her compliments all the time. Even if he did pinch her and try to steal kisses when no one else was looking. He hadn't come back to church, but he had called on her again Tuesday night, and she hadn't told him to stop coming.

AJ seemed to think he had some claim on her, but if he wanted to claim her, he sure had a funny way of doing it. She couldn't decide how she felt about AJ. She liked rambling over their two farms and the back roads with him, talking about what berries were getting ripe, or how Shiloh's training was coming, or when it would be time to plant the wheat. She liked seeing his broad shoulders and ropy arm muscles bent to some task.

"Ma, can I run over to the Swaney's real quick and see Cynthia, before we start the washing?"

Her mother hesitated. "You always think of some way to sneak out of here on wash day… oh, all right, but make it a quick visit, Sophia."

"I will, Ma." She ran all the way to the neighboring farmhouse and pounded on the door.

"Come in, Sophia, you look ragged. Has something happened?"

"No, Mrs. Swaney, I just want to talk to Cynthia about something."

"Well, then, come in. Would you like a biscuit?"

"No, thank you, ma'am." Sophia looked around the kitchen. "What's Mr. Swaney and AJ up to today?" she asked innocently.

"Mr. Swaney is getting ready to plant corn. AJ went off again with Reverend Hagans. I declare that boy is worrying me lately, with all this running around. He looks downright peaked."

"Oh, AJ's not here?" Sophia said.

Cynthia came into the room with a wicker basket full of sheets in her arms. "Ma, is there anything else... Oh, Sophia, what are you doing here?"

"Just wanted to talk to you for a minute."

Cynthia's brow furrowed. "Has something happened since we saw each other yesterday? Is your grandma all right?"

"No, nothing's happened, not exactly. Grandma's still all right."

"Well, come help me get the washwater and we can talk while we're doing it."

The two headed to the spring carrying pails. The washtub was already set over a low fire in the yard. "I just wanted to ask you what you really think of your cousin Tip Swaney," Sophia said.

Cynthia tilted her head and looked Sophia full in the face. "You ran over here just to ask me that? Oh, I think he's fairly handsome, and a lot of fun. I used to be sort of sweet on him, but he never paid much attention to me. Are things getting more serious with you and Tip?"

"No... not yet, anyway. But he's asking me to go out with him some more. He wants me to go with him to some dances over the summer and I was wondering if maybe you might like to go with us, sort of like a chaperone. Ma and Pa don't want me to be by myself with Tip."

"Oh, that would be fun!" Cynthia cried. "I don't get to go much of anywhere. I don't have a beau, you know." She stuck out her lower lip in a pout.

Sophia laughed at her and stuck out her tongue. They busied themselves for several minutes dippering the cold spring water into the pails and splashing each other like children. "So, how is AJ doing?" Sophia finally ventured.

"He's been awful busy lately. You know he's been talking about enlisting after Lincoln called for all those soldiers. He wants to join the cavalry for three years. And maybe Harry too, which is breaking my heart. AJ and Harry are going to ride all the way to Wheeling for a week, to go to some big meeting there."

"Three years! But why? He don't *have* to go, does he?"

"I know, Sophia, ain't... isn't it terrible? He's an awful tease but I'll miss him and worry so much. We all will. I don't know what Pa will do without him." She sighed. "Things just don't turn out like you expect, do they, Sophia? You know I really hoped you and AJ would get married—I didn't count on any old war coming along, or Tip Swaney neither."

"Well, I don't know about *marrying* Tip. He's fun, but..."

"But what?"

"Oh, I just don't know, Cynthia. Let's finish carrying this water. I have to get home and get our laundry going, or Ma will tan my hide."

CHAPTER FIVE

Give Me Liberty or Give Me Death

May 10–May 15, 1861

National Hotel in Beallsville, Pennsylvania

FRIDAY, MAY 10, 1861, 9:00 AM
PENN CENTRAL RAILROAD STATION
PHILADELPHIA, PENNSYLVANIA

"All aboard!"

Ben Kelley sat in the first row of his first-class coach and listened as the conductor stood on the platform, yelling, "Last call, all aboard, last call, folks, all aboard!" Moments later the Pennsylvania Central engine, puffing smoke and steam, slowly pulled out of the Philadelphia Station headed for Wheeling, Virginia. The conductor, starting down the aisle to check tickets, smiled at him, obviously recognizing his passenger as the new freight agent of the B&O Railroad in Philadelphia.

"Good mornin', Mistah Kelley," The conductor said with a wink. "I won't tell anybody that you abandoned the B&O to ride in a *great* first-class coach."

"Good morning to you too, Bob. Now you know us so-called Union men must be careful these days on the B&O. The Virginia militia are parked over there at Harper's Ferry. You wouldn't want anything to happen to me, would you?"

"No sir, Mistah Kelley! Us Pennsylvanians are happy that so many folks like you want to stay in these United States, and not run off and join that Confederacy."

Kelley chuckled and said, "I'm going back to Wheeling as a colonel, to take command of a regiment of mountain soldiers, to try to keep us in the Union."

"Sir... I mean Colonel, congratulations! Are all those muskets we're carrying yours?"

Kelley lowered his voice and looked around the coach. "Umm, maybe, but let's keep that our secret. We don't want anything to happen to this train."

"My lips are sealed, Colonel. I better be moving along now. Best of luck to you."

Kelley had decided to take the job offered him by Wheeling's Mayor Sweeney. President Garrett of the B&O was happy to have a commander who really knew his railroad line, and a military man as well, to protect the railroad and help keep northwestern Virginia in the Union.

Kelley had communicated with his children still living in Wheeling. They all wanted him back and said they were proud he would be leading the first infantry regiment in western Virginia. All the boys wanted to join his regiment.

Kelley had telegraphed his decision after he heard that ten companies were already forming and all they needed now was for him to take charge of the regiment and start a training program. The soldiers were ready to fight, had their own muskets, and knew how to use them. But marching together, standing in line and delivering volley fire, along with many other crucial skills of an infantry soldier, would have to be taught to them—and there was no time to lose.

It was a long traveling day and he went over in his mind everything he had learned at the Partridge Military Academy. By the time he arrived in Wheeling, he had nearly filled a notebook with names of officers, training schedules, and a list of tasks that he needed to do before and after taking command.

FRIDAY, MAY 10, 1861, 3:00 PM
NATIONAL PIKE, BEALLSVILLE, PENNSYLVANIA

WANTED
A few Brave Men
to join the
RINGGOLD
CAVALRY

The handbill hung next to the entrance door of the National Hotel and caught AJ's eye as he and Harry rode into Beallsville. "What's this, Harry? Somethin' we need to look into while we're here?"

The two men were weary after their long day's ride on the National Road. When they had made their plans for their trip to the Wheeling Convention, Beallsville was to be their first night's stop. It was about thirty miles from Smithfield—the number of miles each day they planned to spend in the saddle, in order to cover the almost ninety miles to Wheeling by the opening of the convention. Both young men were invigorated by their plans and hopeful that the Convention would help them answer many of the questions they had about their own, and the country's, future. AJ had talked seriously about the journey with his father, explaining what he hoped to learn by it. He felt guilty about taking time from spring plowing and planting, but his father had agreed to handle the corn planting in AJ's absence, with the help of John and a hardworking son of a neighbor. John didn't mind one bit being kept out of school for a week.

When they started out that morning, Harry had told AJ that he was looking forward to being on the National Pike with him. "This Road's a piece of our history, AJ, the first Federal highway. So many famous people, and so many settlers heading west, have gone this way before us," he said.

The pair had found the going easy along the wide, macadamized road, but traffic was lighter than expected and many of the taverns and businesses were closed and boarded up, or turned into private residences. "Wish we could have seen it back in the '40s, in its heyday, before the railroads came in," Harry commented. "They say it was nothing to see twenty stagecoaches and a hundred six-horse wagons lined up on the road in those days."

They wore comfortable riding clothes and carried their personal necessities, along with oats for their horses, in saddle bags. They planned to sleep out at night under the stars. Each carried a blanket roll covered with a rubber blanket. Fastened together over a horizontal pole with uprights, the rubber blankets could be made into a two-man tent, essential for rainy nights. They would buy food along the way and graze their horses when they took breaks. They brought money, tucked safely away in their riding boots, to pay for tolls, ferry crossings and a boardinghouse when they arrived in Wheeling. For safety, each carried a flintlock horse pistol with powder and lead balls, and a hunting knife.

Intrigued by the cavalry handbill, they dismounted and walked into the shade of the hotel porch. "Look here, Harry." AJ pointed to a name and address of the person to contact—Dr. John Keys. "Let's ride over and talk to him and see what this is all about." AJ and Harry asked directions from a woman entering the hotel, and then rode to the address, just a few blocks away.

A sign on the door read:

Dr. John Keys

Medical and Surgical Practice

Please Knock

Harry stepped up and knocked loudly on the door. AJ hung back a few paces, his hat in hand. After a moment, a tall, slim man, appearing slightly older than Harry, opened the door and looked quizzically at them.

"My practice is closed today, gentlemen. Can I help you in any way?" he said. His manner was businesslike, but cordial.

Harry replied, "Good afternoon, sir. Sorry to interrupt you after hours. My name is Harrison Hagans and this is my friend Alexander Swaney. We were riding through town and noticed the handbill on the National Hotel about the Ringgold Cavalry. We are from Fayette County on our way to Wheeling to attend a convention. We're both very interested in joining a cavalry unit."

The man smiled and gestured for them to enter. "In that case, please come in, gentlemen. My name is John Keys. Whereabouts in Fayette County? I too was born in that county, on a farm about six miles east of Brownsville."

"We're both from Smithfield, about six miles south of Uniontown," Harry said. "I'm a minister of the gospel and Alexander is a farmer… everyone calls him AJ, by the way."

"It's nice to meet both of you. AJ, I was once a farmer, before I went to medical school. Hard work, but I loved it." He ran his fingers through his unruly black hair. "Well, let me get right down to it, and tell you I'm sorry to say that if you've come to enlist in the Ringgold Cavalry Company, so far I've run up against a stone wall in getting my company into the service of our country. I've written Governor Curtin and offered our cavalry, but he wrote back saying that Mr. Lincoln didn't want any cavalry. I intend to go to Harrisburg soon and speak with the Governor, because this makes no sense to me. If there's going to be fighting, we *are* going to need cavalry!"

Harry replied, "Right now we're just trying to find out if there are any cavalry companies we could join. We're both experienced with horses. AJ is the finest horseman I ever had the pleasure to ride with. He has a well-trained horse and can shoot the eye out of a squirrel from 150 yards, using his horse's back to sight from. Beats anything I ever saw!"

"Now that *is* an impressive feat. I would surely like to see you do that, AJ. That's a nice horse you have. A Morgan, I believe, is it not?"

"Ye-yes, sir, it is," AJ stammered, his face flushed from the unaccustomed praise and attention. "He was a gift from my pa."

Dr. Keys continued, "I'm quite willing to tell you everything I know about the cavalry. I was about to close my office and get something to eat. If you haven't had supper, why don't you come to my farm and have supper with me and my family? My place is just about a mile out of town. If you wish, you can keep your horses in my barn and spend the night. That way I can tell you about the Ringgold Cavalry company, you can ask any questions you have, get a good night's sleep and leave when you wish in the morning."

"We were going to sleep out under the stars, but how can we refuse such a kind invitation? And we're very eager to learn more about the cavalry," Harry replied. AJ nodded his agreement, happy that they would apparently get some of their questions answered by this knowledgeable man.

"Then it's settled. My horse is out back grazing in the yard. I'll go saddle up. Wait for me here."

As the three rode together to Dr. Keys's farm, he explained the history of the Ringgold Cavalry. The company had started in 1847 at Monongahela, Pennsylvania, a small town about 15 miles northeast of Beallsville on the west bank of the Monongahela River. The company was named Ringgold in honor of Major Samuel Ringgold, who served with distinction in the Mexican War. Keys was the third captain of that proud company, which had been training for years as a Pennsylvania cavalry unit.

On arrival at Dr. Keys's two-story frame house, four tow-headed girls ranging in age from about 5 to 16 ran to greet their father. He patted their heads and kissed each of them affectionately. AJ and Harry offered to care for the horses while Dr. Keys went to tell his wife that he had brought guests for supper. At Dr. Keys's suggestion, they released all three animals into a small, lush pasture near the house, where they could graze all night and have plenty of fresh water from the creek. Harry and AJ then joined Dr. Keys at the house. He introduced them to Mrs. Keys, a plump, harried-seeming woman of about 30, and his two-year-son John Junior. Harry apologized to Mrs. Keys for adding to her household burden for the evening, but she smiled and said, "Don't you worry. I'm used to it!"

The supper was plain but filling and was enlivened by the chatter of the children. After the meal, Dr. Keys shooed the children away and took his two guests into his study.

"As you might imagine," he said, "I had to learn a lot about cavalry training before I was elected as the Ringgold's captain. I'm sure you both know that the horse and rider are partners who need to understand one another very well. But that's not enough to make a good cavalry horse or a good cavalryman. A cavalryman's horse must learn how to get along with other horses, and the rider must learn how to cooperate with other cavalrymen.

"For example, the cavalry horse must be able to ride side by side with other cavalry horses and remain side by side as they jump fences and other obstacles. As with infantry, we call it 'holding the line.' The cavalry horse must be able to run in line behind or ahead of another line of cavalry horses without trying to pass the line ahead or fall back on the line behind. The cavalry horse must know how to wheel right and left while keeping a straight line. Cavalry horses with even more training can turn on their haunches to allow the rider to use his sword or other weapons effectively against an enemy cavalryman.

"Of course, the cavalryman must know how to give his cavalry horse all these commands and know an almost bewildering number of bugle calls. Most importantly, a cavalryman pays attention to the feeding and comfort of his horse *before* his own. But you both obviously know that."

Keys paused in his monologue to take a breath. He smiled. "I can see by the glazed looks in your eyes that I've overwhelmed you with detail. A problem I have. I know this seems like a lot to learn, and it is. I can give you a list of books that you might order from the publisher, if you want to practice with your horses. I understand that a cavalry manual written by Philip St. George Cooke will be out soon, so you may want to get yourself a copy. I still feel that I have a lot to learn, especially when companies are formed into regiments and regiments into brigades, which are then supposed to work as a single team. So far, I've only drilled our men by platoons and as a company…

"But I've talked far too much! It's a subject very near to my heart, as you can see. What questions do you have for me?"

AJ was intimidated to hear of the amount of training needed, but at the same time he was challenged and thrilled by it. He felt sure that Shiloh was capable of being an excellent cavalry mount. Hesitant, he asked, "Could I bring my own horse?"

"Yes," Dr. Keys replied. "I can't recall how much, but the government will pay some amount of money to you per day for use of your horse and will place a value on your animal. So, if your horse should be killed in the line of duty, you would receive that money."

AJ's heart gave a lurch as he thought about Shiloh being killed in battle.

"What about bringing our own arms?" Harry asked.

"I'm sure you could bring some of your own arms, but not too many of us have our own sword. I suspect we'll see more pistols and carbines come into service as they're developed by arms manufacturers. I'm very interested in your long rifle, AJ. I know during the Revolutionary War Morgan's men made good use of those rifles, in the battles of Saratoga and the Cowpens, and I understand the mountain men from Tennessee won the Battle of Kings Mountain using those rifles."

"Yes, I know a little about those battles," AJ replied eagerly. "My grandfather left me his long rifle that he got from a German gunsmith over in eastern Pennsylvania. It's very accurate and I taught myself how to change the powder load for different ranges and how to handle drop and windage. But you can't load a long rifle as fast as you can a musket, so for close-range volley fire it's not so good. But you can't beat it for long shots."

AJ's enthusiasm for the subject overcame his natural reticence, and the three talked well into the night. They exchanged mailing addresses so they could write and keep in touch. Dr. Keys expressed his hope that they would join his cavalry company, if and when he got approval. Also, he wanted to be kept informed of the developments in the western part of Virginia. He told them that, from what he had read in the Wheeling newspaper, it seemed that many counties west of the Alleghenies were determined to stay loyal.

That night, Harry and AJ slept in a back room. The next morning they rose early, before the children were awake, and had a hearty breakfast prepared by Dr. Keys, who let his wife sleep a little longer. Harry and AJ then headed west to the town of Washington, their next stop on the National Pike.

SATURDAY, MAY 11, 1861, 9:00 AM
LEE'S OFFICE, RICHMOND, VIRGINIA

General Lee stared at the letter he had received from Major Boykin four days ago. Twice now he had tried to answer the letter and ended up throwing those drafts in the fire. He wondered, *Was my telegram of April 30th to Boykin so unclear? 'Muster into the service of the State volunteer companies from the northwest counties, assume command, go to Grafton, protect the B & O Railroad, don't interrupt the peaceful travel on the road, don't annoy the citizens using the road, and tell me if a force is needed at Parkersburg.' How could I have been clearer?*

Boykin's letter stated that it was "impractical" to hold Grafton with a small force. The citizens were very bitter and disposed to support the Union. The area was "verging on a state of actual revolution." One of their leaders, John S. Carlile, openly proclaimed the laws of the State should not be recognized. And Boykin strongly suggested that at least one battery and 500 men from the eastern counties should be sent to Parkersburg.

General Lee would try once more to draft a reply. This time he told Boykin: *You must persevere and call out companies from well affected counties and march them to Grafton. Four hundred rifles and some ammunition have been ordered from Staunton to Major Goff at Beverly. I do not think it prudent to order companies from other parts of the State to Grafton, as it might irritate, instead of conciliating, the population of that region. On Colonel Porterfield's arrival at Grafton communicate this letter to him.*

SATURDAY, MAY 11, 1861, 6:00 PM
NATIONAL PIKE, 3 MILES WEST OF WASHINGTON, PENNSYLVANIA

As AJ and Harry left Washington, the traffic on the National Pike noticeably increased. Wagons carrying a variety of farm produce rolled west toward Wheeling, and wagons from Wheeling loaded with kegs of nails, leather products, bricks and other manufactured goods were heading back east. Herds of cattle, horses, sheep, pigs and turkeys with their drovers traveled the road in both directions. Once, the two travelers rode past a line of ragged male slaves tied to a cable in pairs, trudging toward Wheeling, being driven like cattle. AJ, wide-eyed, turned to Harry. He had seen free blacks in Uniontown, but never slaves tied together like that. The young pastor shook his head, sorrow in his eyes. "They're probably fugitives being taken to Wheeling, either to be returned to their owners or sold at the auction there. Human beings treated like animals, AJ. We have much to answer for..."

They rode west together in silence for a long while. AJ couldn't get the image of one slave's face from his mind. The man's skin was about the color of Shiloh's coat, and he was tall, well-muscled, and carried himself in a dignified manner. He had lifted his head as they rode past and stared at AJ's horse and had suddenly smiled at AJ, showing even white teeth. AJ felt an instant connection with the man, obviously an appreciator of beautiful horse flesh even in his current misery. AJ had heard the arguments: that the blacks weren't fully human; that they were better off enslaved here, being fed and cared for, than free in heathen Africa; that God had ordained slavery and the Bible approved it. He wasn't sure how he was supposed to feel about it all, but that smile from the black man had told AJ that the man was certainly a fellow man and a fellow horse lover.

"That looks like a good, quiet place to bed down for the night," Harry said, pointing ahead to the right as the last light began to fade. He indicated a level grassy spot at the base of a hill, near a clump of hemlocks. "It's well off the road, and the sky's clear. There's a meadow over there, and a small stream."

AJ nodded his approval. They removed the saddles, saddlebags and bedrolls from the horses, led the horses to the stream and then turned them loose. Neither horse was staked since they had abundant grazing and never strayed far from their owners.

AJ soon had a fire going. Both men spread out their bedrolls, leaned against their saddles and chewed on biscuits and beef. A gentle breeze occasionally caused the fire to flicker. As twilight approached AJ pointed to a spot in the western sky and announced, "There's the first star, Harry."

They both stared up into the deep indigo sky as other stars flickered into view.

After a companionable silence, AJ said, "I liked watching the men marching around the parade grounds in Washington. That could be us sometime soon, Harry! They said they were going to be with the 12th Pennsylvania volunteer infantry. The 90-day infantry, that is. But nobody seemed to know anything about any cavalry companies forming. One officer told me to check about the Ringgold Cavalry in Beallsville."

Harry chuckled. "We're ahead of them there, aren't we? Those men I talked to were also very eager to hear news about what's happening in western Virginia. They clearly approved when I said I was certain the western counties would stay with the Union."

"Some of 'em told me they read the Wheeling paper. So I figure they'll get the news of what happens at the Wheeling Convention almost as soon as we do."

"One more day in the saddle and we'll be there. Good night, AJ. Don't forget—tomorrow is Sunday. We'll have services together right here, in God's cathedral, before we start out in the morning." He sighed softly. "I'll be thinking of our church back home, you know. I don't like to miss a Sunday of preaching, but I know Reverend Miller will tend the flock in my absence. When—or if—you and I leave to join the Army, I'm hoping he'll take over my church while I'm gone. He had a long career as pastor of a church north of Uniontown, but they recently hired a younger man. I don't think retirement suits him. And he's too old to be called up by the military. God always provides, AJ." Harry turned over and adjusted his saddle blanket to use as a pillow.

AJ smiled. "You know nobody can really take your place, Harry. Good night." AJ closed his eyes but sleep didn't come. His mind was uneasy, with the future still so uncertain. Images of soldiers drilling, the clattering of wagons, and the face of the black man in the sad line of slaves flashed before his eyes. He listened to Harry's light snores till long into the night. Then, in restless dreams, he told Sophia he loved her and wanted to marry her.

SUNDAY, MAY 12, 1861, 2:00 PM

WHEELING, VIRGINIA

AJ stared at the dark clouds of lingering smoke filling the sky from the surrounding iron furnaces. Most of the iron in these parts was used to produce nails—Wheeling's nickname was "The Nail City." The mighty Wheeling Suspension Bridge came into view, rising high above the Ohio River as the two horsemen rounded the north loop of Wheeling Creek. They stopped in amazement to watch a steam-powered paddlewheeler puffing dense clouds of smoke into the already gray sky, as it headed upstream and passed under the bridge. At 1,000 feet long, measured from the bridge pier on the east bank of the Ohio River to the bridge pier on Wheeling Island, this had been the longest suspension bridge in the world when it was completed in 1849.

Wheeling was now the fourth largest city in Virginia, trailing only Richmond, Petersburg, and Norfolk in population. The city had grown rapidly since the National Road arrived in 1818 and was extended across the Ohio River by the suspension bridge. But it was not only the National Road and bridge that provided transportation here. The Ohio River, the Northwestern Turnpike, the B&O Railroad, and the Pennsylvania Railroad provided transportation systems for goods of all kinds to and from the north, south, east, and west. It was this confluence of so many transportation systems that made the city one of the most vital commercial centers in the country.

The National Pike joined Market Street as the pair headed south to Washington Hall where the Convention would be held. Even though it was Sunday, Market Street was humming with commerce. They saw businesses of every sort: fruit and vegetable stands, blacksmiths, saddlers, tanners, hatters, hotels, bars, and clothing stores were just a few of the enterprises, all open for business. The odors were almost overwhelming, from food of every description, human and animal excrement, and other acrid crowd smells distinctly human.

As AJ watched the swarms of people, black and white, squeezing along the streets with their packages, his heart pounded and he struggled to catch his breath. For a moment he was afraid of falling from his horse. He had never been in a big city or in a large crowd of people. An image came to mind of the fish he caught back home and threw onto the bank to flop and gasp. *Like a fish out of water. Yessir, that's what I am!* He pressed his hand to his chest, trying to still his heart, and turned to gaze at Harry. His friend was stoically surveying the street scene, a slight smile on his lips. *Harry feels at home everywhere,* he thought. Resolving to follow Harry's example, he took several deep breaths and his dizziness passed. The pair neared the end of the street and both gazed up at the imposing three-story structure of Washington Hall, where the Convention would be held. AJ swallowed hard and Harry whistled in awe.

A man in the crowd apparently thought they were delegates and in-quired if they had already found a place to stay. "No," said Harry, "we came just to listen to the delegates. Can you direct us to an inexpensive establishment where we could board our horses and sleep?"

"Yessir, happens I know the cleanest and cheapest boardinghouse in town," the man said as he handed Harry a card with the boardinghouse address, "but I'm a'feared they might charge a big price on account of the big meetin'. Make sure you tell them folks at the desk you all are just spectators, else they'll raise their prices on you, sure as shootin'."

"Thank you, kind sir, for your help and advice," Harry said, "and good day to you." The man smiled and tipped his none-to-clean hat and went on his way. AJ and Harry decided to go to the boardinghouse by way of Main Street so they could take in the sights along the riverbank. Like Market Street, Main Street was also very busy. Boats of all sorts were lined up at the docks where men loaded and unloaded cargo into waiting wagons, while other men negotiated prices.

When AJ timidly asked one of the teamsters if it was usually so busy and crowded at the docks, the man spat a stream of brown juice on the ground and said, "Hell, no, this is a Sunday and lots a' workers won't work on a Sunday. Come by tomorrey and you'll see so many boats in the river you can almost walk across 'em to Wheeling Island!"

AJ and Harry finally wound their way through the crowds and reached the boardinghouse. The clerk behind the desk first quoted a very high price for a shared room and board for their horses. AJ watched and listened as Harry negotiated back and forth until he got the three-day price down to a more reasonable amount. *Harry knows how to handle just about anything we come up against,* he thought. He found the city unsettling and once again he envied Harry's confidence and calm demeanor.

Monday, May 13, 1861, 11:00 am
Washington Hall, Wheeling, Virginia

AJ and Harry arrived early and found seats in the spectator section. After election of a temporary chairman and secretary, Reverend Peter Laesterley offered a prayer to open the proceedings.

After that, it appeared to AJ and Harry that General John Jackson and Mr. John Carlile wasted most of the morning. Only one delegate spoke frankly as to the purpose of the Convention, Mr. Burdett of Taylor County, who said: "For my part I did not come here to talk. I came here for action. While we are talking, the chains have already been forged for us, and the bayonets are threatening invasion. In my town of Grafton, Letcher has ordered his troops to rendezvous. I tell you it is no time now to debate and evince feeling. I trust there will be no more of this, but calm, solemn, stern deliberation, and a resolve to do what is right to defend and protect ourselves!"

At dinner time the convention adjourned until 3:00 PM. When it reconvened, things finally became more exciting to the pair when General John Jackson of Wood County took the floor and expressed his opposition to the Convention taking any decisive action, as he thought it would be premature, and too "revolutionary." He proposed merely passing a series of resolutions condemning the wrongs done to the northwest counties of Virginia and waiting to see the results of the people's coming vote on secession on May 23 before taking any further action.

Mr. Burdett interrupted Jackson in midtirade: "Suppose in the meantime, while waiting, Letcher should throw his troops into this part of the state to intimidate the Union men and carry the election by violence and force, as they will do in the East; what do you propose to do in such a case? We must meet this emergency now!" Many of the delegates burst into loud applause. Burdett continued as the applause died down: "Are we to wait till a military despotism pervades our country from one end to another, and freemen's mouths are closed and we are threatened with ropes around our necks?" AJ and Harry looked at each other and nodded. Burdett's reaction concurred with their own.

John Carlile took the floor and replied to Jackson: "If I had supposed the deliberations of this body were to be limited to the adoption of a few paper resolutions, I would not have endured the fatigue, and passed the many sleepless nights, and expended the hundreds of dollars I have for the furtherance of what I supposed would be the action of this Convention, to maintain the liberties of a patriotic people."

Carlile was a popular spokesman and the applause for him was thunderous. He continued in the same vein, stating "western Virginia is already in a revolution because of the 'usurpers' in Richmond stealing the people's power to make their own decisions." He recommended immediate and decisive action. The delegates interrupted Carlile frequently with loud applause and cheers. AJ felt his own heart pounding with excitement and he had to fight an impulse to rise to his feet and cheer.

Carlile continued saying, "We are the only portion of this State that is not now under a military despotism. The order has gone forth and is even at this hour being executed, by which we are to share the same fate that has been imposed on other portions of the State. The soldiers have been ordered to rendezvous at various points in this part of the Commonwealth. No people ever remained free or ever will, that were not willing to spill their last drop of blood for the maintenance of their liberty. Show yourselves worthy to be free; and while I am not a professor of religion, yet I have the confidence which a pious mother instilled into me to believe that the Almighty, who seems to be distrusted now, will come to our aid and protect us in our freedom." Harry nodded enthusiastically and joined in the respectful applause that greeted the last statement.

General Jackson interrupted Carlile, saying, "I wish to know how prompt action would overcome the difficulty."

Carlile responded, "Let this Convention show its loyalty to the Union, and call upon the Federal government to furnish us with means of defense, and they will be furnished."

Many delegates again applauded, and Carlile continued saying, "There are 2,000 Minnie muskets here now" (the delegates cheered) "and more on the way, thank God." (The delegates cheered again.) "Let us act! It is useless to cry peace when there is no peace; and I for one will repeat what was said by one of Virginia's noblest sons and greatest statesmen, *Give me liberty or give me death!*"

The delegates rose from their seats with great and prolonged applause, and AJ and Harry joined in. Finally, Waitman Willey rose to give a speech supporting the position of General Jackson, and Cambell Tar of Brook County gave a speech supporting the position of Carlile. The Convention adjourned to reassemble at 10 AM on Tuesday. AJ and Harry left the hall to return to their boardinghouse, greatly stirred by what they had seen and heard that day.

MONDAY, MAY 13, 1861, 11:00 PM
WASHINGTON HALL, WHEELING, VIRGINIA

That night, after the Convention had adjourned for the day, one of the delegates, George M. Hagans, wrote in a letter to his friend, Major General George B. McClellan:

> *...I urge the immediate taking of the B & O R.R. The opinion is that the Confederates are now arranging for such a step themselves. You need not fear of wounding State pride of western Virginia. The people here will welcome the presence of U. S. forces. There is no doubt on this point for I have talked to the leading men of every county and this is their unanimous judgement. The U. S. arms here at Wheeling ought to be instantly distributed along the Rail Road; and decisive steps inaugurated at once. The people are with the Federal Government, and instances are narrated to me of their spirit and the determination in this regard, as furnish incontestable evidence that they are now ripe for movement...*

TUESDAY, MAY 14, 1861, 8:00 AM
MCCLELLAN'S HQ, CAMP DENNISON, CINCINNATI, OHIO

Now it's complete, McClellan thought. He held the latest telegram from Washington, that expanded his Department of Ohio to include the western counties in Virginia and Pennsylvania, in addition to the states of Ohio, Indiana, and Illinois. *Now,* he thought, *I can finally respond to all the letters I've been receiving from Virginia citizens in the western counties, asking for my help!*

TUESDAY, MAY 14, 1861, 9:00 AM
B&O RAILROAD STATION, GRAFTON, VIRGINIA

As the train pulled into the Grafton railroad station, Colonel George Porterfield of the Virginia militia looked around for the expected company of soldiers, led by Major Boykin, to greet him. All he could see were a few passengers waiting to board the train before it continued on to Wheeling. *Perhaps Boykin did not receive my telegram,* he thought. He walked over to the Grafton Hotel to speak to the telegraph operator.

"Good morning. I sent a telegram yesterday to Major Boykin. Do you know if it arrived here?"

The telegraph operator stared at Porterfield's uniform and frowned. Nevertheless, he turned and searched through the telegrams from the day before and found one addressed to Major Boykin, Grafton, Virginia. A note was attached.

"Yes, it did arrive," the operator replied.

"Do you know if it was delivered to Major Boykin?"

"The note attached to the telegram says 'undeliverable.'"

"What does that mean? Could you not find Major Boykin?"

"I can't say. I wasn't on duty yesterday."

"Do you know Major Boykin?"

"I've heard of him."

Porterfield shook his head impatiently. *This rascal is skirting the boundaries of impertinence.* "Well, do you know where he can be found?" he asked.

"Last I heard he skedaddled out of Grafton for Fetterman."

"And when was that?"

"Hmm, maybe a week ago."

Realizing this operator was not likely to provide him with any further information, Porterfield gave terse thanks, retrieved his horse from the station master, and headed up the road toward Fetterman in search of Major Boykin.

TUESDAY, MAY 14, 1861, 10:00 AM
WASHINGTON HALL, WHEELING, VIRGINIA

AJ yawned. He wondered if he had dark circles under his eyes, like those under Harry's. They had stayed up late the previous night listening to several men talk about the military companies in Wheeling and surrounding areas that were forming up to fight the "rebs." They spoke of a "sesh" Major Boykin who was in Grafton, trying to get men to sign up for "that dang Confederacy." These men laughed and made jokes about the Major. One of the men, who clearly had one too many whiskeys, said, "He sure left in a hurry when we told him he had better git back on that train and not come back. We should've dipped that feller in molasses, rolled him in cotton and run him out of town on a rail!"

Despite the fact that he had gone to bed after midnight, it took AJ a long time to fall asleep. Then he awakened before light to see to the comfort of their horses, which were housed in adjacent stalls in the boardinghouse stables. "That was quite a night," Harry whispered to AJ.

"It sure was. Those fellows talked like a war's already started here in Virginia..."

Harry interrupted AJ by holding up a hand. "Waitman Willey has the floor now. Let's listen to what he has to say."

"It seems my remarks made last evening have been misunderstood. Some are saying that I believed the proper course of this Convention was to adjourn until after the election, without taking any action whatever. I want it understood that what I intended to say differed from Mr. Carlile only with regards to his approach. I wish to declare a distinct and unequivocal position in condemnation of the usurpation at Richmond, and lay down a platform upon which to organize the public sentiment for a separation of the State."

Mr. Wheat then rose and presented eight resolutions. Harry whispered to AJ that these resolutions were similar to those he had heard before, at other meetings he had attended.

Next came a convoluted legal debate that AJ had trouble following. It involved the popular Mr. Carlile wishing to explain a "New Virginia" state resolution he wanted to introduce. AJ yawned and glanced at Harry, who was completely engaged in the discussion. Harry was nodding slowly, as though he agreed with every word Carlile was saying.

Mr. Carlile was called to order because, it was said, he was arguing *for* his resolution instead of explaining it. Carlile agreed for the sake of harmony to adjourn until later. When the delegates reassembled, the report of the Committee on State and Federal Relations was read, which consisted only of the paper resolutions. Carlile's "New Virginia" state resolution was not included.

On motion the Convention then adjourned to 9 o'clock the next day. After the adjournment, someone proposed three cheers for New Virginia, which went up with a wild and almost ferocious yell. Three more were given for Carlile. Then the spectators and delegates dispersed.

On their walk back to the boardinghouse, AJ and Harry conversed on the day. "It seems to me like Willey always waits till the very end to criticize Carlile," AJ remarked.

"Yes, I've been wondering about his motives. I think his criticisms have a hidden purpose. Maybe to actually make Carlile look good, or maybe he wants to wait until after the people of the State vote on the 23rd. I think he has good intentions."

"You might be right. Carlile and his proposed State of New Virginia certainly got all the cheers this evening. I didn't hear many cheers for Willey."

WEDNESDAY, MAY 15, 1861, 6:00 AM
FETTERMAN, VIRGINIA

Reveille? Was that the sound of a bugle calling reveille? Am I dreaming? Am I back at Virginia Military Institute? Colonel Porterfield's eyes opened. He looked around him and remembered that he was in the village of Fetterman, Virginia about two miles northwest of Grafton, at a camp beside the Tygart Valley River.

The events of yesterday slowly came back to him. He had found Major Boykin with a small company of men from Fairmont under the command of Captain William P. Thompson. They called themselves the Marion Guard and Captain Thompson was the son of Circuit Judge George W. Thompson of Wheeling. To his pleasant surprise these men at least had arms but no ammunition. The other companies Major Boykin had located, and which were now apparently marching to this camp, had no arms *or* ammunition.

"Why did you choose this spot to camp and not Grafton?" he asked Boykin upon arrival at the Fetterman camp.

"Because Grafton is full of people loyal to the Federal government, not our State of Virginia government. It's dangerous. They have a company there called the Grafton Guards under the command of Captain George R. Latham. He nailed a United States flag to his door and drills his company every day in the town. Here, the Fetterman postmaster is loyal to our State, so we can at least send and receive letters," Boykin replied.

Boykin also gave Porterfield a recent letter from General Lee to read, plus all past correspondence between Lee and Boykin. Porterfield read those letters carefully. They made him wonder, *Do General Lee and Governor Letcher really understand what is going on with the people in this part of the State?* The past letter from Boykin to Lee clearly pointed out that the companies joining Boykin had no uniforms, or arms, and little to no military training.

Porterfield decided to write a letter to Adjutant-General Garnett explaining the situation more clearly. After breakfast, he ordered Captain Thompson to send a courier to Beverly to post the letter, find Major Goff, and determine the location of the 400 rifles and ammunition General Lee said had been ordered from Staunton to be sent to Beverly.

"Good morning, Colonel," Boykin said as he handed a mug of coffee to Porterfield through the flap in his tent. "The men are starting breakfast. Would you like to join Captain Thompson and me? We can plan our day's activities."

"I'll be along shortly," he said. *How to get some fighting men and some weapons to fight with—those are the activities we need to plan!*

WEDNESDAY, MAY 15, 1861, 9:30 AM
WASHINGTON HALL, WHEELING, VIRGINIA

After the session preliminaries were over, AJ and Harry listened carefully as Mr. Willey took the floor and resumed his argument from the previous night.

"I reiterate that I'm opposed to the organization of a provisional government. It would be treason against the State Government, the Government of the United States and against the Government of the C.S.A. It will inevitably bring war and ruin upon this part of the State. I will never lend myself to an insurrectionary or unconstitutional means of accomplishing an object which I think can be accomplished according to law."

Mr. Carlile then rose and announced that a resolution had been adopted by the committee that he believed would, in a short time, bring about their hopes of a New Virginia. The resolution called for the appointment of a committee to possess all the powers of the Convention, and which could recall the Convention in any emergency. He pronounced himself satisfied, for the time being.

Applause followed Carlile's speech. After prayers, the singing of "The Star Spangled Banner," and three hearty cheers for the Union, the Convention adjourned.

AJ and Harry made their way down the steps with the crowd of spectators. Two loud men in front of them expressed their opinions that the Convention had accomplished nothing. They were disgusted that the delegates had not all agreed to support Carlile's "New State" resolution. Two men behind just as loudly expressed their opinion that Carlile was a hothead and that Willey and General Jackson had saved the day.

Once they were outside the building, AJ asked, "What do *you* think about how it turned out, Harry?"

"We heard some excellent debates from men who understand our Constitution very well. I think we witnessed democracy in action, where free men can speak and debate different points of view without fear. I trust that they have chosen the right path to follow, for now. After all, until the people of Virginia vote on May 23, they don't know if Virginia will definitely secede or not."

"Oh, come on—we already know that vote on May 23 is goin' to be for secesh! Carlile and his gang don't want their freedoms taken away while they know something still can be done to stop it."

"But until that vote happens, Virginia is legally in the Union. So, if the people take actions that are against the Constitution of the United States, such actions would be treasonous in the eyes of the Federal government, whose support they seek. So legally, all the westerners can do is wait until the results of the vote are made public. Don't you see?"

AJ thought it over. "You're right. Maybe that's what Carlile meant when he said, 'I'm satisfied that nothing more than is now incorporated in the committee...' or something like that. I'm anxious to see how the vote goes. But I bet you anything it's goin' to be for Virginia to leave the Union."

As AJ and Harry walked back to their boardinghouse to pack for the trip home, Harry said, "I'd like to stop in Waynesburg on our way back, to visit the Cumberland Presbyterian Church. I met the minister a few months ago and he wanted me to visit there, to see his church and the Christian school they've built."

"That's all right with me," replied AJ. "Maybe there's a cavalry company formin' in Greene County."

"Maybe. Perhaps we should also visit Morgantown on the way home and see what the folks there are doing about answering the President's call for militia."

AJ yawned. "Let's go to bed early tonight, so we can get on the road at first light. I'm a little homesick. And I want to see how far Pa got with the corn plantin'.

.

CHAPTER SIX

Saviors, Not Invaders

May 16–May 30, 1861

Ohio Troops Landing in Parkersburg on May 27, 1861

THURSDAY, MAY 16, 1861, 6:30 AM
AJ AND HARRY EN ROUTE TO WAYNESBURG, PENNSYLVANIA

The riders got off to an early start Thursday morning on their homeward journey. Clouds of smoke rising from the nearby iron furnaces obscured the sun as it peeked above the surrounding mountains. AJ hated the smoke, and his spirits rose as they left Wheeling. Last night they had carefully planned the route they would take. They would meander across the border back into Pennsylvania and then head southeast, through the wooded hill country, and into Virginia, to stop in Morgantown before heading home. They were in hopes of finding someone starting a company of loyal cavalry in Morgantown. Along the way, they would visit a pastor friend of Harry's in Waynesburg, Pennsylvania, so Harry could see Cumberland Presbyterian Church and a Christian college there.

Their route took them first on the National Pike headed east, to a turn-off to follow the Waynesburg Road. It looked easy enough on Harry's map, but neither could remember seeing a road sign to Waynesburg when they travelled to Wheeling. Moving slowly along the Pike, they crossed over into Pennsylvania and finally found the inconspicuous Waynesburg Road turn-off on the east side of the little village of West Alexander. Both men sighed in relief as they left the Pike and trotted off down the dirt road toward Waynesburg. Unlike the broad, macadamized National Road, this little road was overhung with trees. Birdsong filled their ears.

"Well, did you like the big city, AJ?" Harry asked after they had traveled a mile or so.

AJ pondered the question for a minute before answering. "I surely wouldn't want to *live* in that city. The smoke from those iron works was terrible, and the streets smelled like a horse stall that needed cleanin'. Just didn't seem like a healthy place to live. And all the folks seemed to be in such a big hurry. I thought the Ohio River was mighty impressive, but with so many boats, I was surprised we didn't see any accidents. To me, that suspension bridge was the most amazin' of all. How did it carry all those heavy wagons and horse teams, with those tiny wires?"

AJ could see from the expression in Harry's eyes and his suppressed smile that he was amused by AJ's reactions to the first large city he'd ever encountered. Embarrassed, AJ added, "But I'm a farmer, you know... I'm sure you liked it just fine, didn't you? Lots of souls to harvest there!"

"Actually, I agree with most of your views, but I do think I could enjoy living in Wheeling. It seems like the center of power for the western Virginia counties, and it has so much energy, with so many souls, as you say, living there. I especially liked the new Custom House. You know, it was designed by the famous architect Ammi B. Young, who used a new kind of construction, with steel beams and girders. That building will most likely be around many, many years! And, yes, that suspension bridge *was* marvelous."

AJ, knowing little about architecture and nothing about Ammi Young, decided to change the subject to a question that was bothering him. He said, "Getting back to that conversation we was havin' yesterday, Harry—what do you think is going to happen if the Virginians vote to secede on May 23?"

After a pause, Harry said, "As I recall, the last resolution at the convention stated in that case the people of the represented counties would appoint delegates to a General Convention, to meet in June. I suspect they *will* hold a second convention in Wheeling and look for some ways to get Federal government protection for the western counties that don't want to leave the Union."

AJ frowned. "But what do you think that will mean to *us*?"

"That protection could take many forms, I guess, but I think Ohio or Pennsylvania, or both states, will send troops over the state line into the western counties of Virginia. Western Virginians are already creating loyal militia companies. Those companies will likely be formed into a regiment in Wheeling. I also heard that eastern Virginia has sent officers to organize those western Virginians who favor secession. If that's true, then it will be just a matter of time before those forces collide and start fighting each other. I truly think they'll start a civil war inside Virginia, AJ."

AJ's eyes were wide with concern as he replied, "And I bet our own Pennsylvania governor won't just stand by and see our state threatened by the secesh Virginians. I'm sure he'd rather see Virginia tore to pieces by war than our own state."

"You're right. And that's true for Ohio as well. And the railroad companies, who are also threatened. I don't think it will take long for General McClellan to send Union troops into western Virginia. And once out-of-state troops are brought in, a war between the states will likely start here. You and I, and other Pennsylvanians like us, are going to be drawn into all of this. And it won't be too far into the future. I can just feel it coming, like a storm."

AJ's head was reeling. *War a reality, not just a "maybe"! And there's nothing we can do to stop it,* he thought. He had to admit to himself that, while the unknown nature of war was frightening, he was also thrilled by it. As a boy he had loved to play soldier with his cousins and the neighboring farm boys, but never expected to be a real soldier.

"It scares me to think about it, Harry. But I guess I'd rather volunteer now and be a part of a loyal western Virginia army, so I can help those folks we listened to at the convention protect their homes *and* keep the war away from Smithfield."

Harry turned in his saddle and looked closely at AJ for a moment, then nodded approval and said, "I agree with you. I too would rather join up with a western Virginia unit. After all, my family still lives near Morgantown, and I lived there many years. We need to keep in touch with Dr. Keys, and we need to find out if anything is happening in Morgantown."

The two rode on in silence, each lost in his own visions and fears of the war to come. They stopped for water, food and a brief rest at noon, then continued on the road toward Waynesburg. Late in the afternoon, as the light was fading, Harry said, "I think we should stop soon for the night. We'll be able to reach Waynesburg tomorrow, in the late morning."

"How long did you want to spend with your pastor friend in Waynesburg?" asked AJ.

"Not more than two or three hours. I saw him recently at a meeting in Uniontown, and I promised to visit him if I was ever near Waynesburg," Harry responded.

They found a spot, some distance from the road, near a stream and a meadow with thick spring grass. There they made camp, watered their horses and turned them loose to graze. It was a clear spring night and stars were appearing, looking close enough to touch. A half moon provided enough light for them to find and assemble a cold supper from their saddlebag stores, without the need for a campfire. They talked quietly for awhile, then bedded down. Harry, as usual, fell asleep quickly. His soft sputtering snores kept AJ awake as he fretted and worried about his future. *I never thought I would actually* want *to go to war... but it ain't exactly wanting to go. It feels more like I* have *to, to protect my family and keep the country together.*

It seemed to AJ that he had placed himself into a trap. He wanted to protect the people he loved, but was going to war the right way to do this? Did he really have to leave the place and people he loved in order to protect them? It didn't make total sense to him. *Does God really want me to kill people, other Americans, wrong-thinking as they might be?* Over and over, questions and worries ran through his mind until, exhausted, he finally fell asleep.

Thursday, May 16, 1861, 3:00 pm
Colonel Porterfield HQ, Fetterman, Virginia

Colonel Porterfield heard hoofbeats approaching. He looked up from his map-covered table and listened. A heavily breathing horse arrived in camp and the rider called out for someone to walk his horse. A moment later he heard rapid footsteps approaching his tent.

"Colonel Porterfield, sir, it's the messenger you sent to Beverly. May I enter?"

"Yes, come in, son. What news have you brought me from Beverly?"

"Sir, I found Major Goff. He knows nothin' about them muskets, or any supplies for you."

Shocked, Porterfield stared at the messenger, then shook his head in disbelief. The messenger, who appeared badly fatigued and road-weary, fumbled in his jacket and held out a folded sheet, saying, "Sir, here's the written reply. Do you have any more orders for me?"

"One moment, son. Are you *sure* it was Major Goff you spoke with, and that he understood what you were asking?"

"Yes'r, I know'd it was Goff because I asked folks in Beverly where he was. Everyone was friendly and knew the Major. I found him and gave him the message you wrote. The Major read it while I was standin' there, and wrote his answer out right then."

"Please tell Major Boykin I want to see him right away."

"Yes'r."

Shortly, Major Boykin stood in front of Porterfield's tent and announced his presence. "Colonel, you wanted to see me?"

"Come in, Major. The messenger has returned with a letter from Major Goff. It's bad news. Goff has not received any arms and was not even informed to expect any muskets or supplies. I want you to assist me in writing a letter to General Garnett, Lee's Adjutant General."

Boykin and Porterfield worked together hastily to express their concern in the letter to Garnett:

> *A message from Major Goff stated no rifles were in Beverly and Goff had not been informed to expect any. This was a serious disappointment. The men under my command are green and will not for some months be more effective than undisciplined militia. The men lack uniforms, arms, ammunition, and other essential equipment. The people in the area are bitter and apparently on the verge of civil war. They are in the process of forming their own companies and regiments that are well supplied with the means to oppose us.*

The letter was rushed to the post office in hopes that it would reach General Garnett within a few days.

FRIDAY, MAY 17, 1861, 3:30 AM
AJ AND HARRY'S CAMPSITE ON THE ROAD TO WAYNESBURG

AJ's eyes flew open. He had awakened suddenly from a bad dream, one in which Shiloh had stumbled and fallen down a steep bank, rolling over and over, screaming in fright and pain. The dream faded quickly as he realized where he was, but then he heard Shiloh's shrill call again. This was no dream! Wide awake now, he jumped to his feet and grabbed his pistol. *Could be a big cat nosing around!* he thought.

"Harry, get up!" he shouted. "I think somethin's after the horses!" The half moon provided enough light to make his way through the meadow, but AJ stumbled over rocks and protruding roots in his haste to reach his horse.

As his eyes adjusted to the night, he could make out Shiloh's dark form half-rearing and striking out with a foreleg. Then he heard another sound: it seemed to be human, a cry of pain. AJ reached his horse and pointed the pistol at a person moaning on the ground. "Whoa, easy there, boy." AJ touched his horse to calm him and discovered a piece of twine knotted around his neck.

"Who *are* you? What d'you think you're doing? You're trying to steal my horse, you good for nothin'..." A hot bolt of anger surged through his body. Petty thievery he'd encountered before, but a horse thief—that was something else!

"Get up, you!" He grabbed the man by the arm and, with the strength given him by his anger, yanked him to his feet and held the gun in his face. The dark figure, cradling his right arm, cried out and said, "He kicked me—I think my arm's busted. Don't shoot me, mistah!"

Even in the low light, AJ immediately recognized the chiseled black face of the slave they had passed on the National Road—the man who had admired Shiloh and smiled up at AJ as they rode by. The man he had felt sorry for, even felt a momentary kinship with, was now trying to steal his horse!

"I know who you are. You're from that gang we saw on the Pike. How did you get away? And why're you trying to steal my horse? You better talk, if you want to save your no-good hide!"

Shiloh pranced and neighed, made nervous again by his master's agitated voice. The dark man shrank from the horse. AJ, breathing hard, tightened his grip on the man's arm. "I've a mind to just shoot you right here, like the miserable thief you are!"

"Please, mistah, I know'd it was wrong, but I *got* to get away from here—get back to my fam'ly! I'd a found some way to get him back to you, nice horse like him."

AJ could see the dim figure of Harry making his way toward them. "What's going on, AJ?" called Harry, still wiping the sleep from his eyes. "Why are you holding this man at gunpoint?"

"This... rascal tried to steal my horse!" AJ shook the man by the arm and he cried out again in pain. "Look, I know him, Harry—he's one of those slaves we saw coming into Wheeling and he's trying to run."

"Take it easy," Harry said. "Let me talk to him."

"Talk? I've a good mind to throttle him!" AJ responded, the angry heat still running high.

"Just calm down now, AJ. Count to ten, like I told you before. Quit shaking him and let him answer." Harry spoke in a quiet but commanding voice. "Mister, who are you and what are you doing here? You've no right to molest our horses. Explain yourself."

The man replied in a trembling voice, "My name's Abraham Blackman, suh. From up around Pittsburgh, and I gots to get back up there. My fam'ly..." He broke off, with what sounded like a choked sob.

"How did you end up down here on the Pike, with that slave catcher? And how did you get away?" Harry asked.

"I'm a *free* man. That ol' white man knock me on the head one night and haul me off, was gonna sell me. And my poor wife got no idea where I be! I thought if I could cotch your horse, mebbe he could get me away from here. I swear I would'a found some way to get him back to you, oncet I got away..."

"Do you have your free papers?" asked Harry.

The dark man looked down. "Naw, suh... I lost 'em. I don't have no papers. That's why I has to sneak and hide."

"Tell us the truth, man!" urged Harry. "We're not slaveholders and you're in Pennsylvania now. You have nothing to fear from *us*."

The man was obviously reluctant to tell them more. He stared at the ground, holding his injured arm. Finally, AJ brought the pistol back up to his face. "Tell the truth, if you know what's good for you! My friend here's a minister of the gospel."

Abraham looked at Harry, doubtful. Then he decided to talk. "'Bout two year ago, I ran, got away from a real mean master down in North

Carolina. *Real* mean man. Made it up to Pittsburgh and started workin'
up there. Got me a wife and baby. I *cain't* go back to being no slave, no
more. No more."

"How'd you get away from that man we saw you with?" asked AJ.

"Jest dumb luck. He warn't all that smart. He got all likkered up with
some other white man, the night afore we got to Wheeling. Passed out. I
allus carry an ol' Indian rock I found a long time ago hid in my clothes,
an old spearhead. Carry it all the time, for luck, I guess, and... jest in
case. I got the ropes sawed through and slipped off."

For a moment, AJ found himself feeling sorry for the fugitive but,
remembering his attempted thievery, hardened his heart. "Well, stealin'
my horse surely ain't no way to act," he blurted. "That's just trading one
wrong for another. And there ain't *no way* you'd ever be able to find me,
to give him back. That's just a lie! So you can just quit saying that!" He
could feel the blood rising to his face.

"AJ, don't get yourself all worked up again," said Harry. "This man's
in a desperate situation. You might have done the same yourself, if you
were forcibly separated from your wife and baby."

"But, *horse thievin'*, Harry! And how do we even know he's telling the
truth?"

"We don't. I'm just asking you to show some compassion and forgive
this man standing here, like our Lord forgave us."

"But, what are we going to do with him? We can't just let him go,
can we? It's against the law! We're supposed to turn him in."

At this, the man struggled to get away but AJ still gripped his arm.
"No, you don't!"

"Both of you, *stop!*" shouted Harry. The two stopped struggling.

"AJ, we're not turning him in. That would be unjust. We're going to
trust that he's being honest with us, and we're going to help him get back
to his family in Pittsburgh." Harry turned to Abraham. "And, Mr.
Blackman, I strongly suggest that you cooperate. And should you get

home to Pittsburgh, you should move your family further north, perhaps even to Canada. You've been captured and brought back to the South once, and it can happen again."

AJ stared at Harry, open-mouthed. "But, Harry, we could get in a lot of trouble for helpin' him. You may not like the Fugitive Law, but it's still the law!"

"As you well know, I answer to a higher law, AJ," Harry said. "Let him go. Some other time I'll explain to you the way I see things. Right now we need to make a plan. Come on, Mister Blackman, we'll build a fire up and see to your arm, and you could probably use a bite to eat. And then we'll talk about options. AJ, you check the horses to be sure they're both uninjured, and then come on back to the campsite." Harry turned and started back.

When AJ let go of his arm, Abraham stood for a moment, looking at Harry's receding back, as if pondering whether he should run again. He looked at AJ and the pistol in his hand. "Op-shuns?" he asked quietly. AJ shrugged. "I don't know what he's talkin' about half the time either. You better just go with him." Abraham finally nodded and hurried off in Harry's direction.

AJ was confused and frustrated. His parents had taught him right from wrong, and to stay on the right side of the law, always. *What is Harry doing?* He felt as though the solid earth were breaking up under his feet. His whole body still shook, from the fear and anger he'd experienced. He turned to Shiloh and ran his hands over him, feeling for any cuts or swellings, glad he had trained his horse so carefully, so he knew to respond to no one but him. He removed the length of twine knotted around Shiloh's neck and head. The horse was calm now, nuzzling AJ, searching for a carrot or a sugar lump. Betsy had wandered over to investigate, and AJ inspected her as well, going slowly, giving himself time to calm down, to stop shaking. Finally satisfied that both animals were relaxed enough to start grazing again, he walked back to the campfire where

Harry and Abraham sat, absorbed in their discussion... *just like old friends*, he thought in disgust.

FRIDAY, MAY 17, 1861, 7:30 AM
WAYNESBURG, PENNSYLVANIA

The remainder of the road to Waynesburg was rough traveling, nothing but a narrow, rutted dirt road that carved its way through wooded knolls and grassy, rolling hills. Harry insisted Abraham have a turn riding. "He's not riding *my* horse," AJ responded.

"Very well, that's up to you. He and I will take turns walking and riding Betsy then."

Abraham spoke little during the trip. He took his turn on Betsy when Harry instructed him, and only responded when spoken to. AJ supposed that came from being a servant. He did notice that the man knew horses. He had a calm way about him and he looked out for Betsy, checking and adjusting her saddle and girth, making sure they weren't rubbing galls. He also plucked succulent blades of grass for Betsy to nibble when they stopped for a rest. He even enticed Shiloh to eat grass out of his hand.

But he tried to steal my horse! AJ could not get past that fact. The night before, Harry wrapped Abraham's arm, which turned out to be badly bruised but apparently not broken. Then Harry questioned the fugitive closely, and finally announced to AJ they would take Abraham with them to Waynesburg, to Harry's pastor friend. He seemed to think the pastor would be able to help Abraham get back to his family in Pittsburgh.

"But what if we're seen on the way?" questioned AJ. "People are bound to be looking for him. He's worth a lot of money. We could face big fines, Harry, or even prison, for helping a fugitive!"

"Fortunately, this road is lightly traveled. If we're questioned directly, let me talk," responded Harry. "I will say that Abraham belongs to me, that I purchased him in Wheeling, and that we are returning to our farm near Morgantown. When we get to Waynesburg, we will turn Abraham over to Pastor James, who can help to return him to Pittsburgh. He will provide him with clean clothes, some money, and freedom papers, for safe travel."

"How do you know this preacher can, or will, do all this, Harry? That's asking an awful lot of him, ain't it? And I still don't trust this 'Abraham'… What if he knocks the good pastor on the head and steals everything he has? And it'll be our fault for bringing trouble down on him."

"Trust me, and trust in the Lord. It will turn out all right."

"But, Harry, he's already got you breakin' the law and ready to lie for him, and that's a big sin. And you a preacher yourself. Listen to me, Harry! I just can't feel right about all this."

Harry sighed and rubbed his forehead, as if trying to rub away a pain there. "I understand your concerns, AJ, believe me, but I have to ask you to trust me in these matters. I'll explain more to you later."

AJ shook his head and walked away. What they were doing was wrong; that's all he could see. Why couldn't Harry see that? It was black and white.

It was late morning before they came in sight of Waynesburg, the county seat of Greene County, named after the legendary "Mad" Anthony Wayne, a Pennsylvanian who won honors during the Revolutionary War. The village boasted the stately Cumberland Presbyterian Church, poised on a hill, with a graceful spire. Nearby were the Union School, courthouse, hotel, and all the shops and homes necessary to handle the needs of a growing population of about a thousand people. To the south of town flowed the South Fork of Tenmile Creek which, to the occasional eagle flying overhead, might have appeared as a cradle for the city.

Shiloh caught sight of the village first, his ears perking as he spotted the church spire. As they came into the main street of the town, they saw a few people on the sidewalks, wandering into the stores and the hotel. Several eyed them curiously. AJ's heart hammered in his chest and his throat was dry from nervousness. He expected to be accosted by officers of the law at any minute.

They rode up to the church, and tied their horses to the hitching posts. A wooden sign reading "Office" hung on a door at the side of the church. Harry knocked and a kindly looking middle-aged man about six feet tall, with large hands and a broad chest, opened the door.

"*Harry!*" the pastor exclaimed in a booming voice, clasping Harry's hand in his large ones. "It's so good to see you! What a wonderful and unexpected visit, and who, may I ask, are these gentlemen with you?"

"Could we come in, Brother James?" Harry said. "I have a few things I need to talk over with you." He glanced over his shoulder, making sure they were not being observed by passers-by.

James stepped aside to allow the three men to come into his office, an untidy cubicle, furnished with several old but comfortable-looking chairs and a large, scarred wooden desk covered with books and papers. Opened crates containing more books sat on the floor.

"Pastor James, this is Alexander Swaney, a very close friend of mine. We call him 'AJ' back home in Smithfield. And this fellow is Abraham Blackman. He's the one I need to talk to you about. Do you think you and I could go into the sanctuary for a bit, to talk?"

AJ and Abraham were left to themselves in the office. They chose seats on opposite sides of the narrow room, avoiding each other's eyes. AJ, hat in hand, looked around at the framed diplomas and Sunday School certificates hanging on the plaster walls. Abraham sat quietly, head down, cradling his injured arm.

After 20 minutes of sitting in silence, AJ stood and rubbed the small of his back. He had never been one for sitting or doing nothing. He sighed and looked at Abraham. The man hadn't moved or spoken since they had sat down. "This is a lot of trouble you're putting us through,"

AJ said frowning. "I don't know why Harry's riskin' our hides to save yours."

Abraham finally raised his eyes to meet Harry's. "Neither do I, suh. But I praise the Lord for it. You are savin' my life. I hopes to pay you back some day. And I'm truly sorry for all the trouble."

AJ had to admire the man's dignity. "What do you work at, up in Pittsburgh?" he asked.

"Farrier. Shoe horses. I l'arned the trade under my first mastuh. A decent man, he was."

So that explains why he's so good with the horses. "That's hard, hot work, ain't it? I watch our horseshoer and he's sweatin' no matter how cold it is."

"Yessuh, but it gots to be done. I like the work. And I like the animals."

AJ sat down and tilted his chair back against the wall. They fell quiet again and soon Harry and the pastor returned. The pastor carried a parcel in his arms, which he handed to Abraham. "Some clean clothes for you to change into, Abraham, more suitable for a freeman. Follow me—you're going to stay here for a couple of days while we look into who might be chasing after you, and then we'll soon get you moving north again."

Abraham stood, a relieved smile stretching his lips. He offered his hand to Harry, who shook it vigorously, saying, "I'll pray for your safe return to Pittsburgh and your family. And remember what I said about Canada." The black man nodded, then turned to AJ and held out his hand. It stayed there, suspended in the air for a few seconds, while AJ stared at it. Then, slowly, AJ stretched out his arm and shook the hand. "Good luck to you," he mumbled.

"I'll never forget what you done for me," said Abraham, standing up straighter, as if to salute them. He held up his hand in farewell and then followed the pastor through the door.

The two friends were alone together for the first time since Abraham had tried to steal Shiloh the night before. AJ couldn't look Harry in the eye. He was still angry and confused about this strange turn of events, and Harry's willingness to put them both at risk to help a fugitive. "You know the law says we could both be thrown in jail for six months, Harry, and fined $1000 for what we've done, helping that colored man!"

Harry nodded. "Yes, I realize that. Fortunately, Brother James says this town is mostly supportive of fugitive slaves and the officers of the law tend to look the other way. And I'm sorry you had to be brought into it. But maybe it's the Lord's doing. You need to know some things, AJ, with this war coming our way. Sit down. We have to talk."

AJ listened in silence to what Harry told him, about the harsh conditions of life under slavery. About what Harry thought this war was really going to be about, to end the evil of slavery in the country that called itself "the land of the free." And, most shocking to AJ, about Harry's activities with the Underground Railroad around Uniontown, helping fugitive slaves who passed through the area find safe hiding places and papers, and moving them on to the next "station" further north, out of reach of the slave catchers.

Harry seemed like a different person to him now. He thought he knew everything about his friend, after their long travels together. He had almost idolized Harry, he realized. *But I really don't know him at all.*

"You're... you're a criminal, Harry," AJ whispered. "You've been breaking the law all this time."

Harry nodded. "That's one way to look at it. But I look at it as doing God's will, trying to play a small role in correcting a horrific evil. Slavery *is* evil, AJ, and we each have to decide how we stand. I stand firmly against it. And if this war comes to us—as we both know it will—that is why *I* will be fighting."

"But you have to tell lies to help the runaways. Don't the Bible say telling lies is always wrong?"

"Yes, lying is wrong. The Commandment says 'Thou shalt not bear false witness against thy neighbor.' This commandment was meant to avoid slander and injustice. What I do is also meant to avoid injustice. When I lie for this purpose, which I try to do as little as possible, I ask God's forgiveness and ask Him to lead me on the right path in His eyes. He is a merciful God."

AJ mumbled, "It just ain't right."

Harry sighed. "You know, AJ, the Bible has some instances where lying appears to be acceptable when done in the service of mercy and justice. In the chapter of Joshua, when two Israelites went to Jericho as spies to see the land that God had promised them, the woman Rahab gave them refuge and lied to their pursuers while helping them to escape. She was not punished by God for this and indeed was praised in the New Testament in the books of James and Hebrews for her actions in helping the Israelites."

AJ felt his brain was melting. He rubbed his eyes and slumped in the chair. Harry patted him on the shoulder. "We need to stay here till after dark," he said, "so we're not observed leaving without Abraham. We don't want to take any unnecessary chances. Go stretch out on a pew in the sanctuary and try to rest up. I'll visit with Brother James."

As AJ entered the cool, dark sanctuary, he thought, *No "unnecessary chances"? So all this risk you've put us in was necessary, Harry?*

Saturday, May 18, 1861, 10:30 AM
Morgantown, Virginia

Leaving Waynesburg after midnight, AJ and Harry crossed over the Mason-Dixon line back into Virginia. After several miles of riding, they could see the mountains covered in their new spring leaves, in brilliant shades of yellow and light green. The Monongahela River lay in the valley below, reflecting the clear blue sky as it snaked its way toward Pittsburgh to help form the Ohio River. To the left, a fork in the road descended to the river, where they could see a ferry taking passengers and horses to the other side. To the right the other fork in the road led south to a suspension bridge crossing the river into the heart of Morgantown. They could see the towering tops of the bridge.

Harry said, "I've heard that crossing the river over the bridge costs only one cent. My guess is the ferry would cost us more. Shall we continue south along the high road and cross over on the bridge?"

AJ nodded. He had spoken little on the ride to Morgantown, trying to come to terms with all that Harry had told him the night before. The solid ground that he had thought he was building his life on appeared to be giving way under him. First, Sophia had turned her back on him and apparently had chosen someone about as different from him as it was possible to be. Now Harry, the person in his life that he most admired, had turned out to be a criminal. No wonder he had the glooms.

However, the thought of crossing the impressive bridge on their horses was an interesting one, as a training exercise. Shiloh had never been on a large bridge with other traffic, and he wanted to see how his horse reacted.

Harry was obviously thinking the same. "Knowing how obedient Shiloh is," he said, "it might be a good idea if you take the lead across the bridge."

AJ nodded. "We could walk them across, but I'd like to try riding them."

A few miles further on, the pair rode up to the tollkeeper, dismounted, and asked the amount of the toll.

"You're in luck today, there ain't no charge for crossin' the bridge. Where you from?"

Harry replied, "From Smithfield, Pennsylvania. Right now we're on our way back from the Wheeling Convention."

"Say, did you get to hear our Mr. Waitman Willey up there? He and Mr. Dent are delegates from this county."

Harry replied, "We certainly did. Willey's an inspiring speaker, one of the best orators I've ever heard."

"That he is, sir. He's spoken many times to the folks around here and most of us believe we'll stay with the Union, like he urges. Some folks here speak of secession, but mostly behind closed doors now. They ain't too pop'lar these days."

AJ asked, "Is there any talk here about formin' a Union cavalry company?"

"Well, posters are all over town asking for 1,010 brave men to form a reg'ment of infantry in Wheeling. I hear somebody named Kelley from Wheeling is going to lead that reg'ment. Both Willey and Dent are tryin' to get the men here to enlist. You should talk with that dentist, McGee, in town. He's a good horseman and I hear he's been tryin' to form a company of cavalry."

Harry and AJ looked at each other. At last! "Do you know where we could find Mr. McGee?" asked Harry.

"It's Saturday, so he might be home today. His office is on Walnut Street, near the intersection with High Street. Just ask folks over there. Everybody knows him. Someone will tell you where he lives."

"Thank you, kind sir, we'll head over that way," Harry replied.

As they mounted their horses, a man and woman in a little one-horse buggy started across the bridge at a trot and waved at the tollkeeper. AJ and Harry followed side by side. Both horses pricked their ears and arched their necks when they first stepped onto the bridge. Betsy stopped and balked briefly, but when Shiloh moved ahead, she followed. Both horses soon settled down. Once on the east side of the river it was easy to locate the courthouse. Several men stood around reading the posted signs. Harry dismounted and approached the group. "Excuse me, gentlemen, can any of you tell me where I can find Mr. McGee, the dentist?"

A well-dressed man in his forties pointed down the street and said, "Yes, he's still in his office on High Street near the corner with Walnut. You can't miss him. He has a dentist sign on his door."

AJ and Harry watered their horses and then tied them to a nearby hitching post. It was just a short walk to the dentist's office. When they knocked on the door, a clerk invited them in.

"The dentist is busy with a customer right now. Who shall I say is calling?" the clerk said.

"We're from Smithfield, Pennsylvania on our way back from the Wheeling Convention and would like to speak with him about joining a cavalry company," Harry replied.

The clerk left the room and soon returned with the message that the dentist would see them in about 15 minutes. "We can wait," Harry responded. He and AJ sat in the waiting chairs, talking quietly about their hopes of soon finding a suitable company to join, now that their minds were made up. An older man walked by holding his jaw and left the office. Moments later a tall, white-jacketed man came out and offered them his hand. "Hello, gentlemen, my name is Lowry McGee," he said.

AJ and Harry rose to their feet, shook his hand and introduced themselves, explaining their mission and the outcome of their trip to Wheeling. "We understand you might be forming a cavalry company and we're both very interested in joining it," Harry said.

"Well, it sounds like you both are well informed on the Virginia politics and I thank you for wanting to help us western Virginians. You're right, I've made it known to our delegates, Willey and Dent, that I'm available to form and lead a company of cavalry. So far, I've been told to wait until after the election on May 23. I think this is a big mistake. I know eastern Virginians are already forming cavalry companies and they have good leaders with experience. Cavalry is needed *now* because it takes a long time to train cavalrymen and their horses," McGee said.

"We stopped in Beallsville, Pennsylvania on the way to Wheeling and spoke to Dr. Keys of the Ringgold Cavalry," said Harry. "He told us the same thing about how long it takes to train cavalry. Dr. Keys told us that Governor Curtin won't accept cavalry units because President Lincoln doesn't want them in his call for 75,000 militia."

"Yes, that is pretty much the story I've gotten. In the meantime, the eastern counties will be way ahead of us. I don't know what to tell you, gentlemen. Please leave me your addresses and take my card. Let's keep in touch by letter. Mr. Willey apparently thinks like you. He believes the Second Convention will form a new Virginia state government to replace the one that seceded—or should I say, that will *likely* secede, come the vote on May 23. That likely means the Convention will elect a new governor of Virginia and he will authorize forming up infantry and cavalry regiments. Mr. Willey is a very clever man, so we may get our cavalry company sooner than we think."

Harry said, "Dr. Keys told us a new cavalry manual is available. Have you heard of it?"

"No, I haven't," McGee replied.

"I'll try to get a copy and let you know if and where I find it. I want to study cavalry training and tactics," said Harry. "In the meantime, AJ has probably the best-trained horse I've ever seen and he's a crack shot with a long rifle. Watching him ride, jump and shoot is impressive, and a bit intimidating."

"Well, if you boys join a cavalry company, I surely hope it will be the one I help organize. I have another customer to see right now. Can you stay awhile?"

Harry said, "Thank you very much, Dr. McGee, but I need to get back so I can prepare my sermon for tomorrow."

"Then I'll say goodbye to both of you for now. Please take my card and leave me your addresses so we can stay in touch."

Harry's elaborate praise of him and his horse had embarrassed AJ. *I wonder if he's just trying to make it up to me, about him being a law breaker,* he thought. AJ wished things could be the same between them, but doubted they ever would. At least he felt satisfied that they had learned as much as they could about the prospects of the coming war and the likelihood of joining a cavalry company. They would probably have to wait for the outcome of the Second Wheeling Convention. They already were sure they knew the results of the coming Virginia vote on the Secession Ordinance.

SUNDAY, MAY 19, 1861 7:30 AM

SWANEY FARM, SMITHFIELD, PENNSYLVANIA

AJ arrived home late Saturday night and rose early Sunday morning to feed the animals and milk the cows. He told his pa what they had learned from the trip regarding the likelihood of war and the determination of the northwestern Virginians to remain in the Union. He did not mention a word about Abraham Blackman or the Underground Railroad.

His father listened carefully to all that AJ told him, and said he would make plans with nearby farmers to save food and animals in the event Confederate cavalry might decide to raid the Smithfield area. He understood AJ and Harry's decision to look for a cavalry company to join, but asked that AJ stay, if he could, to help with the harvest.

Everything had apparently gone smoothly while he was away, to AJ's relief. The spring planting was almost done. He wanted to ask about Sophia—whether his pa had seen her, whether Tip Swaney still came around—but didn't. *I've put all that behind me.*

This morning the whole family rejoiced to have AJ at home again. They pelted him with questions about city life and the sights of Wheeling. Cynthia wanted to know if he had met any pretty girls or handsome men. John wanted to know when they could target-shoot again.

Between bites of thick fried bacon, AJ looked up at Cynthia and, trying to keep his voice even, said, "How are the Mosiers? Is Sophia's grandma doing all right?"

Cynthia's lips curled in a tiny, satisfied smile and she stared at AJ with a knowing look that annoyed him. "She's doing as well as can be expected." She paused and then said, "Oh, I forgot to tell you, AJ—Sophia came over here a morning or so before you left, looking for you. You and Pa were out somewhere."

AJ choked on the lump of bacon he was swallowing. "Looking for me?" he croaked, when he had regained his breath and composure. "What did she want?"

"I'm not sure," Cynthia replied, the tiny smile still on her lips. "She wanted to tell you something."

Their mother shot a sharp look at Cynthia. "I thought she came to see *you*, not AJ," she said.

Cynthia squirmed. "Well, me too, but she told me she had something to tell AJ."

"And she didn't tell you what it was?" her mother responded.

Cynthia shook her head.

"Humph, must not have been so important then."

AJ's throat had closed up. He couldn't eat another bite. He wondered what Sophia had wanted with him. She hadn't even spoken to him since the night by the spring. Or was this just Cynthia's cruel teasing?

"AJ, eat your breakfast! And you all stop asking him so many questions," his mother finally exclaimed. "He looks like he didn't eat a bite on that trip. He's like a scarecrow."

"Ma! I ate, but we did a lot of riding and that always trims me down," AJ replied.

"Now don't argue with me," his ma replied. "I want you to eat a good breakfast, and start puttin' some meat back on those skinny bones.

And AJ, if you're going to join the cavalry, you're going to have to promise me some things."

AJ knew he was in for one of his mother's medical lectures. She was an herb doctor, of sorts, who knew hundreds of remedies. She spent hours in the woods and fields collecting roots, leaves and bark. Some of this knowledge had been passed down to her through generations of her family. But she also read every health journal or book she could get her hands on, and took every opportunity to talk to their local doctor about the latest findings. She cared for the health of her family in every way she knew.

"Now listen, AJ," She pointed at him with her knobby finger. "I want you to keep yourself clean and wash your hands ever' chance you get, with soap when you can get it. Disease follows dirt, I know that for a fact. Sleep outside when you can—next to cleanliness, fresh air is the best remedy. And watch what you eat—try to find vegetables and fruits. I don't 'spect Mr. Lincoln is going to be giving his army much of that. Pick berries and wild onions if you got nothin' else. A body needs some green, live food."

"Yes, Ma. Look, I'm eating."

"And one more thing, son. I want you to promise your pa and me that you won't take any extra chances while you're out there fightin'. I'm heartsick about you goin' anyway, and I know how young men are—always havin' to be showin' off and testing their mettle. You just do your duty, but don't put yourself in harm's way any more than you have to. Don't be a hero! Promise me."

"But, Ma, we haven't even found a company to join yet."

"Promise me, I said!"

All right, Ma. I promise."

AJ looked up to see tears in his mother's eyes.

WEDNESDAY, MAY 22, 1861, 9:00 AM
GOVERNOR DENNISON'S OFFICE, COLUMBUS, OHIO

Major General McClellan sat in Governor Dennison's office, discussing the news that had just arrived from across the Ohio River.

"George, thank you for coming up here to talk with me. I wanted to congratulate you personally on your impressive and well-deserved promotion to Major General in the U.S. Army, and to discuss a few items that concern me."

"Thank you, Governor, and what items are on your mind?"

"What do you make of this information about secessionist troops assembling at Grafton?"

"I am concerned, Governor," he replied. "Grafton is right at the junction of the B&O Railroad to Wheeling and the Northwestern Virginia Railroad to Parkersburg. It's a strategic point. If the Virginia militia gains control of that junction, they could send troops to occupy those two cities, and then use them as a base to launch an attack on Ohio."

"We must do something to prevent that! I don't want to just defend our borders, George, I want to go beyond them. Have you given any thought to invading Parkersburg and Wheeling, to force any battles to take place on Virginia soil, instead of Ohio soil? What do you recommend?"

"I've received many letters from responsible citizen leaders in the western Virginia counties, asking me for troops to help them repel invasions ordered by Richmond. I talked this over with Colonel Kelley, who's already formed a regiment of Virginia infantry volunteers loyal to the Union and is now forming a second infantry regiment. Kelley hasn't wanted to make a move against the secessionists until after all Virginians vote on secession tomorrow, and I agreed with him. Lincoln also has been unwilling to invade Virginia until after the vote is final. Kelley is willing to place himself and all his men under my command."

"What's your opinion of this Colonel Kelley?"

"He has a good military education from the Partridge Military Academy in Vermont. Some say the schooling there, taught by a tough and brilliant West Point graduate, is harder than the schooling at West Point. Kelley also knows the B&O Railroad inside and out, since he worked for that line for a long time. He's friendly with John Garrett, the President of the B&O. Kelley's a good man to have over there. Protecting that railroad is a top priority. He says the folks in the western Virginia counties mean to stay in the Union. They've already begged Washington for arms and I understand the governor of Massachusetts sent them over a thousand muskets and ammunition. It's to our advantage to have these men on our side, and we should do everything we can to help them and keep them supplied."

"What should we do next, George?"

"As you know, Governor, Washington has now placed me in command of the Department of Ohio, which has been expanded to include western Virginia and western Pennsylvania. However, I haven't yet received any direct orders from Washington. They are slow to answer my requests. The secessionists in Maryland cut Washington's telegraph and rail lines a while back, and that fouled up our communications for awhile, but there seems to be a decided apathy in Washington. And as I said, Lincoln hasn't wanted any troops sent into Virginia until after the public vote on secession, which is tomorrow."

"This is a crisis. Let's both of us send telegrams to Washington and get you some orders. I'll send one to General Scott, and you send one to Secretary of War Cameron. Maybe that will shake things up."

McClellan hesitated. *Scott isn't going to like us putting pressure on him like this*, he thought. But then he considered his increasing frustration with Scott and the old general's refusal to consider McClellan's plan for winning the war quickly, obviously believing it to be hasty and ill-considered and always suggesting more patient plans of his own. *He ap-*

pointed me Major General, the highest military position in the country except for his own, but he won't listen to me. Scott is old and has lost his edge, he thought. McClellan tried to be diplomatic and conciliatory toward the aged general, whom he admired for his past military accomplishments, but found himself increasingly frustrated with being under the command of a man obviously past his prime. *It's time for his mantle to fall on my shoulders.* He resolved to send the telegram Dennison desired and let the chips fall where they may.

Governor Dennison and McClellan sent their separately drafted telegrams to Washington, asking for urgent replies. In his telegram to General Scott at the War Department, Dennison advised the general that Confederate troops were advancing on Grafton and Clarksburg in western Virginia and the situation was dire, needing direct action.

In his own telegram to Cameron, McClellan advised that Cumberland should be occupied at once to stop movements through it to western Virginia, and he told the Secretary that he had received no orders, instructions, or authority to act. He said that his "hands were tied" due to the lack of orders.

It wasn't long until a reply to both telegrams arrived. Both replies came from General Scott. The answer to the Governor's telegram told him that McClellan was in charge of the Department of Ohio and to take up this matter with him, not Scott.

When McClellan read his own lengthy, scolding telegram from the old general, he could feel his face turning red. Secretary Cameron had obviously passed his communication on to Scott to handle, and Scott was angry. He instructed McClellan to take charge and do his job, saying that he was "surprised at your complaint to the Secretary of War against me that your hands are tied." He reviewed all his prior instructions and communications to McClellan and added a terse line: "It is not conceived what other instructions could have been needed by you."

It was a slap in the face and McClellan did not take kindly to the rebuke. He resolved to act, and act swiftly. He took his leave of Dennison, saying that he would keep him informed. He was heading to a military conference in Indiana to discuss several strategic military decisions that would affect the course of the war. He resolved to use all the power of his personality to sway those in attendance to his point of view. If he could keep the northwestern counties of Virginia on the Union side, then all of Ohio and the states west of the Ohio would be safe, as well as the industrial center at Wheeling and the industrial might of Pittsburgh. *Let the eastern Virginians secede*, he thought. *I will make sure the Confederacy spends little time in my Department.*

He could see now that the only solution was to get rid of Scott. He just had to determine the best way to do that.

WEDNESDAY, MAY 22, 1861, 8:00 PM

COLONEL PORTERFIELD'S HQ, FETTERMAN, VIRGINIA

Lieutenant Daniel Wilson and Private Thornsbury Bailey Brown of the unionist Grafton Guards militia unit were returning from a recruiting trip to Pruntytown, about four miles west of Grafton. As they approached the intersection where the Northwestern Turnpike crossed the B&O Railroad, they ran into pickets from the Letcher Guards in Fetterman, where the secessionist forces under Porterfield were headquartered.

"Who goes there? Give me the sign or I'll fire!" one picket yelled.

"Brown! Quick, shoot him," Lieutenant Wilson ordered.

Without hesitation, Brown drew his pistol, aimed, and fired at the picket. The sound from the pistol echoed through the pastoral countryside.

"Damn you! You shot me in the ear!" the picket screamed.

With blood pouring down one cheek, the injured picket raised his musket and fired at the men silhouetted against the twilight sky. Wilson heard no screams, only a grunt and the thump of a man hitting the ground. "Brown!" Wilson cried. There was no response from the man on the ground.

Oh, my God! Wilson spurred his horse and galloped away in the dark. He heard a shot and felt an impact on his right foot but no pain. A bullet apparently hit the heel of his boot. He made his way back to Grafton to inform others.

THURSDAY, MAY 23, 1861, 9:00 AM

GRAFTON, VIRGINIA

The news of the death of Private Brown, a native son, shocked the town of Grafton. The event, occurring on the eve of the vote on the Richmond Convention secession ordinance, served to amplify the townsmen's hatred of Richmond. Emotions ran high as the people of Grafton cast, unanimously, their vote against secession. In the midst of crying and mourning, many threats against "Letcher and his henchmen" were heard in the streets. Many citizens wanted to arm themselves, march to Fetterman, and take revenge on the traitorous soldiers camped there. They were held back by Captain Latham, in charge of the Grafton Guards, who assured them taking revenge would only result in civilian deaths.

THURSDAY, MAY 23, 1861, 9:00 AM

FETTERMAN, VIRGINIA

While most of the secessionist soldiers understood that their picket was doing his duty, many knew Brown well and grieved his death. For everyone in the camp it was a shocking reminder they were not playing "soldiers." As far as anyone knew, this was the first death of a unionist soldier under fire during the present conflict. Colonel Porterfield had considered making a show of force by marching troops into Grafton, to deter the people there from voting in today's referendum, but out of respect for Brown and the mourners in Grafton, he decided against it. *The Grafton votes will probably "get lost in Richmond" and not be counted anyway,* he thought.

Whether the Grafton votes were counted or not, on May 23, 1861 Virginian's citizens ratified the ordinance to secede from the Union. *Well, it's official,* thought Porterfield. *Now all hell is free to break loose.*

SATURDAY, MAY 25, 1861, 9:00 AM
COLONEL PORTERFIELD'S HQ, FETTERMAN, VIRGINIA

Porterfield sat at his table sipping a cup of coffee when Boykin announced that his informant had just ridden into camp. "Come on in and bring Jim with you," he told Boykin. Jim did not look the part of a spy. At five and a half feet tall, and a little on the chubby side, he intimidated no one. He was softspoken and gregarious. He got along with everyone and could easily take on the role of a unionist or a secessionist, depending on who he was talking to. He could have been a spy for a Union colonel as well as a spy for Porterfield. *Perhaps he is,* Porterfield thought. *If so, he's damn good and his information is almost always correct. As it should be—he's being paid well enough for it.*

"What do you have for me, Jim?" Porterfield asked.

"Well now, Colonel," the little man said, rocking back on his heels, "I took a trip on the train to Parkersburg, a packet boat trip up the Ohio to Wheeling, with stops, of course, at Marietta and Bellaire just like you asked. Then I took the train from Wheeling back to Grafton, just like you told me to do."

"Go on, Jim. What did you find?"

"Well now, Colonel, I found out that General McClellan is massin' infantry troops with a battery of cannon at Marietta and the same at Bellaire. Countin' flags in their camps, I would say a brigade is at each location. Mighty fine-looking soldiers, I might add. They had on new uniforms, *that fit*, and rugged looking new polished shoes. They marched together real nice, and had shiny new muskets and bayonets. Every soldier had a haversack and a bedroll on his back. They looked to me like they just got there. Their pretty white tents, all lined up in straight rows, looked brand-new.

"Then I went to Wheeling and stood in line to sign up for General Kelley's Second Infantry regiment that's formin' up right now. I met some nice fellers standing in that line. They told me Colonel Kelley's First Infantry regiment is all full now and ready to fight. They have nice new uniforms, shoes, and muskets too. Ten companies in that regiment and each company, they told me, has exactly 101 men, not countin' officers. That second regiment already had four companies ready for combat and it looked like there were still a thousand men in the line I was in."

"Did you sign up?" Boykin asked with a smirk.

Jim forced out a nervous laugh. "Well now, Major, I thought about it, but then I remembered I had to hightail it back here, to tell you boys the news."

"Could you tell if the men from Ohio or any of Kelley's men were preparing to move out?" Porterfield asked. "Tell me exactly what you saw."

"Well now, Colonel, I couldn't rightly tell that. There are so many boats travelin' up and down that big muddy river between Parkersburg and Wheeling, those troops might just walk across from boat to boat without touchin' any water a'tall. It's amazin', it is. But I guess it wouldn't take any of them boys too long to get across that river, jump on the train, and come visit you here in Grafton."

"Thank you, Jim," Porterfield said as he handed the man his usual payment. "Help yourself to something to eat. Come back and give me more details after you've eaten."

"Thank *you*, Colonel. That's mighty kind of you, sir." Jim had a big grin on his face as he left the room.

Porterfield was worried. He turned to Boykin and said, "This is bad news, Major. Here we sit with very little equipment and our muskets are… who knows where? We have enough men now for a small regiment but hardly anything to fight *with*. Prudence tells me I must assume those brigades at Marietta and Bellaire are going to attack us down here either directly, or in support of an attack by Colonel Kelley's regiments. I believe they mean to save the railroad for themselves and drive us out. Or worse yet, they may mean to capture everyone and put us all in prison. We have no secure base to fall back on and we don't know the location of our promised supplies. We must take defensive measures to slow any attack by them and fall back towards Beverly. Perhaps, if supplies arrive in time, we might be able to make a stand at Philippi. I will telegraph General Johnston at Harper's Ferry for assistance."

"I agree, Colonel, we're much too vulnerable here."

Porterfield stroked his chin whiskers as he thought for a moment about how best to protect his position. He consulted a map on his desk, and then said to Boykin, "I want you to call for volunteers for two bridge-burning details. At least one officer and a squad of men should be in each detail. The first is to take the B&O train toward Wheeling and burn the two railroad bridges that cross Buffalo Creek near Mannington. I want this done tonight. That detail is to return here to Fetterman. The second detail will take longer and those bridge burnings should occur tomorrow night, or the following. Order that detail to take the Northwest Virginia Railroad train toward Parkersburg and burn the railroad bridge across the North Fork of the Hughes River at Toll Gate, and burn the one across Goose Creek at Petroleum. That detail is to return to our camp at Philippi. Go and select the men, give them their orders, and report back to me." *That should buy us some more time,* Porterfield thought.

Sunday, May 26, 1861, 5:00 am
McClellan's HQ, Camp Dennison, Ohio

"General! Wake up, sir!"

Fighting his way out of a deep sleep, George McClellan looked around and saw only darkness. *Where am I?*

"General McClellan! Wake up, sir!"

"What do you want?" McClellan demanded of the voice in the dark.

"Sir, it's Colonel Lander. I have a telegram you need to read right away."

Lander was a bear of a man, a flamboyant adventurer, and a noted explorer who offered his services to McClellan as a volunteer *aide-de-camp*.

"Come in, Colonel," said McClellan. "I think I'm awake now. Bring in a lamp and read the telegram to me."

"Sir, the telegram is from Colonel Kelley in Wheeling. Last night, Kelley says, he received word that someone burned two bridges on the B&O Railroad near Mannington. Kelley thinks Porterfield's rebels, camped at Fetterman, are to blame. Kelley wants to know if you have any orders for him."

"My God, has that damn Colonel Porterfield decided to start a civil war in his own state, against his own people? Light my lamp too while I get out my maps, so we can find the location of those bridges."

Together they spread the maps on the table and placed lamps to light the approximate area of interest. Warming their hands from the heat of the lamps, they searched for Mannington.

"Here it is!" Lander exclaimed.

"And here are the two bridges crossing over Buffalo Creek," McClellan added. "I want you to send a telegram to Kelley right away and order him to spend today preparing his regiment for an extended stay and assembling the supplies he'll need to repair those bridges. He is to proceed early tomorrow morning toward Fairmont, repair the railroad as he advances, post guards at all important bridges, and report to me his progress by telegraph at least daily. Have each man carry rations for one week. Emphasize to Kelley that it is most important to prevent any further destruction of the railroad. Sign my name to the telegram. Is that clear?"

"Yes, sir, I think that will suffice."

"Then go ahead and get that telegram sent and come back here as soon as possible. And bring me a fresh cup of hot coffee. Make sure it's brewed fresh—not that horse piss that sits all night!"

While Lander handled the telegram, McClellan pondered the precautions he should take against flank and other attacks by the enemy forces and how best to protect his supply bases. While he thought about the railroad line to Parkersburg, the aroma of coffee came wafting into his tent.

"General, here's your fresh coffee. The telegram to Kelley has been sent."

"Thank you, Colonel." McClellan took a sip, then another, paused to make sure he was wide awake, then said, "I've been thinking about sending several Ohio regiments over the border to help Colonel Kelley and secure the railroad over there. We don't know yet what we're dealing with and I don't want to chance any setbacks. What do you think?"

"Those regiments are well trained, well equipped, and probably anxious to get into a fight. But, how are the Virginians going to take to this? Are they going to welcome us with open arms, or resist us as an invasion force?"

"I'm almost certain we'll be welcomed by the westerners. I've received many letters over the last few weeks from their leaders asking us—no, begging us—for help. Kelley assures me that most citizens of northwestern Virginia will look upon our men as saviors, not invaders. I'm sure there will be some, however, whose sympathies lie first with their state and not with our country, who will look on our boys as invaders. I'll inform Washington of my actions and I'll issue a proclamation today to the people of western Virginia explaining our intentions. I'll also issue another proclamation for our soldiers, explaining the behavior I expect of them. You prepare orders for the Ohio regimental commanders so we can get them started early. On your way back, get the cook to prepare some breakfast and another pot of coffee."

Alone in his tent, he wondered, *Have I thought of everything?* Then he took one more precaution. He wired Brigadier General Thomas A. Morris in Indianapolis to move with two regiments to Wheeling or Parkersburg, depending on circumstances which he would wire later, and keep his movement secret. If asked, Morris should give Pittsburgh or some other city as his destination.

MONDAY, MAY 27–30, 1861
WHEELING, VIRGINIA; B&O RAILROAD; GRAFTON, VIRGINIA

The men on the B&O station platform stood at ease holding onto their muskets as yard crews loaded the final items of bridge repair and telegraphic communications equipment onto the train. The tall man in a Union officer's uniform carried a lantern, carefully checking off every item. As railroad men closed latches on the baggage cars, he climbed the stairs to the platform and gazed down the long line of his soldiers. They smiled at him as he walked along briskly, signaling the conductors to open the doors to the passenger cars. These men, the first regiment of Virginia infantry soldiers loyal to the Union, adored him. Although they had not yet been given tents, haversacks, cartridge boxes, canteens or any other articles essential to their comfort, they all had muskets and their pockets were full of ammunition. They were confident that Colonel Benjamin Franklin Kelley, the man they called "Old Ben," knew what he was doing and would look out for them. To show their appreciation, they gave him three loud cheers as he ordered them to board the train. All hoped to see some action soon.

Kelley and his staff were the last to board. Sitting down beside Kelley, his regimental surgeon, Joseph Thoburn, said, "Colonel, you've done amazing things with these men."

"Thank you, Joe, and thanks again for stepping in to be the surgeon for the regiment. Please, call me Ben."

Kelley had an immediate liking for the dark, full-bearded doctor with the kind face, who had signed on with his regiment for the three-month enlistment. He felt instinctively that Thoburn was a man who could be trusted with his life, whether as a physician or on the battlefield.

"Then 'Ben' it is. I hope I can be of assistance, whatever comes to pass in these uncertain times. I haven't had any military experience before now, but perhaps my experience overseeing an Ohio lunatic asylum will prove pertinent!"

Kelley chuckled. "That might be particularly appropriate if you end up in Washington!"

They both laughed heartily. "I understand you received arms for the regiment from Massachusetts, Ben. I'm curious—how did that come about?"

"Several of our leading citizens made applications to the Secretary of War. I understand the folks in Washington were reluctant to provide arms to us western Virginians, for fear they would fall into the hands of the rebels. Finally the Secretary of War referred our delegation to Massachusetts Governor John Andrews, who agreed to send us arms."

"Incredible! I also heard you had some trouble getting this train from the B&O. Was that a big problem?"

"No, not really, I can spot secession sympathizers a mile away. When I applied for transportation yesterday, the yard manager refused on the grounds that the B&O proposed to be neutral between warring factions and would not carry troops or munitions for either side. This man already knew the railroad bridges near Mannington were burned on the 25th. I could have contacted President Garrett, but I needed to handle this matter quickly, so I told the yard manager that this was war and railroads could not be their own masters. He would have the train ready by 4:00 AM today or I would throw him in prison. I came down early with one of our companies, to be sure he got the message. He was assembling the train, but I still don't trust him, so I'll replace him today with a yard manager loyal to the Union. I also have men on this train that I can trust, to replace telegraph operators suspected of secession sympathies at each station."

"I was also curious about how you got General McClellan to finally send troops across the river to help us."

"We need to thank Colonel Porterfield for that, not me. Tearing up those bridges last Friday night was just what McClellan needed to act. I'm sure he worries about a Virginia invasion of Ohio, and with that act of sabotage, he could finally respond to all the calls for help that our citizens have sent him. All I did was send a telegram to McClellan informing him of what had happened and asking for orders. He responded quickly by sending me orders to repair the railroad and move toward Grafton. He also informed me he would send Ohio Volunteer troops to Parkersburg and Benwood."

"I thought you said our destination was Fairmont," Thoburn said.

"Yes, but McClellan left it to my discretion to proceed on to Grafton. I suspect Porterfield is trying to buy himself time by burning those bridges. He probably knows from his spies I have a full regiment of a thousand men and I suspect he's having a hard time getting western Virginians to sign up to fight for him. So maybe he has fewer soldiers than I have and has decided to pull back from Grafton. McClellan asked me to place guards at bridges along the way, to prevent further destruction of the railroad."

149

"Ben, I hope you're right about Porterfield pulling back. You're the military man, and your reasoning seems good to me. I appreciate you taking time to discuss strategy with me. I want to learn as much as I can."

"You never know, Joe, you might be in command of this, or some other, regiment someday. I'm glad you're interested."

Joined by Colonel James Irvine's Sixteenth Ohio infantry regiment at Benwood station, Kelley's regiment proceeded cautiously along the railroad line, stopping at each bridge and station to place guards and to replace telegraph operators with trusted Union men. They encountered no opposition and arrived near Mannington just before sunset.

Over the following two days, Kelley received telegrams from McClellan advising him that more troops from Ohio and Indiana were on their way to support him. When Colonel Milroy's Ninth Indiana regiment arrived, Kelley, having encountered no resistance thus far and now well reinforced, sent McClellan a telegram that he planned to proceed to Grafton. McClellan replied that Brigadier General Thomas A. Morris and his Indiana infantry brigade would meet him in Grafton to take overall command. Confident, Kelley then proceeded to Grafton and on May 30 occupied the town. He found no enemy there or in nearby Fetterman and learned from citizens that Porterfield and his secessionist Virginia men had departed for Philippi, hoping to gather reinforcements and supplies.

Kelley passed orders to his staff and the other regimental commanders to set up camp. Then, weary, he retired to his room in the Grafton Hotel to rest and plan a strategy to defeat and capture all of Porterfield's command. Although he was physically tired, his brain was active. He knew sleep would not come easily until he found a plan that could work. Plan after plan ran through his mind, based on how many men he expected Porterfield to have and how many men General Morris would have under his command. After a restless night, tossing and turning, dreaming and thinking, he arrived at a simple envelopment plan requiring Morris's force to be divided into two parts, one of which he would lead.

This will work, he thought. When General Morris arrived the next day, he would go over his plan with the staffs of all brigade commanders. Finally, he slept.

MONDAY, MAY 27, 1861, 8:00 AM

ABOARD STEAMBOAT OHIO 3 NEAR PARKERSBURG, VIRGINIA

Tensions ran high among the men of the 14th Ohio Volunteer Infantry Regiment as they formed on the cargo deck of Steamboat OHIO 3 as the boat maneuvered toward the dock on the Virginia side of the Ohio River. The men had just been given the order to fix bayonets. Many wondered what would be waiting for them when the ramp of the steamboat dropped down on the wharf. Would it be a line of Confederate muskets, as some believed, or would it be cheers from a crowd of western Virginia unionists welcoming them into their state with open arms, as others believed?

"Men, the honor of Ohio is in our hands!" The voice of their commander, Colonel Steedman, rang out in the morning stillness. "We come to Parkersburg this morning to aid our friends in Virginia who still hold high that star-spangled banner. When the ramps are lowered, I expect to see Virginia citizens welcoming us. But because we are soldiers, we prepare for the worst and pray for the best. We are entering a Virginia that has seceded from our Union. We have heard that those Virginians who voted for secession far outnumber the loyal Virginia citizens. If any who favor secession greet us, let us show them our steel. We shall not falter. We shall not fail. Our cause is just."

The ramps lowered. There on the wharf and in the streets stood men and women waving American flags. A band struck up a rousing marching song for the soldiers as they marched up 6th Street on their way to the Western Virginia railroad terminal. The men could no longer hear the commands of their officers over the cheers of the crowd, but they knew they could find their way despite the tears in many of their eyes. They came prepared to secure Parkersburg and this railroad for these patriots and for the Union.

Steedman kept a copy of his orders from General McClellan on him at all times. It read:

> *You will on receipt of this, cross the river and occupy Parkersburg. The 18th (Ohio) regiment at Athens, is ordered to report to you. You will at once move toward Grafton, as far as can be done with prudence, leaving sufficient guards at Parkersburg and the bridges as you advance. Avail yourself of the assistance of the armed Union men, preserve the strictest discipline, and do all in your power to conciliate. If you have to fight, remember that the honor of Ohio is in your hands. Communicate fully. See that the rebels receive no information by telegraph. See that the rights of the people are respected, and repress all attempts at negro insurrection.*

After securing his base at Parkersburg, Steedman set out for Clarksburg 80 miles away. It took him four days to reach Clarksburg. The bridges at Petroleum, across Goose Creek, and at Toll Gate, over the Hughes River, suffered extensive damage and needed rebuilding. McClellan sent his trusted aide-de-camp to Parkersburg, to assist in gathering needed materials. They would not enter the town of Grafton until June 1.

TUESDAY, MAY 28, 1861, 9:00 AM
COLONEL PORTERFIELD'S HQ, FETTERMAN, VIRGINIA

Boykin's daily walk to the post office finally paid off. "I have two letters addressed to Colonel Porterfield," the postmaster said with a smile. Boykin took the letters and ran off like a boy, to tell Porterfield.

Colonel Porterfield looked at the letters; one was from General Johnston and the other from General Lee. He opened the one from Gen. Johnston first. It read:

I regret to inform you that conditions here dictate that I must keep all my forces at this location. If conditions change I will send a battalion of infantry to assist you.

"Looks like we can't count on any help from Johnston," he said, frustrated, passing the letter to Boykin to read.

The letter from General Lee read:

I have to inform you that I have ordered one thousand muskets, with a sufficient supply of powder and lead to Beverly, escorted by Colonel Heck and Major Cowan. Any instructions you may have for Colonel Heck address to him at Beverly. Colonel Heck has been instructed to call all the volunteers he can along his route.

Porterfield's face turned purple and he shook his head angrily. Handing the second letter to Boykin, he said, "Another announcement from General Lee that he is sending us arms! Why does he not say when these arms are scheduled to arrive in Beverly? I wonder what happened to the *other* arms he said were coming?" He sighed and gestured to Boykin. "Major, send a messenger to Beverly and tell him to *wait* there until Colonel Heck arrives with the muskets. Tell him to lead Colonel Heck, and any troops he might have gathered, to our camp at Philippi. Pass the orders, we march to Philippi today!"

TUESDAY, MAY 28, 1861, 4:00 PM
ON THE ROAD TO PHILIPPI, VIRGINIA WITH
COLONEL PORTERFIELD

Colonel Porterfield rode up and down the column as his soldiers marched easily on the macadamized turnpike. He wanted to observe for himself the progress of these green troops in their marching training. *Not a pretty sight.* Even some of the company commanders and the platoon officers had trouble at times keeping step. Recalling his marching days at Virginia Military Institute, these men barely looked like soldiers to him. He rode ahead to find Major Boykin, who he had sent with two platoons to teach the skills and duties of skirmishers in protecting the front, rear, and flanks of the main column of marching men.

"How's the training going, Major?"

"A few of the men are eager to learn, but I'm afraid most think what we're doing is punishing them. They want to walk on the smooth road, not out there in the field with the briars and chuck holes."

"We've got to keep after them. When we get to Philippi I want you to teach the men how to stand picket duty. Until we get more information, we must assume that Kelley and his unionist friends from Ohio are still after us."

"I will do my best, Colonel. Is that a flag of the Confederacy that I see flying on top of that courthouse?"

"I'm not sure I know what that flag looks like, to tell you the truth. I'll take a look through my field glasses. Hmm, looks more like the United States flag. No, it doesn't have enough stars or stripes... I think. If it *is* a flag of the Confederacy, do you think the people know we are coming?"

"Wouldn't surprise me, Colonel. Everyone in these parts seems to know things before we do."

As the column descended toward the town of Philippi, Porterfield looked for a suitable campsite. The turnpike ran though the massive covered bridge over the Tygart Valley River and south through the town, which lay on the east side of the river, then weaved around the mountain toward Beverly, about 30 miles south. Downstream of the bridge stood a working gristmill and further downstream on the east side of the river lay a meadow, which would make a fine camp away from the town, yet close enough to the pike leading south to Beverly. Porterfield decided to explain their needs to the town's leaders and seek their approval before setting up the camp. He wasn't sure which flag that was, but Philippi had the reputation of being a secessionist town, so he was optimistic that they would cooperate. The courthouse, businesses, and shops along the main street and the surrounding homes looked so peaceful set against the brilliant spring green of the surrounding hills. *Might not be peaceful long*, he thought.

WEDNESDAY, MAY 29, 1861, 6:00 AM
COLONEL PORTERFIELD'S HQ, PHILIPPI, VIRGINIA

"Colonel, you are not going to believe this," Major Boykin said, pulling back the flap on Porterfield's tent.

"What is it, Major?"

"You have to take a look for yourself, sir."

Colonel Porterfield pulled on his clothes and walked out of his tent. There in front of him a colonel, in a grey uniform with gold braid, stood in front of a wagon with a company of well-dressed and armed cavalry.

The colonel in the grey uniform came to attention, saluted and said, "Colonel Heck at your service, sir. I have a wagon full of muskets, lead, and powder for you."

For a moment Porterfield thought he might be dreaming. Then he returned the salute and replied, "How many muskets did you bring, Colonel, and is the powder in caps and the lead in balls that fit the muskets?"

"My orders were to bring you 1000 muskets. The lead is all in balls sized to fit the muskets. The powder is in kegs, not in caps, sir."

"Are powder horns in the wagon?"

"No, sir."

"Am I supposed to teach green soldiers to load muskets and fire four times a minute using a spoon or their fingers to load powder?"

"I'm sorry, sir, this is what I was given to bring to you."

"What about this cavalry unit—whose command are they under? Are they to be under my command?"

"They were assigned to me as escort to insure the safe delivery of the rifles. They are from Rockbridge and I suspect they're looking for a good fight. If you want them, I'll place them under your command."

"I only have 500 men, Colonel. Were you able to find any more volunteers along the way?"

"Sorry, sir, the men on the other side of the mountains have already joined regiments. I tried to get men on this side of the mountains, but it seems most call themselves 'unionists.' Sir, I need you to sign the voucher for the equipment I brought."

"In just a minute! Can I keep that team of horses with that wagon?"

"I'm sorry, sir, my orders are to bring the team back to Staunton. I did notice horses and rigs for sale when I passed through Beverly. You could try there."

"Colonel, I *insist* on keeping that team with the wagon. I have the enemy near here and I need that team to protect the rifles, which I can't use right now. You can 'requisition' a team when you pass back through Beverly."

"You're in charge, Colonel. I'll add that team and harnesses to the voucher you need to sign."

"Yes, that will be fine. Tell the commander of the Rockbridge Cavalry company he and his men are now under my command."

"I'll tell them, Colonel. I'm sure it will make them happy. As I said, they're looking for a fight."

"Colonel Heck, I'll sign those vouchers now. Be sure to relay to those in command at Staunton what you see here today. I don't have enough men for offensive actions and what you see are mostly green militia still in training. It will take months of training to get these men in fighting condition. If those soldiers in Ohio cross our border in large numbers, as I believe they will, I'm not going to be able to stop them."

The two colonels saluted each other and Colonel Heck rode off to Beverly. The captain of the Rockbridge cavalry company came over and introduced himself to Porterfield. Altogether there were 108 cavalrymen.

THURSDAY, MAY 30, 1861, 9:00 AM
PHILIPPI, VIRGINIA

The mayor and other town leaders met with Colonel Porterfield and Major Boykin. The mayor introduced himself and his staff and asked if he could do anything to assist the Colonel.

"Thank you, sir, but I believe the men are now settled in their camp downstream of the gristmill, the location you suggested. All of our needs have been satisfied. I told our men yesterday that they were to be on their best behavior and treat all citizens of Philippi as honored hosts. Is there anything you need from us?" Porterfield didn't entirely trust these people yet, remembering his experience with the unionists of Grafton, but he believed in diplomacy.

"Thank you, Colonel Porterfield. There is one small favor we would like to ask of you and your men," the mayor replied.

"Why, of course. What is it?"

The mayor cleared his throat and said, "We would like to ask, if you are going to do battle with your enemy, that you please take the fight down the road and away from our town. We have many women and children living here, you see."

Porterfield was taken aback by the naive request. He replied, "Mr. Mayor, I can only promise that we will *try* to honor your request, but we cannot control the behavior of the enemy, should they come down the road from Grafton and attack us here. We've chosen a spot for our camp on the outskirts of your town, which I hope will allow us to take up defensive positions far from the village center, and I pray the enemy soldiers will not intentionally harm the village and its inhabitants. But war is not a game, sir, and we have no control over the enemy's location or actions. My apologies. I do hope you understand." He nodded at the mayor, a tight smile on his lips.

The mayor sheepishly said he understood and nodded back.

Later that day a company of soldiers joined the camp from Upshur County. They had little training and few had arms. They received rifles and ammunition and a quick lesson on how to load and fire the rifles. This company now brought Porterfield's total force to about 600 infantry and 108 cavalry.

He knew all of the men under his command were undertrained and underequipped and they were in a most precarious position. The colonel's sinking feeling came back. *We've been hung out to dry,* he thought.

CHAPTER SEVEN

The Philippi Races

June 1–June 15, 1861

Grafton Hotel at the junction of railroads to Wheeling and Parkersburg c. 1857

SATURDAY, JUNE 1, 1861, 3:00 PM
GRAFTON, VIRGINIA

Kelley met most of the regimental commanders and observed their troops as they arrived in Grafton. He gave special treatment to Brigadier General Thomas A. Morris when his brigade arrived, as Morris would be the overall commanding officer and Kelley wanted to personally show him and his staff to their rooms in the Grafton Hotel. They talked for awhile and Kelley suggested assembling all the troops to a brief change of command ceremony, so all soldiers knew Morris was now the overall commander. Morris agreed. The ceremony began with a regimental band playing "The Star Spangled Banner" and ended with Kelley leading the troops in three hearty cheers for General Morris.

After the ceremony, Kelley informed General Morris of his proposed plan to defeat and capture all of the enemy forces now located in the town of Philippi. Kelley proposed a meeting with staff to go over this plan. Morris agreed and after all the commanding officers were assembled in one of the hotel's meeting rooms, Kelley spread out a large map of the area on the table and began his presentation.

Pointing to the small town of Philippi, he said, "My most recent information indicates that Colonel Porterfield is camped here, at Philippi. My plan uses a simple surprise and envelopment strategy that will involve two forces. The first force, which I propose to lead, will take the train to Thornton and then march along these back roads to a place south of Philippi on the Staunton-Parkersburg Turnpike, which leads from Philippi to Beverly. My force will be in position to capture Porterfield's force when he tries to retreat south toward Beverly.

"The second force will take the train to Webster and then march south on the Staunton-Parkersburg Turnpike and stage here west of the covered bridge that spans the Tygart Valley River.

"Upon a signal from artillery placed here on this hill, the second force will attack through the covered bridge and drive Porterfield's men through the town into the arms of the first force, resulting in the capture of Porterfield's force.

"I don't know exactly where Porterfield's camp is located. There are two possible places. The first is north of Philippi downstream of the covered bridge. The second is south of the town and upstream. Officers may be boarding in family houses. The men are likely in tents visible from the hill where our artillery is placed. The artillery will be able to reach both campsites. I estimate the size of his force at a thousand men or less."

Kelley paused to let the general and his staff study the map for several minutes. Finally, the general said, "Colonel Kelley, a most impressive plan! Well done. What else do you want to present before we let the staff critique it?"

"As I said, the first force would go by train to Thornton. We can pass the word among those men to talk instead about Harper's Ferry as their destination. If any spies are in the crowd at the station, they might think that's our destination.

"The second force would go to Webster by the train to Parkersburg. At Webster they would detrain and then march along the turnpike to Philippi. Of course, we need to work out the details as to which regiments will be in each of the two forces. I recommend Milroy's Ninth Indiana and Irvine's Sixteenth Ohio go with me, since we've already worked together."

The general nodded. "Any comments on this plan from the commanders or their staffs?" he asked.

"How are we going to coordinate the attacks by the two forces?" Colonel Milroy asked.

The general scratched his head. "Let's use watches and plan to start the attack, say, at 0400?" Kelley nodded; yes, that would work.

"We probably still need a loud starting signal," Colonel Dumont added. "How about if I fire a shot from one of my cannons as close to

0400 as possible? That way we can be sure the cannons are ready and it will signal Kelley to start his attack from the south, while we start the attack from the north."

Kelley watched the general closely to see if he approved. The general tilted his head as he contemplated the suggested plans. Then he rapped sharply with his knuckles on the map. "Let's go with everyone in place as close to 0400 as possible, followed by the infantry attack immediately following the first shot from the cannons." Kelley released the breath that he had been holding—his carefully thought-out plan was going to work.

"How close do you think Porterfield's pickets will be to the turnpike?" Dumont asked.

"Not sure," Kelley replied with a grimace. "But it will still be dark and maybe they won't have pickets out too far from their camp. I suspect Porterfield's boys are still pretty green and might not like being too far away from camp in the dark."

Everyone laughed at Kelley's comment, even though it had some truth in it, as bushwhackers were known to be in the area of Philippi.

The general said, "If you have no more questions or comments, let's take the rest of today for planning. Bring me, on or before 1800, your detailed plans on when the troops should board the trains. I'll prepare orders for Colonels Kelley and Dumont."

As he left the room to prepare for the operation, Kelley smiled to himself. *It will take a bit of luck, but I have a good feeling about this one.*

SUNDAY, JUNE 2, 1861, 8:00 AM

GRAFTON, VIRGINIA

Kelley and his surgeon Joseph Thoburn stood together near the engine trying to talk over the hissing sounds of steam building in the boiler as the fireman added more wood to the firebox. Smoke drifted upwards from the big inverted conical stack, carrying the aroma of a damp campfire on the moist morning breeze. Kelley's column, consisting of six companies of his own 1st Virginia Infantry, nine companies of Milroy's Ninth Indiana infantry, and six companies of Irvine's Sixteenth Ohio infantry—a total of about 1,600 men—readied their equipment. The men talked among themselves as they prepared to board the cars that would take them east to Thornton about six miles away. Prepped beforehand by their officers, they spoke of their long trip ahead to Harper's Ferry, so any spies among the crowd that had gathered to watch might conclude they were on their way to attack the enemy force at that station. After all were aboard, Kelley smiled as he noted that some folks in that crowd rushed off to their horses as the train pulled out. *Perhaps,* he thought, *to warn the rebels at Harper's Ferry.*

"Well, Ben, do you think our feint worked back there?" Surgeon Joseph Thoburn asked after the train cleared the station. Kelley turned to look at his companion. Their friendship had grown and he admired Thoburn not only for his medical skills but also for his curiosity and interest in all that was taking place around them militarily and politically.

"Let's hope so," Kelley replied. "I saw a few in the crowd running for their horses. We also told our loyal telegraph officer to allow folks to prepare telegrams and pay for them, but to send only those wires addressed to Harper's Ferry. And one of our operators at Thornton will tell anyone desiring to send a telegram that the lines have been cut."

"Ben, you do think of everything!" The surgeon clapped him on the back, "Do you really know all those back roads and trails from Thornton to Philippi?"

"No," Kelley admitted. "But Captain Fordyce has engaged a guide, a backwoods farmer, a Mr. Baker, who knows the roads."

Both men smiled as they contemplated the cleverness of the plan. *By noon the rear guard company should be disappearing into the forest,* Kelley thought.

Sunday, June 2, 1861, 4:00 pm
Colonel Porterfield's HQ, Philippi, Virginia

It had been a quiet and peaceful Sunday in Philippi. Most of Colonel Porterfield's men had attended morning church services. In the afternoon sun, rare in these days of almost constant rain, the men lazed, enjoying some time off from the countless marching drills, musket practices, sentry instructions, and the seemingly endless other tasks that are the lot of new recruits. Porterfield sat in his tent, writing a letter home.

Suddenly, Major Boykin announced outside Porterfield's tent, "Colonel, your favorite spy, Jim, is here. He just arrived from Grafton and wants to talk to you."

"Bring him in," Porterfield said, recalling he had last told Jim to take a room at the Grafton Hotel and keep his eyes and ears open for trouble. "What news do you have for me, Jim?" he asked.

"Well now, Colonel, to start with, a part of Colonel Kelley's regiment and a bunch of soldiers from Ohio and Indiana arrived in Grafton in the morning on May 30, lookin' for you, they was. I think they was downright disappointed that you'd run off. Them was their words, not mine, Colonel, you understand."

"I'm not offended, Jim, so go on." *Will this man* ever *get to his point?* he thought.

Jim hooked his thumbs in his suspenders and rocked back on his heels, a wide grin on his face. "Well now, these fellows took over the Grafton Hotel and told me to git. Now that warn't very nice of them, Colonel, don't you agree?"

"Yes, I *agree*, Jim. *Please* go on."

Jim grinned again and scratched his head. "Well now, I hung around there and several captains tried to get *me* to enlist. I told 'em my wife would hunt me down and shoot me if I left her." Jim laughed and waited for a reaction from the colonel, who stared at him in stony silence. "Now you know, Colonel, I ain't even married, so I was tellin' 'em a little lie, which I might add is much at odds with my gen'ral principles. You understan', don't you, Colonel?"

Colonel Porterfield steamed for several seconds, then replied in a steely voice, "*PLEASE* go on. I'm paying you good money for this. I need to know how many men they have and if you think they know where I am!"

"Well now, Colonel, simmer down, I'm a little bit on the slow side, you know. Looked to me like they had about 2,000 men and I heard some talk about Philippi, so I reckon they know you're here."

Porterfield's face flushed. "Damn! They've obviously repaired the bridges we burned near Mannington and they have more than three times the number of men we have here. Did you hear them say anything about bridges being burned along the line from Parkersburg?"

"Well now, yesterday a lot more soldiers arrived and I did hear 'em talkin' about it takin' a lot of time to repair two bridges on the Parkersburg Railroad."

Porterfield jumped to his feet and exclaimed, "How *many* new soldiers arrived yesterday?"

"Well now, Colonel, don't go getting yourself all excited, 'cause I got a lot to tell you. But to answer your question, I reckon 2,000 more soldiers."

"Dammit, Jim, that's *bad* news. Don't you have any good news for me?"

"Well now, Colonel, you're scarin' me. Maybe I do, and maybe I don't. I reckon I'll tell you ever'thing if you just calm yourself and sit back down!"

Porterfield sat down, gritted his teeth, and said, "*Continue!*"

"Well now, I watched Colonel Kelley board a train with almost 1,600 men at 8:00 this mornin' and they was headin' for Harper's Ferry."

"How do you know that?" Porterfield asked. *That would be a fortunate turn of events, if true.*

"Well now, Colonel, I heard sev'ral men talkin' about where they was goin' and they had with 'em plenty of supplies for a long stay, and to fix railroads."

"What about the 2,000 new men—where were *they* going?" Porterfield asked.

"Well now, Colonel, I reckon I don't know 'bout *that.* They looked like they was tired and needin' rest. I heard Charleston mentioned a couple times. Do you want me to ride back out and try to find out where they're headed to?"

"No! Unless you have more to say, get yourself something to eat from the cook and let me know how much I owe you for your hotel room and your trip. Don't leave just yet—I might need you to go back to Grafton."

Just then Major Boykin returned and said, "Colonel, there's something you need to know. Two young women from Pruntytown just showed up and said that about 5,000 Union troops are coming this way. I don't think this is a good place to make a stand, Colonel. We're in a valley and if the enemy should bring artillery, they could place it on that hill and rake our camp."

Porterfield could feel cold sweat sliding down his face. Pulling a handkerchief from his pocket, he wiped his brow and took a deep breath. "Major, I'm thinking we should leave here and head for Beverly. If we had well-trained troops and some artillery, we might make a stand here by digging in on this side of the river and burning that covered bridge. The people here, of course, would hate us for that."

The colonel continued to wipe his face, his brain ticking off various options. Finally, he said, "All right then, Boykin, let's put out the best of your trained pickets tonight. Place them far enough out so they can hear if men and artillery come marching down the pike. Pass the word to the men to sleep on their arms. Unless we get word that the Federals are close during the night, we'll plan to depart right after breakfast and march to Beverly. It looks like the rain may start up again. If so, the Federals will have a slow time of it getting through these mountains, and maybe it will deter them altogether. But have everyone stay on high alert."

SUNDAY, JUNE 2, 1861, 8:00 PM
UNION COLONEL DUMONT'S HQ, GRAFTON, VIRGINIA

Colonel Dumont waited 12 hours after the first train left, supposedly for Harper's Ferry, for a second engine and its train of cars to arrive at Grafton. The train would carry a part of his force, consisting of eight companies of his own 7th Indiana destined for Webster near the WVRR. Colonel Lander, aide to General McClellan, joined him just before the train departed at 8:30 PM. Dumont and Lander sat together and talked. Learning of Lander's years of varied experience, Dumont asked, "Do you want to take charge of the artillery and its placement on that hill General Kelley showed us?"

"Yes, I would like that. It'll give me something to do and will make me feel like I'm not just McClellan's spy."

Both officers laughed and Dumont jokingly replied, "Why, Colonel Lander, I would *never* think our God-fearing Major General McClellan sent you here to spy on me."

On arrival at Webster, Dumont formed up with five companies of Colonel Steedman's 14th Ohio with two fieldpieces, Colonel Critten's 6th Indiana, and some of his own 7th Indiana. He now had a total of about 1,400 men. Around 10 PM Dumont's force started the march on the Pruntytown-Philippi Turnpike toward the town of Philippi. As they marched, Dumont noticed the evening sky turning pitch-black. Thick storm clouds set in, blanking out the starlight and making it difficult to stay on the road. An hour or so later heavy rain pounded the men, soaking their clothes, and increasing the load they had to carry. But the rain also had a cloaking effect, Dumont thought. And the noise would make it difficult for any enemy pickets to hear the marching column, and it would silence squeaking wheels on the cannons and caissons.

MONDAY, JUNE 3, 1861, 3:45 AM
KELLEY'S COLUMN, NORTHEAST OF PHILIPPI, VIRGINIA

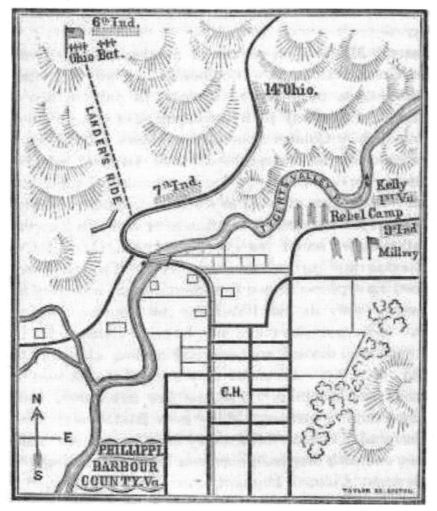

Philippi - Showing Troop Locations Prior to Battle

This rain could ruin everything, thought Kelley. Their 22-mile march had been a grueling one. Around midnight heavy rains muddied the steep roads, slowing the marching column. Mr. Baker, their guide, had a heavy mountaineer's accent, which was hard for the soldiers to understand, and the noise of the downpour made it even more difficult to communicate. From the start the farmer had trouble understanding the soldiers as well. When they came to a crucial fork in the road, Baker tried to explain where each fork would take them, but the men could not understand what he was trying to tell them. So the farmer took them on the road that led just behind the town.

Kelley hunched over to block the rain and pulled out his pocket watch. It was nearing the time when the two forces were to spring their trap. He peered through an opening in the forest and suddenly realized they had taken the wrong fork. Just then a cannon fired. Disoriented at first, Kelley asked an aide, "Is that the enemy firing on us?"

"No, Colonel," his aide replied, "look at the men in the enemy camp. I think the shell from that cannon just hit that man who fell. It's Dumont's artillery, firing the signal from that hill to start the attack!"

Kelley squinted as he peered through the rain. He could barely see Dumont's men forming to charge across the covered bridge. "Yes, I see it clearly now. We came too far north, but let's make the best of it! Pass the order for the men to form a battle line. We'll charge their camp and bag the whole bunch of them!" Kelley's heart raced and now his prancing horse sensed his excitement and tugged hard at the reins. "Charge!" Kelley yelled, and his lines surged forward.

Porterfield's men were in disarray. Although they had been warned of a coming attack and were already planning to move out to Beverly early in the morning, the torrential downpour had lessened their sense of urgency. In the face of overwhelming numbers of enemy soldiers coming at them from two directions, they ran—some in bare feet, with no clothes or arms, some with partial clothes and shoes. Some grabbed their muskets only to drop them in the mud as panic set in. The cavalry mounted and tried to stop the men from running, but there were not enough of them. The panicked men just pushed through and soon the cavalry joined the retreating foot soldiers.

"Come on, men, after them!" Kelley screamed as he led the chase, thinking of nothing but the victory ahead. Kelley on his horse was closing fast on the retreating foot soldiers. Suddenly the colonel saw, as if in slow motion, one soldier hiding behind an overturned wagon turn and fire a pistol directly at him. At first Kelley thought the shooter had missed him, and that he had simply hit a low overhanging tree limb when he instinctively ducked. Touching his chest and finding blood on his hand, he cried out, "Men, I've been hit." He was having trouble catching his breath, yet he managed to wave his men on, yelling, "Keep up the chase, don't let them escape!"

His aide, noticing the colonel's horse slowing and the colonel slumping in his saddle, ran to his side, grabbed the colonel's horse by its reins, and asked, "How bad is it, Colonel?"

"I'm feeling dizzy..." Kelley replied as he slumped to one side of his saddle. The aide caught him and lowered him to the ground, then yelled and gestured for the surgeon, who appeared almost immediately at Kelley's side.

"Keep the men after them," Kelley whispered, grasping Thoburn's jacket and trying to pull himself up. The surgeon gently pressed the colonel back to the ground. He scanned Kelley's bloodied jacket and then opened his clothing to look at the wound. He said, "Hold on, Colonel. Just lie there for a moment and let me look at you. Your men know what to do. You've trained them well."

A few of the men stopped to see if the doctor needed help. "You men, use your blankets and form a shelter," Thoburn ordered. Kelley looked down to see blood, diluted by rain, still pouring from a hole in his chest. Breathing required a definite effort, but so far he felt little pain.

"How does it look, Joe?" Kelley gasped.

"One of you men run back and bring up an ambulance, double quick!" Thoburn ordered. Then turning to his patient, he replied, "Ben, you've been hit in the right chest. I need to lean you forward to see if there is an exit wound on your back."

Kelley groaned and said, "I expect I'll have to die." Silently he prayed the Lord's Prayer. *I'm ready to meet my Maker.* Yet he thought of his children with regret—he hated to leave them just now. He felt that he still had much to accomplish.

The doctor explored the wound. "I see an exit hole, and it doesn't look like you're hit in the spinal column, the heart, or any of the great blood vessels. That's a very good thing, Ben. I'm pretty sure we'll be able to patch you up." Kelley could hear the relief in his surgeon's voice.

"Looks like you've been shot in the front of your chest between two ribs. The ball went through your right lung and may have hit a rib in the back. I'm going to load you in the ambulance, take you to one of these houses so I can examine you more closely and try to stop this bleeding."

The ambulance arrived and Kelley felt himself being loaded into it, but fog seemed to be filling his brain. They took him to the nearest house. The occupants were friendly and helped the ambulance crew carry Kelley inside. The family in the house said they were on the side of the Union, but had bided their time while Porterfield's army occupied their town. *I'm sure they all say that now,* thought Kelley.

Surgeon Thoburn was able to stop the bleeding and gave Kelley medicine to ease his pain. *Thank God for Joe,* he thought as consciousness faded. The colonel drifted into a relatively peaceful sleep.

Several hours later Kelley suddenly awoke, coughed, and looked around the room. His surgeon was still seated by his bed. Kelley asked, "Did I hear... Lander yelling... awhile ago... or was I dreaming?" He was nearly out of breath by the time he got his question out.

"You weren't dreaming, Ben, that was him," replied Thoburn. "Some of your boys were outraged when they saw you shot and blood all over you. They captured the shooter and were fixing to kill him. Colonel Lander appeared, looked at you, and then ran to our boys and stopped them, telling them to take him as a prisoner of war."

For Kelley to speak at all now required great effort. Nevertheless, he continued to try to talk and said, "Good, fair… brave."

"Take it easy, Colonel, don't talk. I've stopped the bleeding and don't want it to start up again." The surgeon inspected the wound and applied another dressing. "Oh, by the way, Ben," he said as he finished, "I heard something about Lander that you might find amusing. Apparently he was the one in charge of the artillery and ordered that first shot. When he saw you show up and start your attack, he vaulted on his horse and, some say he liked to have *flown* down that briar-covered hill, which is nearly a 45-degree slope, jumping fences and all. I'm sorry I missed it! I still hear some of Dumont's men talking about 'Lander's wild ride.'"

A slight smile played around Kelley's lips. "Many rebs… killed?" he asked.

"It's hard to say, Ben. I heard the walking wounded ran off. There are maybe 10 or so dead. One boy in their cavalry got hit by that first cannonball. Dr. Robinson, the surgeon with the Sixteenth Ohio, amputated his leg. Probably saved that boy's life."

"Need… cavalry," Kelley gasped.

Thoburn pressed a finger to his commander's lips. "Don't talk, Ben. I can talk enough for both of us."

Kelley smiled.

"Yes, you're right. If *we* had cavalry we could have stopped their hasty retreat. I'll wager the papers will be calling this the Kelley Races or maybe the Philippi Races, instead of the Battle of Philippi! You could hardly call this a battle. I never saw troops run so fast. Our boys gave up the chase.

They're exhausted from all that mountain marching in the rain and mud."

Kelley nodded.

Thoburn continued. "I'm not sure how we're going to get cavalry. I understand Lincoln doesn't want it because he thinks it costs too much to train and maintain. Why, I even heard he thinks the war will be over before a regiment, or even a company, of cavalry could be trained. The rebs are ahead of us in the use of cavalry, all right. I'm told they already have several regiments and they're using their own horses. Maybe it will take a battle where the Confederate cavalry runs after our retreating boys to make our leaders understand why we need cavalry."

Kelley nodded, then said, "Porterfield... done for."

"Yes, probably this will be the last we'll see of him. Looks like we had a great victory, thanks to your clever plan, and he certainly seemed surprised by our attack. I've read the telegrams we've intercepted and it's clear General Lee sent Porterfield up our way to form an army to occupy Parkersburg and Wheeling and take charge of the railroads. Lee probably wants to use those towns to invade Ohio, occupy Morgantown, invade Pennsylvania and maybe even capture Pittsburgh. So Porterfield will be Lee's scapegoat and probably get sacked."

Kelley nodded, but before Thoburn could tell him to stop talking, Kelley said, "They... be back..."

Thoburn growled at Kelley, then replied, "Yes, I believe so too. And probably with a bigger force. But they know now it's not going to be easy! If they do send another force, let's hope McClellan comes over here, brings more troops and artillery, and takes charge. Now, stop talking, Ben! I mean it!"

Kelley held up one finger to signal one last question, and then asked, "I... get... well?"

"Yes, you will. I've already sent a telegram to alert a surgeon I know well in Wheeling to prepare for surgery. He's the best around and I want to get you there just as soon as I know you are well enough to travel. I'll be with you all the time. Now get some rest. Doctor's orders! *No more talking now!*" Kelley's heart was full to see how concerned and caring Thoburn was for his welfare. *I owe him my life*, he thought. He prayed a silent prayer of thanksgiving. He was glad to stay on earth for a while yet. Things were getting interesting.

MONDAY, JUNE 3, 1861, 4:30 AM
ON THE ROAD TO BEVERLY, VIRGINIA

Porterfield watched as his men fled down the road toward Beverly. He couldn't believe the Union troops had actually marched all night in that downpour! He had thought he would have plenty of time to move to Beverly before the Federals arrived. *And where were my pickets?* he thought. Porterfield yelled at Boykin to mount up and pointed south. "Let's ride through them and we'll try to get them to form up and retreat in order down the road to Beverly, as we'd planned."

The Federal footsoldiers, soaking wet and tired, could not keep pace with the fleeing rebels. They slowed to a walk and finally gave up the pursuit. Further down the pike Porterfield's men slowed when they saw their colonel and Major Boykin in the road with sabers drawn and pistols in their hands.

Porterfield fired a shot into the air, then yelled, "Stop and reform, damn you, or we'll shoot and saber anyone who tries to get past us. The cavalry boys are covering your asses in the rear and the Federals have no cavalry to run you down!"

Faced with being shot, his men stopped, formed a column, and retreated to Beverly in good order.

WEDNESDAY, JUNE 5, 1861, 8:00 AM
SWANEY FARM, SMITHFIELD, PENNSYLVANIA

Cynthia came running into the house, out of breath. "Where's AJ?" she asked her mother.

"Calm down, girl, AJ's working down at the barn. What are you so heated up over?" Ma said.

"Oh, Harry's coming up the lane and I can't help it. Every time I see him I get all in a twitter."

"Well, that's no way to get a man, girl. Calm yourself down and walk slowly to the barn and let AJ know Reverend Hagans is here. If you wait just a minute as he rides up, you can say hello. Then walk away like you're not interested in them at all... anyway, I think the Reverend's too old for you."

"Ma! How can you say that? I'll try your advice, but you know how AJ teases me about Harry."

Cynthia smoothed her apron, tucked in a stray strand of hair behind her ear, and forced herself to walk sedately to the barn.

"AJ, I see Harry is coming up our lane. I suspect he has some news for you about your war," Cynthia said.

"Thanks, Sis. Are you going to stick around and make eyes at him?" AJ asked.

"Oh, AJ, stop it! How many times do I have to tell you I'm not interested in him?" she said, coloring.

"Have it your way, Sis, but you're welcome to hang around and hear what he has to say."

Harry rode up on Betsy, tipped his hat to Cynthia and greeted her politely saying, "Good morning, Miss Cynthia. How are you this fine morning?"

Cynthia smiled at Harry and in a quivering voice replied, "I... I'm fine, thank you... and..."

Before she could say anything more, Harry turned to AJ and said, "The *Wheeling Intelligencer* is calling the battle at Philippi the 'Philippi Races.'"

"Wait a minute, Harry, what are you talking about?"

"Oh, sorry, AJ, I forgot you might not have heard the news. Philippi is a little town about 16 miles south of Grafton on the Staunton-Parkersburg Turnpike, and a battle took place there two days ago—the first land battle of our war! Virginia forces loyal to the Union, and forces from Ohio and Indiana, surprised and attacked Virginia secessionist soldiers camped in that town. The secessionists were asleep in their tents. They were awakened by cannon fire and when they saw they were being attacked, most of them just ran down the road toward Beverly with the loyal forces running after them—the 'Philippi Races.' It will probably be all over the nation's newspapers before long. Colonel Kelley, from Wheeling, was leading the charge and got shot in the chest. They think he might die."

"Harry, it's happening just the way we thought it would! Virginia is breaking apart. Did the paper say how many men were killed?"

"Yes, they think about six men were killed or wounded, all secessionists from western Virginia. I brought the paper with me if you want to read it."

"I do."

AJ read the article, shaking his head at the loss of life and violence so close by. He and Harry leaned on the fence for an hour and discussed the battle, and its implications. AJ's brain was full of troubled thoughts. *Now the war is real. What part will I play in it? And will I be up to it?*

Cynthia, hurt by Harry's lack of attention, ran back to the house, tears streaming down her cheeks.

WEDNESDAY, JUNE 5, 1861, 8:00 AM
LEE'S OFFICE, RICHMOND, VIRGINIA

General Lee got up from his seat and stood at attention as Governor Letcher walked into his office carrying several newspapers and telegrams.

Lee saw the look on Letcher's face and knew an angry tirade was coming. Letcher threw the papers and telegrams on Lee's desk and asked, "Have you read what the press in the North, and even in the South, is saying about that disaster at Philippi?" Not waiting for an answer, he said, "They are calling it the 'Philippi Races' because our boys outran that traitor Kelley and those invaders from Ohio and Indiana. That colonel you placed in charge couldn't stop them. Look at those telegrams President Davis received from Southern governors. They want heads to roll around here! All this had to happen just when I'm about to issue a proclamation handing Virginia's military forces over to the Confederate States of America. I put you in charge of all Virginia militia and soon you'll be under President Davis. So what are your plans?"

Lee sat calmly pondering this outburst from Letcher. Inside he fumed. *How dare this governor single me out for blame for the Philippi mess? How many times had Letcher promised me muskets would be sent to Staunton for delivery to Colonel Porterfield, and then they end up elsewhere? Yes, I am partly to blame, but so is Letcher, and even President Davis. They knew as well as I do that western Virginians had been mistreated by eastern Virginians for a long time. And they ignored Major Boykin's warning that the northwesterners were rebelling, just as I did. Well... firing back at Letcher will not solve anything and is certainly not the way this gentleman handles problems.*

Lee took in a deep breath and calmly replied, "Yes, Governor, I have read several newspaper accounts of the engagement at Philippi. It does not surprise me that some of our Southern governors are disturbed. But I can tell you, Governor, this is not the end of our problems in the western part of our state—it's only the beginning. We must stay calm and plan what needs to be done, particularly with our rebellious citizens in the northwestern counties. As for transferring Virginia's military forces over to the Confederacy, I look forward to this. President Davis is a friend of mine."

"Well, General Lee, you still work for *me* and I want that colonel you sent up there relieved of command and censured!"

"I've already sent a telegram recalling Colonel Porterfield. He is demanding, under military law, a Court of Inquiry. He believes he did no wrong. He had green troops with little to no training in the use of muskets. After many promises that muskets would be sent to him, he received them only a few days before the engagement. And he claimed the powder sent to him was difficult to use. His men had no powder horns and the powder was not in caps. Contrary to what the northern papers are saying, Porterfield says he posted pickets and most of his men retreated in an orderly fashion. He has a right to be heard, Governor, and because he is under my command, *I* will let him be judged by officers in a Court of Inquiry."

Taken down a peg by Lee's forceful manner, Governor Letcher replied, more calmly, "Then you handle him as you see fit. More importantly, have you given any thought as to what we should do to get those northwesterners back on our side, and how to get those damned Federals out of Virginia?"

"Yes, of course I have. I think we have both a military and a political problem. Many folks living in northwestern Virginia don't trust us easterners. They have a long history of grievances about taxation and representation. So I recommend you issue a proclamation to these people reminding them that they are citizens of the State of Virginia and that the majority of Virginia's citizens elected to leave the Union. They should abide by the majority, as we always have done in the past. It is their duty to do so now. You should also remind them that a majority of Virginia's citizens voted to remove the inequality in taxation regarding the slave property tax issue that they've been complaining about for so long."

He could tell that he now had Letcher's attention. The governor nodded thoughtfully.

Lee continued, "I think your proclamation should identify a town in Virginia where the northwesterners can rally with fresh troops we must send. Together they could drive out the Federal invaders. I will confer with my Adjutant General, Colonel Garnett, today and determine the size and location of our new force and the best place for the northwesterners to rally. We should also send a large force to the Kanawha Valley, where we know many citizens are more in favor of the Confederacy."

"All right, General Lee. Go ahead and make your military plan. I'll work on a proclamation to the people of northwestern Virginia. Let's meet again in two days to finalize a plan that you can submit to President Davis on June 8 when the Virginia military forces will be transferred to the Confederacy."

Lee stood at attention as the governor walked out of his office. Then he sent an orderly to notify Robert Seldon Garnett, his 41-year-old Adjutant General, to come to his office. When the slim, handsome officer entered the room some time later, Lee noticed his sad eyes. Garnett had lost his wife and young son, his only child, to a fever several months ago, and had recently returned from a sabbatical in Europe, only to be thrust into the chaos of secession and impending war. Lee pitied him, but believed he was the man to straighten out the mess in western Virginia. Garnett's record was impeccable: a graduate of West Point, class of 1841, served as an instructor of tactics, served as an aide to General Zachary Taylor in the Mexican War and was twice brevetted for gallantry. In 1849 while shipwrecked during a mission to California, he designed that state's great seal. He had returned to West Point as commandant of cadets, under Lee.

Lee was fond of him. "Rob, I've just spoken with Governor Letcher about the Philippi skirmish. We need to assemble a large force to drive the Federals out of northwestern Virginian, retake the B&O Railroad all the way to Wheeling and Parkersburg, and establish fortifications to secure the Shenandoah Valley. I would like you to take command of this force, replacing Colonel Porterfield. I will help you plan your campaign and assist you in gathering together all the men you will need. We will have to get approval of the plan from President Davis, since all Virginia's military forces will be turned over to the Confederacy two days from now. When we submit the plan, I will ask President Davis to promote you to the rank of brigadier general. I'm sure he will honor my request."

Garnett hesitated for a moment and then responded, "Permission to speak freely, sir?"

Lee nodded. "Of course, Rob."

"General, you know I will go wherever you need me. However, I want you to know that I think this is a Herculean task you're giving me. We gave Colonel Porterfield this same task, did not support him properly, and we didn't listen to him when he explained the difficulties he and Major Boykin had recruiting soldiers in that area. I subscribe to the *Wheeling Intelligencer.* The people in the northwestern counties are in full rebellion against our government in Richmond. Now that citizens of Virginia voted to secede from the Union, the northwesterners have set a date to commence their Second Wheeling Convention and I'm certain they'll try to form a new state out of Virginia's territory. It's very clear to me that it was the leaders of the northwestern counties, backed by their constituents, that asked for help from General McClellan in Ohio. Furthermore, those Federal soldiers were welcomed by most, if not all, of the people in Wheeling, Parkersburg, and elsewhere, with open arms."

Lee frowned. He did not believe that things could be this bad in western Virginia. *It must be Rob's depression talking,* he thought.

"But surely, Rob, you must be wrong in your interpretation of the desires of our citizens who live out there. I am certain that the majority are true citizens of Virginia and are being misguided by a few bad men. Surely most citizens of western Virginia think like you and me. It is their duty to Virginia to follow her wherever she leads, as we have always done. No, General, I cannot, and will not, believe that any citizen of Virginia could ever fight against the Old Dominion. But let us not argue these political matters, General. We are soldiers and we must do our duty. Let us spend our time planning your campaign."

With Garnett's words brushed aside, along with the papers on his desk, Lee spread out maps so they could make detailed plans. Then he said, "Rob, I believe your campaign can be conducted in two phases. In the first phase you will fortify the Staunton-Parkersburg Turnpike to prevent any Federal forces from entering the Shenandoah Valley and interrupting our supplies at Staunton. Perhaps 5,000 soldiers would suffice for that part of your campaign. In the second phase you will take charge of the B&O Railroad by first occupying Grafton. From there you will launch attacks on Wheeling and Parkersburg to drive out the Federal invaders. Perhaps another 5,000 more soldiers would be needed, but I pray that citizens of Wheeling, Parkersburg and others west of the mountains will come to your aid. What are your thoughts, Rob?"

Garnett said, "I think we should place fortifications at two places. One here, at the base of Rich Mountain, to block passage from Parkersburg, and the other here, near Belington, at Laurel Hill, to block passage from Wheeling down through the Tygart Valley River. I would place about 1,500 men in a well-fortified position at Rich Mountain in such a manner as to flank both sides of the turnpike. I would place four pieces of artillery to protect the Rich Mountain fortifications—one on each flank and two in the middle. I would locate the larger contingent of my force, about 3,500 men, at Laurel Hill where I suspect Federals from Grafton might try to attack. They will need another four cannons."

"Yes, very good," Lee replied. "This will secure what I think of as the gates to the northwestern country. As soon as all the fortifications are in place and manned, I will send you enough men to increase your total force to about 10,000 soldiers, plus perhaps another 5,000 western Virginia recruits will join your ranks. With a force of that size you can advance on Grafton and take charge of the forks of the B&O Railroad. From there you can take Wheeling and Parkersburg.

"Now, Rob, see to your duty of planning the details. I will want you to be in Huttonsville by June 15 to start receiving citizen recruits from the western Virginia counties to help you with your tasks. That is the village that will be named in Governor Letcher's proclamation as a rallying point for the recruits."

After Garnett saluted and left his office, Lee notified President Davis of the need to have a brigade move on Charleston to prevent Federals from entering the Kanawha Valley and mentioned the promotion of Garnett to general. He thought back, with some anxiety, on Garnett's warning to him about the rebellion of the westerners. He shook his head trying to clear those thoughts. *No, they will do their duty to Virginia.*

FRIDAY, JUNE 7, 1861, 1:00 PM
OFFICE OF PRESIDENT JEFF DAVIS, RICHMOND, VIRGINIA

"Come in," the President said as he motioned for General Lee and Governor Letcher to sit.

"Mr. President, it is my honor to present you with a copy of my proclamation, released to the press this morning, informing all Virginia citizens that Virginia's military forces are now under the direction of the Confederate States of America," Letcher said.

Smiling, the president said, "Thank you, Governor, and I see you brought along my friend, General Lee, to give to me."

"Well, the General is now yours to command, sir, but I wanted him with us so he could explain his military plans to handle our western Virginia problem. I had a small part in helping to create this plan by preparing a proclamation to the citizens of that area that will hopefully help us recruit more men, so together we can drive out the Federal invaders," Letcher replied.

"Go ahead, General, I'm anxious to hear your plan. As you probably already know, I received a lot of complaints from other governors over what the press is calling the 'Philippi Races.' The point is we're missing out on a great opportunity to take this coming war to the enemy. We need to control the industrial center at Pittsburgh, Pennsylvania as well as in Wheeling, so we can build weapons we'll need to fight a war. I envision a fleet of gun boats controlling that long border along the Ohio River and keeping Ohio and states west, and the western part of Pennsylvania, isolated. Controlling the B&O Railroad will allow us to transport men and supplies to and from the heartland of our new country."

Lee was shaken by Davis's strategic views and did not speak immediately to explain his plan. He had given no thought to the grand strategy the President espoused. Nevertheless, the plan he and Letcher had devised this morning was a start. The two phases discussed with Garnett ran through his mind. The first phase would secure the Shenandoah Valley, the very important breadbasket of the Confederacy. The second phase would then secure the B&O Railroad. Taking a deep breath, Lee started his presentation by saying, "Mr. President, the plan we developed has two phases which should fit nicely into your grand strategic plan to win the coming war…"

At the end of his explanation Lee expressed the need to have Robert Garnett commissioned as a brigadier general and the need to have a small army in the Kanawha Valley.

President Davis said, "Yes, I think this has a chance of working. I'll prepare a commission for Garnett and give consideration to who to send to the Kanawha Valley. And thank you, General, for reminding me of the importance of the Shenandoah Valley to the stomachs of our soldiers. If there are no further discussions let's adjourn our meeting and get to work implementing the plan. Governor, send me a copy of your proclamation."

SATURDAY, JUNE 15, 1861, 5:00 AM
MCCLELLAN'S HQ, CAMP DENNISON, OHIO

McClellan tossed and turned in his bed. *So much to think about since our victory at Philippi!* His brain refused to turn off. The Second Wheeling

Convention was in session and John Carlile had already presented "A Declaration of the People of Virginia," which clearly aimed to divide the state of Virginia into two states. Carlile's document called for the reorganization of the government of Virginia on the grounds that, due to Virginia's decision to secede from the United States, all Federal government positions held by citizens of the State of Virginia had been vacated. From his study of the Constitution, a new state could be created from within a state, but only if that state's House of Delegates approved the division. Then both houses of the Federal Congress had to approve it as well. So, he wondered, *Is reorganizing the government of Virginia going to be the first step in the process of forming a new state? Will the House of Delegates of the reorganized government of Virginia approve the division of the state?*

He had just learned that Letcher, the governor of the seceded State of Virginia, had issued a proclamation calling on the "People of North-Western Virginia" to rally behind seceded Virginia. He chuckled as he read the first part stating: "That our people have the right to institute a new Government..." He supposed Letcher conveniently forgot that he swore allegiance to our country and to defend its constitution. But what bothered him the most was the last part, referencing the village of Huttonsville in Randolph County as the place where all the "People of North-Western Virginia" were to meet with their arms and help "drive the invader from your soil." That could only mean Letcher and Lee had already agreed to send another force of Confederate soldiers to Huttonsville and the so-called "invader" was, of course, his Ohio and Indiana troops in Grafton, Parkersburg, Wheeling, and distributed along the B&O Railroad, protecting it from the destructive activities of Virginia secessionists like Colonel Porterfield's command.

He scratched his head. *What can Letcher and Lee be thinking? Do they not realize that the "People of North-Western Virginia" now view the seceded State of Virginia as the enemy? Do they not realize that it was the "People of North-Western Virginia" who asked me for help in driving out the eastern*

Virginia invaders like Colonel Porterfield and his troops? Do they not read the Wheeling Intelligencer *that speaks for the "People of North-Western Virginia?"*

Well, I will teach these southern dreamers another lesson. I, Major General George Benton McClellan, will personally go to "North-Western Virginia" with even more soldiers, find whoever Lee is sending and "drive the invader" from the soil of the "People of North-Western Virginia" and destroy him and his force.

He got out of his cot invigorated and determined, opened the flap on his tent and called out to an orderly to send his aide-de-camp to his tent with a pot of coffee right away. Moments later Colonel Lander walked into his tent with hot coffee and said, "Morning, General, what's on your mind?"

"Lots!" McClellan said with a smile. "Sit down, we have much work to do."

Jack W. Lewis

CHAPTER EIGHT

Battle of Rich Mountain

June 15–July 14, 1861

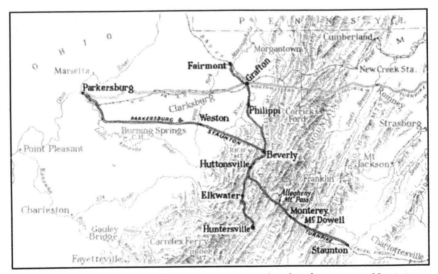

Map showing major turnpikes, rivers, towns and railroads in western Virginia

SATURDAY, JUNE 15, 1861, 6:30 AM
GENERAL GARNETT C.S.A. HQ, HUTTONSVILLE, VIRGINIA

It had been a long, uneventful march along the turnpike from Staunton to Huttonsville, the town that Governor Letcher had proclaimed as the rendezvous site for recruits from the western Virginia counties. General Garnett met Colonel Heck on arrival in Huttonsville and the colonel had introduced him to the officers of the infantry companies, the one cavalry company, and the one artillery company that Heck commanded. Heck explained that many of the infantry and the cavalry company had been at Philippi and others were recent recruits. These men knew they were still mostly green but were "rarin' to get another chance" to clear their name and prove they could fight as well as the Yankees.

Heck and other officers had trained them during the ten days since Philippi. Still, Garnett could see they were not up to his standards and indeed he found them to be in a miserable condition. The men preferred to walk instead of march and when they tried to march, they could hardly keep step. But, as he reminded himself, *at least they have muskets now.* Heck told him they had powder in caps and knew how to load and fire on command. Garnett's thoughts wandered back to the letters he had received from Colonel Porterfield. *No wonder so many of these men ran from the surprise attack at Philippi.*

Garnett had a bad feeling about this whole operation. He was undermanned and undersupplied, and he knew from following the news that the western counties of Virginia were disaffected and did not support the move to secede. Since the deaths of his wife and infant son, his long mourning sabbatical in Europe, and his difficult decision just a month and a half ago to resign from the U.S. Army and offer his services to Virginia and the Confederacy, his world had turned upside down on every front. Jefferson Davis had promoted him to brigadier general, which brought him no joy. But at least he was glad of the challenges of command and the distraction they provided from his almost disabling grief. *Marianna,* he thought, and felt the painful stab in his heart, unlessened in the two years since her death. Her snapping blue eyes and piquant, slightly mocking smile floated before his eyes. *Her beautiful face—at least it has not dimmed yet. I can still recall every detail.*

He thought of their joy when their son Arthur was born, naming him together, her pleasure when they chose Nelson for his middle name in honor of her fine family. Garnett suffered from overwhelming guilt at his own role in their deaths. *I dragged my young vibrant wife, a lady of incomparable gentility and refinement, across the entire country, to live in hardship on an Indian reservation in Washington Territory. My own selfishness—my desire to have her with me—caused her death.* No matter that she had insisted on accompanying him. He should have left her in New York, safe with her family. It did not seem real that she and his tiny son were both gone, just as it did not seem real that he was no longer in the U.S. Army and was now heading off to fight that army, which had been his only home for so many years. He sighed and called himself back to the present, surveying the sorry, ragtag lines of soldiers. *I have only Duty to live for now, and I will do that duty, as it is presented to me.*

The other troops General Lee had promised had not yet arrived, so Garnett put Heck's men to work, constructing fortifications at a key pass near the base of Rich Mountain, overlooking the important Staunton-Parkersburg Turnpike. Heck, obviously aiming to please the popular new general, suggested they name the fortress "Camp Garnett" in his honor.

Later that afternoon, Colonel John Pegram arrived with his Twentieth Virginia Infantry Regiment. *Now, these are fine-looking soldiers,* Garnett thought, *well equipped, and they know how to march and keep step.* He congratulated the short, goateed Pegram, who in turn assured him that, although still green, his boys were "itching for a fight." They would not run in the face of the enemy, the colonel assured him. Garnett knew Pegram's reputation as a haughty Virginia aristocrat—he had been one of the first U.S. Army officers to offer his services to Virginia after the secession vote.

Pegram's regiment brought the total strength at Camp Garnett to about 1,300 men. Garnett, always a stickler for military protocol, placed Pegram in command of the fortress, not because Pegram had a better-trained regiment, but because he had discovered the date of Pegram's commission preceded the date of Heck's commission.

Over the next two weeks, Garnett was pleased, and relieved, to see 3,500 additional Virginia and Georgia troops arrived, bringing his total force to about 5,000 men. He sent the new troops to Laurel Hill, near Belington in Barbour County, to build fortifications. That camp would be several miles north of Beverly, where the road extended over a low ridge near the Tygart Valley River.

When the fortifications at Camp Garnett were finished, Garnett's inspection showed the earth and log entrenchments to be very strong. He reasoned the fortifications would be able to hold off an enemy force triple the size of the number of men he stationed there. He warned Pegram that during his inspection he found an overgrown road leading to a little-used footpath that led to his right flank. Garnett then took command at Laurel Hill, where he had more men but less extensive fortifications. He wanted to be along the Beverly-Fairmont Pike, where he expected an enemy attack would first take place. Laurel Hill lay closer to Grafton, where the railroads to Wheeling and Parkersburg met. *Close enough*, he thought, *so the enemy will first want to drive me away.*

MONDAY, JUNE 21, 1861, 9:00 AM
MCCLELLAN'S HQ, PARKERSBURG, VIRGINIA

McClellan, with his *aide-de-camp* Lander, boarded the train in Parkersburg heading to Grafton. He intended to take no chances in defeating this new force of Confederates, who he knew had been sent to capture the B&O Railroad and chase him out of his Department. With him were about 20,000 men in 27 infantry regiments, four artillery batteries of six guns each, and two companies of cavalry. *Many of these men are green,* he thought, *but I've ensured they're well trained and most, if not all, will do their duty when the time comes to drive the rebels out of my Department—or, better still, bag the whole lot and send them off to prison. It will take time to distribute these new men in positions along the railroads from Parkersburg and Wheeling to Grafton. I will, of course, retain enough men and equipment to defeat this new enemy force.*

Lander, sitting beside him on the train, interrupted his thoughts with news from the Second Wheeling Convention, now in session in Wheeling, and the still-in-session Richmond Convention.

"It's very interesting what's going on in northwest Virginia right now," he said. "I've just read that the Second Wheeling Convention delegates voted unanimously for an ordinance to restore a loyal government of Virginia, since the seceded State of Virginia left the Union. The delegates elected officials to represent this new 'Reorganized Government of Virginia.' Francis H. Pierpont of Marion County was unanimously elected as Governor. Members were elected to the House of Delegates, who then appointed Representatives and Senators to the United States Congress. I understand U.S. Representatives and Senators have already been accepted and seated in Washington, and President Lincoln sent a letter to Governor Pierpont welcoming his State of Virginia back into the Union!"

McClellan smoothed his carefully groomed mustache, as he contemplated how these events might affect his own plans in western Virginia.

Lander continued, "Very clever move on the part of those western Virginians, I think. They're one step closer to having their own state, which they've wanted for decades. I can only shake my head though when I contrast that with the news on the same day that the seceded State of Virginia Convention in Richmond adopted the constitution of the Confederate States of America. The poor deluded people in Virginia are being led off a cliff by rabid, secessionist politicians!"

McClellan nodded, and said, "Excuse me, Colonel," as he rose to depart the train, which was slowing to make another of several stops to deploy his soldiers to protect the railroad. Each time he appeared on a station platform, grey-haired men and women, mothers holding up children, and other wellwishers, cheering and crying, had reached out to touch him, calling "God bless you!" This time, he lifted a hand and nodded to the crowd of about fifty people, who gave him three cheers. These displays of affection lifted his spirits and stiffened his resolve to do his best for these patriotic people. *I feel humbled to be their deliverer from tyranny—yes, that's a nice touch to add to my next letter to Nelly.* He couldn't wait to pass on to his wife news of the ovations, confirming she had made the right choice of husband. Seeing the crowds' enthusiasm also convinced him just how out of touch Richmond was with these northwestern Virginians.

When the train moved on, he returned to the discussion of the news Lander had given him. "Lander, can it be any clearer now to the eastern Virginians that northwestern Virginia has seceded from the seceded State of Virginia?" Lander laughed and McClellan smiled wryly. "Whoever Lee sent to Huttonsville will likely find few, if any, northwesterners willing to help him. When we get to Grafton, I'll prepare my own proclamation to the citizens of western Virginia."

WEDNESDAY, JUNE 23, 1861, 9:00 AM
MCCLELLAN'S HQ, GRAFTON, VIRGINIA

McClellan read over his proclamation one last time. He wanted to be sure it did not strike the pleading tone of Letcher's earlier proclamation to the citizens. He meant to simply state facts and warn those who commit criminal acts against loyal citizens of Western Virginia that they would be severely punished. He was proud of the final draft, thinking it reached just the right proportions of sternness and restraint. His proclamation read:

Proclamation of Major-General McClellan.
HEAD-QUARTERS DEP'T OF THE OHIO,
GRAFTON, VIRGINIA,
June 23, 1861

To the Inhabitants of Western Virginia:

The army of this Department, headed by Virginia troops, is rapidly occupying all Western Virginia. This is done in co-operation with, and in support of such civil authorities of the State as are faithful to the Constitution and laws of the United States. The proclamation issued my men, under date of May 26th, 1861, will be strictly maintained. Your houses, families, property, and all your rights will be religiously respected. We are enemies to none but armed rebels, and those voluntarily giving them aid. All officers of this Army will be held responsible for the most prompt and vigorous action in repressing disorder and punishing aggression by those under their command.

To my great regret I find that the enemies of the United States continue to carry on a system of hostilities prohibited by the laws of war among belligerent nations, and of course far more wicked and intolerable when directed against loyal citizens engaged in the defense of the common government of all. Individuals and marauding parties are pursuing a guerrilla warfare, firing upon sentinels and pickets, burning bridges, insulting, injuring and even killing citizens, because of their Union sentiments, and committing many kindred acts.

I do now, therefore, make proclamation and warn all persons, that individuals or parties engaged in this species of warfare, irregular in every view which can be taken of it, thus attacking sentries, pickets or other soldiers, destroying public or private property, or committing injuries against any of the inhabitants because of Union sentiments or conduct, will be dealt with in their persons and property, according to the severest rules of military law.

All persons giving information, or aid to the public enemies, will be arrested and kept in close custody; and all persons found bearing arms, unless of known loyalty, will be arrested and held to examination.

GEO. B. MCCLELLAN,
Maj. Gen'l U. S. Army, Comd'g Dept.

MONDAY, JULY 1, 1861, 9:00 AM
MCCLELLAN'S HQ, BUCKHANNON, VIRGINIA

As McClellan toured and inspected his Western Virginia Department, he set up a telegraph system allowing him to communicate with all his troop commanders, Governor Dennison, and Washington. He was particularly proud of this field telegraph communication system for he knew it was the first use of the telegraph for field military tactical use. It consisted of more than just wires and men who could send and read Morse code. His system consisted of a corps of men who, with rolls of wire, poles, wagons, mules, picks, axes and sundry other equipment, could install telegraph systems as fast as his troops could march. He even had portable stations at his and his generals' battlefield headquarters and men using ciphers to encode/decode military messages.

After his troops were in position to defend key points on the B&O Railroad and major towns, he turned his attention to removing rebel troops from his Department. He had learned from loyal Virginia citizens and his scouts that General Garnett, Lee's former Adjutant General, was now in command of the rebel soldiers in his Department. They were constructing fortifications at the base of Rich Mountain along the Staunton-to-Parkersburg Turnpike and at Laurel Hill near Belington. McClellan had served in Mexico with Garnett, who was older than McClellan by four years, and he knew the opposing general to be an honorable and intelligent commander. Yet he wondered about the structures Garnett had constructed and the attitude of the soldiers inside. Fortifications, he believed, were defensive in nature and the soldiers inside would have defensive thoughts, at least for now. He reasoned the fortifications were probably built to keep his army from attacking Staunton in the Shenandoah Valley. Offensive forces, intending to capture Grafton, or retake or destroy the B&O Railroad, might use these fortifications to quarter offensive soldiers, but none of his sources had reported seeing any rebel forces out scouting the countryside, trying to locate or determine the size of his offensive forces. *Perhaps,* he thought, *Garnett has too few men for offensive operations and is waiting for offensive troops to arrive. If so, I am in position to destroy Garnett's forces before any offensive forces arrive.*

"I will strike first!" he said out loud, jamming his closed right fist into his left hand. "I will model my campaign after General Scott's advance against the Mexicans fourteen years ago."

McClellan knew that he had learned a valuable lesson from Scott during those days in Mexico. He would, like Scott, not move until he knew everything was ready. Then he would move swiftly and forcefully. And, like Scott, he would try to gain success by maneuver rather than by pitched frontal battle with enemy troops.

Still, he faced an age-old military problem—he did not know the size of Garnett's forces. Local citizens provided him with comparative size estimates, but they seemed to be guessing at the actual size of each force. They told him the forces with Garnett at Laurel Hill were larger than those with Pegram at Rich Mountain. Even his scouts could not estimate the sizes of forces at each location.

So he decided on a battle plan which, at the start, would provide the missing information on size of the enemy. He would attack Garnett's forces with two columns, one from Philippi under General Morris, the other from Buckhannon, about fifteen miles west of the fortifications, commanded by himself.

Brigadier General Morris's brigade had about 4,000 men. He ordered Morris to attack the Laurel Hill fortifications, which supposedly had the most troops, and determine its size and strength. Morris's force would repeatedly attack in such a manner as to make General Garnett think that the bulk of his army would be attacking there. The rest of his forces, almost four brigades with eight cannons, would comprise the second column. They would attack the smaller, but well entrenched, forces at Rich

Mountain to determine their size and strength. McClellan reasoned that if he could defeat the Rich Mountain force first, Garnett's superior force at Laurel Hill would be vulnerable to an attack from the rear, which might force Garnett to abandon that fortification.

MONDAY, JULY 1, 1861, 8:00 AM

SWANEY FARM, SMITHFIELD, PENNSYLVANIA

With all morning chores done, AJ quietly sat on Shiloh waiting for Harry to arrive. Birds whistled their morning songs while he surveyed the green fields of wheat and corn and fenced livestock pastures around him. To the east the sun peeked over the Laurel Mountains, casting rays that started to burn away the mist crouching in the lowlands. It was good to be alive on a morning like this. But, as the sun's first rays touched his bare arm, their warmth announced a hot day to come for riding.

Today, he remembered, Governor Pierpont of the Restored State of Virginia would take office in Wheeling. Would the new Governor now authorize the formation of cavalry companies, or maybe even a cavalry regiment or two? Harry had found out that Dr. Keys's Ringgold Cavalry company had received orders from Pennsylvania Governor Curtin to muster for duty in Grafton, Virginia. Surely now Dr. McGee would be allowed to muster in a company of cavalry. Harry had missed yesterday's Sunday services again, in order to travel to Morgantown to talk with Dr. McGee. Hopefully, Harry would bring good news today.

AJ's thoughts turned to the incident with the escaped slave Abraham and his own conflict with Harry over it. He had told no one about the incident, but it had been constantly on his mind since he had returned from their trip to Wheeling. He turned it over and over in his brain. In a way he could not believe it had really happened. He had mulled over what Harry told him about the sorry conditions of southern slavery and he had come to terms, he thought, with Abraham's desperate attempt to steal his horse. But he still wrestled with the fact that Harry was on the wrong side of the law and actually helped runaway slaves to find freedom in the North. His idol had cracked—he had seen the truth about Harry, but he still wasn't sure what to think about it. Was Harry a hero for helping the downtrodden, or was he a criminal who turned his back on the law of the land? Could a good man be a lawbreaker?

Shiloh's soft whinny was the first sign that Betsy and Harry were near. Soon AJ saw them coming at a trot, kicking up dust along the way. The two horses nickered at each other and both men smiled. AJ still felt awkward around his friend, now that he knew the truth about him. He wondered whether Harry was hiding anything else from him.

They trotted down the lane side by side. AJ finally broke the silence: "So tell me the news from your trip to Morgantown—I've been thinkin' about it all morning."

"I will, my friend, but first let's get a good start on my rounds. I think it's going to be a hot day."

They kicked their horses into a canter. Once on the main road, Harry slowed Betsy to a trot, turned to his friend, and said, "Well, AJ, our wishes have come true. Dr. McGee received permission to form a cavalry company."

"That's great news! How'd it come about?"

"All the officers who were at the Philippi battle, especially Colonel Kelley, knew Porterfield escaped because the Federal forces had no cavalry. Porterfield had a company of cavalry, which helped cover his retreat. McGee told me Colonel Kelley helped arrange the assignment of the Ringgold Cavalry to Grafton."

"But, how did McGee finally get permission to form his cavalry company?"

"It's kind of a long story, but the short version is that McGee got permission through Waitman Willey. While Mr. Willey was at the Second Wheeling Convention he visited Kelley, who was still recovering from his wound. Colonel Kelley told Mr. Willey about Philippi and how he needed cavalry. Mr. Willey told Colonel Kelley he would go back and form a cavalry company in Morgantown, name it 'Kelley Lancers' in his honor, and send it to him as a gift from Morgantown. When Mr. Willey returned to Morgantown, he told McGee about the promise he made to Colonel Kelley. McGee agreed to form the company and be its captain. McGee and Mr. Willey already selected the first and second lieutenants. He asked me to join."

"Harry! That's… wonderful. Are you goin' to do it?" AJ was almost afraid to hear the answer. He suddenly realized that the thought of being separated from Harry frightened him.

"Yes, but under one condition."

"Condition! What condition?"

"That you join up with me."

"You made *me* your condition for joinin' up?" Astonished, AJ replied, "Why, Harry?"

"Simply because you're my friend, and we've been through a lot together. Besides," Harry said with a grin, "you're the best horseman and rifleman I've ever seen and I'm selfish—I want you by *my* side."

Without hesitation, AJ said, "Then, Reverend Hagans, I'll join too!" AJ's hair seemed to stand on end and his skin tingled with excitement and pride, that Harry felt this way about him. His second thoughts about Harry vanished.

But second thoughts about himself quickly appeared in their place. "Seriously, Harry, are you *sure* about me? I worry a lot about what kind of soldier I'll make. I'm still not sure I could kill somebody."

"As I told you I would, I've been delving into the Bible, looking for what the Lord has to say about killing in times of war. Throughout the Good Book, forces of evil appear that must be stopped, and bloodshed is sometimes the result. Whether a Christian should serve in the military is a matter of conscience, but I believe killing an armed combatant in war is not sinful in itself. In Ecclesiastes 3:8 the Bible says there is a time to love, and a time to hate, a time for war, and a time for peace…"

"But, Harry, the men we're supposed to fight look and talk just like us, and they worship the same God. How can God decide who lives and dies in a war like this one?"

"I don't know!" Harry exclaimed. "I trust God will see that justice is served in the end. But I have no idea what He has in mind for all of us. None of us do. But I feel certain God sees slavery as an evil and will use this war as an opportunity to rid this land of slavery."

AJ didn't speak for several minutes. His brow furrowed. Thinking about it was giving him a headache.

The day got hotter. After making several house calls, AJ and Harry stopped in the shade of trees near Monroe and ate the dinner they had brought with them. Harry asked, "When do you think you could be ready to go to Morgantown to enlist? McGee wants to start recruitment on July 18. That's when a new dentist is coming to take over his practice."

"I'll talk it over with Pa tomorrow and make a plan. He knew this day was comin'." AJ fell quiet again as his mind mulled over all that he needed to do to prepare. "What are we supposed to bring, Harry? Can I bring Shiloh and my rifle?"

"McGee said to bring your horse, rifle, anything you can stuff in your saddlebags, and a bedroll on a sling over your shoulder. He's pretty certain we'll go to Grafton for training and other supplies." Harry looked at the sun's position and said, "Let's go—we need to get moving if we want to finish my rounds and get back in time for your milking and feeding."

As they continued their ride, AJ pondered what it might be like to be in the cavalry and to have to kill someone with a saber, pistol or rifle—a subject he found deeply disturbing. He had killed lots of wild and domestic animals and butchered cows and hogs. But killing a human being, that was a different thing. *Perhaps*, he thought, *the cavalry training will help*.

After Harry's last home visit, the two started their return trip. Harry said, "I've been reading the Wheeling *Daily Intelligencer* and their coverage of the Second Wheeling Convention. Our friend Mr. Carlile did a masterful job writing the *Declaration of the People of Virginia*. Pierpont is now the Governor of Virginia, and Mr. Carlile is arguing that the Loyal Government of Virginia could now give permission for a new state to be created from the western counties, all in accordance with the U.S. Constitution. I think that might actually happen!"

"Maybe so, but I'm bettin' that will take a while," AJ replied.

During the rest of the ride, they conversed and speculated about what would happen in Virginia. When AJ got home, he first brushed, fed, and checked the feet of his horse. Then he fed and milked the cows, taking his time so he could think of what to say to his pa. He was anxious about leaving his family to fend for themselves. *How will my folks feel if I'm kilt?* he thought. *I wonder if Sophia would even care.* His eyes filled with tears which he dashed away with one hand. *Now ain't that something, cryin' for my own funeral, before I'm even dead and gone!*

Sunday, July 7, 1861, 10:00 am
General Morris U.S.A. HQ, Laurel Hill, Virginia

General Morris had his orders from McClellan to "amuse" General Garnett. He would attack what he believed to be a superior force to determine its size and strength, and keep Garnett thinking the main attack would come from him. As McClellan had told him, "General, feel the enemy out and see what he is."

He placed his four regiments in battle lines, chased Garnett's pickets out of the woods in front of the fortifications, and waited while Garnett's men took their positions. His plan was to count battle flags and cannons

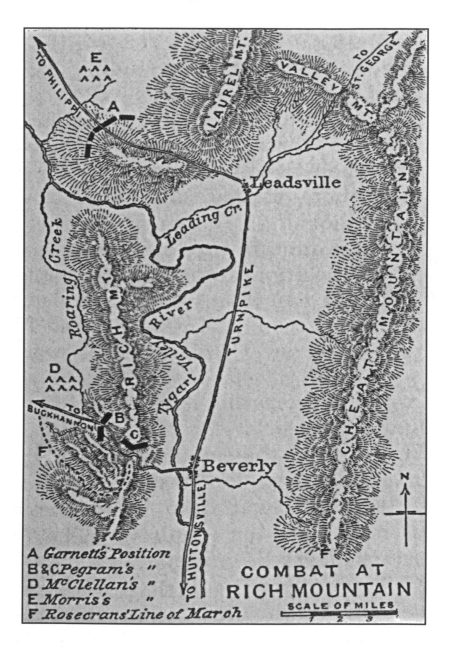

A *Garnett's Position*
B & C *Pegram's* "
D *McClellan's* "
E *Morris's* "
F *Rosecrans' Line of March*

COMBAT AT
RICH MOUNTAIN

SCALE OF MILES

before and during his charge, hoping to make a fair estimate of the number of Confederate forces inside the fortifications. With his men exposed, he noted two cannons firing, attempting to get the range of his forces. He ordered the men to charge and noted the cannons were still range firing. Before he reached the range of Confederate muskets, he halted his line and fired one volley. While his troops reloaded, he watched as the Confederates manned the fortification and he counted their battle flags. The return volley from the Confederates fell short. Morris retreated but with his troops stopping on command to fire a volley. He remained in front of the Laurel Hill fortification and marched his regiments around so they appeared to be receiving reinforcements. He telegraphed McClellan his estimate: Between 3,300 and 3,800 soldiers were in the fortification with at least two cannons. *What a surprise*, he thought. *That rebel has fewer men than I have.* McClellan will get a good laugh out of this, since he chewed me out when I asked for more men awhile back.

Tuesday, July 9, 1861, 4:00 pm
McClellan's HQ, Roaring Creek, Virginia

McClellan reached Roaring Creek, about a mile west of the Rich Mountain fortifications. He was full of nerves, as this would be the first battle in which he was present and in charge. The responsibility of command lay heavily on him. For the sake of his country and his own reputation, he wanted the coming battle to be a success for the Union. He thought he had an overwhelming number of men, but now he had doubts and needed to make sure. He studied the enemy camps through his field glasses for several hours. Then he called Lieutenant Orlando Poe, his chief engineering officer, Colonel Lander, his aide-de-camp, and Colonel Key to his tent.

"Gentlemen, tomorrow morning I want you to conduct a reconnaissance in force on those rebel fortifications. Advance as far as you can and test their strength. Bring back an estimate of the number of soldiers and cannons inside."

Turning to Lieutenant Poe he said, "Lieutenant, you will be in charge. Use all your engineering skills to size up this fortification and estimate how many enemy soldiers are inside."

To Lander he said, "I want you to go along and bring back your independent estimate of the number of soldiers."

Finally, he addressed Colonel Key saying, "I'm depending on you to use your brigade cautiously. I know your men will be looking for a fight, but you must control them. Move as close as you dare without bringing on a battle. Try to capture a few of their pickets while minimizing your losses."

WEDNESDAY, JULY 10, 1861, 9:00 AM
MCCLELLAN'S HQ, ROARING CREEK, VIRGINIA

Lieutenant Poe, along with Colonel Lander and Colonel Key leading his brigade of Ohio and Michigan troops, cautiously advanced to within 300 yards of the fortifications before Confederate pickets opened fire, supported by artillery from within the fortifications. One of Key's soldiers was killed and two were wounded. Poe had not seen men die or wounded in battle, and it shook him. Steeling himself, he ordered the advance to continue. They were able to capture several Confederate pickets before Poe finally called off the advance.

Poe chose two captured privates, took them aside and said, "You men killed one of my soldiers and wounded two others! If you want to save your hides, tell me quick, how many men are inside your fortification?"

The two trembling, obviously green, soldiers looked at one another with trepidation. One private responded immediately, "Don't shoot us, sir! I'll tell ya… we got around 8,000 men inside and I hear tellin' more are on the way."

"To help us lick you Yankees!" interjected the second private, apparently a bit pluckier than his comrade.

Poe tried other interrogation techniques on the remaining pickets. All gave him numbers ranging from 7,000 to 9,000 men. One gave detailed descriptions of the fortifications saying, "They can't be taken even if the best of you Yankees tried. You all will be kilt and your mangled bodies'll lay in heaps in front of us."

When Poe was done with his interrogations, he believed the fortifications could not be assaulted from the front without great losses to McClellan's forces. Colonels Lander and Key, who sat in on the interrogations, both thought the pickets were telling greatly exaggerated lies, but the lieutenant believed their stories. Lander was particularly skeptical. He knew many sentries were taught to exaggerate the size of their force, under interrogation by the enemy. *Besides*, he thought, *this fort has fewer soldiers than Garnett does at Laurel Hill so they probably have no more than 1,500 to 2,000 men.*

WEDNESDAY, JULY 10, 1861, 8:00 PM

MCCLELLAN'S HQ, ROARING CREEK, VIRGINIA

McClellan received the report from Poe of his interrogations of the rebel pickets and his belief that a frontal charge would needlessly take the lives of many of his green soldiers. Poe also mentioned that Lander and Key believed the pickets were exaggerating their numbers. McClellan stewed over this information. He did not want to make a frontal attack. He had seen in Mexico what cannons could do to charging infantry and he wanted no part of that. Even if Poe's estimates were far too high, a frontal attack would still get many of his men killed, and a defeat of his forces could be disastrous to the Union and his own reputation. He had to find another way to defeat this fortification and that meant maneuvering.

He called a council meeting of his staff and senior brigade commanders to discuss alternate plans. McClellan looked around at the council members. General Rosecrans, who would lead the frontal attack if one was made, had not arrived. McClellan did not think highly of Rosecrans, having called him "a silly, fussy goose" in a recent letter to his Nelly, and his lateness to this important meeting only reinforced the low opinion.

"I want each of you to speak your mind on this matter, before I make the final decision on our strategy," McClellan told the group. Many felt the estimates of the Confederate pickets were exaggerated and a bold frontal attack should be ordered. Still reluctant to take that risk, McClellan was about to voice his decision when the flap on the tent opened and in walked Rosecrans.

An imposing figure, Rosecrans had piercing eyes, a scarred yet handsome face, a sharp temper, and a brilliant mind. He graduated fifth in his West Point Class of 1842. He held the same reservations as McClellan about making frontal attacks on enemy fortifications.

Rosecrans saluted and started to explain his lateness. He tended to stutter when excited, which exasperated McClellan. "For-for-forgive my lateness, Gen-General McClellan, I have some go-go-good news. One of my r-regimental officers detained a y-young civilian named Da-Da-David Hart earlier to-today near our pi-picket line."

"Catch your breath, and slow down, General!" barked McClellan.

Rosecrans breathed deeply for a moment, and started again. "Hart cl-claimed he was returning to his home on top of Rich Mountain from a v-visit with a friend when he was stopped. H-Hart was brought to me for questioning. I gr-grilled him and threatened his life if he was lying. Hart stuck with his st-story and said I could shoot him if he was lying. Hart lives in the gap at the top of Ri-Rich Mountain and says all in his family are for the Union and he knows a way we can fl-flank attack those fortifications. Hart says he can lead us along a mountain path that c-can't be seen from the fortifications. Hart says his farm is often used by the soldiers from the fortification for a small r-rear guard."

He stopped for another deep breath. "Go on, General," said McClellan, now anxious to hear the rest of the proposed plan.

"We can destroy the rear guard and attack the fortifications from the rear, while you, G-General, lead the rest of our forces in a frontal attack. Now, General, if you will allow me to take my brigade, I will take Hart as a guide and, by a night's march, surprise and d-defeat any enemy soldiers in the gap, get possession of it, and hold their only l-line of retreat. You can then take him on the front. If he gives way, we shall have him; if he fights obstinately, I will leave a portion of my f-force at the gap, and with the remainder fall upon his rear."

General McClellan's father-in-law, Inspector General R. B. Marcy, spoke up and said, "Excellent plan—what a stroke of luck! We should proceed immediately!"

McClellan responded with a frown. "I'm not totally convinced, General. There are too many unknowns here, too many things to go wrong, just as they did at Philippi."

The council officers argued among themselves while McClellan listened and pondered the best strategy. Finally, he made up his mind. "All right, I'll approve the plan under the following conditions. First, I will interrogate David Hart myself and determine if that young man is a unionist, is telling the truth, and really knows the backroads where he would lead Rosecrans's brigade. Secondly, I must receive hourly reports by cavalry couriers from you, General, describing your progress, so the plan can be changed if need be. And finally, I want Colonel Lander, my aide-de-camp, to travel with you." The meeting ended with a nod from Rosecrans indicating McClellan's terms were acceptable.

Thursday, July 11, 1861, 3:00 am
General Rosecrans's HQ, Rich Mountain, Virginia

Rosecrans's aide came into his tent to awaken him as ordered, but found the general already wide awake, thinking about the day ahead. Rosecrans agreed with McClellan that green soldiers' lives would be wasted making a frontal attack on the Confederate fortifications. But he didn't like McClellan not trusting his own ability to alter plans should events suddenly force him to change them. Yet he understood McClellan's hesitation. If somehow he led his brigade into a trap and his men were killed or captured, it would be McClellan who would be blamed for the disaster, not him. So Rosecrans had received his orders to make the attack. McClellan in turn agreed to make his frontal attack only after Rosecrans was ready to make the rear attack and had sent a message to McClellan confirming that his brigade was ready.

Rosecrans's brigade formed on the turnpike. His four regiments totaled 1,842 infantrymen—the Eighth, Tenth, and Thirteen Indiana, and the Nineteenth Ohio. Seventy-five troopers of Burdsall's cavalry were with him. Hart and Colonel Lander led the way and Rosecrans and his brigade followed. Around 5 AM all veered off the pike and took to the woods. Almost immediately, delays slowed their progress. Downed trees with thickets of nearly impenetrable laurel, grapevine, and greenbrier blocked the way. The rugged terrain of deep gullies and almost impassable cliffs made it clear this march was going to be slow and grueling .

At 6 AM Rosecrans's heart sank as rain started, adding soaking water to the weight the men had to carry up the mountain. Through slippery mud and across swollen freshets they climbed. At first the rain was light, then it turned heavy. Lander, hunched on his horse with water pouring from the brim of his hat, dropped back to consult with Rosecrans and said, "This feels like the march to Philippi, but without any road to guide us."

Rosecrans's temper, already on edge, flared. "You had it easy compared to what we're going through now! Go back to the front of the line and keep a close watch on that Hart boy. I want him shot if he's leading us into a trap."

The march at times slowed to a crawl. Still Rosecrans urged his men on and on. Time ticked away. Looking at his pocket watch, he realized the three-hour flanking march had consumed almost five hours, with no destination in sight. Neither the horses nor the men could make time in the countless tangled muddy paths and turns. Hourly progress messages to McClellan went out with cavalrymen who never returned. He assumed the couriers were lost.

Thursday, July 11, 1861, 9:00 am
McClellan's HQ, Roaring Creek, Virginia

McClellan paced and worried while his brigades stood ready to make a frontal attack. It was now 9 AM and Rosecran's "hourly" reports, growing more infrequent, had stopped. He was sure it was Philippi all over again, with pouring rains rushing down paths that could no longer be followed and men getting lost. He pondered his next move. Finally, he decided to recall Rosecrans's brigade. He dispatched a cavalry courier to inform Rosecrans of his decision. He thought of dismissing his brigades, but instead ordered them to rest.

Thursday, July 11, 1861, 9:30 am
Colonel Pegram's HQ, Camp Garnett,
Rich Mountain, Virginia

"Colonel Pegram, we have captured a Union cavalry sergeant. Do you want to question him? We found a dispatch on him, sir."

Pegram took the dispatch from the soldier and read it: "General McClellan orders General Rosecrans to abandon the attack and return to headquarters." Deeply concerned, Pegram asked the captured sergeant, "What attack?"

"I'm not sure," the sergeant replied, his eyes evasive. "I think a flanking attack of some kind."

Pegram remembered that General Garnett had earlier alerted him to an overgrown road leading to a little-used footpath that led to his right flank.

"Was it my right flank?" Pegram asked the sergeant.

"I'm not sure... maybe... Yes, I think it was your right flank," replied the sergeant.

Pegram thought the Federal cavalry sergeant was being purposefully vague, but he could not take chances. He had McClellan's message and the warning from General Garnett. Pegram moved almost half his troops from his left flank to the right flank and ordered 310 men with one of their four artillery pieces to the area of Hart's farm, to guard against any Federal attack from the right flank.

Thursday, July 11, 1861, 12:00 noon
General Rosecrans's Field HQ, Rich Mountain, Virginia

The rain let up a little and Rosecrans gave his men a badly needed rest. His temper flared again. His "three-hour march" had now slipped to over eight hours. He called for Hart and, frowning, questioned, "Exactly how much farther is it, boy?" Hart, obviously nervous under questioning, said, "General, the road slopes down gently from where we now stand to our farm about a mile ahead. From there you can march down the mountain and attack the rebel fortifications from the rear. You won't be beaten!"

Rosecrans thought the boy appeared sincere. He dispatched a cavalry courier with a message to McClellan stating their location and the fact they were far behind schedule. He stated he would stop sending messages until he had something of importance to communicate. He waited impatiently while his men rested, then deployed them in line for battle. This took much longer than expected because of the irregular terrain. By 2 PM he finally had his regiments in battle line and ordered out skirmishers. Within minutes his skirmishers were fired on by rebel pickets near the Hart farm. Rosecrans had not expected to encounter pickets this far from their fortifications and guessed they were shielding a rear guard that Hart had previously mentioned were sometimes posted at the farm. Some of his men fell when the rebel pickets fired, so he ordered a volley that drove the Confederates back to the farm.

Once in position, the rebels opened fire with an artillery piece, which brought Rosecrans's men to a halt, some falling back to take cover. The rear guard, thinking Rosecrans was beaten, cheered loudly. Rosecrans was surprised by the Confederates' effective use of their cannon, which at times fired at the rate of about four times a minute, but he was far from defeated. He watched as most of the cannonballs harmlessly went over the heads of his men. After reconnoitering the area, he confidently formed his men into a more advantageous battle line and ordered a bayonet charge. After a short, vicious fight, the rebel cannon was silenced and the artillerymen lay dead. All together, over a hundred rebels were killed, badly wounded, or captured. The rest of the rear guard scampered around in the mountains trying to escape. The clearing out of the rear guard had cost him time. It was now almost 6 PM.

THURSDAY, JULY 11, 1861, 2:30 PM
MCCLELLAN, IN FRONT OF CAMP GARNETT,
RICH MOUNTAIN, VIRGINIA

The hours passed slowly for McClellan and his men that morning. He received General Rosecrans's dispatch stating no more communications would be sent to him until "something of importance" happened. Earlier he formed his men for a frontal attack, but after many hours of waiting, they now sat or lay on the ground resting and chattering while he and his staff went back to his tent to plan a bombardment of the rebel fortress and the placement of his cannons on a ridge Lieutenant Poe had discovered, which looked down into the fortress.

Suddenly, everyone in his entire camp grew quiet. All could hear musket fire and the thunder of artillery echoing near the top of Rich Mountain. Thousands of his resting men sprang to their feet. McClellan and his staff rode up on their horses. All eyes were on him and he knew what they were thinking. *The moment has arrived, General McClellan, to order us to attack those rebel fortifications.*

He turned to his staff and said, "Something is going on up there! Where is the dispatch from Rosecrans telling me what's happening? The man has already disobeyed my recall order and now he leaves me in a quandary as to who is firing those muskets and cannons. The cannon fire can't be coming from Rosecrans; he took no cannons with him."

"General," Inspector General Marcy urged, "we should attack those fortifications now! Maybe Rosecrans didn't receive your recall order. The trooper you sent with that dispatch never returned. Perhaps the messenger was captured."

McClellan's own thoughts raced and Marcy's remarks did not fully register with him. To himself, but loud enough for his staff to hear, he said, "As we agreed, I will wait for Rosecrans's dispatch before giving the order to attack those fortifications. Besides, Lieutenant Poe has not yet placed our cannons on that ridge he found, where we can fire inside that fortress."

In a short while the sounds of muskets and cannons from the mountains died out. McClellan raised his field glasses and viewed the fortifications. A rebel officer rode into the fortifications and, moments later, wild cheering could be heard from inside.

Disgusted, McClellan said to his staff, "That can only mean one thing. The rebels have been victorious. This is the result of Rosecrans disobeying my orders!"

"George!" Marcy exclaimed, "That rebel officer couldn't get down the mountain that fast. The silence could mean Rosecrans is repositioning his men to silence those cannons."

"We have no way of knowing that," McClellan snapped. "Perhaps additional rebel brigades came up the east side of the mountain from Beverly and have him surrounded. I cannot chance sending any of our men in a frontal attack on those fortifications. We will wait here for a dispatch from Rosecrans before taking any action."

They all turned their eyes toward the mountain as the musket and cannon fire from the top started again.

Thursday, July 11, 1861, 2:30 PM
Colonel Pegram's HQ, Camp Garnett,
Rich Mountain, Virginia

Pegram heard the firing at the top of the mountain. He had prepared for an attack on his right flank but the musket fire seemed to be coming from his left flank. Turning to Colonel Heck he said, "Is this the enemy attacking our rear guard?"

Heck replied, "The bulk of the musket fire seems to be aimed at our left flank, but I think the cannon volleys are coming from our forces on the right flank."

"I need to know what's going on up there," Pegram said. "Select one of our companies and tell the captain to get up there quickly and determine what is happening."

The selected captain arrived just as the rear guard was cheering what they thought was a victory over the attacking enemy. The captain surveyed the battleground area, then returned and told Colonel Pegram what he found. Word of the supposed victory spread quickly through Camp Garnett, and led to wild cheering.

Pegram, however, did not cheer. He was nervous and lost in thought over what else the captain had told him. The captain had said, "There are many more enemy soldiers and they greatly outnumber our rear guard. However, I could not spot any enemy artillery and our boys were firing our cannon at the rate of three to four shells in a minute. That rate of cannon fire seemed to be making up for the imbalance in numbers of soldiers."

Pegram thought for a moment. "But one cannon can fire in one direction only at a time, and at that firing rate the cannon will soon be out of ammunition. What happens if the enemy flanks our cannon or it runs out of ammunition? Thank you, Captain, for that information. My apologies, I already know the answer to my question. Return to your company."

Pegram knew the tide of battle could turn against his forces at any minute, and if the rear guard were overwhelmed, his fortification forces would be trapped between Federal forces in his rear and Federal forces in his front. He decided to leave Heck in charge and send additional men to reinforce the rear guard, along with a second cannon and more ammunition. The forces he selected were mostly artillerymen and their horses, and a small company of covering infantry—about fifty men. He would lead this force himself.

By the time Pegram reached the mountaintop the firing was dying down. His reinforcements were "too little and too late." The enemy shot the horses pulling the second cannon and, dismayed, he watched as the cannon rolled down an embankment, followed by enemy soldiers crowding around the prize. He appealed to the soldiers that were left of the rear guard, but they were too demoralized to rally and fight again. Sending those men through the woods toward Beverly, he stumbled back to Camp

Garnett, not reaching the fortification until almost midnight. His attempt at a counterattack was over and all was quiet on the top of the mountain.

THURSDAY, JULY 11, 1861, 6:00 PM
McCLELLAN, IN FRONT OF CAMP GARNETT,
RICH MOUNTAIN, VIRGINIA

"I have decided to withdraw our forces to Roaring Creek. Poe, I want that road to the bluff finished tonight and our artillery placed in position. Position the Ninth Ohio where they can guard our artillery tonight. I want everyone ready to launch an attack on those fortifications after breakfast tomorrow morning," he said to his staff.

"Have you given up on General Rosecrans?" Marcy asked.

"I have not received any additional communications from him. I can only assume the worst: he has been defeated and captured."

Marcy walked away in silence, making a conscious effort to keep his head from shaking. But he couldn't stop the questions racing though his mind, *Is my son-in-law a fool or a coward… or both?*

THURSDAY, JULY 11, 1861, 6:00 PM
GENERAL ROSECRANS FIELD HQ, RICH MOUNTAIN

While Rosecrans had successfully cleared the rebels from the field around the Hart house, he was far from satisfied. He had not heard any action from down the mountain and wondered why McClellan had not made the frontal attack as planned. He got Lander aside and asked, "You know McClellan's mind better than me. Why do you suppose *your* General did not attack the rebel fortifications today?"

Lander hesitated while he thought over how to answer Rosecrans. *After all*, he thought, *he's your general too.* Finally Lander replied, "*Our* general likes to have everything in his orders strictly obeyed. Did you send hourly reports to him? If you didn't, I'm sure he got mad and may even have recalled you. Did you receive any dispatches from him?"

"The answer to your first question is 'yes' at the beginning of our march, and 'no' after the cavalry informed me they could no longer get their horses through. The answer to your second question is 'no.' I did send him a message when we reached the top, saying I would discontinue hourly reporting until I had something to report."

"Did you send him a report after the rebel rear guard was defeated?"

"No."

"Then he is probably still waiting for that dispatch before he attacks."

"Thanks for your assessment, Lander. Interesting. Now let me pose a problem to you. It would appear on first glance that if we spend the night where we are on top of this mountain, we're in a bad position. To the west and down the mountain we have the rebels in the fortifications, who could attack us. To the east and down the other side of the mountain, we have rebels, apparently the Forty-Fourth Virginia Regiment, according to a prisoner we captured, who could attack us from Beverly. But if we look at our position another way, we're in a good position. We have the turnpike blocked so the rebels are caught now between us and McClellan, and we stand in the way of any rebel relief forces coming up the turnpike from Beverly. So what would you do in this situation, if you were in command of my brigade?"

"Well, General, the men have put in a good day's work and need rest. So I would stay here for the night, but only after preparing the men for a counterattack from the fortifications, *or* an attack from that relief force in Beverly. My preparations would include placing the two captured rebel cannon on the turnpike facing in opposite directions and doubling up the number of pickets in both directions. I would ask the men to sleep with their clothes on and with their muskets by their side. I would send a dispatch to McClellan informing him that we'll be in position to attack the rear of the fortress at daybreak."

216

Rosecrans laughed. "Lander, you should be promoted to brigadier general and given a brigade to command. That is *almost* exactly what I plan to do. My only exception is, I will hold off on sending the message to McClellan until we reach the rear of the fortification in the morning." As Rosecrans turned and started to walk away, he stopped, turned back to Lander and, smiling, said, "On second thought, maybe you should be promoted to *Major* General." Lander smiled, but made no reply.

THURSDAY, JULY 11, 1861, 8:00 PM

CONFEDERATE GENERAL GARNETT HQ,

LAUREL HILL, VIRGINIA

In the distance Garnett could see a lone rider making his way toward his camp. In his field glasses, he could see it was the Confederate cavalryman who carried dispatches to and from Beverly. Garnett had spent most of the day peering through his field glasses at the enemy, waiting for a frontal or flank attack from McClellan that he thought would come soon. Every few hours the Federals in his front bombarded his position with their artillery. But for the most part, their cannonballs did little damage. He had communicated earlier with Colonel Scott to hold his Forty-fourth Virginia regiment in Beverly, ready to assist Colonel Pegram should he need help.

The cavalryman dismounted, walked toward Garnett and said, "General Garnett, sir, Colonel Scott sends his regards and asked me to hand deliver this dispatch to you."

"Wait here while I read it," he replied.

As he read, he could feel his heart beating faster. The dispatch told him a disaster had occurred on top of Rich Mountain, and Colonel Scott said he was unable to provide aid to that small, courageous band of embattled soldiers. He thought Scott's explanation as to why he did not attack the enemy was weak. *Now he tells me that the Federals hold the turn-*

pike at the top of the mountain and will most likely attack the rear of Camp Garnett in the morning. But surely, he thought, *Pegram would abandon the fortress and either try to reach me here at Laurel Hill or join forces with Scott and hold Beverly until I arrive. But what if the Federals were to quickly occupy Beverly? Then where will I go?* All he knew for certain was the way to his rear was now open to an attack by the Federals. With at least a brigade of Federals in his front, he would be trapped. *I must pull out soon*, he thought. *Tonight, under the cover of darkness, makes the most sense.*

He quickly wrote a note to Colonel Scott stating that he would abandon Laurel Hill tonight and march to Beverly. He asked Scott to hold the town from falling into Federal hands and to rendezvous with Pegram, if he could. If he were unable to hold Beverly, he should retreat to Huttonsville and make a stand there.

"Take this dispatch to Colonel Scott with my regards," he said to the cavalryman. As the messenger rode off, he sadly recalled the conversation he had had with General Lee a week ago as they planned these defenses. He still could hardly believe Lee's reply when he had told Lee that the northwesterners had given up on Richmond and would not come to their aid. Lee, he remembered, said, "But surely, Rob, you must be wrong in your interpretation of the desires of our citizens who live out there. I am certain that the majority are being misguided by a few bad men. Surely most citizens of Virginia think like you and me. It is their duty to Virginia to follow her wherever she leads, as we have always done." Garnett had thought then, as he did now, *Lee is out of touch with reality and is sending me to my death. All of Lee's talking and Letcher's grand proclamation gained me a grand total of twenty-three recruits, with no weapons, no shoes and no training.*

Trying to shake off his depression, he made plans to pull all of his men out of the Laurel Hill trenches and silently move south to Beverly. Orders were given to leave campfires burning and tents in place. Men were to leave all equipment that made noise as they marched and remain silent as they left camp. By midnight almost all of his men and wagons were on the road to Beverly. Along the march some of the men from Pegram's force wandered out of the forest and informed him that the Federals now held Beverly. Bitterly disappointed, he reversed course and headed north, intending to move around the northern end of the mountain back to Staunton. It would be a long and arduous march.

FRIDAY, JULY 12, 1861, 1:00 AM
COLONEL PEGRAM, CAMP GARNETT,
RICH MOUNTAIN, VIRGINIA

When Pegram returned from his ill-fated counterattack, he found a tired, wet, hungry, and disheartened force. He was in much the same condition. Heck and the men in the fortification had already heard of the defeat of the rear guard. And McClellan had robbed them of the opportunity for revenge by not making a frontal attack. Pegram convened a war council of the officers. He said, "Gentlemen, we are in a tenuous position. The Federals on top of the mountain have the road to Beverly blocked and, by the grace of God, we were spared today from an attack by McClellan's forces. Surely if we are still here in the morning, we will be caught between the two Federal forces and slaughtered or forced to surrender. I know the men are tired and hungry, I know we have sick and wounded men, and I know it is pouring rain, but I think we must abandon this fort tonight. As I see it, we can attempt to join forces with General Garnett at Laurel Hill, or go to Beverly and join forces with Colonel Scott of the Forty-Fourth Virginia and then either march to Laurel Hill or retreat to Huttonsville."

Colonel Heck suggested, "Sir, I think our map maker, Hotchkiss, should lead the way and that we should go directly to Laurel Hill to support General Garnett. The General will also feel exposed to attack by the Federals, once Camp Garnett is abandoned."

Most officers agreed with Heck. Pegram then asked, "Are there any more suggestions?"

Others asked about equipment to take. Pegram replied, "We need to be very quiet when we leave. Any personal equipment that can make noise must be left behind. This will be a long march in wet weather, so tell the men to take only what is absolutely essential."

Around 2 AM the column began their departure for Laurel Hill, with Hotchkiss leading the way followed by two infantry companies chosen by Colonel Heck, who was now commanding the move, as Pegram had decided to stay behind with Dr. Taylor and the sick and wounded. However, Dr. Taylor soon convinced Pegram to go on with the last column moving out, as he thought the Federals would not take a doctor prisoner, but they would surely place Pegram in prison since he had been an active U.S. Army officer.

The rear end of the long column was just about to leave camp when Pegram joined it. His fatigue was almost immobilizing but he wanted to resume command. He sent his orderly forward to halt the column, so he could inform Colonel Heck that he was taking over again. The rain and darkness made any maneuver difficult and halting the column was no exception. His orderly, coming up on Colonel Heck, thought Heck was at the head of the column, so the orderly did not move all the way forward. When Heck passed the order to stop, Hotchkiss and the two lead companies continued on toward Beverly, not realizing the column had stopped behind them.

"Why did you order the column to stop?" Heck asked Pegram when he finally reached him.

Pegram, having neither the strength nor the will for a long explanation, simply replied, "I'm taking charge of the column now."

To his dismay, Pegram soon learned that Hotchkiss, their guide, had gone ahead and was now out of sight and could not be followed. *What else can go wrong this night?* he wondered. *Is Heaven itself out to destroy us?*

He led the column himself, almost aimlessly picking his way through the dark, stumbling over rocks and downed timber. At dawn they finally reached the outskirts of Beverly. However, Pegram, looking through his field glasses, spotted a small military group in the distance and thought it was Federals. He decided to stay in the mountains to avoid capture and do his best to reach Garnett.

Pegram was near exhaustion. He had fallen from his horse during the morning skirmish and the injuries he received were becoming incapacitating, so that he was barely able to walk. He sent some of his men to a small farmhouse they passed, to see if they could get some food, but they returned with no rations. The farmer said he had no food to give them, but he did give them the bad news that they were surrounded by Federal troops. Most of Pegram's men had collapsed and were sleeping, huddled together on the ground in the fence corners and wherever they could get a bit of shelter from the rain and cold.

Gathering his officers for another council, Pegram told them, "Gentlemen, the farmer says we are surrounded by Yankee soldiers. I can see the men are weak and exhausted, as I am and as you are. I fear if we run into those Yankees they will open fire on us. Many of us will die, as we have no dry powder. I see no alternative but to surrender to General McClellan."

The officers were subdued. Most resisted the idea, but without powder their men were at the mercy of the Federals. Colonel Heck spoke first, with a show of bravado.

"Colonel Pegram, I did not volunteer for our army to surrender without a fight. I would rather die fighting than go to a Yankee prison."

"What are the opinions of the company officers who know the condition of their men?" Pegram asked.

All of the other officers, except one, agreed that it was best to surrender.

Colonel Heck spoke up again, saying, "It's obvious that I'm in the minority. I don't want my regiment to suffer. I will go along with the plan to surrender."

Colonel Pegram, with despair in his heart and his hands shaking from cold and hunger, wrote a note to McClellan offering the surrender of the exhausted men under his command as prisoners of war.

FRIDAY, JULY 12, 1861, 3:00 AM

GENERAL ROSECRANS - FIELD HQ,

RICH MOUNTAIN, VIRGINIA

Rosecrans awakened suddenly and listened. All he could hear was the rain, like falling buckshot, hitting his tent. Then he rose from his cot as someone called out, "General Rosecrans, are you awake, sir?"

"Yes, I'm awake, who's calling me?"

"Sir, it's one of your guards. Our pickets captured a rebel soldier who is wet, exhausted, and hungry. The prisoner says Colonel Pegram abandoned Camp Garnett. Do you want to talk with the prisoner?"

"Yes, yes! Give me a moment to light a lamp. Make sure he's unarmed and bring him inside."

"Colonel, he is shivering badly. We checked him for knives and pistols, and he has no weapons."

"Send my orderly to fetch a dry woolen blanket and some hot coffee. Then bring him inside."

While the two guards stood on either side of the prisoner, Rosecrans held his lamp close to the prisoner's face and noted a scared boy, maybe eighteen years old, in wet ragged clothing, shivering almost uncontrollably.

"Take it easy, son. Take off your wet clothes and wrap yourself in this blanket. I have hot coffee on the way."

Shivering and hardly able to talk, the young man slowly removed his wet clothes and wrapped up in the warm woolen blanket.

"What's your name, son?" Rosecrans asked.

"Jes... Jessie, si... si... sir," the prisoner replied.

The orderly entered with two cups of hot coffee.

"Jessie, just sit there awhile. Drink this coffee and get yourself warm."

A few minutes later after Jessie's shivering died down and the coffee was gone, Rosecrans asked, "How long ago did Colonel Pegram leave?"

"'Bout two this mornin'."

"How many men are left in camp and are any wounded?"

"Maybe a hunderd or so... half 'em wounded and half sick."

"Is a doctor tending to the wounded?"

"Yes. Doc Taylor."

"Do you know where Colonel Pegram was heading?"

"Not sure. The column headed north. I heard them sayin' General Garnett and Laurel Hill."

"Where were you going when my pickets caught you?"

"I left near to the end of the column. I was so tired I fell out and got lost. I slept a little. I was tryin' to take the pike to Beverly when your picket caught me."

"All right, son. You go now with the guards. They'll get you something to eat and some clean clothes to wear, if we have any. You won't be harmed, but you must understand that you are now a prison of war. Don't try to escape, or the guards will shoot you."

Rosecrans organized his men to march down the pike to investigate Camp Garnett. Pickets were stationed around the main marching column to cover the front, both flanks, and rear of the column as his brigade moved cautiously down the mountain. He reached Camp Garnett at 6 AM and found about seventy sick and wounded men under a white flag, being attended by Dr. Archibald Taylor. Two remaining cannons, four caissons and ammunition, 19,000 cartridges, two stands of colors, a large quantity of clothing, tents, camp equipment, wagons, horse teams and personal items were strewn about the camp.

Rosecrans's temper started to rise again as he viewed the scene. He thought, *An opportunity to capture all of Pegram's force has been lost because McClellan did not attack the fortification as promised. For now, I will set my feelings aside, but I will not forget or forgive.* Then he sent a dispatch to General McClellan informing him that the rebels were gone and he now occupied the fortifications.

FRIDAY, JULY 12, 1861, 6:30 AM
McCLELLAN'S HQ, ROARING CREEK, VIRGINIA

As General McClellan prepared to bombard Camp Garnett prior to his planned morning frontal attack, he saw a cavalryman riding up to his tent. For a moment, he thought the trooper looked like one of the men from the cavalry company that had been assigned to General Rosecrans. As the cavalryman got closer, he saw that the trooper was from Burdsall's cavalry. *Is this a dream, or is this horse and rider a ghost?* he wondered.

"General," the cavalryman said, "General Rosecrans sends his regards and asked me to personally hand you this dispatch."

Shocked, surprised and almost speechless, he managed to say, "Is this dispatch you are carrying really from General Rosecrans?"

The trooper replied, "Yes, sir."

Still finding it hard to believe, McClellan inquired, "Is the general in good health and what is the state of his brigade?"

"He's in fine health, General, and his brigade is in good shape. We lost a few men in the battle yesterday, but we killed and wounded many rebels and took many prisoners. And we silenced that damn cannon they had. Them rebs could sure load and shoot that thing… about as fast as our infantry can load and fire a musket!"

Still somewhat doubting his senses, McClellan inquired, "Where's General Rosecrans now?"

"Why, General, he's over in those fortifications with his whole brigade, trying to figure out where those rebels skedaddled to. The General thinks Pegram's tryin' to hook up with that rebel general at Laurel Hill."

The trooper handed him the dispatch. Finally, it sunk in, Rosecrans was not dead and Rosecrans's brigade had not been captured. Success!

"Thank you! Give my regards to General Rosecrans and tell him I'll be over to see him just as soon as I can undo some orders and write new ones to break camp."

He read Rosecrans's dispatch with a big smile. He had written off that general and now he appears, as if from the dead, ready to chase down the fleeing rebels. He thought, *I admit it, I was wrong about that man. I'm proud of him.* He passed the good news to his commanders and soon cheers roared down the valley while regimental bands played "Yankee Doodle." His orders to his brigade commanders were brief: "Up tents and after them."

Then he gathered his staff and rode proudly into the fortifications with much fanfare. He got off his horse, walked over to Rosecrans, shook him by the shoulders, and said loudly, "General Rosecrans, you are this day a great Union hero. You and your fine fighting brigade of brave soldiers should all be wearing wreaths of laurel. All of you have singlehandedly defeated an entrenched enemy." He then stepped back, and saluted Rosecrans. The Rosecrans brigade, watching this display of affection for their general, let out three cheers for General Rosecrans, followed by three, a bit less enthusiastic, for Major General McClellan.

McClellan felt almost giddy. He thought of the telegrams he would send to Washington praising the accomplishments of his army, and the gloating letter to his Nelly.

When the impromptu victory ceremony ended, General Rosecrans got him aside and said, "General, the way is now open to Beverly. We need to occupy that town before Garnett escapes!"

Rosecrans is right, he thought, *but with so many matters to attend to it might be noon or later before I can send someone to occupy Beverly.*

FRIDAY, JULY 12, 1861, 5:00 AM

GENERAL MORRIS HQ, LAUREL HILL, VIRGINIA

"General Morris, sir, wake up!" the picket called outside of the general's tent.

Morris rose from his cot and asked, "Who's calling me?"

"General, it's one of your pickets, sir. I believe the rebels have abandoned their trenches on Laurel Hill."

Pulling on his pants and boots, he grabbed his field glasses and surveyed the trenches where he expected to see Garnett's forces. The tents were in place, but there were no men to be seen manning the trenches.

"I do believe you are right," he said to the picket.

"Do you want me to send out more pickets to take a look around, General?"

"Yes, but first have the gunners send over a few rounds. That usually gets their attention. If you don't see any movement after a few rounds, take a dozen men and walk over there and make sure no one's home."

It was late morning when the pickets returned with confirmed information that the rebels had abandoned their defenses at Laurel Hill.

Morris, anxious to pursue Garnett's forces, called Captain Benham to his tent, and said, "Captain, are you and your men up to pursuing General Garnett and his forces?"

Captain Benham, McClellan's Chief of Engineers, graduated at the top of his West Point class of 1837. While still only a captain, he was nevertheless an officer with years of military experience from the Mexican

War. As a regular Army captain, he outranked the militia colonels of Morris's command.

"How much of a lead do they have on me, General?" Benham asked.

"My best guess is they have about 12 hours. But they took their wagons and artillery and that will slow them down," Morris replied.

"Do you have any idea where Garnett is headed?"

"I suspect he's headed for Beverly, but maybe, just maybe, McClellan captured that town before Garnett got there. If so, Garnett will likely backtrack and take that wagon road that runs along Leading Creek toward the Cheat River, and then try to pick up the Northwestern Turnpike at Red House, Maryland. It would be the only way to get back to the Shenandoah Valley."

"If he did have to backtrack, then that would cut his lead time down quite a bit. I've got 1,800 men, eager as bloodhounds for a chase. I'll make sure my men lighten up their personal load so they can move fast. We'll take no wagons that can slow us down. Maybe we can catch up to him," Benham said.

"The trail might be easy to follow," Morris said. "My guess is all those green troops will be dropping their gear all along the path, to lighten their loads."

"I suspect you're right. With your permission, General, I'll get my men ready and start off right away on the chase."

"Permission granted. Good hunting and may the Lord look after you and your men. I'll follow you with the rest of the brigade as soon as I can."

FRIDAY, JULY 12, 1861, 9:00 AM
CAPTAIN BENHAM, LEADING CREEK ROAD, VIRGINIA

Benham's force—Steedman's Fourteenth Ohio, Dumont's Seventh Indiana, and Milroy's Ninth Indiana—played the odds and headed immediately toward Leading Creek, as the most likely route Garnett would have taken *if* he had to backtrack from Beverly. The odds favored Benham. Garnett *had* backtracked and Benham easily found their trail. The heavy rains turned the trail into deep mud, worked into a jelly by the plodding feet of men and horses and the turning and churning of wagon wheels. Abandoned personal gear and equipment littered the trail.

Soon hastily constructed rebel barricades, darkness, and heavy rains forced Benham to halt for the night to rest himself, his men and horses. The men built fires and huddled around them, trying to warm their chilled bodies. Exhausted, muddy and wet, they sprawled wherever they could find a dry spot.

SATURDAY, JULY 13, 1861, 5:00 AM
CAPTAIN BENHAM, VILLAGE OF NEW INTEREST, VIRGINIA

At the first light, Benham walked quietly among his men. They got to their feet quickly without any prodding. These bloodhounds, as Benham liked to call them, would need to set a furious pace today.

At the small village of New Interest, the fleeing rebels had turned east on a mountain road, barely wide enough for a wagon to pass. Along this road, the deep tar-like mud held discarded equipment, including stools marked as belonging to General Garnett, fine blankets, and heavy duck tents. All were tramped into the ever-deepening mud and destroyed by the feet of the infantry and the incessant rain. Wrecked wagons perched upside down in trees over high cliffs. To Benham, the trail no longer looked like that made by a retreating army; instead, it resembled the chaos left by a stampeding mob. Such sights made his men move faster, as if they could smell they were on the very heels of their rebel quarry.

Further up the mountain, the road got even worse and the rain fell harder. Benham's men encountered barricades of timber which they sometimes chopped through using the axes left by the rebels.

By noon Benham's force neared Shavers Fork, a tributary of the Cheat River. Turbulent from the rains, the river slowed the rebel retreat. As Benham crossed the creek, he saw the rebel baggage train resting in a meadow on the bank. Storming through the water refreshed his men and washed away the mud caked on their boots and clothes.

The pursuit turned into a running fight; shots rang out, wounding soldiers. Three miles downstream Benham approached a crossing known as Corricks Ford. He saw rebel wagons stalled in the deep rocky riverbed, a frantic scene. Rebel teamsters cursed their teams, whipped them and cursed again. Benham looked on, astonished. A rebel regiment faced them across the creek. About 80 feet above them on a bluff sat three cannons. "It's one of the best natural defenses I ever saw," he said to his staff.

Without orders, his bloodhounds knew what to do. He watched his regiments and artillery take position and return the fire coming from the rebels. As the fight raged on, one of his battalions flanked the rebel forces, which began to melt away, leaving their cannons. Benham looked at his watch. The skirmish had lasted maybe 30 minutes.

The sounds of the skirmish caught the attention of an obviously high-ranking Confederate officer. Benham saw the man, silhouetted against the sky in a black overcoat, ride fearlessly among the retreating rebels. He ordered some of the fleeing men to form a skirmish line. Benham saw another officer stop and attempt to get the high-ranking officer to fall back, to no effect. *This is truly a courageous leader!* Benham thought. Moments later, Benham's men fired a volley and the finely dressed officer fell from his horse. The slight figure of a young rifleman took aim at the advancing Federals, and then he too fell beside his officer. The rest of the Confederates fled through the woods, leaving the bodies behind.

Benham and some of his staff crossed the ford for a closer look. The dead officer had stars on his uniform. Benham watched as one of his staff members respectfully closed the man's eyes and bound his jaw with a handkerchief. They weren't sure of the identity of the courageous man, but Benham thought, *It must be Garnett. How sad.*

Major John Love, an aide to General Morris, soon arrived on the scene and informed Benham that the fallen officer was indeed General Garnett, who had once been Love's roommate at West Point. Benham saw tears in Love's eyes, and indeed his own eyes were wet. The troops filed by in hushed reverence, paying their respects to this general officer, so highly regarded by both sides.

Benham ordered an ambulance brought forward to carry Garnett's body to Beverly. He had lost his enthusiasm for the chase and could see that his men badly needed a rest. General Morris, who had been following Benham's pursuit at some distance in the rear, ordered the pursuit taken up again by a nearby brigade guarding the B&O Railroad. That brigade set off with orders to cut off the fleeing rebels in western Maryland.

Captain Benham couldn't get the gallant general out of his mind. *It seems clear that Garnett needlessly—but so bravely—exposed himself to our fire,* he thought. He took some comfort in the knowledge that Garnett would now be united in heaven with his wife and son. *Perhaps that's what he had in mind all along.*

SUNDAY, JULY 14, 1861, 8:00 AM
McClellan's HQ, Beverly, Virginia

Most of the soldiers took advantage of the opportunity to attend Sunday services and thank God for their victory and that they were still alive. General McClellan waited for the guard and his staff to make the arrangements on the parade ground, where he would formally accept the surrender of Colonel Pegram and 553 officers and men, He perused the telegram he received from General Morris, stating that Captain Benham had caught up with General Garnett's retreating force from Laurel Hill at a place near the Cheat River called Corricks Ford. Garnett had been killed, along with a dozen rebels. Many rebel prisoners were taken.

Everything, McClellan thought, *has fallen into place just as I had envisioned. First General Rosecrans's brilliant flanking maneuver started the fall of both fortresses. It was like dominos standing on end and when the first is tipped over, the others fall.*

He thought about what his army had accomplished. Even though many Confederates retreated and perhaps would escape capture, more than 700 had become casualties of his Rich Mountain campaign. The B&O Railroad, at least in his department, was secure, the Restored Government of Virginia was now a secure reality, and the gates to the Shenandoah Valley now lay open, making the Shenandoah Valley vulnerable to attack by the Union. Now, he even had his troops guarding the Staunton-Parkersburg Turnpike at Cheat Mountain. Only one Confederate force, commanded by former Virginia Governor Wise, remained in his department and recent telegrams from General Cox, whom he had sent to the Kanawha Valley, indicated Wise had already packed his bags and was headed out.

After formally accepting the surrender of Colonel Pegram's forces, McClellan spent hours drafting telegrams to Washington praising his men and enumerating the accomplishments of his army. The northern papers had already picked up the stories of his victory and apparently were casting him as a national hero. McClellan reveled in the glory, but when he was alone, his thoughts wandered to his dead defeated foe. General Garnett had been an 1841 graduate of West Point, five years before McClellan. They had served together in the Mexican War, and he thought very highly of the man. One of McClellan's colonels had reported that his men, on scene at the time of General Garnett's death, believed Garnett purposely exposed himself at Corricks Ford. McClellan wondered whether this was so, possibly because of the humiliation of defeat. He wondered how he himself would respond to a defeat, having tasted the sweet wine of a conclusive victory so early in the campaign. He hoped he never had to find out.

McClellan turned his thoughts to the future, the next move in this game he was playing with the Confederates. *Who will they send next to try to take control of these northwestern counties, now in the Restored State of Virginia? No matter—we'll be ready.*

CHAPTER NINE

Jine the Cavalry!

July 16–September 13, 1861

Column of marching Union cavalry

Tuesday, July 16, 1861
East of Grafton near Tygart Valley River

The boy was crying. He couldn't help it. Wet, weak, cold, hungry, and lost, he wished now he hadn't lied. If only he could go home to Georgia. Back home his friends told him they was going up north on a joy ride, to whip them Yanks. It was all going to be such fun. So he lied about his age of 15 years, so he could join up. It was easy. After all, he was almost six feet tall, his voice had changed, and the regiment enlistment officer wouldn't know any different. Besides, he reckoned, those enlistment fellers were just trying to fill their ranks as quick as they could.

But the fun had ended for good that night when his regiment and the rest of Garnett's army left Laurel Hill. The boy thought, *It didn't take them Yanks long to catch up with us when we ran. Somewhere in that miserable mud and rain, when the Yanks were on our heels like dogs, they started shootin'. I ran and didn't stop.*

When he walked and crawled back the next day, he found no one around but the dead. He couldn't tell if they were Georgians, Yanks or who. They all lay scattered, covered in mud or floating upside down in the water. So he reckoned they didn't need their clothing, or boots, or the bits of soggy food he found on them. He gathered everything he could carry. He left all the dead for someone else to bury and headed for home—he'd had enough soldiering. But after days wandering the rough mountains, not knowing which way was north or south because of the incessant rains, he was out of food, his clothes were just wet rags, he was shivering, his shoes were worn through, and his crying wasn't helping. He must find something to eat or die trying.

So when he spotted a couple of tumble-down shacks, looking more like woodpiles than houses, his spirits lifted. He hoped to meet a kind lady, like his ma, who would give him a bite of food and tell him how to get home to Georgia. He would promise to do some work in return, when he got his strength back.

He pounded on the door of one of the shacks. A skinny hound, curled on the sagging porch, raised his head and barked halfheartedly. The boy was disappointed to see a bent old man answer the door. The old man looked him up and down, smiled a toothless smile and motioned for him to come inside. The shack was cluttered and had a sour smell, but a hot fire was burning in the fireplace. The boy knelt on the dirt floor as close to the fire as he could get without scorching himself. "Please, sir, could you spare a bite of food?" the boy asked timidly. "I'm about to faint."

The old man grunted. "Might have a little squirrel stew left. Look in 'at pot." He indicated an iron pot on the hearth, coated in a layer of grime. The boy grabbed the pot and began to ladle the congealed brown stew into his mouth with his hand. The old man watched him eat for a few minutes before the questions started.

"Whar you from, boy?" the old man asked.

"Georgia," he answered.

"Whatcha doin' up here, boy?"

"I come up with a Georgia regiment and the Yanks beat us up purty bad."

"You a sojer from Georgia, fightin' them dam Yanks?"

The boy nodded, still trying to scrape a few bits of burned meat from the bottom of the pot.

"Where's your rej-ment, boy?"

The boy looked up at his questioner, hesitating before forming his answer. "They took off without me. Must'a thought I got kilt."

"Yore a de-sorter, boy, now ain't ya?"

The boy ducked his head like a frightened rabbit at the accusation. "Nossir, I ain't! I'm just tryin' to find my regiment."

The old man looked toward the door and tilted his head. "Wait right here, boy, and get warm by that there fire. I be back." He painfully got to his feet and left.

The boy was ill at ease. He didn't fully trust the old man, but at least he had given him food and maybe he could get an old blanket from him, something to cover up with. And the fire was making him sleepy. He dozed off, his head on his chest.

The old man soon returned with three slouching men, all of them dressed in tattered, stained, homespun clothing. As they entered the shack, the odor of unwashed skin and tobacco came with them. Each had a long scraggly beard, a hat made of animal skins, wet from the rain, and fierce-looking eyes. Two of the men carried old muskets and one carried a coiled leather bullwhip that showed signs of long use. The boy looked at these men and their weapons and his mild unease turned into fear. He was sorry he had been lulled into a feeling of safety by the warm fire and the leftover stew. He quickly got to his feet.

The old man said, "This here is Hank and his two boys, Junior and Bobby. They been out huntin'. They wanna have a little talk with ye, sojer boy."

Hank, the older man with the whip, spoke first. "This here old man said you a de-sorter, from Georgia. Is that so, boy?"

The boy's hands began to shake. In a quivering voice he replied, "I ain't no deserter, I told him. I just got lost durin' the fight with the Yanks. I'm tryin' to get back to my regiment."

"Don't lie, boy. You know what they do to de-sorters, don't you?"

"Yessir, I know they get shot. But I *ain't* no deserter, I said!"

"Don't 'sir' me, boy. I ain't one of your damn osso-fers. We don't like sojers and we hate osso-fers. And we sure'n hell don't take kindly to no de-sorters. Now, one more time, boy, answer me true, are you a de-sorter?"

Shivering so he could hardly speak, the boy said as loudly as he could, "N-no!"

Hank said, "Well, boy, we gonna see if you tellin' us true."

Turning to the two men with the muskets, Hank said, "Junior, Bobby, y'all strip this here boy down and tie 'im to one of them truth-trees out back."

The boy tried to run for the door, but was overpowered by the three men, while the old man giggled and danced a little jig, in anticipation of the coming entertainment.

Junior and Bobby lay down their muskets, stripped all the wet rags off the boy, and drug him to a tree behind the second shack. They tied him, while Hank snapped his whip in the air and asked, "One last time, boy, you a de-sorter or ain't ye?"

The pale and shaking boy once again answered, "No, I'm tellin' you the truth!"

The whip tore down his back, buttocks, and the back sides of his legs with a pain so great that he screamed. Again and again the whip tore into his flesh until he could no longer stand the pain and fainted. The boy bled profusely from the cuts of the whip as Hank paused to wipe the sweat from his forehead. The old man he-he'd and shouted, "Gettin' tired a'ready, Hank?"

"Shut up, old man, or I'll give you a lick or two. Junior, th'ow a bucket of water on 'im. See if he's still livin'," said Hank.

The boy's body flinched when the cold water drenched him, but he did not scream or gain consciousness. Bobby walked over to the boy, pulled his head back by the hair, and asked, "Are you a de-sorter, boy?"

The boy did not answer. He hung limply by the wrists where they had tied him. Blood continued to pour from the many cuts on his thin body, profusely from some. Hank cut him with the whip several times more but the boy didn't move or make a sound. Another bucket of cold water failed to arouse him. His face had turned blue and Bobby said, "He ain't breathin' no more."

"Git rid of 'im," Hank ordered, disgusted.

Junior and Bobby cut the boy down, dragged him away from the dilapidated buildings, into the woods.

"He might start stinkin', if it ever gets warm enough," said Bobby.

"Somethin' will eat 'im first," Junior said. "At least he saved us some powder and lead, since we didn't have to shoot 'im."

They walked away and left the boy lying in the leaves for the buzzards, wolves, and bears.

TUESDAY, JULY 16, 1861, 10:00 AM
PRESIDENT DAVIS'S OFFICE, RICHMOND, VIRGINIA

News of the Rich Mountain disaster and the death of General Garnett struck Richmond like a lightning bolt. Telegrams poured in from southern governors and piled up on the desk of President Davis. Particularly harsh were the telegrams from the Governor of Georgia. The First Georgia Infantry regiment was the pride of their state due to its glorious exploits during the Mexican War. The famous regiment had been sent to Virginia at the request of Davis, to be trained alongside the Virginia troops near Richmond by General Lee, before being sent to Garnett.

Lee sat uneasy at a small table, discussing with Davis how to renew efforts to save western Virginia. "I am sure many of those governors are blaming me for this disaster, but my biggest fear," said Lee, "is the Federals under McClellan will now move on Staunton and into the Valley of Virginia."

Davis replied, "We can't let that happen. We're going to need all the men Beauregard and Johnston have to counteract the movements of those ninety-day volunteers that Lincoln has been training. I'm sure they're going to make a move on us soon."

Lee pondered his response. He was heartsick over the death of his friend and protégé, Garnett. *But I have to move on*, he thought. *No time to mourn an old friend and comrade.* He gathered his thoughts.

"Georgia General Henry Jackson took over command of Garnett's forces when Garnett was killed. Somehow, Jackson managed to get those sick, hungry, and demoralized troops to the safety of Monterey, a small town on the Staunton-Parkersburg Turnpike, and he set up a defensive position there. He wants to be relieved, so let us order General Loring with several fresh regiments to the area to relieve Jackson, organize a proper defense, hold the mountain passes, and protect the Virginia Central Railroad at Staunton," said Lee.

"Good," replied Davis, "but we have another problem lurking out there. This problem is with our ex-governor Wise and his 'Wise Legion.' He's been chased out of the Kanawha Valley by the Federals and now swears the entire region is 'wholly disaffected and traitorous.'"

Lee shook his head and sighed. "Yes, I know about Wise's exploits. Can we send General Floyd and his force out there and put him in charge of Wise?" offered Lee.

Davis hesitated. "If we do that, we could be making more trouble for ourselves. Floyd, as you know, is also an ex-governor of Virginia and those two are bitter rivals. I realize I'm the one who appointed them to their current positions, but it was a political necessity—I had to do something to keep them out of my hair, Lee! Floyd is senior by two days... but I'm not at all sure Wise would take orders from him."

"But surely, Mr. President, they love the Old Dominion as much as we do and would place our cause above their disagreements."

Davis sighed and didn't respond for a moment. Then he said, "I hope you're right, General. Go ahead and prepare orders for Generals Loring and Floyd."

WEDNESDAY, JULY 17, 1861, 8:00 AM
MCCLELLAN'S HQ, BEVERLY, VIRGINIA

Lieutenant Poe and Colonel Lander sat comfortably with McClellan inside the large home of Bushrod Crawford who, as a delegate to the Virginia Convention, had voted for secession and fled south with his family, leaving their large house vacant as the Federals approached Beverly. McClellan took the home for his headquarters. Poe and Lander had just returned from a scouting expedition east along the Staunton-Parkersburg Turnpike to find out where Garnett's forces had gone and to look for places to built fortifications to secure the western counties.

"Well, gentlemen, what did you find on your travels?" McClellan asked.

Poe replied, "When we started out we intended to travel east along the Staunton-Parkersburg Turnpike to the outskirts of Staunton. We found no Confederates in Huttonsville and folks friendly to the Union told us all of Garnett's forces that escaped are now in Monterey, under the command of a general with a deep southern accent, and that many of his men are in rags and look like they're starving. We think the general they're talking about was in charge of the Georgia regiment assigned to Garnett at Laurel Hill."

McClellan nodded. "What about sites for fortifications?" he asked.

"We continued on toward Monterey and inspected the two mountain passes between Huttonsville and Monterey—Cheat Mountain and Back Allegheny Mountain. Cheat Mountain is closest to Huttonsville and, with an elevation of 4,600 feet, is the tallest of the two. It also has the best defensive terrain. It's an ideal spot for a fortress. The surrounding terrain is rugged and there's no way for the fortress to be flanked or bombarded from above."

"Anything else?" McClellan asked.

"We also travelled south to Huntersville. There's a good road leading south which folks told us provides access to Lewisburg on the James River and Kanawha Turnpike. Of course, that route also gives any Confederate forces access to Beverly, so we would need a defensive structure at Elkwater," Poe replied.

Following the reports, McClellan, who thought the best defense was a good offense in this case, sent a telegram to General Scott proposing to move on Staunton, capture that town and take control of the Virginia Central Railroad, provided such a plan fit in with the War Department's overall strategy, he had added. McClellan had decided not to rock the boat too much with Scott at this early stage of his command. He recollected with satisfaction the flattering words he had received from the old general recently, following his successful operations in Virginia. *I do still value the old man's praise... even though he's long past his prime and should no longer be in command.*

THURSDAY, JULY 18, 1861, 4:00 AM
SWANEY FARM, SMITHFIELD, PENNSYLVANIA

AJ slowly awakened, rubbed his eyes and remembered. Today he would travel with Harry to Morgantown and join the cavalry. As he dressed he recalled the send-off party the evening before. Every member of his family had been there, except for his cousin Tip, and he'd been glad not to see him. Everyone there had shaken his hand and wished him well.

Even Sophia had dropped in for a while. AJ's eyes had been on the door the whole evening, to see if she would come, and finally he saw her with her family, carrying a basket of food covered with a dishcloth. *Like I had died or somethin'*, he thought.

Furtive glances passed between them. Finally when he was alone for a moment, she had come up to him and said, very quietly, "I'll miss you, AJ. We all will. Please come back to us. Promise me you will."

He had nodded, and then looked into her eyes for a brief moment, trying to memorize their color. She held his gaze before turning away, and he thought he saw her eyes fill. But he wasn't sure. There was so much he wanted to say, but couldn't. She had left with her family shortly after that.

Cynthia, Earsala, and John had cried when they hugged him goodbye last night before going to bed. AJ had to fight back tears himself. *Their big brother going off to fight a war is more than they should have to bear,* AJ thought. He had carefully cut locks of his hair to leave as keepsakes with Cynthia and his mother. They tied them up with red silk thread and carefully wrapped them in parchment paper.

Although they had said their goodbyes the night before, he found his mother and father waiting for him in the kitchen, a fire going. His pa hugged him long and hard, and told him again how proud he was. They ate together, talking of planting and harvest. When he stood to leave, his ma pulled out a small wooden box and handed it to him.

"You're prob'ly going to run into some sickness in the Army, AJ, and you'll need these medicines. You know what most of them is for, and I've wrote names on everything." She reached up and patted his cheek, and smiled, a sad smile.

He hugged his mother one last time and finally left for the barn.

Shiloh pranced and nickered as AJ tossed the saddlebags onto his back, packed with his necessaries. AJ figured his horse knew they were going on another long ride. Then he tied on his blanket roll, slid his Pennsylvania long rifle into its saddle holster, and slipped his powder horn and ammo sash over his buckskin jacket. With his buckskin pants and riding boots, he felt like a frontiersman from a previous century.

Soon Harry and Betsy came up the lane, as they had done so many times before. *But this time is different,* thought AJ. *A new and unknown road. Will I ever return?* Then he shook his head in an attempt to shake out the negative thoughts. *I have to return... I promised Sophia.* A new sprout of hope was trying to poke forth. He wasn't sure whether to let it grow, or pull it out by the roots.

THURSDAY, JULY 18, 1861, 1:00 PM
MORGANTOWN, VIRGINIA

The painted sign on High Street read "KELLEY LANCERS VOLUN-TEERS FORM HERE." AJ and Harry joined the end of the line, already about 50 men long. Newly arriving volunteers fell in behind them. One man hollered as he walked up, "Whoo *ee*! Jinin' the cavalry!" and the group chuckled. As they introduced themselves to the men standing near them, they found many were from Morgantown, but others were from western Pennsylvania and as far away as Ohio.

The line got longer. AJ could feel his heart pounding. Since his trip with Harry to Wheeling, he had been more interested in seeing and experiencing more of the world. Still, his mind continually drifted back to his farm and his family. And the vision of Sophia bobbed up into his mind's eye, like an apple in a barrel. Despite his hurt pride, he knew he still carried deep feelings for her, and probably always would.

Someday, he thought, *God willing, I'll return to my home, where I know how to earn my own living.* He would never hesitate to tell anyone that he was a farmer. He was proud of the knowledge and skill that he'd acquired over his short lifetime. But now he was turning his face to a new direction, where he was unsure of himself, unsure of his abilities to learn all the new skills that faced him, and mostly unsure of his suitability for the possibly violent life of a soldier. He promised himself that he would work as hard as was needed to master the difficult job ahead of him. He would do his best. He always did his best.

AJ snapped out of his thoughts when the young dentist they had met in Morgantown stepped to the front of the line and boomed, "Men, give me your attention!" He paused to allow the men to stop talking and turn toward him. "For those who do not know me yet, my name is John Lowry McGee and I've been selected to form a company of cavalry, to be known as the Kelley Lancers. I will be your captain and Mr. Lemley, standing here beside me, will be my first lieutenant." He indicated the man beside him, who smiled and touched his cap.

"You might be wondering, why the name 'Kelley Lancers'? Kelley is for Colonel Benjamin Kelley from Wheeling, who was seriously wounded at the recent Philippi battle and is still recovering from that wound. Attached to his name is the word 'Lancers.' A lance is a long pole with a sharp spear at one end, somewhat like the lances the knights of the Middle Ages carried into battle. Lances were very effective in the past against infantry. During the Mexican War, many Mexican cavalrymen carrying lances were known as 'Lancers.'" He chuckled. "I'm not sure if we'll really carry lances or not. We'll find out when we get to Grafton."

The young captain continued, "We'll start the day with a medical examination to see if you're fit to become a cavalryman. This job is strenuous work, so you must be physically very strong, 18 years old or older, and have good teeth. I notice many of you have come here with horses and weapons. That's good! It shows me you are at least fit enough to ride a horse and know how to use firearms. Dr. Mackey will be performing the physical examinations. He will ask you to strip down and he'll poke and prod you, to make sure you're fit for duty. If you pass the physical exam, you'll come back here to my desk. I'll check the condition of your teeth and record your full name and physical characteristics."

There was some mumbling among the men and McGee waited for them to quiet down before continuing.

"Around 1700 hours, the ladies of Morgantown have agreed to prepare a hot supper for everyone. I ask you to be on your best behavior and act as gentlemen with the ladies—no flirting and no alcohol allowed. For those with no place to stay, I've arranged with several families to put you up tonight in their homes or in the haylofts of their barns. They'll also give you breakfast. Of course, you are also welcome to sleep out under the stars. There are many grassy spots down by the river to camp.

"We'll meet here tomorrow morning at 0600 hours dressed and with your horse, if you brought one, saddled and loaded with your equipment. We'll bring one wagon loaded with a kitchen and food. We'll then form a marching column and proceed to Grafton, where all of us will be officially mustered into service by a U.S. Army officer, who will have you take the oath of the United States Army. We'll be two days marching and we'll have marching drills, and other instructions, along the way. Everyone needs to bring a bedroll, and water. Any questions?"

One volunteer asked, "Please, sir, what time is seventeen hundred hours and oh six hundred hours?" Some of the men in line laughed, but others nodded.

"These are military times, based on a 24-hour system for telling time. A day begins at 0000 hours and ends at 2400 hours, which are two different ways to represent midnight. So 0600 hours is 6 AM civilian time and 1700 is 5 PM civilian time. Military and civilian times are the same for the morning hours from midnight to noon. They differ for the afternoon and evening hours. Military afternoon time is civilian time plus 12 hours. From now on we will only use military time, so learn how to use it. Any other questions?"

Another volunteer asked, "Will we be paid for our horses? And how much will we be paid for being a soldier?"

"Once you muster in at Grafton, you will become a private in the United States Army. You will be paid 40 cents a day for your horse and the Army will provide the feed. A value will be placed on your horse that will be paid to you should your horse be killed in the line of duty. Each private soldier will be paid a monthly wage of $12.00 and another $3.00 each month to cover the cost of your clothing. You will be given a uniform, weapons, boots and some other necessaries. For those who did not bring a horse, one will be issued to you along with tack and saddle. Any property issued to you, such as a horse, tack, saddle and firearms, remains the property of the U.S. Army and must be returned when your enlistment is up or when you leave the service for any reason. Any other questions? Then form a line at the doctor's office for the physical. After you're done, come back and line up at my desk so I can check your teeth. You'll get used to standing in lines in the Army, so you might as well start now." The men laughed.

"And don't forget to bring the results of your physical to me," McGee added. "I'll enter your name, age, and physical description in my company record book."

By 5 PM, 100 men, a full company, had passed the physical and dental exams and were signed up in McGee's record book. Several men were turned away who were too young, too old, or did not pass the physical. All the recruits appeared to enjoy the hot supper prepared by the Morgantown ladies and all the men behaved as well as they knew how—at least they behaved as their mothers had taught them to behave around women. Some of them chose to sleep out under the stars in a grassy spot, where they could hear Deckers Creek flowing into the Monongahela River.

Captain McGee invited AJ and Harry to spend the night with him and his wife. AJ was impressed that Harry seemed to know several of the officers from his days living near Morgantown. They greeted him warmly. Again, he wondered why a man like Harry, with his education and connections, was friends with him.

FRIDAY, JULY 19, 1861, 6:00 AM
MORGANTOWN, VIRGINIA

As 6 AM approached, AJ and Harry headed for the meeting place. The men gathered around in a loose group, talking quietly to each other, unsure of what they were to do next. Some stood stiffly next to their horses and some lounged near their equipment, trying to look soldierly. AJ stood next to Shiloh, checking and rechecking his gear.

At exactly 6 AM, Captain McGee rode up and greeted the recruits. He seemed in good spirits. "Good morning, men. I've been informed that the patriotic citizens of Morgantown have arranged a send-off celebration for us that will commence in a few hours. They've asked that we march past a reviewing stand so all can see us. I would like to go over the formation we'll use for this review, and also during our march to Grafton. We will form in four side-by-side columns, with 25 men in each column. Those of you who are without horses will be in front and those with horses will follow."

The men practiced the formation and Captain McGee, with the help of his lieutenants, made adjustments and assignments so the marching column looked balanced. He also instructed the men on foot to try to stay in step as they marched.

By the time the men finished the formation and marching practice, a crowd of people from the area had gathered to listen to a speech by Marshall Dent, editor of the *Virginia Weekly Star*, and to cheer the new recruits. American flags appeared everywhere in the crowd and on the buildings, fluttering in the summer breezes. A local band played "The Star Spangled Banner" while everyone sang.

AJ looked on in disbelief. He had never seen nor imagined, nor had he expected, such a colorful celebration. *And all for us.* He turned to see how Harry was handling the fanfare.

At that moment everyone hushed and gathered around to hear the speech. AJ and the rest of the company stood up tall and tried their best to look like soldiers. Dent was a familiar face and voice to AJ. He and Harry had heard him speak at the first Wheeling Convention nearly two months ago.

Dent began, "We are gathered here today to praise these young men who have willingly volunteered to dedicate their lives to keeping the State of Virginia in the country we love. Some of these young men are from other states in our Union and are here because they share with us a common belief that we are all citizens of just one country. A country that believes that *all* men are created equal and that no man should be a slave to any other man. This, the United States of America, is a country they believe is worth fighting for.

"We live in troubled times, make no mistake about it. Our State of Virginia has been split apart over fundamental moral issues. Here in Morgantown and other counties west of the Alleghenies we have learned to live by trading with friendly neighbors from Pennsylvania, Ohio, Kentucky and other states. Few of us make a living on the backs of slaves. Our brothers on the eastern side of the Alleghenies never understood us and now they wish to enslave *us*, and force us to fight for a cause we do not believe is righteous. These men, standing before us today, are willing to fight for a cause that is morally just. They believe, as the founders of our country did, that no people ever remained free, or ever will, that was not willing to spill their last drop of blood for the maintenance of their liberty. These men know that the United States of America is a country worth fighting for.

"And so we say to you men, thank you and Godspeed. And with His help, stay the course until all Americans are peacefully reunited in one nation, the United States of America, a country that will always be worth fighting for."

The crowd cheered wildly. Tears welled in AJ's eyes. Until that moment he had never been able to fully express his own feelings about joining the cavalry. He wished he had a copy of Dent's speech to send home to his ma and pa.

When Dent finished, a local minister prayed, and then Lieutenant Lemley formed the men into a marching column. Captain McGee rode his horse to the head of the column and barked the order, "Forward... march." The band struck up a patriotic marching song and Mr. Dent led the crowd in three hearty cheers for the Kelley Lancers. AJ could hear the band and the crowd cheering all the while he marched with the column across the bridge over Decker Creek, and the noise still rang in his ears for miles down the road. He felt his own heart beating in unison with the sound of the marching—the most exhilarating moment of his life so far. Even Shiloh arched his neck and pranced until the band could no longer be heard.

SUNDAY, JULY 21, 1861, 6:00 PM
GRAFTON, VIRGINIA

The Kelley Lancers arrived in Grafton on Saturday and were immediately mustered into service for three years, effective July 18, 1861. Lieutenant Samuel Williams, aide to Major General George B. McClellan, administered the oath. A campsite was assigned near the campsite of the Ringgold Cavalry. AJ and Harry received their uniforms and were assigned to different tents. The tents were large conical affairs, similar to the tepees of the Plains Indians, holding 12 men each, which AJ found rather crowded.

Today, the Sabbath, was a day of rest for the Kelley Lancers. After religious services, led by a pastor hired by the Ringgold men, Harry suggested that they visit the Ringgold camp and seek out Captain Keys.

"Captain," Harry said as he and AJ approached their acquaintance from Beallsville, "AJ and I wanted to explain to you why we decided to join the Kelley Lancers instead of your Ringgolds."

"Good day, my friends. No explanation necessary. What's important is we're on the same side. Besides, it took far too much time getting Governor Curtin to make up his mind. In fact, I think if it hadn't been for your Colonel Kelley, the Ringgold Cavalry might still be sitting in Beallsville. Kelley actually wrote to Governor Curtin about us. I think his request broke the political log jam."

"I'm glad it all worked out," AJ said, and Harry nodded his agreement.

Captain Keys replied, "It looks like we'll be seeing a lot of each other over the next few weeks. Colonel Kelley asked me to be the head instructor for training the Kelley Lancers. We'll start the training tomorrow." AJ was pleased to hear that they would learn the essentials from Keys, since he knew him to be knowledgeable.

Later that evening, word spread quickly throughout the Grafton camp of a telegram from Washington announcing a major defeat of the U.S. Army at a place in northeast Virginia near Washington, called Bull Run. The news cast a gloom over the group. AJ immediately went to Harry's tent to commiserate.

"It's a disaster, Harry! Everybody says so!" AJ said. "What'll this mean for us?"

His friend, who was organizing his sleeping bag and camp chest, turned and looked him in the eye, frowning. "AJ, a war is not lost by the outcome of a single battle. This defeat will undoubtedly be a sign to both sides that this is going to be a longer and bloodier war than anyone thought. My faith in God is not shaken. In the end, I believe God *will* banish slavery and those who believe in it. Take heart, my dear friend, some good *will* come out of this disaster."

"All right, Harry, if you say so." AJ was embarrassed about his doubts and his need for reassurance. He missed his family and decided to write to them. Perhaps if he eased their fears in writing, it would help to calm his own.

Grafton, Virginia - July 21, 1861

My dear family,

I'm writing to let you know that all is well with me and Shiloh. We had a grand time in Morgantown. We started with a medical exam, I past with flying colors. We then signed Capt McGee's record book and he wrote down the color of my complekshun, hair, eyes and how tall I am (5 ft 11 in). Later the Morgantown ladies treated us to a hot supper and our Captain invited Harry and me to stay the night with him. Him and his wife are very frendly folks. The next morning before we marched off to Grafton, where I am now writing this letter, the folks in Morgantown put on a big send-off party. Mr. Dent, one of the Morgantown lawyers we saw in Wheeling, gave us a fine patriotic speech. He asked for three cheers for our company. Then we marched off while a band played marching music and I think every one of us held our head high.

It took us about a day and a half to get to our camp here in Grafton. We had lots of marching and riding drills on the way. Some of the men did not have horses and they had to walk. I felt sory for them and sometimes I let some of them ride Shiloh, while I marched next to him, just to be sure he didn't buck them off. When some of the other men with horses seen me giving rides, they let some others ride too. Shiloh held up real well.

By now you probly heard the news about our loss at Bull Run. Please do not worry yourselfs over this. I'm sure old Abe Lincoln will take akshun. Rumors here say that Gen McClellan has been ordered to Washington to take command and that Abe will call up more soldiers before the army has to fight again. Of course, I'm hoping Lincoln will finally call for some more cavalry regments.

I will tell you a little about camp life. We do everything here by someone blowing a tune on a bugle. They blow a tune at 0600 hours (that's 6 AM) to get up. Some men think that's early. I'm guessing they don't live on a farm. They blow a different tune for Roll Call and you better not miss that or you get double watch Duty. They blow yet another tune for brekfast which means you have to feed your horse first before you can eat. Then they blow another tune to water your horse and that means taking him down to the nearest creek. The bugle calls go on and on until 2100 (9 PM) when the tune is played for bedtime we must go to sleep.

12 men sleep in a tent. I have made a frend in my tent, Oliver Swink, from Ohio. He's 19 and a little homesick like me. He has found a stray kitten and it sleeps with him.

You can share this letter with any one you think might be intrested. Please write soon. I love and miss ALL of you.

Your son (and brother), Alexander

AJ thought about writing a letter to Sophia, but since he hadn't asked her permission to write, he decided it might not be proper. He hoped she would write to him.

Tuesday, July 23, 1861, 9:00 pm
McClellan's HQ, Beverly, Virginia

McClellan read again the telegram received on the 22nd from the War Department in Washington: "Circumstances make your presence here necessary. Charge Rosecrans or some other General with your present department and come hither without delay."

He had already sent a telegraph to General Cox in the Kanawha Valley informing him of his orders to go to Washington, and instructing Cox "if possible, drive Wise beyond the Gauley Bridge," referring to a 500-foot-long wooden bridge on which the James River & Kanawha Turnpike crossed over the Gauley River before continuing on to Charleston.

Next he summoned General Rosecrans to his office to discuss the transfer of command of the Department of Ohio.

"General Rosecrans, it's my pleasure to offer you command of all forces in the Department of Ohio. I've discussed this appointment with General Scott, who agreed with me that you are the best man for this job. Do you accept?"

"Yes, I do, General, but I trust we still have time before you depart to brief me on your strategic plans for this department."

Handing Rosecran sheets of handwritten plans, McClellan said, "I've left you this memorandum detailing plans for going on the defensive, which General Scott believes is necessary, given the outcome of Bull Run. At present I don't know who the Confederates will send against you, but I feel certain they have not yet given up on their attempts to reclaim the western Virginia counties. It will be up to you to carry out defensive actions to keep the territorial gains we achieved and, when the opportunity arises, to go on the offensive and drive once more the Confederates out of this department."

"Yes, I agree we should be on the defensive for the time being. I have other items I would like to talk over with you. Can we ride together to the Grafton station and discuss them on the way?"

"Of course, stay with me and let's talk until my train departs."

Rosecrans and McClellan discussed the problems associated with long supply lines and the difficulties defending the western Virginia mountains with the Federal forces scattered and isolated throughout the area. McClellan emphasized the use of the telegraph to keep all commanders informed and to give orders. It was the battlefield innovation he was most proud of.

As McClellan boarded the train for Wheeling, where he would transfer to the Pennsylvania Central Railroad headed east to Washington, he accepted Rosecrans's salute and they wished each other success. He thought, *That was a smooth transfer, but I have to admit, I'm worried. The Confederates will most certainly be back, their confidence restored by this success of theirs at Bull Run. They'll want to drive our forces out of western Vir-*

ginia. Despite his orders to go on the defensive, I hope Rosecrans will still think offensively. Well, I have to leave it to him now as I have my hands full elsewhere. Hope he's up to it.

THURSDAY, JULY 24, 1861, 9:00 AM
CONFEDERATE GENERAL H. R. JACKSON HQ,
MONTEREY, VIRGINIA

Confederate Brigadier General William W. Loring looked around at the bands of ragged, demoralized men as he entered the Confederate camp at Monterey. *So this is what's left of General Garnett's defeated force,* he thought, as he rode towards the headquarters tent occupied by Georgia's Brigadier General Henry R. Jackson.

Loring, a native of North Carolina, was an experienced and proven soldier. As a young boy of 16, he had run off to fight in the Seminole Wars in Florida. With only one arm—his left arm having been shattered in the battle of Chapultepec during the Mexican War—he was still an imposing figure. Three times he had been wounded in the Mexican War and two times he was brevetted for bravery.

Jackson welcomed Loring into his tent and after introductions Jackson said, "Not a pretty sight, are they? Many more men are still laid up sick and some are still suffering from malnutrition. They all wanted to disband and go home after their ordeal, but I stepped in and did the best I could to buck them up and put some flesh back on their bones. But these men are still afraid of the Federals and it will take awhile to rebuild their courage. In the meantime, I separated out the best of them and established defensive positions. I certainly hope you are bringing some well-trained fresh troops in, so these boys can remember what proud Southern soldiers look like."

"Have you ordered some clothes, shoes, and firearms for these men?" Loring asked.

"Yes, I did that as soon as we entered Staunton. But it seems that everything in the way of supplies went to the men under Beauregard and Johnston," Jackson replied.

"How did the men respond to our victory at Bull Run?" Loring asked.

"Some gave out a few cheers, but many of them just don't seem to care. They are very homesick," Jackson replied.

"Well... Richmond is sending us three fresh regiments and I'll telegraph them to send clothing, shoes and other supplies for these men. Now, I've heard some good things about you, General. Don't you have any good news for me before I relieve you?" Loring asked.

"I'll tell you what I've done and let you be the judge whether it's good news or bad. Between here and Huttonsville to the west there are two mountain passes. The highest is Cheat Mountain, the closest to Huttonsville. It's now occupied by the Federals and they've built a very strong fortress up there. Except to reconnoiter that position, I've made no attempt to attack or get past that fortification. The second mountain pass and the closest to Monterey is called Back Allegheny Mountain. There I've stationed my best regiment, the twelfth Georgia under Colonel Edward Johnson with the Third Arkansas and Fifty-second Virginia regiments in reserve.

"There is also a pass across the Alleghenies on a rough road running from Millborough on the Virginia Central Railroad, where I've posted the Twenty-first Virginia commanded by Colonel William Gilham and the Sixth North Carolina. What you see here is the Thirty-seventh and Forty-fourth Virginia and the First Georgia," Jackson replied.

"General Jackson, I'm impressed with what you've accomplished. I'll relieve you of command and I'll stay here a few days so I can become familiar with the men and the terrain. My intention is to find a way to flank that Federal fortress on Cheat Mountain and defeat those Federals, so I will be heading west. I'll keep you informed."

MONDAY, JULY 29, 1861, 2:00 PM
MONTEREY, VIRGINIA

Lee watched the scenery from his rail car. He took several deep breaths, to try to allay the anxiety that gripped his chest and gut. He was heading to Staunton, and from there by horseback to Monterey, to take command of Confederate forces in western Virginia. He had been President Davis's second choice for this job. After Joseph Johnston's impressive performance at Bull Run, Davis had asked if Johnston would take over in western Virginia. Johnston refused. Lee had accepted, reluctantly. He felt obligated to go, especially after the death of his friend Garnett. He still felt a load of guilt on his shoulders over that tragic event.

It was a dismal situation, he felt. He had finally come to realize what Porterfield and Garnett had tried to tell him—many, perhaps most, of the western Virginians did not support secession and were determined to break away from Confederate control. They wanted to secede from Virginia and they supported the Union troops pouring over their border from Ohio and Pennsylvania. To make things worse, Davis had not given him full command in the same sense that Rosecrans was given command of all the Federal forces in western Virginia. He was being asked to "inspect and consult" the plans of the generals Loring, Floyd and Wise in the area and use the force of his personality to "persuade" these generals to get along together, and accept his advice. *It is as if the Confederate War Department leadership knows nothing about the concept of unity of command at the highest command level. I'm sure Johnston knew what this assignment entailed and that is why he refused the offer,* he thought.

Lee, along with his staff of two, disembarked from the train at Staunton and continued on to Monterey on horseback. There Lee saw for the first time the sickness and demoralization of the forces that had been Garnett's army. Lee conferred with General H.R. Jackson for a few days, during which he learned that Jackson had already been relieved by Loring and that Loring had moved his quarters to Huntersville, where he was planning a flanking movement on the Federal forces on Cheat Mountain and at Elkwater. Lee and his staff prepared to set out to find Loring.

Friday, August 2, 1861, 9:00 pm
Grafton, Virginia

The bugle sounded the last notes of the day. AJ could hear the soft snores of his friend Oliver on the bunk next to him, but sleep wouldn't come. He tossed and turned on his bed sack—a mattress ticking bag stuffed with straw—as he thought back on the grueling first week of cavalry training. It was not what he had expected. Every muscle hurt, including several he didn't even know he had. Being a cavalryman obviously called for the use of different muscles than farming. Captain Keys led the training, as expected, because he was the best and most experienced cavalryman in the camp. AJ recalled Keys's brief speech on the first day of training.

"Many cavalry experts will tell you it takes at least two years to become an acceptable cavalryman. I know this to be true, as it has taken me that long to be where I am today in my training and I still don't know everything I would like to know. You will probably receive at most a month of training before you see action. In this time, I've been ordered to teach you the basics all cavalrymen must know. Keep in mind that training is never-ending and you will do well to practice, *all the time*, everything you learn in these four weeks. It is only through practice that you can expect to better an enemy cavalryman in a fight. In short, what you learn this month can save your life.

"Your Captain McGee and his officers have told me they want to be student cavalrymen just like you. I'm impressed by your officers, for I believe leaders can only lead men if they first know what they are asking from their men. 'Follow me!' should be the cry of every officer who leads men into battle."

The captain had explained that he had divided the Kelley Lancers into four platoons and asked four infantry sergeants from a nearby Ohio infantry regiment to be in charge for this first week of dismounted marching training. They were experienced, tough men who wouldn't tolerate any back talk. Keys instructed the Lancers to listen well to what the sergeants had to say and to do exactly what they told them to do. "If you don't know your right foot from your left, learn it now, before the sergeants have to teach you, using their rather unpleasant method," he warned.

AJ tried again to fall asleep, but it seemed he could still hear Captain Keys and the infantry sergeants barking commands: "platoon, right face, platoon, left face, platoon, right oblique, platoon, forward quicktime, march, platoon, halt, platoon, about face, platoon, left oblique, platoon, forward double-quicktime, march, platoon, halt." At first AJ had chuckled along with the other men as they ran into one another and stepped on toes. Once he and his friend Oliver had turned the wrong way and knocked each other down, which brought forth gales of laughter. But Captain Keys and his sergeants were not laughing. Keys yelled, "*Think* about what you are doing, men! You must learn these steps and many more as you'll perform them side-by-side on horseback at a walk, trot, canter and gallop. If you run into one another and knock your friend down now, what do you think you will do to your horses when you're mounted? Do you want to wound or perhaps even kill your horse?"

So the week slowly passed and the aches and pains grew. The sergeants took no pity on them. They yelled at everyone, called them disgustingly profane names, stamped on their feet, and slapped them on their heads. By the end of the week, almost everyone in the company was bruised and hurting, but they had learned all the marching commands.

His friend and tentmate, Oliver Swink, was an eager nineteen-year-old from southern Ohio, a stocky lad with orange-red curly hair and the beginnings of a mustache around the corners of his mouth. Many times the cavalrymen were lined up in alphabetical order, so he and Oliver had often found themselves next to each other and had begun to talk. He was a farmer too, the youngest of four brothers and the only one of them to volunteer so far. He had been ready to leave home—"They all treat me like a baby," he said—but he, like AJ, felt homesick. In their free time the two liked to share their favorite memories of "back home" and play with the stray orange kitten Oliver had adopted, which he called Red. AJ teased him that the kitten must remind him of his redheaded brothers at home.

They also had taken to singing duets together. Oliver had a song-book, a hymn collection brought from home, and in their free time they tried out harmonies on different hymns. They both thought AJ's bass and Oliver's tenor blended especially well on "Am I a Soldier of the Cross." Some of their other tentmates had commented on how well they sounded together. *This is a camp of singing soldiers,* AJ thought drowsily. Often the evening air rang with the sound of soldiers raising their voices around the fires, sometimes a single voice, sometimes blending together in a whole choir of voices.

AJ finally dozed off while vaguely recalling Captain Keys saying, "Next week, men, you will learn how to use a saber—dismounted."

In his half-sleep, he muttered, "Can't wait."

SATURDAY, AUGUST 3, 1861, 6:00 AM
GRAFTON, VIRGINIA

AJ dressed, attended roll call, and rushed over to the stables to feed and groom Shiloh.

"How are you doing, big fella?" AJ dropped Shiloh's feed into his nose bag and carefully inspected the muscular gelding while brushing him. "You're sure full of yourself this morning," he said as the horse nudged him with his big head and almost knocked him down. Shiloh had not been ridden for several days.

Oliver arrived too and began to feed and groom Maggie, the rangy sorrel mare assigned to him. Oliver's family had not had a horse they could spare for him. Today, maybe, the two of them would get to ride their mounts around the camp.

After watering his horse and retying him to the picket line, AJ had a powerful hunger. He headed for the table shaded by a tarpaulin that served as kitchen and dining area for him and seven other men—their "mess." The not-very-savory fare was issued to them on a regular basis, but they had to cook it themselves. He and his messmates had at least built themselves a stove and a crude table with stools hacked from logs. One of the men had just finished frying his bacon in the single pan they all shared, so AJ flung a piece of bacon into the pan for himself and positioned it over the snapping fire. He poured himself a cup of mudlike coffee and stirred a spoonful of brown sugar into it.

He was almost done with his breakfast when he heard the familiar "Good morning, AJ. And how are you this fine morning?" from behind him. It made his heart glad.

"It's real good to see you, Harry! Would you like some coffee, if you can call it that? And how did you like this week's marching training?"

"No, thank you, on the coffee. The training was harder—and more painful—than expected... but most necessary, I'm sure. How about you?"

"Pretty much the same. Tho' I thought the infantry sergeants were brutes. I got the feeling they don't think so much of us cavalrymen. I know a lot of people think it's not real work to ride a horse. Oh, well... that week is over. Heard any news from home, or any news at all?"

"You probably already know that Colonel Kelley was promoted to brigadier general. I understand his surgery went well and he's feeling better. I overheard some of the infantry officers say they expect to see him walking around here soon. For now, he rides in a carriage when he wants to get around. And I hear he's planning to visit his cavalry company and meet everyone."

AJ was astonished. "Kelley here? And meeting all of us? I guess that means more spit-and-polish work for us, don't it?"

"Probably so, but won't it be nice to meet him? I hear he worked for the B&O Railroad for many years and is friendly with the president of that line. Speaking of generals, I overheard some of the infantry officers saying they expect General Robert E. Lee will be sent up our way to take command, after General Garnett was killed at Corricks Ford."

"Now that's sending the big gun, ain't it? I thought Lee was in command of *all* the Confederate forces."

"It's not really clear. I think he's only in command of all the Virginia militia right now, but he's been working under Jeff Davis, the President of the Confederacy... Oh, one other piece of news—apparently next week the Second Wheeling Convention will reconvene. I understand they'll begin to work on statehood for the western counties of Virginia."

"That's really somethin'! What they goin' to call the new state?"

"I've heard some calling it Kanawha and others calling it New Virginia."

"Well, Harry, so long as it's in the Union, whatever it's called, I'll surely welcome it!"

The bugle sounded Sick Call and Harry left to attend to some duties. AJ noticed the number of men heading toward the hospital had steadily increased throughout the week. Several of the men in his own tent had fallen ill, some with fever, some with vomiting and diarrhea. One had measles, he had heard. So far he had avoided any symptoms, but he was glad he had Ma's little box of remedies in his chest. Like she had told him to do, he slept outside when the weather allowed. Often he would roll up in a blanket in the field and let Shiloh graze around him on a long line tied to his halter, rolling over to give him a new spot when he had eaten all the grass. Sometimes Shiloh even laid down beside him.

He wondered, *Is all the sickness caused by our hard training, or the terrible food, or something else?* He recalled his mother several times taking him as a child to a neighbor's house when a child was sick there. She said it was best to get the childhood diseases as a child, not as an adult. AJ had asked her how the diseases could pass from one child to another. She said she didn't know, but she thought something moved through the air that carried the sickness between folks. *I think I got every sickness that came around, so I 'spect she was right.*

At the 1000 hours Drill Call, word was passed to everyone that at the 1400 hours Mounted Drill, General Kelley himself would inspect the company. Everyone was expected to have his horse well groomed and tack shining. Boots were to be polished and clothes clean with no mud spots. Arms would not be worn, since training in arms had not started yet. The company would be mounted and formed in one file for the inspection.

AJ looked forward to the chance to show off Shiloh, as well as the chance to meet the General. He had heard some of the other men in camp praising his horse as he rode by, and although he pretended not to hear, it always made his chest swell with pride. He spent the next two hours polishing his boots and brushing his uniform. Most of the last two hours were spent cleaning his saddle and tack, brushing Shiloh, and polishing Shiloh's hooves. As 1400 hours neared, he and the other men walked their mounts to the parade ground and stood in line next to their horses. General Kelley arrived five minutes later in an open one-horse carriage accompanied by an aide. Captain McGee called the men to attention, and ordered them to salute the general. Then General Kelley asked Captain McGee to have each trooper walk, with his horse, up to his carriage and introduce himself and his horse.

When AJ realized what was about to happen, his stomach dropped. The thought of walking up by himself, being the center of attention for that moment and being expected to talk with General Kelley started him trembling. He feared that his knees would give way and he would tumble to the ground in front of everyone, and that would be the end of his cavalry career. Fortunately, he was in the center of the line and had some time to prepare himself. He rehearsed in his mind, over and over, what he would say. When his turn came, he took a deep breath and briskly walked Shiloh toward the General's carriage and asked his horse to stand. He saluted the General and said, "Sir, my name is Alexander J. Swaney. I'm from Smithfield, Pennsylvania. My horse is a Morgan horse and his name is Shiloh." At the mention of his name, Shiloh's ears perked and he whinnied softly, which made the general smile.

"I am very pleased to meet you, Private Swaney… and you too, Shiloh. Your horse is a fine-looking animal, a hardy breed, and he talks, I see. Tell me, why did you decide to join the Kelley Lancers instead of one of the Pennsylvania cavalry companies, like the Ringgold Cavalry?"

AJ hesitated. He had not expected the general to ask him a question, let alone one that would require a complicated answer. His voice cracked as he tried to speak. He cleared his throat and tried again. "Well, sir, it's kind of a long story. My friend Harry Hagans, who's my preacher and also from Smithfield, asked me to go with him to the First Wheeling Convention back in May. We met Captain Keys in Beallsville along the way and he was very kind to us and talked to us 'bout the Ringgolds, but at the time he couldn't get his company in the service, so we didn't sign up with him. After the Convention, we both wanted to help our Virginia neighbors here keep their freedom. Smithfield, you know, is close to Morgantown, so we stopped there on the way home and met Dr. McGee, who told us later he was formin' the Kelley Lancers, so we jumped aboard. And that's how we decided to join up with your cavalry company."

"Thank you, Private. I'm very proud to have you, and Shiloh, in my company," said Kelley, his face straight but with a twinkle in his eye. The general said nothing further. *Does that mean he wants me to return to my place in line now?* AJ decided to walk back, but first, he came to attention, saluted and said, "Thank *you*, sir, and I am glad to see you're healing from your wound."

After all the men had introduced themselves, the general expressed his pride in getting to know each man in the Kelley Lancers and asked God to bless the men and keep them safe during drills and in future battles.

After Captain McGee dismissed them, Oliver poked AJ in the ribs and teased him for taking up all the general's time and making him stand longer than was necessary in the hot sun. AJ just grinned, ducked his head, and didn't respond. By now he knew never to try to explain why he did something, as it would only worsen the men's teasing.

Later that evening, Harry told him the general had said, "So you're the friend of Swaney, who took him on that long trip to Wheeling?" Even Harry teased his friend about being so talkative with General Kelley. "What's come over you, AJ? You were always a quiet one."

AJ knew it had been only his nervousness, but said, "Maybe your way with words has finally rubbed off on me, Harry." They talked together for an hour or so, and AJ found his feelings for Harry almost returned to normal. Everything was so new and the training so physically grueling that he hadn't really had time lately to ponder that dark time with the slave called Abraham, when he had first discovered Harry's "criminal activities," as he thought of them. Although AJ knew the Fugitive Slave Law was controversial, it was still the law and he couldn't approve of any instance of breaking the law. But now that they were at war and he was fighting to end slavery, among other reasons, he was beginning to see things differently.

SATURDAY, AUGUST 3, 1861, 8:00 AM
GENERAL LORING HQ, HUNTERSVILLE, VIRGINIA

"Halt! Who goes there?" Loring's picket yelled as General Lee and his staff, consisting of Colonel John A. Washington and Captain Walter H. Taylor, reined in their horses.

"Who are you and what do you want?" the picket bluntly asked.

Captain Taylor replied, "This is General Lee and his staff and we are here to see General Loring."

"Oh, is that so? And I'm Abe Lincoln! I need to see some identification," the sentry snapped.

Captain Taylor showed their identification and the orders signed by President Jefferson Davis. It was too much for the sentry to believe. Orders signed by the President of the Confederacy, and a colonel claiming to be a nephew of General George Washington?

"You wait here," the sentry said, as he called to another sentry to get the officer in charge.

The officer came up quickly, recognized Captain Taylor, saluted and said, "General Lee, I apologize for the delay. The sentry is only doing his duty. We're in territory near the enemy and we must take every precaution."

"We understand, son, and are very impressed by your guards. Can you take us to General Loring's office?" Lee replied calmly.

The officer led Lee and his staff to a large tent where Loring and several others were discussing the organization of his supply train and the stocking of his depot. After the officer of the guard announced that General Lee was here and wanted to talk with him, Loring invited Lee and staff into the tent and had some chairs set up for them.

Loring got right to the point, saying, "General Lee, we're very busy organizing my supply train and depot right now. What is the purpose of your visit?"

"General, I have been sent by our President to help coordinate the forces we have sent to western Virginia to drive the Federals out of our state," Lee replied.

"Well, General, I believe that is the assignment that was given to *me* in my orders. Have my orders been changed? Do you or President Davis believe I'm incapable of following my orders? Have Confederate forces other than mine been sent to western Virginia? If so, where are they and why was I not informed?"

Lee was surprised by the barrage of questions and the obviously hostile attitude of General Loring. In his typical gentlemanly manner, Lee explained, "General, President Davis and I have full confidence in your ability to follow orders. Your orders have not been changed and I am not here to take command of your army. General Wise's Legion has been driven out of the Kanawha Valley by Federal forces and General Floyd has been given orders to combine his force with that of General Wise and take charge of operations in the Kanawha Valley."

"Why have I not been informed of these plans for Floyd and Wise? And why are they not under *my* command? We must have one general in command of *all* Confederate forces in western Virginia, in order to drive all the Federal forces out of our state. Is that too much to ask of you and President Davis? Do you think for one moment that McClellan was not in charge of *all* the Federal forces that drove the Confederate forces of Wise and Garnett out of western Virginia? I have far more battle experience than you and President Davis combined. Neither of you have been tested in battle the way I've been tested, and now you have the audacity to come here as an advisor to *me*?"

Lee did not immediately reply. He had learned long ago to wait before speaking when the hot wave of anger and resentment flared in him. That lesson had served him well many times. But he still had his angry thoughts. *How dare Loring talk that way about his President, or me? Davis and I both attended West Point and Loring did not. And Jeff Davis served under President Pierce as Secretary of War for years, and Loring did not. What experience does Loring have in strategic planning? But it will do me no good to bring these facts to his attention. I will take another approach.* Lee sighed and then said, "General, you are correct. We do need to improve our command structure and your battle experience far exceeds that of President Davis and myself combined. But I look upon my assigned role as a brother-in-arms wanting to help you defeat our common enemy in any way I can. I have no *direct* command of an army. I am not in competition with you. I have only a brain full of ideas to share with you. You may ignore any of my ideas as you choose, but I think it better to have the views of two generals when making strategic plans."

Loring sat in silence for a minute, considering Lee's response. Finally, he nodded and smiled. "General Lee, I will work with you and have you review the plans, as my staff and I develop them. But right now, I'm organizing my supply train and stocking my depot. You and your staff are welcome to stay with us as long as you like, but it will be at least two days before we start planning our attack on the Federal forces at Elkwater and Cheat Mountain. If you wish to scout the area, I suggest you base yourself near Valley Mountain and scout north as far Elkwater. As you approach Elkwater, you can see where the Federals are now building a fortification. My scouts tell me they have completed the fortress at the summit of Cheat Mountain. Any plans we make will have to consider these two Federal positions."

"Thank you, General Loring, an excellent suggestion. I will take your advice and move to Valley Mountain and see what I can discover there. I hope to see you in a few days."

Tuesday, August 6, 1861, 8:00 pm
Meeting of Generals Floyd and Wise, C.S.A,
White Sulphur Springs, Virginia

The two generals walked into the meeting room at White Sulphur Springs resort at the same time. They eyed one another, then circled the table like two tomcats meeting for the first time and looking for a vantage point from which to pounce.

"Well!" said Floyd, "They probably gave us this round table so we couldn't fight over who should sit at the head."

"Now, now, General Floyd, you know I don't have to sit at the head of a table to have an advantage over you. I simply use the brain God gave me. For example, I spoke with your Colonel Heath before we entered this room and he told me that his Forty-fifth Virginia regiment was intending to join the rest of your brigade and move *west* to the Kanawha Valley along the same route that I just used to bring my legion *east* and away from that God-forsaken place. Why, the populace there is wholly disaffected and traitorous. Please, General Floyd, enlighten me as to why you would want to do this."

"Well, General Wise, I have orders to immediately regain the ground you just lost and place you and your Legion under my command. I expect us to leave in a day or two."

"That is a foolish plan, General Floyd, for two good reasons. First, my men are exhausted and their supplies almost gone. I need at least two weeks for rest and resupply. Second, I favor drawing the enemy toward us and fighting on ground *we* choose. Let the enemy cope with the transportation problems associated with that forty-mile-long Fayette Wilderness that extends to Gauley Bridge, not us."

"No, no, Wise! We cannot leave the Kanawha Valley in the hands of the Federals. We must drive them away or, unmolested, they will stay."

The back-and-forth bickering went on and on, until they finally tired and left the room. The meeting that General Lee had hoped would mend their relations only worsened them.

SUNDAY, AUGUST 11, 1861
GRAFTON, VIRGINIA

AJ finally had an hour or so to himself. He decided to use it to write home to his family about the past two weeks of cavalry training. His forearm ached and his wrist felt weak from the days of saber exercises, but he picked up the pencil anyway.

Grafton, Virginia - August 11, 1861

My dear family,

Please forgive me for not writing sooner. I was so tired from the marching training that I just fell asleep ever time I tried to write. There is much more to being a cavalryman than I expected. While I'm a good rider, I find I'm not so good at marching and I'm bad at the saber. Most of us seem to have two left feet and we still mix up the marching commands. The instructors laughed at us and as a jibe, told us we can't teach our horses marching commands until we know them ourselves. They told us we would many times be fighting on foot and the quickest way to move a large body of men from one place to another is by marching in step. It makes sense till you get commands like "platoon, by the right flank, march" or "platoon, by the left obleek, march." While all these strange commands are being shouted at you, they expect everyone to stay in step. Lots of funning at the start as men ran into one another and some got knocked down (me), especially when we march quick-time and double quick-time. The instructors didn't laugh. They just shouted at us. So I been prac-

ticing the commands over and over in my mind each night before I sleep.

The last week was the worse yet. Lt Anisansel of the Ringgold taught us how to use the saber. Remember me telling you about Captain Keys we met in Bealsville last May, on our way to Wheeling? Well, he is here leading the Ringgold cavalry and they are much better trained than we are. Lt Anisansel was in the French cavalry, he says, and is very good with the sabre. We started to practice standing alone so we would not butcher our horses, as Lt Anisansel said we might. We first learned the meaning of the right and left side of the gripe; the terms by tierce, and by quarte (I think they mean gripping a sa-ber with three or four fingers), how to draw the saber from the scabard, and return the saber to the scabard. Then we learned the moulinet (sp?). That's not some French dance. It is a way to move a saber in a clockwise circle first to our right, then to our left. Then this is repeated in the other direction. All of this we were told was suposed to "render the joints of the arm and wrist suple." I don' know what supple mean but I can tell you the muscles in my right arm hurt mighty bad and my right wrist feels limp. I can bearly hold this pencil.

Next Lt Anisansel explained the dismounted positions of a trooper and how to use the saber against infantry and enemy cavalry. We lerned guard, point (right, left, front, rear), cut (right, left, front, rear) and parry (right and left against a sabre, against a bayonet, and against a lance). Lt Anisansel showed us all of this from standing and on horseback by using some assistants to play enemy infantry, cavalry, and lancers.

Now I know why our instructors told us it takes 2 yrs to train for cavalry. All during this past week we practiced handling the sabre

from the ground. Right now I think it would be downright danger-
ous to our selves and to our mounts to carry or use a saber while rid-
ing, even at a trot. To try it at a gallop would be madness. It's going
to take us awhile to get used to that weppon.

Next week we start with firearms—revolvers, shotguns, carbines and
muskets. Hopefully that will be easy training since most of us have
grown up hunting with some sort of gun. Capt Keys wants me to
show how to shoot my long rifle using Shiloh to rest and steady the ri-
fle. Harry probly put him up to it, since I would NEVER volunteer
to do it. It makes me feel like a show-off. But the Capt. asked me so I
will do it.

I am staying well. But two men in my tent has some fever. I am
looking after the horse of one till he's up again.

I go to prayer meeting every night they have it. Oliver and me sing a
lot to pass the time. I would like you to hear our harmonies. We get a
few compliments.

Hope all is well there. I have not yet received any mail from you.
Please send your letters to Grafton, Virginia attention Kelley Lancers.

My love to everyone.

Alexander

PS If you have any sheet music or magazines you can spare I would
shurely enjoy them. And please tell the Mosiers that I miss them too.

Monday, August 12, 1861
General Lee HQ, Valley Mountain, Virginia

Much to Lee's pleasant surprise, General Loring and his staff joined him
in his humble headquarters—a large tent where he slept with his two

aides. Word had been passed to Loring that General Lee had just been commissioned as a full general (two ranks higher than Loring's brigadier commission) in the Confederate Army. Lee was now one of just three full generals and Loring, a stickler for protocol, had come to pay his respects and plan with Lee how they could defeat the Federal fortifications at Elkwater and Cheat Mountain.

"General Lee," Loring said on entering Lee's tent, "may I be the first to congratulate you on your appointment to your new rank."

"Thank you, General Loring, that's very thoughtful. I do hope you brought your staff with you, so we can begin our plans together to drive the Union men out of our state."

"I have brought them, sir. They are standing just outside and are ready when you are to start planning. I also brought some additional tents, so we can plan together in one place."

"May I ask before we begin our planning sessions whether you have given instructions to General Henry Jackson to establish that camp we discussed about twelve miles east of Cheat Mountain, along the Staunton-Parkersburg Turnpike?"

"Yes, sir, I have. The camp has been named Camp Bartow and it's located near Travelers Repose Inn. Perhaps you stayed at that inn when you first arrived?"

"Yes, we did. A very pleasant inn… How many men do you have stationed there and how many are stationed here with you?"

"My army is in two divisions. At Camp Bartow are 5,000 men under the command of General Jackson. The division here has about 6,000 men under my command. Of course, those numbers include men who are sick, which has greatly reduced the size of my effectives. As you know we have been stricken with measles here. Why do you ask, sir?"

"Well… some of the ideas I have involve attacking the Federal forts at Elkwater and Cheat Mountain at the same time. Such a plan would require splitting your army into five or six brigades. But before we can fully explore this, or any other plan, we need maps. I understand you have a brilliant mapmaker in your engineer, Jed Hotchkiss."

"Yes, he's very good. An intelligent man."

"Then let us set him to work at once creating maps, while your men scout these mountains to find ways to flank the two Federal fortresses. I do not advise making frontal attacks. Most of our boys are still mostly untested. While I trust they will always bravely do their duty, green troops tend to break and run, as you well know."

"General Lee, I will handle these details. There are three major factors we must take these into consideration in our planning... the incessant rain, cold and sickness."

"Yes, General, I certainly agree. If possible we should have our plans completed as soon as possible to take advantage of warmer weather, if there is such a thing in these mountains. But now, I must leave you and visit with Generals Floyd and Wise, who are contending with the Federal General Cox in the Kanawha Valley and, I might jokingly add, contending with each other. I am afraid their bitter political rivalry is interfering with their military judgment at times. I have also been informed that General Rosecrans is planning a move south to join with General Cox and crush the forces under Wise and Floyd. I must warn them before that happens. I should be gone no more than a week or two. When I return perhaps Hotchkiss will have maps for us and your scouts information to help us in planning our strategy."

SATURDAY, AUGUST 24, 1861
GRAFTON, VIRGINIA

The third week of training went comparatively smoothly for the men of the Kelley Lancers. All understood the advantages and limitations of the various firearms available. As ordered by Captain Keys, AJ prepared to demonstrate shooting his long rifle at a 5-inch target 250 yards away. AJ found the thought of the demonstration embarrassing, but he resolved to hide his discomfort and do his best.

Harry participated in the demonstration with AJ. He held the already saddled Shiloh until AJ got himself into position on the firing range. All involved with the placement and retrieval of the target agreed that AJ was exactly 250 yards from the white target containing a 5-inch diameter black bull's eye. Several officers from infantry regiments had heard about AJ's long rifle and gathered to watch, chatting while they waited.

AJ carefully studied the wind, then loaded his long rifle. He whistled for Shiloh as he had done so many times before and watched as Shiloh perked his ears, snorted until Harry released him, then cantered up to AJ and stopped. AJ positioned Shiloh parallel to the target and asked the horse to stand. Laying his rifle across the saddle, he checked the wind once more and warned Shiloh he was about to fire. Some of the men watching flinched more than Shiloh when the rifle cracked. The target-men ran the 250 yards to the target. The runners returned with the target, big grins on their faces. AJ's ball had hit almost dead center.

The infantry officers gathered around to view the target while Captain Keys congratulated AJ. One infantry colonel asked AJ if he had thought of joining the U.S. Army sharpshooters. He replied, "No, I just want to be in the cavalry." Some shook their heads and walked away. Some patted him on the back and congratulated him before leaving.

Word of AJ's feat spread through the camp and soon he was asked to repeat his performance for General Kelley and his staff. General Kelley asked him to fire at the target five times so he could see the size of his spread. After five shots, the runners left to retrieve the target. While awaiting their return, AJ explained to General Kelley that the size of the spread depended mostly on the variability of the crosswinds. He expected the size of the grouping to be small today because the crosswinds were light and steady.

When the runners returned, all could see that AJ's five shots had ripped out about a 3-inch diameter hole in the bull's eye. General Kelley said, "Private Swaney, I'm impressed with your shooting, and with your horse's training." He patted AJ on the back. "Good job, son."

AJ didn't know how to respond. He was full of conflicting emotions: self-conscious, awkward, but proud and glad that his skill and all the hours of training were valued. He hoped they could be used to win this war, not just to gain him unwanted attention.

When Kelley and those attending him had left, Harry stayed behind. He patted AJ on the shoulder. "Congratulations, my friend. That was some fancy shooting!"

"Well, I was glad the wind didn't kick up. It's a lot harder to shoot straight when it's windy."

Harry laughed. "My friend, all I have to say is I'm glad you're on our side!"

Back at the stables with Shiloh, removing the tack and grooming him, AJ became aware of a deep sadness settling on him. He tried to understand why. He should have been happy that the demonstration had gone so well today. It was Sophia, he decided. If things were different between them, he could have written to her and told her about this afternoon, about General Kelley congratulating him. She would have been thrilled and proud for him. With her, it wouldn't have felt like bragging. She would have understood.

SATURDAY, AUGUST 24, 1861
GRAFTON, VIRGINIA, LATE EVENING

Later that day, Captain Keys met with Captain McGee, saying he had two items he needed to pass on. "First," Keys said, "the Ringgold Cavalry just received orders to proceed tomorrow, via the B&O Railroad, to Mineral County, Virginia. I regret I will no longer be available to instruct the

Kelley Lancers. Most of your men are taking the training very seriously and I know you can handle the last training week yourself. I recommend you combine all the lessons learned in the first three weeks' training into field maneuvers, leading up to a final test in which each man must use all his weapons against an infantry dummy. Please extend my regrets and best wishes to your men."

"Thank you, Captain Keys. You've done a fine job training the men, my officers and me. What is the other item you wanted to pass on?"

"Well, this is disturbing information, but it involves something we need all our cavalrymen to know about. I just learned of a horrifying incident involving a squad of Burdsall's First Ohio Cavalry. Apparently they were on a scouting expedition between our fortress at Cheat Mountain and the Greenbrier Valley. These were good men and were on the lookout for trouble, especially from bushwhackers, who they heard were operating in the area. The squad was crossing a creek and stopped in the middle to water their horses. When they started to leave, several bushwhackers, hidden on a nearby bluff, opened fire with rifles and killed seven of the men. Only one man got away. He thinks there were seven bushwhackers, because all seven men in his squad fell at the same time and he remembers only one volley fired by the bushwhackers."

"My God!" McGee cried out. "Did they catch them?"

"No. Burdsall took the rest of his cavalry company and a company of infantry and combed the area, trying to find their nest. They had run like the cowards they are. The news gets worse—it seems many of the bushwhackers hate anyone in the army, regardless of which side a soldier is on. They are lawless, cold-blooded killers who are taking this war as an opportunity to even old scores with neighbors they don't like. Our men have found civilians hanging from trees and many other outrages. One of our soldiers was found beheaded—his head on a pike with a sign saying, 'Some bloody deeds are done in these hills.' I understand many of our commanders are now taking action to hunt down these killers and give them swift justice."

"Thank you for the warning. I'll make sure our men are informed. I haven't heard yet of any outrages like that in the Grafton area, but it seems those bushwhackers are like a bad disease that can spread anywhere. Good luck to you, Captain, and may God be with you and your men."

SUNDAY, AUGUST 25, 1861
GRAFTON, VIRGINIA

After breakfast, AJ walked through camp to the meeting area for Sunday worship services. He fell in with Harry on the way, who was seemingly lost in thought.

"You all right, Harry?" he asked.

"Hm? Oh, yes, AJ, just a lot on my mind. I was thinking over the news I read yesterday about the debates the delegates at the Second Wheeling Convention are having over the boundaries of the new state. They've been debating, rather heatedly, for almost two weeks and some thought they would never be able to agree. Fortunately, last Tuesday they reached a compromise that was passed by a majority."

"So what's in the compromise?" AJ asked.

"The proposed state of Kanawha will have thirty-nine counties, with a provision that seven more could be included if a majority of the people in those seven counties approve it. Also, counties that would border on the new state could apply for admission to the new state, if the residents desired and the constitutional convention approved."

"Sounds complicated, but I guess they know what they're doin'. When is this all supposed to happen?"

"The plan is to be submitted to voters living in the affected counties for approval in late October. If a majority approve the new state, then a constitutional convention would meet in November to create a constitution."

"Harry, d'you think they'll ever really get there? And then what happens?"

"Like you said, it *is* complicated. Remember, according to the United States Constitution, the new state constitution must be passed by the House of Delegates of the Restored Government of Virginia. If they approve the counties breaking off into a new state, then it will be sent to the U.S. Congress. Both houses must debate and approve the creation of the new state *and* its constitution. Then, if approved by both houses, I think it goes to President Lincoln for final signature. And then—*voila!*—we have a new state!"

"V'wa la?? Sounds like it could be years before all that happens, if it happens at all. Seems like it would be easier just to keep the Restored Government of Virginia, like they have now."

"Maybe, but what if the war ends and the Confederacy is dissolved and the Restored State of Virginia then includes all the counties in the now-seceded State of Virginia. Won't the western counties be back in the same place they were before Virginia seceded? Don't you think the people in the western counties would end up again being treated as second-class citizens, or worse? Remember this conflict between eastern and western Virginia has been going on since our War of Independence. No, I believe the new state would be best off permanently separated from the old Virginia. Those mountains are just too great an obstacle. I agree it will take some time, but I think it could happen by next year."

AJ shook his head. "Makes my head spin. I'm going berrypickin' after church services today. I'm feeling kind of low and I thought maybe that would pick me up some."

Harry looked up. "Are you sick, AJ? The past few weeks have been awful strenuous."

AJ shook his head. "No. Well... maybe homesick."

SATURDAY, AUGUST 31, 1861, 2:00 PM
GRAFTON, VIRGINIA

AJ was satisfied that today's mounted cavalry drill and inspection had gone well. No horse reared or misbehaved when the order was given to draw sabers. The company performed an in-line mock charge at a gallop. Each trooper had a pistol in one hand and a saber in the other. Each trooper shot and slashed infantry dummies. All this was performed almost in unison. And to AJ, the best part was that no horses or men were injured, mostly because each trooper's horse held to a nearly straight line.

It had not been that way all week. Every day at least one man and one horse had been injured by a saber during practice. Most were minor injuries, but one trooper spent a day in the hospital while a surgeon sewed up a wound requiring eight stitches. A vet had stitched up another trooper's horse, which had been slashed by the trooper while falling with saber in hand. Fortunately, neither AJ nor Shiloh had been injured. AJ attributed that to all the time he had spent training his horse before joining the Army and his constant practicing after each day's lesson.

While the men were dressing for the mounted drill, a rumor spread that Governor Pierpont had ordered a cavalry regiment to be formed in Wheeling. AJ ignored the rumor, as he had learned that listening to rumors would detract from his performance at the drill. Once the company was in formation, however, Captain McGee announced that a new cavalry regiment, to be called the First Virginia Cavalry, was being formed in Wheeling and General Kelley had agreed to allow the Kelley Lancers the honor of becoming the first company, Company A, in that regiment. Lt. Henry Anisansel of the Ringgold Cavalry would likely be promoted to colonel and placed in charge of the regiment. Captain McGee had more details, which he promised to provide if the company drill and inspection went well today.

AJ and the other troopers did their best in the drill. As McGee gave the command to dismount and stand at ease, he congratulated everyone on a job well done. Then he explained what they could expect under the new cavalry regiment, once it was formed.

"Men, General Kelley informed me that Henry Anisansel was selected by Governor Pierpont to form the First Virginia Cavalry Regiment. The governor apparently knew Anisansel when he was a music teacher at a school up in Pennsylvania and thinks he's a good organizer. That's the principal reason he was chosen to form the regiment. The regiment will likely consist of cavalry companies being formed in nearby western Virginia, Ohio, and Pennsylvania counties."

Oliver turned to AJ, made a face, and said, "A *music* teacher?"

AJ shushed him and a couple of the men near them guffawed.

McGee glared in their direction and continued. "Kelley said the Ringgold Cavalry was offered the honor of being the first Company A and Captain Keys was offered the lieutenant-colonel position. However, Captain Keys refused the offer, because he wants the Ringgold Cavalry to remain an independent cavalry unit, due to its long history and in honor of its founder."

After the men were dismissed, the rumor mill started up again as several men added to, or subtracted from, Captain McGee's comments. AJ listened and wondered, *How can they know more about the new cavalry regiment than General Kelley or Captain McGee?*

SUNDAY, SEPTEMBER 1, 1861, 10:00 AM

GRAFTON, VIRGINIA

Reverend Jackson, who had been hired by the men of the Ringgold Cavalry to hold religious services, left with the Ringgold Cavalry when they departed for New Creek. The men of Kelley Lancers had often sat in on Reverend Jackson's services, so Harry decided to approach Captain McGee with a proposal to continue holding religious services for the men, at no charge. McGee was delighted and approved the request immediately. So when Private Harrison H. Hagans, a Bible in hand, stepped up onto the bale of hay that Reverend Jackson had used as his pulpit, most of the men looked at each other in surprise. They had no idea Private Hagans was a preacher.

"Men, Captain McGee gave me permission to hold Sunday services. Not many of you know it, but I am an ordained Methodist Episcopal minister." More men joined the group as they saw Harry standing on the hay bale and Harry motioned for them to take a seat.

"In my sermons I usually talk about subjects that are on the minds of everyone in my congregation, and then discuss what the Bible advises, to help us learn what God wants and expects of us. This morning I've chosen the subject of rumors, with which we all are very familiar. Indeed, I hear the rumor mill is hard at work regarding Governor Pierpont's desire to form a regiment of cavalry. Here are just a few rumors I've heard since Captain McGee talked to us yesterday: Governor Pierpont has now changed his mind—no cavalry regiment. General Kelley, not Lieutenant Anisansel, will form the regiment. Only Virginians living in the northwestern counties of Virginia will be allowed to join. Captain McGee will be promoted to colonel and will lead the regiment. The list of rumors on this single subject seems to go on and on."

Some of the listeners' faces turned red and they looked at each other sheepishly.

Harry continued, "What does the Bible say about rumors and gossip? Proverbs 20:19 says, *Whoever goes about slandering reveals secrets; therefore do not associate with a simple babbler.* The Bible is saying that a gossip betrays a confidence, so avoid anyone who talks too much. Proverbs 18:21 says, *Death and life are in the power of the tongue, and those who love it will eat its fruits.* In this verse, I think the Bible is telling us something important: Words are powerful. They can build up or destroy. In James, Chapter 3, it says, *Look at the ships also: though they are so large and are driven by strong winds, they are guided by a very small rudder wherever the will of the pilot directs.* Verse 5 says, *So also the tongue is a small member, yet it boasts of great things. How a great forest is set ablaze by such a small fire!* I think the Bible is telling us that spreading seemingly harmless rumors can cause great destruction. God desires that we use our words to praise Him, according to Psalm 34:1, to speak wisdom, Proverbs 10:13, and to encourage and edify each other according to Thessalonians 5:11 and Ephesians 4:29.

"And the great writer Shakespeare also has some pertinent words in his play *Henry IV, Part 2*:

> *Rumour is a pipe*
> *Blown by surmises, jealousies, conjectures*
> *And of so easy and so plain a stop*
> *That the blunt monster with uncounted heads,*
> *The still-discordant wavering multitude,*
> *Can play upon it.*

"Many of us seem to think of spreading or listening to rumors as entertainment, or a harmless pastime. But are they not also a waste of our time? Time that we could spend practicing and thinking about the skills we are being taught, which could save our lives in battles yet to come. Time we could spend writing home to our families and friends, to reassure them and ourselves. Time we could spend reading good books—and particularly the Bible."

After finishing his sermon, he asked one of the privates to lead them in singing a few familiar hymns and he closed in prayer. One man asked Harry if he planned to continue the evening prayer meetings that Reverend Jackson had held. Harry asked for a show of hands. Almost all men wanted to continue holding evening prayers, so Harry agreed to lead them.

WEDNESDAY, SEPTEMBER 11, 1861
GENERAL LEE HQ, VALLEY MOUNTAIN, VIRGINIA

As General Lee prepared for the battle on the following morning, he carefully went over all the preparations he and General Loring had made, just to see if they had missed anything.

Loring had agreed to organize his Army of the Northwest into six brigades, as Lee had suggested, made up of troops from Virginia, Tennessee, Georgia, Arkansas and North Carolina. Several brigades were already making their way to their assigned positions on Cheat Mountain or near Elkwater. During the several weeks of scouting and map making, a civilian surveyor had discovered a route that might flank the Union fortress on Cheat Mountain. To investigate the surveyor's findings, Loring sent Colonel Albert Rust of the Third Arkansas Infantry regiment back up the mountain with the surveyor to investigate.

Rust, a big man with broad shoulders and a full dark beard, was bold, energetic, and domineering. At well over six feet tall, he towered over most of the men, including Lee.

Lee recalled his meeting with Rust after the colonel had returned from his reconnaissance mission on the mountain. He had told Lee, in his usual domineering manner, that he had pulled out his spyglass and saw the Yankees in their trenches. "I believe we can capture the whole lot of 'em with a surprise attack!" he had told Lee. He had also asked—really demanded, thought Lee—for the honor of allowing him to lead his brigade up the mountain and be the first to signal the attack to the other brigades.

Lee felt awkward. He had been taken by surprise, as he hadn't considered Rust for that job. The man was a lawyer and a Congressman, with little actual military experience. But he was a good friend of President Davis. "Are you certain you can pull it off?" he had asked, and Rust replied that he "had seen it with his own eyes and that fortress can be flanked!" Lee had finally acquiesced to Rust's request to lead the assault.

Now, Lee had second thoughts. *I admire his zeal, but is Rust really the man for this job? It's too late to make a change now. Rust left yesterday and is already enroute to his destination.*

Lee had other second thoughts as well. Was his battle plan too complicated? It required five brigades to attack two fortified Union positions, all at the same time: one at Elkwater commanded by Union General J. J. Reynolds, and the other on top of Cheat Mountain, commanded by Union Colonel Nathan Kimble.

It is a daring plan that requires secrecy and coordination. But if it works, Loring's troops will capture the fortress on Cheat Mountain and then sweep down the turnpike and trap the Union forces at Elkwater. It will be the end of Union defenses in the area and will allow us to reclaim western Virginia. He prayed silently for God's blessing on the battle plan, and for His will to be done.

As Lee lay down for an afternoon nap, the rain started again. It descended in torrents and lashed at his tent. In his half-sleep, he saw visions of Rust's troops struggling up Cheat Mountain and wading knee deep in the icy cold Shavers Fork. As that vision faded another replaced it, of General Donelson advancing his brigade too far beyond Elkwater and about to be discovered. Slowly awakening, he wondered: *Will Rust reach his position? Will the men be able to keep their powder dry? Will it ever stop raining? We could not figure out a way to overcome this terrible weather, and now it's too late to stop the attack. It's in God's hands now.*

Unable to sleep any longer, Lee roused his staff and set out to catch up with General Donelson's brigade. He found Donelson's troops struggling to dry their powder and clean their rifles. Satisfied that this brigade at least was in the assigned position, Lee found a spot near a haystack and, with his staff, tried again to sleep.

THURSDAY, SEPTEMBER 12, 1861
NEAR ELKWATER, VIRGINIA

As the dawn sky slowly brightened, Lee awakened and rode with his staff toward a bluff overlooking Elkwater. Just as they came to the edge of the woods, a troop of Union cavalry raced by them, headed toward Elkwater. "They probably spotted Donelson's infantry and are running to inform Reynolds," he said to his staff. "Thank God they either didn't notice us, or thought we were too insignificant to bother with."

Lee climbed a ridge from which he could see the enemy's tents, a tantalizing view, one that invited him to attack. But he waited patiently for Rust's signal, set to commence at 10:00 AM. As the minutes slowly passed, Lee pulled out his watch and stared at it repeatedly. When his watch said 10:30 AM, he began to pray even harder.

THURSDAY, SEPTEMBER 12, 1861
CHEAT SUMMIT FORT, VIRGINIA

Unknown to Lee, it looked that morning as if his complex plan might actually work. The brigades of Rust, Anderson, and Jackson surrounded the fortress at Cheat Mountain as planned, Rust was about a half mile west of the fortress, Anderson about two miles west of the fortress and Jackson about one mile east of the fortress. These troops, despite being wet, cold, and in a dense fog, were in position, ready to fight. The Union forces under Colonel Kimball remained unaware of their presence. Everything depended on those broad shoulders of Rust, to attack the fortress on schedule and alert the others to begin their part of the drama.

It had not been easy for Rust to get into position. The climb up the mountain had been grueling. When Rust aroused his men that morning from their miserable sleep, they were numbed by the wet and cold. Their hellish trek up the mountain exhausted them. By force of will Rust prodded them into formation and they moved down the ridge to their position. As they picked their way slowly along the foggy road toward the fortress, they captured Federal pickets, who informed Rust the fort held about 5,000 men and boasted that it was absolutely impregnable. He doubted their stories.

Soon, however, through the dense fog appeared a staggering view. He could hardly believe his eyes. There looming over him, like a great medieval castle, stood a large blockhouse with several heavy cannons pointed directly at him. Federal troops lay in the trenches surrounded by many large, sharpened-log spikes pointed in every direction. From the level of the road, the fortress now indeed looked impregnable. Badly shaken, he summoned his senior officers for council. "It will be madness to try to storm this works!" he said. All his officers agreed.

While Rust and his council discussed what to do next, they awakened the men in the fortress. A small force of Indiana infantry, led by Colonel Kimball, emerged and headed directly at Rust's brigade, believing they were dealing with only a small Confederate scouting party.

Startled, Rust's men took to the woods. Kimball's men plunged into the woods after them and opened fire. Rust's 1,600 men broke and ran. Kimball joined in the fracas and, waving his hat, yelled, "Hurrah for Indiana. Trail them, boys!"

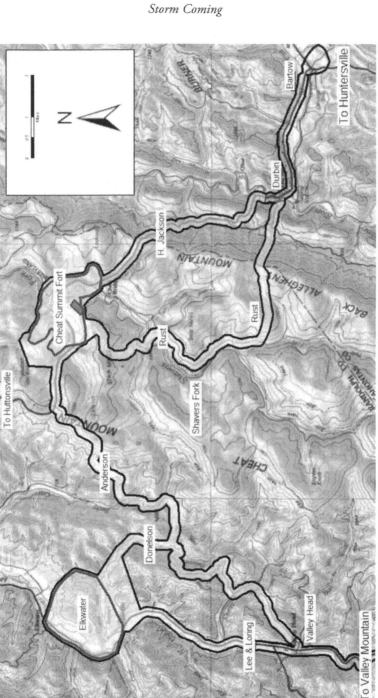

Routes taken by Confederate brigade commanders to be in position to attack Federal forts at Cheat Summit and Elkwater on morning of September 12, 1861

THURSDAY, SEPTEMBER 12, 1861
NEAR ELKWATER, VIRGINIA

Lee, growing more impatient and anxious by the minute, waited for Rust's attack signal. It was now well past 10:30 AM and through the fog and rain he could hear nothing from Rust. Lee went back to talk with Donelson.

"General Lee," Donelson said, "my men are in no condition to attack the Union forces in Elkwater. The storm has drained their strength and their powder is still wet."

Lee ordered Donelson to stand down and withdraw. Lee knew they lost the chance for total surprise when the Federal cavalry sped past him earlier.

After retiring back to Valley Mountain discouraged and disillusioned, Lee gradually discovered what had happened to the other brigades. Donelson's brigade retired down a path running along Becky Creek. His men ran into a group of Federal scouts which opened fire. A few of his men still had dry powder and returned the fire and overpowered the scouts. The Federals withdrew back up the turnpike toward the Cheat Mountain fortress.

The situation got worse. While waiting along the turnpike for Rust's attack signal, General Anderson's brigade encountered ninety Federal infantrymen coming down the turnpike to relieve the Federal scouts Donelson's brigade encountered. The ninety Federal infantrymen fired three volleys into the fog, tearing into the ranks of Anderson's brigade. At nearly the same moment the fifty Federal scouts trying to get back to the fortress fired another three volleys into the rear of Anderson's brigade. Anderson's men, unable to see in the dense fog what they were dealing with, believed they were trapped between two large Federal forces. They quickly moved off the turnpike into the woods and fled.

On the turnpike east of Cheat Mountain waited the third Confederate brigade led by General Henry Jackson. He grew nervous when no signs from Rust were heard. Peering through the dense fog, his men fired at what looked like a Federal force. That force turned out to be their own forward guard. They killed several fellow Georgians. The dreadful mistake deeply demoralized Jackson and his men. They retreated in confusion back toward Camp Bartow, fearing they would find Federals occupying their camp.

Lee sighed and shook his head. It was so painful to contemplate. After Rust's failure to attack, the intricate plan had fallen completely apart. He recalled his second thoughts about Rust as the linchpin of the plan. *I made a big mistake*, he thought. *We had the superior force and the element of surprise with us, but my choice of Rust was weak and the bad weather worked against us... God's will was done.*

FRIDAY, SEPTEMBER 13, 1861
NEAR ELKWATER, VIRGINIA

The following day Lee met in front of Camp Elkwater to confer with General Loring, who had also waited in vain for the signal to attack Reynolds. Loring had managed to exchange a few cannon shots with Reynolds, but then had retired to Valley Mountain. Loring now urged Lee to make a frontal attack on Elkwater, but Lee was not in favor of the plan. It would cost them too much, he thought.

He had no idea what the cost of this campaign was yet to be.

Lee yet hoped to discover some means of flanking the Federals on the right at Elkwater. He sent out several parties to try to discover a suitable route. One of these parties included his son Rooney Lee and his senior aide and tentmate, Colonel John Washington, great-grandnephew of George Washington and the heir to Mount Vernon.

Late in the day he received word that the pair had attempted to capture what they thought was a lone rifleman near the mouth of Elkwater Fork. Federal scouts spied them and fired, three of the balls striking

Colonel Washington in the back and killing him. Rooney Lee's horse was shot from under him, but he jumped onto Washington's horse and escaped.

Lee was devastated. *First Garnett, now Washington,* he thought. Two senior men that he had worked closely with for years and cared for deeply had given their lives in this humiliating, Godforsaken campaign. *And Rooney could so easily have been killed as well!* It was too terrible to contemplate.

John Washington was also a relative of his wife Mary and he knew she would be stricken by the news. When Washington's body was returned to Lee on the following day, he gathered what remained of the colonel's belongings and forwarded them on to Washington's oldest daughter, Louisa. He poured out his sorrow in a letter to Mary:

I am much grieved. He was always anxious to go on these expeditions. This was the first day I assented. Since I had been thrown into such intimate relations with him, I had learned to appreciate him very highly. Morning and evening have I seen him on his knees praying to his Maker.
The righteous perisheth and no man layeth it to heart, and merciful men are taken away, none considering that the righteous is taken away from the evil to come. May God have mercy on us all!

CHAPTER TEN

To Be Called the First Virginia Cavalry

September 31–November 25, 1861, July 1, 1863

Kelley's infantry charging through the bridge to Romney

SATURDAY, SEPTEMBER 14, 1861, 5:00 AM
GRAFTON, VIRGINIA

A horse whinnying awakened him. AJ listened for several minutes, but all he could hear were men snoring around him. Shiloh's welfare was always on his mind, so he wondered whether it was his horse, or a dream. He slipped on his trousers and boots and crawled out of the tent, taking care not to wake the other men, who were quick to curse those who awakened them. In the pale morning light he could see only a mist hanging over the camp. He grabbed his revolver and walked toward the stables. Bushwhackers, he knew, were thought to be operating in the area and might be trying to steal horses. *One shot in the air would arouse the whole company*, he thought.

Now he was close enough to see the horse sheds. A quick look inside told him all the horses were there. Shiloh was calmly munching hay. Then he walked around and behind the sheds, looking for fresh footprints or hoofprints. He could see none. He stood motionless for about ten minutes, listening for any strange sounds. The sun rose and began burning off the mist. Then he spotted him, a short chubby man standing about a hundred feet away. AJ yelled, "Who goes there?"

The man turned towards him and said in a slow drawl, "AJ, it's jest your ol' friend, Jim."

He recognized the friendly infantryman he had talked to a few days before. "What're you doing out here, Jim?"

"Well now, AJ, I jest could not get to sleep. So I made up my mind to go for a mornin' walk and wanted to see and smell me some horses."

"I'd be more careful about your walks, Jim. You're a good ways from the infantry camp here. You know how us cavalrymen are about our horses. Besides, bushwhackers are around, and you could get yourself shot."

"Well now, AJ, I thank you for that good advice and I'll be sure to be more careful 'bout where I take my walks."

Jim seemed to be an engaging fellow, who loved to talk. He had approached while AJ was standing guard duty several days ago and stayed to talk for almost an hour. AJ liked the man all right, yet he thought it strange to find him so near the stables this early in the morning.

"I'll come over and visit you a little later, Jim," said AJ. "Captain McGee is going to muster us in today to the First Virginia Volunteer Cavalry. We're going to be Company A."

Jim turned and said, "Well now, how 'bout me and you walkin' to town tonight for a little fun? Can you get a pass?" AJ wasn't sure what the "fun" would involve but camp life was already getting monotonous and he hadn't seen much of Grafton yet. He knew some of his tentmates had gotten passes to town, so he figured he could too. He promised to meet Jim in the early evening.

He watched Jim walk off, hands in his pockets and whistling. AJ wondered about him. Reveille sounded and AJ went back to the horse shed, fed and brushed Shiloh, and then headed to the cook fire near his tent, to make breakfast. On his way, AJ ran into Harry and told him about his strange morning encounter with Jim. Harry suggested he tell Captain McGee about it.

At roll call, Captain McGee informed the men that today they would be enrolled in Company A, First Regiment Virginia Volunteer Cavalry and mustered in for three years of duty. One man asked if their three-year enlistment started on 18 July or 14 September.

McGee replied, "It will restart on 14 September, because this is a new regiment. Once we muster in as a company, many of you will receive promotions and pay raises based on how well you did during the training. The extra money will more than make up for the extra two months. We'll need at least five sergeants and eight corporals for squad leaders."

AJ felt a bit put out over this unexpected two-month extension. While so far he had mostly enjoyed being in the cavalry and he liked the training, he had told his father that he was signing up for at most a three-year enlistment. The promotions didn't interest him. With promotions, he thought, came more responsibility and more danger. He meant to live up to his promises not to take any undue risks.

When it came time for AJ to sign up with Company A, Captain McGee said, "Private Swaney, I'm very pleased with your progress in the training. The men look up to you and everyone knows you're the best horseman in the company. How would you like a promotion to corporal and become a squad leader?"

AJ stared at his captain, astonished. He had never been offered a "promotion" in his life. All he knew was it sounded dangerous, so he replied, "Sir, I promised my family that I would always perform my duty the best I could, but wouldn't take any extra chances when I could help it. I do appreciate the offer, believe me, sir, and I do thank you for it… but if I took you up on it, I'd feel like I'd be breaking my word."

McGee was taken aback. He had initially thought of offering Private Swaney a position as sergeant, but knowing Swaney's avoidance of any form of bragging, had decided instead to start him as a corporal. "Have to say I'm a bit disappointed, Private Swaney," he replied, "and at the same time impressed with your candor. I don't want to force you to break any promises. However, I think you should write to your people and ask for their opinion, as you'll be turning down extra pay."

"Thank you, sir. I'll write them and ask about it."

"All right, Swaney, you'll take the oath again with all the other men. After that you'll be a private in Company A of the First Virginia Volunteer Cavalry. You're dismissed."

"Excuse me, sir. Would it be possible for me to get a signed pass to walk to town tonight?"

"See my aide—he'll get you a pass."

On the way back to his tent, AJ wondered, *Why didn't I tell Captain McGee about finding Jim at the stables this morning?* He couldn't decide on the right thing to do. Harry seemed to think it was unusual to find Jim "walking" so far from his unit and that the officers should be told. But maybe Jim was telling the truth. AJ didn't want to cause any trouble for the little fellow. He seemed harmless.

SATURDAY, SEPTEMBER 14, 1861, 6:00 PM
GRAFTON, VIRGINIA

They were nearing the main part of town. AJ listened as Jim talked and talked. Up ahead AJ noticed three women in fancy dresses standing on the street. As he and Jim approached, the women stopped talking and stared at the two men. AJ stared back—he couldn't help himself. He had never seen women's dresses with such plunging necklines or such garish colors. The women's cheeks were pink and lips dark red, and a sweetish odor hung like a cloud around them. One woman touched AJ on his shoulder with her fan and asked, "Are you lookin' for a good time to-night, handsome?" AJ didn't know what to say. It seemed rude to walk on without speaking, so he stopped.

"He's with me. Now y'all run along," Jim said.

"Oh," the girl replied, "one of *those?*"

Jim ignored the girl's remark, grabbed AJ's arm and pulled him along. He pointed to a saloon a few doors ahead and said, "Well now, AJ, let's go in there and wet our whistles."

Jim pushed opened the door into the dark, noisy room and headed toward a nearby table for four. Almost immediately, two young women came over and sat down at their table. Both were in off-the-shoulder dresses and were painted, like the girls they had passed on the street, only these two were prettier, AJ thought.

"Betty and Fran, I'd like you to meet my friend, Alexander Swaney. He likes to be called AJ," said Jim, with a wink.

Betty, in a bright red dress trimmed in scallops of black lace that exposed a shocking amount of cleavage, pulled her chair close to AJ's. Batting her lashes, Betty asked, "So, AJ, where you from, honey?"

AJ was flustered. He tried to move away from Betty but she simply reached under the table, patted his thigh and pulled his leg closer to hers. AJ decided to leave it there for the time being. He was too self-conscious to try to move, afraid of insulting her.

"AJ," Betty asked again, "honey, where did you say you're from?"

"Uh, ma'am, I'm from a little place in Pennsylvania, Smithfield, just north of Morgantown. What about you?" AJ stammered. He stared at her cleavage. He didn't think he'd ever seen quite so much of a woman's bosom before.

Before Betty could answer, a waiter came to the table to take their orders. He greeted Jim with a leering smile and a nod. Jim and both girls ordered beer. AJ's family was not given to drinking alcohol and he had never tasted a drink stronger than the rare glass of hard cider. He didn't consider himself a teetotaler exactly, but he had signed the temperance pledge in the family Bible. He told the waiter, "Just a glass of water for me." The waiter looked at him, astonished, and said, "We don't serve no water here!" AJ, face burning, sat in embarrassed silence for a few seconds, until Betty said, "Bring him what we're drinking."

Patting AJ's thigh again, Betty turned her face to him and said, "Never mind that waiter, AJ, he's just a dumb ol' hillbilly. And to answer *your* question, I was born in Richmond and grew up there. But I didn't much like big city life, so I moved out here to Grafton last year. Now tell me more about yourself. Jim tells me you're in the cavalry…"

Betty's animated conversation with AJ continued through the first beer, and grew more inquisitive and more intimate as the beers kept appearing. He didn't much like his first taste of the beer, but it tasted better the more he drank. Betty's pats on his leg turned into long, stroking caresses. Across the table, AJ could see Jim and Fran were kissing. In the warm glow of the beer, AJ felt himself becoming aroused. Then Betty leaned over and kissed him gently on the ear. She whispered, "I like you, Mister AJ. Would you like to take me upstairs?"

SATURDAY, SEPTEMBER 14, 1861, LATE EVENING
MOSIER FARM, SMITHFIELD, PENNSYLVANIA

Sophia awakened suddenly and sat up in bed, her heart hammering. She was having a dreadful dream about AJ. He cried out to her for help. She ran after him, trying to help him, but couldn't find him. *Was it a dream,* she wondered, *or is he really in danger somewhere?* Tears streamed down her face. Quietly she got out of bed, kneeled and began to pray. *Please God, I ask not for me but for AJ. I'm afraid he's in trouble and I can't help him, he's so far away. We've had our fights lately but... I care about him. Please, God, help him! He's a good man.* She felt calmer. AJ, she believed, was in God's caring hands.

SATURDAY, SEPTEMBER 14, 1861, LATE EVENING
SALOON IN GRAFTON, VIRGINIA

Something inside AJ snapped. He jumped out of his chair, ran to the men's water closet, and vomited into a bucket. The room was still spinning as he walked back to the table, wiping his mouth with the back of his hand. Jim and Fran were no longer there, only Betty. AJ held onto a chair to steady himself and said, "Betty, I'm sorry. I have someone back home I care about." The words came hard—his lips didn't seem to be working right. He wiped his mouth again and continued. "I... I don't think she cares for me, but I promised myself I'd stay true to her anyway. You're very pretty, but I can't take you upstairs. D'you want me to w-walk you home?"

"No! It's too early to go home. And you're drunk anyway!" Betty said, scowling. AJ could see that she was already scanning the room, which he noticed was spinning around him. Looking for her next target, he supposed. He staggered to the waiter and asked to pay for all the beers. The waiter took almost all the money he had brought with him. Turning back to Betty, he said, slurring his words, "If you see Jim, tell him I'll see him in camp. And tell him I already paid."

Betty only tossed her head and made a dismissive gesture, as if to shoo him away. He stumbled out the door and swung his head back and forth, trying to remember which direction to walk in.

SUNDAY, 10 AM, SEPTEMBER 15, 1861
GRAFTON, VIRGINIA

It was Sunday morning. AJ recalled most of the events from the previous night and was sick at heart. Besides that, he had a bad headache, and his gut didn't feel well either.

He remembered that he hadn't been able to get Sophia out of his mind on his dreary, weaving walk back to camp. He had felt her close to him at the bar, right before he got so sick.

It was obvious to him that his feelings for her had not lessened. Despite his resolve to stop thinking of Sophia, to forget any thought of love or marriage with anyone, at least until the war was over, she kept appearing in his mind's eye. He supposed he had lost any chance with her. Tip had likely moved in on her in his absence. The thought of Sophia with Tip was painful.

As his head cleared a little, more details about the prior evening came back to him. He recalled that Betty had asked him several questions about the First Virginia Cavalry and where they were headed. Was this a sign that Jim *was* really a spy? Had he arranged the evening to pump him for information, using the women as his accomplices? AJ could not say for certain but he hoped he hadn't given away important information. All he knew was Jim had not returned to his unit this morning. AJ had gone to seek Jim out first thing, to see if he could collect some of the money he had paid for the beers, and one of the infantry men he spoke to in Jim's company told him, "He didn't make roll call. That man is a strange bird. Maybe he deserted. Wouldn't surprise me none." AJ figured that his suspicions had been correct. The money, he guessed, was gone forever. *Serves me right,* he thought.

He took a seat on a straw bale at the midmorning worship service. He feared for a moment that Harry would see right through him and single him out for a sermon on beer drinking and painted women. Coming to his senses, he figured that it wasn't in Harry's nature to do that. It was just his own guilty conscience talking. He looked for his friend Oliver at the morning service, but didn't see him, which was unusual. He hoped he was all right; Oliver had mentioned feeling a little weak yesterday morning. They had made a plan to sing together this afternoon, when their chores were done, if Oliver felt up to it.

Harry mounted his hay bale pulpit and began the service by telling the men that he had learned from couriers that Confederate forces under Generals Wise and Floyd had retreated, another strategic victory gained by Rosecrans.

"Generals Floyd and Wise, both former governors of Virginia, took oaths and swore allegiance, under God, to defend the Constitution of the United States of America. Yet both broke those oaths when they joined with the Confederacy.

"The Bible says in Numbers, *If a man vows a vow to the Lord, or swears an oath to bind himself by a pledge, he shall not break his word. He shall do according to all that proceeds out of his mouth.* And James writes in the fifth chapter of his book: *But above all, my brothers, do not swear, either by heaven or by earth or by any other oath, but let your 'yes' be yes and your 'no' be no, so that you may not fall under condemnation.*

"Being a man who keeps his word is important in life. The great playwright William Shakespeare knew this too, several hundred years ago. Of course it's not Scripture, but he left us some good advice on keeping your word in his play *Hamlet*. In Act I, Scene III the character Polonius advises his son, 'This above all: to thine own self be true. And it must follow, as the night the day, thou canst not then be false to any man.'

"If you make a promise to do something and you keep your word, then you are following God's command. Keep this in mind. You have decided to join the cavalry. As you have learned, this is a dangerous occupation even when there are no enemy soldiers present. You have given your word, under oath to God, to defend the Constitution of the United States of America against all enemies, foreign and domestic. When the battles rage and you become fearful, remember your oath and do not shirk from keeping your word."

AJ left Harry's sermon feeling worse than ever. Last night he had ended up keeping his word to himself, to stay pure for Sophia—despite his efforts to put her out of his mind, he still couldn't imagine marrying anyone else—but he now felt he should have left Jim's company as soon as the two girls sat down beside them in the bar. Public drunkenness! What would his mother and father think? He knew they'd be ashamed. Why did he even agree to go with Jim in the first place? He didn't really know anything about him. And why did he drink all those beers? He resolved to think on what happened last night, pray about it, and maybe talk it over with Harry, to see what he should have done. AJ was beginning to feel that he wasn't cut out for life in an army camp.

After the service the men of AJ's company scattered to spend their afternoon in various leisure activities. Harry had a meeting to attend. AJ's Sunday dinner was a lonely one. He prepared his own coffee and fried a slab of salt pork, then soaked the tasteless hardtack in some water and fried it in the grease from the pork. He looked around for Oliver but couldn't find him; the kitten was in their tent, circling Oliver's empty bunk, mewing piteously. AJ threw it a scrap of pork.

Finally AJ found one of his tentmates, who told him that Oliver was still feeling poorly. He had gone to sick call that morning and he hadn't seen him since. AJ headed to the hospital tents at the edge of the camp to investigate.

Five large walled tents were pitched together to form the hospital. AJ had never been to this area of the camp before and he looked about for someone to ask if Oliver was here. He spotted a short, harried-looking, balding man in a uniform jacket with green medical staff straps and approached him. "Excuse me, sir, are you the surgeon in charge?"

"Yes, I'm Dr. Spooner, Assistant Surgeon. What do you need?"

"I'm looking for my friend, Oliver Swink. He went to sick call this morning and hasn't come back. Is he in the hospital?"

The doctor consulted a notebook that he carried with him. "Swink... Yes, the third tent." He turned to walk on but AJ stopped him. "Sir, can you tell me what's wrong with him?"

"High fever, likely measles but no rash yet. We have several cases in camp." He eyed AJ skeptically. "If you haven't had them yourself, I wouldn't go in there. Highly contagious."

"I had 'em," AJ replied and moved on toward the tent. He stuck his head inside and recoiled at the stench. Twelve men were laid out on straw pallets built up along each tent wall, with an aisle down the middle. Flies swirled around stinking buckets of excrement and vomit. One nurse, a plain middle-aged woman, was tending to a coughing man, his skin red and blotched. AJ spotted Oliver curled on his side, covered by a stained blanket with several moth holes in it. He thought he was asleep but Oliver opened his eyes when AJ moved to his side. AJ laid a hand on his forehead and recoiled at the heat. "You're like a hot stove, Oliver!" The sick boy tried to smile and the effort made him cough.

"You try to rest. I'm going to talk to the nurse," AJ told him. When the nurse left the side of the patient she was tending, AJ approached her. "Ma'am, my friend Oliver over there has measles, or so said the sawbones outside. What are you doin' for him?"

"For measles, the only treatment is rest, and a little whiskey occasionally. He should recover if he doesn't develop pneumonia."

"Don't you have any cots, or better bedding than these dirty blankets?" AJ asked angrily. "How can he get better in here, with this bad smelly air and no clean bedding?"

The nurse stuck her chin out and looked AJ in the eye. "We have been provided with no bedding yet, Private, no bedsacks and no cots. More and more sick are coming in each day. I'm a volunteer from the town, our chief surgeon is absent, and the assistant surgeon does the best he can with what he has to work with."

"Well, Oliver's burnin' up!"

"There's a pan of water and some rags. Soothe your friend with that."

AJ glared at the woman and turned to fetch the water and rags. He bathed Oliver's face for a while until he seemed to feel a little better. "Try to sleep now," he told him.

"AJ," Oliver mumbled, "please look after Maggie, won't you? And Red? Till I'm better?"

"I surely will."

AJ stayed till he saw that Oliver was sound asleep, then headed to the stables to see to the horses. As he walked to his tent after making sure both horses were comfortable for the night, he heard the mournful strains of "Home Sweet Home" played on a banjo, and he wiped a tear from his eye.

Wednesday, September 17, 1861
Lee's HQ, Valley Mountain, Virginia

General Lee picked up the small hand mirror and studied his reflection. He had decided to let his beard grow since it would be easier in camp than shaving. He was surprised to see it coming in completely white. *Mary won't recognize me when she sees me next*, he thought. He sighed, put the mirror down, and turned to the task at hand, writing to his wife, and then to Governor Letcher about the debacle at Cheat Mountain.

He decided to write to his wife first, confiding to her his humiliation and disappointment:

I cannot tell you my regret & mortification at the untoward events that caused the failure of the plan. I had taken every precaution to ensure success & counted on it. But the Ruler of the Universe willed otherwise.

He decided to take another tack in his communication with Letcher. He would not file an official report on the operation. He did not want to place public blame on anyone, even Rust, who he privately did blame for the ultimate failure, when all had, almost miraculously, been in place for success. *But I chose him for the job, so ultimately it is my fault and no one else's,* he admitted.

He began to write the letter, telling Letcher the facts. The troops had all reached their destinations, having traversed twenty miles of steep and rugged mountain passes, the last day through a terrible storm that lasted all through the night and in which they had to stand, chilled to the bone. He waited for the attack signal at 10:00 AM but it never came. The opportunity for surprise was gone. All the provisions were destroyed in the storm. The men had nothing to eat that morning and could not last another day. They had to be withdrawn.

This, Governor, is for your own eye. Please do not speak of it; we must try again.

SATURDAY, SEPTEMBER 21, 1861, 4:30 PM

SMITHFIELD, PENNSYLVANIA

Sophia waited near the door for Tip to arrive. The clouds had broken and the rain had stopped, for the time being at least. She hoped it would finally clear off. She reached up to pat her fashionable new silk hairnet, lined with a pale blue pleated ribbon, that neatly constrained her long curls. She thought she looked rather nice tonight.

Tip would be calling for her shortly, to attend a barn dance in Haydentown. He was engaged to play his fiddle, so they needed to arrive early. The only way her parents would allow her to go was if Cynthia agreed to go too. She had accompanied the pair on two other occasions recently, to a party at a friend's house and to another dance on the outskirts of Smithfield. Cynthia enjoyed the chance to get out and have fun, and Tip didn't object to having two girls—his "harem" as he liked to call them.

Tip. She just couldn't make up her mind about him. He seemed a little bit dangerous and perhaps that's what made him attractive. He was fun, never dull. He usually came to call on Tuesday evenings and brought her little gifts, flowers or candy. He complimented her liberally, saying things that were a bit wild, pushing her to do things that were just a little past what she was comfortable with. But he also made her mad, with his constant groping and pinching and trying to steal kisses. Her parents didn't like him and asked her to stop seeing him, but so far she'd defied them, just as she had AJ. She wasn't exactly sure why. She had to admit there was a wild girl inside of her, that Tip called to.

She heard the clatter of horse hooves outside and grabbed her bonnet and shawl, calling to her mother that she was leaving. "Be home by ten," her father said. Outside, she was surprised to see Cynthia already in the buggy with Tip. She looked questioningly at her friend, but Cynthia avoided her eye, her face flushed pink.

"Good evening, Sophie dear," said Tip, grinning and touching the brim of his cap. She hated it when he called her Sophie but he insisted it was his pet name for her. "I decided to pick Cynthia up first, just for a little change. You know how I like change."

Sophia waited, assuming that Cynthia would get down and let her sit next to Tip on the buggy seat, but Tip said, "Oh, let my li'l cousin Cynthia sit here next to me this time. It's too much trouble to get you both settled again with those damn big skirts!" Sophia frowned at Tip, but gathered up her skirt in silence as he came around and handed her into the seat behind with an exaggerated bow. She arranged her skirt as best she could on the narrow seat. When Tip was back in the driver's position, he put his arm around Cynthia and pulled her closer to him. "Come on over here, Little Cuz," he said. Cynthia's face flamed even brighter. "Stop it!" she exclaimed, trying to slide away from him. "Tip!" said Sophia sternly. "What's wrong with you? If you don't start behaving like a gentleman, you may as well let us out and go on alone!"

"Well, Your Majesty, sorry I offended yore sensibilities!" He guffawed. Clucking to his pony, he turned the gig around and headed down the road. Cynthia turned around and whispered, "I'm sorry, Sophia. I don't know why he's acting like this tonight!"

Tip sang his "Froggy Went A'Courtin'" song at the top of his lungs. Then he turned to Cynthia. "So, what do you hear from my brave cousin Alexander, the gentleman, away at the front, defending us all from the dread secessionists?"

Sophia frowned. This was one of the things that made her particularly mad at Tip, how he liked to poke fun at Alexander for volunteering to join the cavalry.

"He writes us about every week," said Cynthia. "He's mostly been training down in Virginia, no fighting yet."

"If he ain't about the dumbest yokel I ever heard of, up and volunteering before we even know what's going to happen. This ol' war will probably fizzle out in another month or two. I can't believe your pa let him run off like that."

Cynthia turned toward her cousin and hit him on the arm. "Quit talking so mean about AJ, Tip! I think he's *brave* for answering the call to duty. That's more than I can say for you!"

Tip turned to look at Sophia. "What do *you* think, Sophie?"

Sophia didn't answer for a moment. She frowned. *What* do *I think?* The image of AJ came to her mind, his quiet, steady ways.

"I think he's brave too," she finally said. "And my name is Sophia."

SATURDAY, SEPTEMBER 21, 1861, 4:30 PM
GRAFTON, VIRGINIA

Rain pelted AJ as he made his way through the muddy camp to the hospital tents. He carried a canteen filled with warm beef broth he had made for Oliver, from the salted beef that was part of their ration. Oliver had gotten worse instead of better and the last time he visited, the nurse said he wasn't interested in eating. AJ thought he needed something warm inside him and hoped he could swallow a little broth.

When he arrived, Oliver was dozing. At least AJ had been able to find two more blankets to cover him. The tent was still odorous from the open buckets and bedpans filled with excrement. Almost all of the patients had diarrhea, from the bad water, AJ suspected. At the last visit, he had carried some of the full, stinking buckets to the sink, the dug latrine on the outskirts of the camp. The sink was supposed to be covered with soil once a day, but that rarely happened. Most of the men didn't use it anyway—they just went in the woods or behind a bush, wherever they could find a little privacy. The whole camp now stunk from the lax enforcement of the latrine rules.

The same nurse who had been there the first day AJ visited was on duty. She was almost always there, and AJ had developed a grudging respect for her. She was a widow from Grafton. She had a son in the service of the Union, now with McClellan's growing Army of the Potomac near Washington, and she wanted to do what she could for the soldiers. "How is he?" he asked her.

She shook her head, avoiding his eyes. "No improvement. The doctor cupped his chest yesterday in hopes that it would draw out some of the infection, and gave him some opium for his fever and chest pain. He slept some, but he's having trouble breathing."

Oliver opened his eyes. His flushed face was wet with sweat. He breathed rapidly and AJ could hear a crackling sound with each breath. "Do you think you could swallow some beef broth?" AJ asked him.

Oliver didn't answer, just looked up at him. AJ supposed he needed all his energy just to breathe. He lifted Oliver's head and poured some broth into his mouth. The sick boy swallowed some but the effort started a coughing fit and he hacked up a blob of rusty green sputum that slid down his chin. AJ wiped it away with a rag. The effort seemed to exhaust Oliver and he lay back on the blanket and closed his eyes. AJ knelt by his side and took his hand. He could feel Oliver's pulse in his wrist, fast and shallow. He looked up helplessly at the nurse. She shook her head.

He stayed with his friend for an hour, talking softly about the kitten's antics and how his horse Maggie was faring. "They miss you, Oliver," he said. "You've got to get well and come back to them." Oliver moaned softly in his sleep. "Come back to *me*. I miss you too," AJ whispered.

SATURDAY, SEPTEMBER 21, 1861, 6:30 PM
SMITHFIELD, PENNSYLVANIA

Sophia and Cynthia stood against the wall with two other girls whom they knew slightly, and watched the dancing begin. The spacious barn had been cleaned out and swept. It made a respectable dance floor and a sizable crowd was arriving. This was an informal private party, no dance cards, and the rules of social engagement appeared to Sophia to be rather lax tonight. But of course that was the kind of party Tip liked best. Most of the revelers were young. Two older married couples were present as chaperones, presenting at least an air of respectability. Sophia knew one of the chaperone couples slightly.

Some of the young gentlemen approached her and Cynthia without waiting for an introduction, and Sophia politely but coolly declined their offers. Not that she would have minded dancing. That was a problem with Tip usually providing the music at these affairs. She only got to dance rarely, when someone she happened to know well was there, and asked her. She still observed the social niceties, even if Tip didn't care about them.

At least she had Cynthia there to talk to. They watched the dancers and their intricate movements in the reels and quadrilles. She especially liked Tip's lively version of the popular song "Soldier's Joy" and when he played it she felt a momentary pride that he was her escort tonight.

She turned to see a tall young man approach them and recognized Tip's younger brother Daniel, just a year older than her. He was handsome in a lean way, like Tip, but dark where Tip was blonde. "Hello, Cousin Cynthia. And good to see you again, Sophia," he said politely, nodding to them. Both young women brightened. Here was a male acquaintance, actually a relative of Cynthia's, who they might dance with without risking any social impropriety. After conversing briefly, he said to Cynthia, "It appears that Tip has finally gotten warmed up. Might I have the honor of the next dance, Cousin?" Cynthia smiled happily and nodded. She turned to Sophia and asked, "Will you be all right here, Sophia?" and Sophia nodded. Cynthia was pink from excitement and Sophia thought she looked prettier than she'd ever seen her. As she walked onto the dance floor with Daniel, she called over her shoulder, laughing, "Now I'll finally be able to put all that dancing practice to good use!"

Daniel brought Cynthia back after that dance and asked Sophia to be his partner next, and in this manner, alternating between dancing and watching, the two thoroughly enjoyed themselves. Another fiddler had come in, so now two fiddlers and a banjo player formed the energetic dance band. Tip should be able to take a break, Sophia thought. Maybe I'll get to dance with him a time or two.

After several more dances with Daniel, she realized that Tip was no longer playing with the band. She looked around for him, but didn't see him in the barn. Grabbing her shawl from the chair and wrapping it around her shoulders, she stepped outside. The night air was chilly; the half moon and stars shone brightly. She thought there might be a frost tonight. She could see a few shadowy figures outside, cooling off, possibly some couples sneaking a romantic moment.

She walked out a little further, toward the outhouse, and then saw, around the corner of the barn, a lanky male figure that had to be Tip. She saw him lift a jug to his mouth. *Whiskey. So that explains his behavior,* she thought. She had told him early on that the one thing she didn't tolerate was alcohol. She moved closer, intending to confront him.

A female figure passed her in the dark and headed straight for Tip. Sophia caught just a glimpse of red hair and sharp, angry features in the dim light. She stepped back into the shadows.

"Tip Swaney, I found you! Did you think I wouldn't?!"

Sophia could see Tip straighten and put down the jug. He put out a hand to fend off the angry woman. She grabbed him by the shirt and began to pummel him. "You are a no-good scoundrel!" she shouted.

"Ow! Calm down, Lucy," he said, pushing her away.

"Don't tell me to calm down, you… you good-for-nothing. Did you think you could promise to marry me and then just walk out on me? What about our baby?"

"Shh, Lucy, not so loud, sweetheart…," he said, trying to cover her mouth with one hand and hold her off with the other.

"Oh!" Sophia's hand flew to her mouth. She could barely breathe. She saw the woman's silhouette and could make out the swollen belly. So those rumors had been true after all—Tip had gotten a woman pregnant. And apparently had run out on her.

She turned and ran back into the barn, half-blinded by tears, and found Cynthia, who had just come off the dance floor after dancing another reel with Daniel. "Come on, Cynthia, we must go, now!" Sophia said, grabbing her friend's arm.

"Why, what's wrong?" Cynthia asked her, fearful.

"I'll tell you later," said Sophia. Dragging Cynthia with her, Sophia approached the chaperone couple she knew and explained that she felt ill and she and her friend had no way home, since they had come with one of the musicians. The husband offered to drive them the three miles back to Smithfield, and he escorted them to the door.

As they left, the three passed Tip coming in the door, a bruise reddening on his cheek. "Sophia?" he said, reaching for her. She pulled away. "I'm ill and Mr. Bowman has been kind enough to offer to drive us home." Her look was frosty.

"Well, I'll see you then on Tuesday, like usual?"

"No, that won't be possible. I'm otherwise engaged. And I believe you have other… obligations. We must go," she had said. She took Cynthia's arm and they swept through the door to Mr. Bowman's buggy.

SUNDAY, SEPTEMBER 22, 1861
GRAFTON, VIRGINIA

AJ attended Harry's morning worship service and stayed behind to talk to him. He was at his wit's end about Oliver. He had tried all the cures his ma had taught him for pneumonia, which weren't many. The nurse in the hospital tent had told him there wasn't much they could do to treat him. None of the standard treatments the doctor gave Oliver had any obvious effect on the disease. AJ thought if Oliver had only been home, being cared for by his family, in a clean bed, with clean, fresh air to breathe, he might have a chance, but he had no idea how that could happen, especially in his *extremis* condition.

"AJ, my friend," Harry said, frowning, "you don't look well. What's wrong?"

"Oliver is so sick, Harry. The doctor says his measles has turned into pneumony. I fear for him. Could you come with me to see him? I just wish we could somehow get him out of this muddy, filthy camp and back home, to his family, where he might have a chance."

"Come, let's go right now and see what the situation is. He's a young healthy man. Perhaps it's not really as bad as you think."

But when they entered the large hospital tent, they both saw right away that Oliver was bad off. They could hear his raspy, whistling breath from the door of the tent, even over the moans and calls of the other sick patients in the crowded tent. Even though his eyes were open, he didn't recognize them.

Harry shook his head and stared at AJ in dismay. "These conditions, they're shocking. I didn't realize…"

"The big cat… in the river… flying." Oliver mumbled but what he said made no sense. His lips were dry and peeling, like paint off an old building. He plucked constantly at the blanket as he tried to draw in air. AJ saw that his fingernails had turned blue.

The doctor came in while they were there and told them that he could give Oliver some morphine for his chest pain, but he had no other treatment for him. AJ turned to Harry with pleading eyes. "Ain't there somethin' we can do for him?" he asked.

Harry nodded. He bowed his head and prayed aloud, fervently, for healing for Oliver, for protection for all of them. "Thy will be done. Amen."

The two men sat together, keeping watch over Oliver. AJ talked to the sick man, even though he didn't think he could hear. He told him how the training was going, that it rained near about every day and the camp was a mass of sticky mud. Told him that Red the kitten was growing fast and liked to hide under the corner of the bunk and jump out on his feet. He didn't tell him that Oliver's mare Maggie had already been assigned to another trooper. Finally, he ran out of things to talk about.

"Sing to him, AJ," said Harry. "He loved singing with you. I think he can hear you."

So AJ sang, as many verses of as many songs, both popular and sacred, as he could remember. He sang "Amazing Grace," "Am I a Soldier of the Cross," "Lorena," "I'm a Pilgrim and I'm a Stranger," "Listen to the Mockingbird," "There Is a Land of Pure Delight."

While he was singing "Home Sweet Home," Harry reached over and gripped AJ's arm. "AJ... Oliver's home now."

SATURDAY, SEPTEMBER 28, 1861
GRAFTON, PENNSYLVANIA

His day's duties over, AJ slumped on a log outside his tent and wrote a letter to his family.

My dear ones,

I'm homesick something turreble. I have some verry sad news to relate to you. My good friend Oliver, who I wrote to you about before, has died. He first got measles but it turned to newmony. Harry and me was by his side when he died. He was a brave boy only 18 years, and a good boy too. I wrote to his family to tell them how good he was. He left his kitten Red to me to look after.

311

I miss you all more than I can say. I didn't know homesickness
hurt so bad. Please write to me. Direct your letter to the same address
as prior. Much love,
Your son and brother,
AJ

SUNDAY, SEPTEMBER 29, 1861
MOSIER FARM, SMITHFIELD, PENNSYLVANIA

Sophia and her mother cleared the table after Sunday dinner and washed
and dried the dishes. The older pastor substituting for Reverend Hagans
while he was away, Pastor Miller, had dined with them and he and Sophia's father were outside at the barn, looking over the stock. He was a
good-enough preacher, Sophia thought, but no real comparison to Harry.

Her mother sat down to read the Bible and Sophia picked up a piece
of embroidery she had been working on, but quickly lost interest and put
it down. She felt nervous, unsettled. Now that she'd had a week to think
about the disturbing incident with Tip, she was filled with regret. Not for
breaking it off with Tip, but for how she'd treated AJ. He had only acted
out of concern for her, she realized, but she hadn't listened.

She picked up paper and pen and began to write:

Dear AJ,
I hope you are well. I worry about you. We get news of battles
and such very late, it seems. I hope you are safe somewhere and not
fighting right now. I'm sorry for not having writen before. I have
thought of it many times but just didn't do it 'til now. You are much
in my thoughts, my friend. I wish we had made it up before you left.
I miss talking to you. My biggest fear is that you don't come back and
I never get to tell you I'm sorry for how I acted.
We are all well. Pa had a cold last week but seems over it now.
Things go along about as they always did, but without you here it's
not quite the same.

*My grandmother finally passed away last week and Pastor Mil-
ler preached her service yesterday. I'm sad but it was her time. She's
in a better place. The neighbors were real good about bringing food
in for us. Your ma and Cynthia brought us over some chicken and
two apple pies.*

As for me and Tip,

Sophia stopped writing. She sighed and sat motionless for several
minutes, rereading what she had written. Then she tore up the letter and
threw the pieces in the fire.

EARLY OCTOBER, 1861
SEWELL MOUNTAIN, VIRGINIA

Following the abortive battle at Elkwater and Cheat Mountain, and the
retreat of the Confederate armies of Floyd and Wise when confronted by
General Rosecrans's forces at Carnifex Ferry, Lee had consolidated most
of his Confederate forces remaining in western Virginia at Sewell Mountain. The troublesome Wise had finally been recalled to Richmond,
which was a relief. The Wise Legion was combined with Floyd's army of
the Kanawha. Lee asked Loring to bring his forces to Sewell Mountain.
All together, Lee now had about 9,000 soldiers.

He was thinking about his next move. General Rosecrans had combined his force with that of General Cox, a total of 8,550 men, and pur-
sued Lee to Sewell Mountain. Now the both of them had taken positions
on strongly defensible ridges separated by a deep gorge. *We've been facing
off now for two weeks, waiting it out, firing our cannons at each other, with
no decisive results,* Lee thought. He had hoped Rosecrans would be reck-
less enough to attack him directly. But no such luck.

In the early morning hours of October 5, Lee was hopeful again, an-
ticipating an opportunity. He and his staff had heard the sounds of
Rosecrans's troops, cannons, and wagons moving during the night. Lee
felt certain Rosecrans was preparing to attack today and finally provide

him with the opportunity to destroy the Union army. But when dawn broke and Lee peered through his field glasses, he could see no enemy soldiers and he realized that Rosecrans had decided instead to withdraw his forces. He lowered the glasses. "The bird has flown," he sadly told his staff.

He contemplated pursuit, but decided against it, as he would have to extend his supply lines, which were already mired in miserable mud from the record-breaking rains. *Thus ends the battle of Sewell Mountain,* Lee thought. *The battle that never was.*

SATURDAY, OCTOBER 19, 1861
WASHINGTON CITY, DISTRICT OF COLUMBIA

Buford awakened to a sudden jolt of his passenger car. He looked down at the front of his uniform to see if he had drooled on himself during the night of miserable sleep. He stared out the window in a futile attempt to see if they were near Washington.

"Good morning, Captain." Wesley Merritt, stretched out by his side, greeted him cheerfully.

"Did I keep you awake with my snoring?" Buford inquired.

"No, sir, I've been awake for an hour or so, wondering about what's in store for us when we get to Washington."

"Anything will be better than being on this train. Has it really been almost a week since we left Missouri?"

"It has, Captain, and we're supposed to arrive sometime today in Washington. I've been sitting here thinking about Colonel Cooke being reassigned to St. Louis. What do you think about that, sir?"

"I don't know, Wes. It's a bitter pill to swallow, having our regimental commander reassigned after enduring that long march with us from Fort Floyd in Utah. Then they order us to turn over our mounts before getting on the train, and then we find out our regimental name will be changed from the U.S. Army Second Dragoons to the Second United States Cavalry. I'm not sure what to think!"

"Well, sir, it feels like we just had thirty years of history wiped out, and to make matters worse, our officer ranks have been depleted by all the defections to the Confederacy."

"Don't remind me of that. I still think those who left to join the Confederate army should have been thrown in prison, or shot for breaking their oaths. The politicians in Washington are responsible for all this. We should have been recruiting new officers and troopers many years ago. Surely Washington could have seen this damn war coming! It's the same old story played out over and over again, Wes. In peacetime, everyone forgets about the needs of the Army and few even know, or care, what a dragoon does. So here we sit, a depleted first-line national defense regiment of regular U.S. Army dragoons, with no horses, no modern equipment, and no regimental commander, being summoned to Washington to put out the fires they started!"

When they arrived in Washington later that day, those officers who greeted them knew little about their orders. The regiment was assigned to a camp near many other regiments of volunteer cavalry. The volunteers were inexperienced and ill-trained, but had new equipment and fine-looking mounts. Captain Buford and his seasoned troopers seemed out of place. It was clear their unit was no longer considered the first line of national defense.

Buford felt depression setting in, but he refused to succumb. Instead, he resolved to marshal his resources and start managing his own career and not wait around for orders from who-knows-where.

He knew he wanted to be a cavalryman in the service of the United States, but from what he saw of the volunteer cavalry regiments around him and what their colonels had told him, no one seemed to know how to use cavalry in this war. He wanted that to change. He envisioned a day, hopefully soon, when he might be a major general in charge of a division of cavalry. He would make sure they all were trained as true dragoons—equally skilled in the art of a cavalier fighting on horseback with sabers and pistols, and as dismounted cavalry fighting with rapid-fire repeating rifles. In short, the cavalry division he envisioned would be a mobile fighting force of 16,000 men, led by the best cavalry colonels and brigadiers, capable of destroying any enemy cavalry as well as any enemy infantry, while maintaining a close watch over the movements of enemy armies.

Buford decided to work toward making his vision a reality, starting here and now in Washington, exploring every contact he ever had. He would start at the top by going to see Colonel Randolph Marcy—the father-in-law of Major General McClellan—who he had known since 1857 when Marcy led a daring rescue mission to the New Mexico Territory, to keep the main body of the Utah Expedition from starving. Buford would take any job, provided he received a promotion and an opportunity to advance toward his determined goal.

SATURDAY, OCTOBER 19, 1861 8:00 AM

GRAFTON, VIRGINIA

Even though General Kelley knew his wounds had not fully healed, when General Scott sent a telegram ordering him to take temporary command of a new War Department—the Department of Harper's Ferry and Cumberland—he accepted. Scott informed him that General Frederick W. Lander was now being groomed to become the permanent commander and would relieve him in a few months.

Kelley and the flamboyant Lander had become close friends after Philippi and it was Lander who recommended that Kelley be appointed as the temporary department head. Lander and Kelley thought alike. They both believed that aggressive action won battles and they had long conversations on military strategies each time Lander came to visit Kelley in the Wheeling hospital after his chest surgery.

Kelley had heard that Major General McClellan had taken Lander with him to Washington, having recognized a keen fighting spirit in this brave and audacious aide. Lander was subsequently awarded the rank of brigadier general and placed in charge of an infantry brigade on the Maryland side of the Potomac River overlooking the area near Leesburg, Virginia. Kelley suspected it was a command ill-suited to his restless friend, who much preferred to engage, rather than watch, the enemy.

Kelley considered Lander's recent bold moves, to get himself back in the action. Lander had offered his resignation to McClellan and then approached Scott about taking command of the new war Department that contained 120 miles of the B&O Railroad line that had earlier been torn up by the Confederates. Lander threw himself into learning all he could about rebuilding the railroad, the resources available to him, and the name and background of his Confederate antagonist.

Lander had quickly recognized the importance of the town of Romney in protecting the railroad and urged General Scott to commit a large-enough force to capture Romney. He told Scott that Kelley was the man for the job. Scott agreed and hence Kelley's recent orders, to capture Romney. Kelley had called in all of his senior officers yesterday and gave them orders to prepare to depart for New Creek on Monday.

Saturday, October 19, 1861 10:00 am
Grafton, Virginia

AJ stood at morning quarters, anxiously waiting to hear what Captain McGee had to say. He hoped they would be moving to a new camp soon. He was sick of Grafton—the camp smelled like a latrine, the mud was ankle deep… and even worse, he couldn't escape his sad memories of Oliver.

McGee began his address on the stroke of 10 AM: "Men, this will be your last weekend in Grafton. On Monday we will depart by train for New Creek. New orders will be issued after our arrival. I suspect we will engage the enemy. For most of us this will be the first time we may find ourselves in harm's way. Prepare yourselves for a long campaign. Write letters to your family and friends and get all of your gear ready, as if you expect never to return to Grafton.

"You have had almost six weeks training in the use of your weapons and getting to know your horses. Hopefully that training has prepared you to do battle with enemy soldiers. It is natural to have fear at this time. I have no better advice to give you than that offered by Reverend Hagans in one of his recent sermons when he said, 'You have given your word, under oath to God, to defend the Constitution of the United States of America. When the battles rage and you become fearful, remember your oath and do not shirk from keeping your word.'"

Captain McGee dismissed the company, but asked AJ and Harry to remain behind for a moment. McGee said, "I know I gave permission for you two to take Sunday off so you could visit Philippi. I will not break that promise. Just be sure all your gear is packed and ready to go. We'll depart early Monday morning. Enjoy your ride to Philippi, but make sure you're back here on time."

"Thank you, sir," said Harry. He grabbed AJ's arm and led him back toward the tents before AJ could speak.

"What's this about, Harry?" AJ asked. It was the first he'd heard of a ride to Philippi.

"Sorry it got sprung on you like this. I wanted it to be a surprise. Your spirits have seemed low lately, AJ, and I thought it might cheer you up if we got out of camp and went for a long ride together, like we did back in Smithfield. I chose Philippi so we could see where the first battle of the war took place. What do you think? "

AJ nodded his assent but he felt none of his old eagerness. *What's wrong with me?* he thought. *A ride with Harry used to be one of my favorite things.* He sighed, as they turned to walk back to their tents to pack their gear.

SUNDAY, OCTOBER 20, 1861
GRAFTON, VIRGINIA

It was a beautiful but chilly fall day. The sky was finally clear and many of the leaves were off the trees after the hard rains. Harry had held Sunday services earlier than usual that morning to accommodate their ride to Philippi.

Harry carried their passes and both knew the ride wouldn't be exactly like the ones back home. They were in the Army and had to follow strict camp regulations. Both men had to be in uniform at all times. Since they would be leaving the Grafton city limits, both men had to carry the minimum of prescribed weapons for their unit. In their case that meant a revolver and sword. AJ, of course, always carried his long rifle in a saddle holster and today was no exception. They had to leave a copy of their travel route and estimated time of arrival back at camp. If they exceeded the estimated arrival time by 30 minutes, a squad of mounted troopers would follow their route and attempt to find or rescue them.

The route Harry had recorded at the guard station was south along the east banks of the Tygart Valley River to Philippi and return via the Staunton-Parkersburg Turnpike. Their estimated time of arrival back at camp was 1600 hours, 4 PM, well before dark.

The red tape out of the way, AJ and Harry mounted their horses and trotted out of town. Once along the grassy east side of the Tygart River, Harry kicked Betsy into a canter, saying "Come on, AJ!" After a mile or so they were both in a full gallop. Harry threw out his arms and yelled as loud as he could. AJ had to smile at his companion's exuberance, although his smile felt forced. He wished he could feel as Harry felt. They galloped along side by side for about a mile and then slowed their mounts to a walk.

"AJ," Harry said, "isn't it good to be alive? Isn't God wonderful to make such a day as this for you and me?"

AJ nodded and tried to smile again, but his old spark just wasn't there. He felt numb.

Harry pointed ahead of them. "Look about a half mile up there. See that wooded mountain spur that extends almost to the river bank? Looks like there's an open space next to the bank for one rider to squeeze by. Let's race to see who gets through it first."

AJ agreed. Perhaps a race would be the kick he needed to feel again. He moved Shiloh alongside Betsy and Harry counted down to start the race: "3... 2... 1!"

Off they flew, galloping side by side for the first hundred yards. Then Shiloh started to fall back and AJ could feel an irregularity in his gait.

"What's wrong, big fella?" AJ asked as he slowed his horse to a walk and then stopped and dismounted.

AJ looked ahead and saw that Harry had already disappeared around the spur of the mountain. *He'll come back looking for us,* he thought as he lifted Shiloh's front right foot. AJ dug the mud from the foot and tapped on the shoe and the frog. Shiloh did not flinch. It appeared there was nothing wrong with that foot. Next he lifted the left front leg and did the same methodical check. Again Shiloh did not move or try to jerk his leg away.

While moving to check the back feet, AJ looked to see if Harry was coming back yet, but saw no one. Checking the left rear foot revealed nothing, although he noticed a small thorn in Shiloh's left pastern. He watched Shiloh as he slowly pulled out the thorn. Shiloh did not wince and the puncture didn't bleed excessively. *No, that's not it.* He moved to the horse's right rear and again looked to see if Harry was coming back, but no Harry. *That's odd*, he thought, as he lifted Shiloh's right rear foot. *Harry should've noticed by now that we're not behind him.*

This time when he cleaned out the mud, Shiloh flinched and tried to jerk his foot away. Carefully AJ cleaned around the frog and found a sharp stone wedged between the shoe and the frog. As he removed the stone, Shiloh jerked again, and then pricked his ears and whinnied. AJ looked up to see if Harry had returned, but saw only a riderless horse approaching them. As the horse came closer he could see it was Betsy. He frowned, puzzled. *Did Harry take a tumble?*

He ran his eyes over the mare as she came closer. Her eyes were wide and her nostrils flared. He spotted blood on her rump. It came from a long, narrow bleeding laceration. It looked like she had been hit by a whip. The hair on the back of his neck rose as the realization hit him: *Harry's in some kind of bad trouble.* His first instinct was to vault onto Shiloh and ride to the rescue, but he held himself in check and remembered his training. *If I'm going to help, I must not ride off half-cocked and run into the same trouble Harry's in. Think, I've got to think what to do.*

He could feel the blood pounding through his entire body. His heart was beating so hard and so fast that he could hear it thumping in his ears. He tied Betsy securely to a nearby tree so she would not follow them. He quickly checked Shiloh for soundness and noted no limping now. The sharp stone had apparently been the problem. He pulled out his long rifle, rammed powder and a minie ball in the barrel and primed the weapon. He checked his revolver and found it loaded. He loosened his sword in its scabbard and climbed aboard Shiloh.

As he rode on he looked for a spot where he might better see Harry and the person or persons who had hit Betsy. As he entered the woods on the mountain spur he dismounted and slowly crept to a spot where he could see the grassland and the Tygart below. He heard voices and moved as silently as he could in that direction, as though he were stalking wild game, peering through the trees.

Then he saw Harry. His arms were tied in front of him to a large tree and his back was stripped bare. Three lank, scruffily bearded men dressed in dirty, nondescript clothing were gathered around the tree, shouting at Harry and at each other. One had a long black whip curled in his hand. Another had a musket pointed at Harry, and the third man was laughing. AJ saw a second musket leaning against the tree. Blind rage filled him as he took in the scene. *These are damn bushwhackers!* He took a deep breath to calm himself and prayed a silent prayer: *Lord, guide me, please.* A surprising calm descended on him. It was the same calm that came over him at home when he was about to shoot a deer. He slowly moved Shiloh into position, methodically lifted his long rifle from its holster, estimated the distance and crosswinds, and asked Shiloh to stand as he was about to fire. He took careful aim through the trees, now nearly bare of their leaves, at the man holding his musket on Harry… and fired.

In the split second it took AJ to remount, he saw the man with the musket fall to the ground and the other two men looking around wildly to see where the shot came from. AJ screamed like a banshee and rode at a gallop toward the men. In one hand he gripped his pistol, in the other his saber. The man with the whip in his hand yelled, "Bobby! Shoot 'im!" But Bobby was shaking and not fast enough. By the time he grabbed his musket, loaded it, and tried to take aim he was too late. AJ shot him in the head with his pistol.

"You son-of-a-bitch, you done kilt my boys!" spat the man with the whip, his face a mask of disbelief and rage. He tried to unravel his whip but Shiloh suddenly stopped, wheeled on his hindquarters and charged at him. The man raised his arm, frantically trying to swing the whip. AJ thrust his saber into the bushwhacker's chest. The man stood, arm raised, paralyzed. He tried to fling the whip forward, but instead it fell from his raised hand. He could only stand, helpless, as the trooper leaped from his horse, came up to him and jammed the saber into his chest up to the hilt.

AJ stared into the face of his adversary and watched the life fade from the man's eyes. He twisted his saber and then yanked it from the body, as he had been trained to do. The dead man fell to the ground, still twitching, as blood poured from the hole left by the saber, pooled around the body and darkened the leaf litter under and around him. AJ stood and stared, his chest heaving as he sucked in air. He couldn't think or move; his limbs were frozen. Sometimes this happened to him in dreams, when he needed to run but couldn't. *Can this be real?* he thought, surveying the bloody scene.

Harry, still tied to the tree, twisted his head around trying to see what was happening. AJ saw his friend stare, wide-eyed, as if he too couldn't believe his eyes. Harry's lips were moving but no sound came from them.

"Harry? Are you well?" AJ finally broke the silence.

Harry didn't answer for a moment. Sweat ran down his neck and back, mixing with blood oozing from a few scratches. He turned his head away and rested his forehead on the tree trunk. Then he seemed to gather himself. "Yes, my friend. Thank God for you. I owe you my life."

AJ's whole body began to shake and he was able to move his limbs again. He had to sit down on a log for a moment, feeling that his knees were about to give way. He waited for his strength to come back. "I'll untie you in just a minute," he said. "My hands are shakin' so bad…"

Harry sighed, and said, "I'll wait." AJ stared at him and then laughter welled up from inside. He laughed so hard that he had to hold his stomach. Harry joined in, leaning against the tree for support. AJ didn't know where the laughter was coming from, but then, as if a switch were flipped, it turned to sobs that shook his whole body. He covered his eyes and waited for the emotional spasm to cease. Finally it did.

AJ felt cleared out then, like the freshness in the air after a thunderstorm. Wiping away the tears from his eyes and cheeks, he said, "I'm sorry," and rose to cut his friend lose from the ropes that bound his arms to the tree. He led Harry to the log, avoiding the three bodies. They both sat for a moment to regain their strength and composure.

They could hear the gurgle of a nearby spring. AJ got up to wet his handkerchief and returned to wipe the blood and dirt from Harry's back, and from his own saber. He retrieved Harry's shirt and uniform jacket from the laurel thicket where the guerrillas had flung them.

"Well, AJ, I'm glad you didn't follow my advice about counting to ten this time," said Harry with a grimace, as he buttoned his jacket.

AJ shook his head. "Harry, I don't know what come over me. When I saw you there and those three about to hurt or kill you... Something just took me over. It was all like a bad dream."

Harry nodded. "It was your training, AJ. That's why we drill so much. As for me I was praying the whole time. Which seemed to make those men even angrier. When you arrived, it was as though God had sent his avenging angel for me. And indeed, that's what you were."

They talked quietly for a time, Harry describing to AJ how he'd been ambushed and tied and his horse whipped when she tried to bite one of the attackers. AJ reassured him that Betsy was safe. As far as Harry could tell, the men were Confederate partisans operating in the backwoods on their own. "Although, from the past killings they talked about, I don't think they had respect for either side. I got the idea that they'd ambush, kill, and steal from anyone who happened along. They thought I was alone and they could take their time. They continually bragged about how many men they'd killed. I was preparing to meet the Lord... but hoping you'd come along."

AJ and Harry decided to leave the dead bushwhackers on the ground for the time being and ride back to camp immediately to report the incident. Together they rode Shiloh to where Betsy was tied. AJ cleaned her wound, and then they made their way in silence back to camp. AJ still felt shaky and a little sick to his stomach. He stopped and dismounted once to heave and vomit by the side of the trail. Harry waited patiently until he mounted Shiloh again.

When they arrived at camp they sought out their captain and told him what had happened. A squad of cavalry was sent to investigate, but when they returned they reported no bodies to be found, just blood on the ground and the ropes where Harry had been tied. Someone had obviously been there—perhaps the bodies had been thrown into the river or carried away. The squad searched but found no one else in the vicinity.

All agreed no further action could be taken, as there were no bodies to be found. Harry apologized to AJ saying, "My dear friend, I intended our outing to be a time of refreshment and renewal for us both. Instead I'm afraid I've added to your load of misery. I'm mightily sorry for that."

AJ shook his head. "No, Harry—it wasn't your doin'. I'm glad those bushwhackers are dead and can't hurt anybody else."

Word of AJ's administration of instant justice to the three bushwhackers spread among the Kelley Lancers and even to the nearby Ohio and Indiana infantry regiments. More than one soldier came up to AJ to shake his hand, which generally caused AJ to blush and hang his head. He didn't like being called a hero, and flatly refused requests to tell the story to those who wanted more details. He suspected the rumor mill would soon fill in all the details and then some.

AJ realized it was an experience he would carry with him to his grave. He had killed a man—three men to be exact. He wasn't sorry, although he did pray for forgiveness for the act of killing. *I know now I can kill, at least when someone I love or deeply care about is in danger.*

Death was no longer a stranger. Oliver's death had shaken him much more than killing those three murderers, he thought. And seeing Harry in the hands of violent men had made him realize the precarious position they all were in. The gift of life, which he had taken so much for granted until recently, could be taken away at any moment. He might never go home again, might never see his family, or Sophia. He could barely let himself think about her. *Why did I leave without telling her how I feel?* The ache was almost unbearable. He preferred the numbness.

MONDAY, OCTOBER 21, 1861, 8:00 AM
GRAFTON, VIRGINIA

It was a cool crisp fall morning. The waiting train belched smoke and steam. Passenger cars for the men, cattle cars for the horses, and flat cars for the artillery pieces sat motionless, ready for loading. Men and horses stood at attention, the cavalrymen next to their mounts, the artillerymen next to their horses, caissons and cannons, and the infantry with their muskets. General Kelley walked onto the platform with his staff.

"Men," he said in his usual booming voice, "you are impressive. Makes me almost feel sorry for the rebels we're going to chase out of their quarters when we reach our destination. Now get onboard and enjoy the ride."

One cavalryman raised his cap and yelled, "Three cheers for the General!" The men joined in with enthusiasm. Then they began the long process of loading and boarding.

AJ had first planned to ride in the passenger car assigned to the Kelley Lancers and seek out Harry, to congratulate him on his promotion to quartermaster sergeant. But after watching the horses being loaded, AJ had another idea and decided to approach Captain McGee.

"Captain, I'd like permission to ride in the cattle car with my horse. It's the first time he's been on a train, and I can calm him if he starts to act up."

"He's going to be with a lot of other horses who've never been in a railroad car either. If they all kick up a commotion, you could be hurt," McGee replied.

"I can help keep them calm, Captain. The horses are mostly still green, like us. And they'll be nervous."

The captain grinned and said, "Yes, I've watched you around horses, Private. Seems like you speak horse language quite fluently. All right. If you don't mind a two- to three-hour ride with the horses and their associated manure, you have my permission. Not a bad idea. Carry on."

AJ was relieved. He had another reason why he wanted to ride in the horse car, and that reason was Red, Oliver's little tomcat that AJ had adopted. He had agonized about whether to leave him behind and had decided he couldn't. Now he went back to the platform where his bags and gear sat, waiting to be loaded, and retrieved the lumpy canvas sack with holes poked in it, which he had devised to carry the cat. He could hear a tiny "mew" as he picked it up and held it close. "Just hold on, Red, I'll let you out soon."

Shiloh recognized AJ as soon as he opened the sliding door, raising his head and pricking his ears toward his master. AJ gave him a pat and a soft word, and then walked by the whole line-up of horses, studying them closely as they munched hay. He checked their tethers, reaching out here and there to stroke a glistening neck or pull a burr from a forelock. His eyes missed nothing, like a mother hen checking her chicks. They all seemed comforted by his presence.

Being with the horses like this reminded him of back home and he was hit with a new wave of homesickness. He couldn't seem to shake the constant sadness that had settled on him. At home he loved to sit in the barn and breathe in the fragrance of hay, feed and animals. He preferred communing with animals over most people.

People were more complex. Many of the men he had met in the Kelley Lancers seemed intent on trying to make his life harder. They were full of bluster, unwanted advice, complaints, feuding, and teasing. And worse. Some were violent, some malingerers, some thieves. He had learned more about human nature in the last couple of months than in his entire previous life.

Oliver had been an exception of course. But no one else was like his ma and pa, or like his brother John, or Harry. *Or Sophia.* Her face floated into his mind. In his vision, her lips curved in a smile, and he smiled back, lost in his reverie.

A sudden jolt told him the train was ready to roll. Red was mewing loudly now and scratching at the bag to get out. AJ released him into the train car and he yowled for a moment, scolding and switching his tail. Then he curled up on a hay bale and AJ sat down beside him. *One good thing about cats, they sleep a lot of the time,* he thought. Most of the horses spread their legs instinctively as the cattle car began to move, and munched their hay. A few rolled their eyes and pulled against their rope tethers, but a soft word from AJ quieted them.

AJ and the horses swayed together as the train sped up and found its regular rocking rhythm. He closed his eyes. *I need to prepare myself for what is coming. What will it be like going into battle? The sixth commandment says you shall not murder. Harry says being a soldier is not a sin and killing in war, under orders, is not the same as murder.* Even though he had no regrets about killing the three bushwhackers, he was still haunted by their faces. His thoughts wandered back to Smithfield, to Sophia, to Ma and Pa, to his sisters and brother, to the horses munching hay, to the rocking of the cattle car. His head nodded.

AJ was awakened by the blast of the engine whistle as the train neared their destination, the New Creek station. He peered through the slots and saw the Potomac River to the north, and to the south he saw village shops and a large brick mansion towering above them, surrounded by Army tents.

The town appeared larger than he had expected. With the coming of the railroad in 1852 the small village of New Creek, occupying the bluff of land lying south of the North Fork of the Potomac River and west of New Creek, had developed rapidly. The land had changed hands often and now belonged to Colonel William Armstrong, the largest landowner and most prominent businessman in the area, who was now serving with the Confederates.

Armstrong had built the brick mansion, which AJ heard would soon become General Kelley's headquarters and house most of the senior officers. Colonel Armstrong had been a delegate to the Richmond Secession Conference, but had voted against secession. However, his loyalty to the state of Virginia had led him to join the Confederate Army and he was now posted in eastern Virginia. General Kelley passed orders not to damage the mansion.

AJ stuffed Red back in his canvas sack, slinging it over his shoulder, and detrained. He joined in the unloading operation, making sure each horse was carefully led from the rail car and secured. He watched Captain McGee and the other officers from the corner of his eye. He had the feeling, from the way they looked and behaved, that the Kelley Lancers would soon see action.

McGee quickly assembled the Lancers and they marched to a campsite near the Ringgold Cavalry, where they pitched their tents and exchanged greetings and handshakes all around. Red seemed to take the new location in stride and was quickly stalking birds nearby.

AJ could see determination in everyone's eyes and in the set of their jaw. He wondered if he looked the same. There was much work to be done tomorrow. He welcomed the work. It would help him forget.

TUESDAY, OCTOBER 22, 1861, 6:00 AM
NEW CREEK, VIRGINIA

Following the normal morning routine, all officers met with General Kelley to go over the preparation for the coming expedition to capture Romney from the Confederates. McGee was to supervise the farriers and check the feet of all the horses. He ordered AJ to assist him and had him check every shoe on every horse. While the horses were being checked and shod, McGee assigned sergeants to supervise the preparations for their march that was planned to start tomorrow.

329

When the preparations were finished and he had some free time, AJ sat with the Ringgold men and listened intently to their stories. Many told of encounters with bushwhackers, who were thick in the neighborhood and much despised, described by the men as "nothing but cold-blooded murderers." AJ considered telling his own story, but kept quiet. He wanted to forget it rather than relive it.

He was most interested in the details of the Ringgold's expedition to Romney a month earlier, as he hoped to learn something useful for their upcoming attack on the same town. Many of the stories he heard embellished the truth a little, he thought, but the Ringgold men obviously deserved their reputation for boldness and courage. He learned why Romney was so important to capture, as an outpost to protect the crucial B&O Railroad, a major supply artery for the army, both in the east and the west. He was glad the Kelley Lancers were teamed with these experienced cavalrymen.

The purpose of the earlier expedition had been to eradicate the secessionist newspaper in Romney that was abusing and misrepresenting the U.S. government. The expedition had succeeded in destroying the printing press, but two Ringgold cavalrymen were wounded and one horse killed. The 8th Ohio Infantry regiment had several men killed, captured, or wounded, he learned. Colonel Quirk, who commanded that Ohio regiment, had later resigned, giving as a reason that he was not competent to hold the position. *Do any of us feel "competent" to shoot and kill other countrymen?* AJ wondered.

WEDNESDAY, OCTOBER 23, 1861, 6:00 AM
NEW CREEK, VIRGINIA

AJ arose before reveille to watch the sunrise and the early light playing on the mountainside, first purple, then pink, then orange as the sun hit it full on. It was a glorious day and he wished Sophia was there to share in the beauty of it—she loved the fall. He no longer had thoughts about killing or being killed. He knew he would do his duty when the time came. He had decided to leave it in the Lord's hands.

Captain McGee soon informed the men they would not depart until early on Thursday, since the Fourth Ohio would not be arriving until late that evening from Camp Pendleton. The Ohio soldiers would be weary after their sixty-mile march and would need rest before continuing the march on Romney. The Ringgold Cavalry was asked to prepare supper for the Fourth Ohio Infantry and the Kelley Lancers pitched in to help. AJ stayed busy all day building fires, cutting meat, and grinding coffee by wrapping the beans in rags and pounding them with rocks. When the infantry finally arrived, AJ was happy to see the tired, hungry men eating, and relishing, the food he had helped prepare. At dusk the cavalrymen divided their tents with the visitors and all turned in for a rest.

THURSDAY, OCTOBER 24, 1861, 6:00 AM
NEW CREEK, VIRGINIA

AJ awakened early again, sure they would finally move out today. But Captain McGee informed the men that, because the Fourth Ohio had arrived so late, this day would be spent getting the army ready for departure. AJ sighed and wondered, *Are we ever going to leave this camp?* He realized he was learning firsthand the Army tradition of "hurry up and wait."

However, the day turned out to be busy, the time filled by cooking rations for a three-day march, cleaning weapons, and readying ammunition. Orderlies hustled through the camp carrying dispatches to the various commands. The bugle for lights out came early—everyone was told to be ready to leave camp at 0500.

FRIDAY, OCTOBER 25, 1861, 6:00 AM
NEW CREEK, VIRGINIA

The army rose to an early bugle and finally broke camp at 0500 hours. Captain Keys and his Ringgold Cavalry took the advance, as they were familiar with the route. The Kelley Lancers provided wing and rear guard picket duty. The army moved upstream along New Creek until they reached the Northwestern Turnpike leading to Romney. AJ was struck by the beauty of this pike, passing through high mountains toward the Shenandoah Valley of Virginia. At Burlington, in the pastoral Patterson Creek valley, the army halted for dinner. Then they pushed on toward Romney for the expected encounter with the Confederates, who were under the command of Colonel McDonald.

AJ had asked some of the Ringgold men what they knew of their opponent. Colonel Angus McDonald C.S.A. was in his sixties, an old man, they told him. He was a graduate of West Point Class of 1817, and had served two years of duty mostly in New Orleans and Mobile Bay, Alabama before resigning his commission and entering into the fur trade in the west. After returning from the west he had a varied career. For one thing, he had been the superintendent in charge of constructing the very turnpike they were on. Apparently, McDonald was expecting reinforcements from General Thomas Jackson, who was now being called "Stonewall" after the Battle of Bull Run. AJ hoped those reinforcements wouldn't arrive.

FRIDAY, OCTOBER 25, 1861, 1:00 PM
ROMNEY, VIRGINIA

When Kelley's army came in sight of the road leading to Moorefield, a picket of twenty-five to thirty enemy cavalrymen opened fire with shotguns. Captain Keys boldly charged the pickets and chased them for about three miles until they almost entered Mechanicsburg Gap. There the enemy turned and got behind a twelve-pound howitzer which lobbed twelve-pound shot at the Ringgold Cavalry. Keys hastily directed the men to take cover and wait for the rest of the army to arrive. The army then pushed through the mountain gap, only to meet the enemy artillery lined up across the South Branch of the Potomac, in a position to fire directly into the gap.

There Keys and his men awaited the arrival of General Kelley, who came up in a carriage, as he was still suffering from the wound received at Philippi.

Captains Keys promptly informed the general of the situation saying, "The river is impassable for our infantry and artillery. The enemy is holding the covered bridge with three pieces of artillery. The Ringgold Cavalry and your Lancers are currently hidden from view in a ravine. Perhaps we can move down that ravine, find a way to ford the river, and get behind their artillery."

Kelley's bushy eyebrows formed a V as he thought for a moment, then replied, "That seems too risky, Captain Keys. I do not want to see good cavalrymen sacrificed."

"But, General," Keys persisted, "if we can find a way to ford the stream undetected, I think we can surprise them. May we at least try to locate such a place where we could ford?"

"I want you to be absolutely sure you are undetected before you attempt to cross the river. How do you propose to do that?"

"You can watch the enemy, General. They are now lined up, waiting for a frontal attack from us. If you keep feinting an attack, that should keep their attention focused on you. If you see a body of rebel cavalry or infantry moving from their positions, then they've detected us. Start your artillery firing and we'll know we've been detected. If, on the other hand, you hear us across the river yelling and firing our revolvers, then move your infantry and artillery double-quick across the bridge. You'll know we caught them by surprise and maybe we can confuse them with attacks from two directions."

Keys felt strongly that his plan would work, but Kelley still resisted, arguing that they would likely be annihilated. After a few more arguments against Keys's plan, all of which were carefully refuted by Keys, General Kelley reluctantly agreed to give it a try. Keys was elated. He and McGee moved their two cavalry companies quietly down the ravine to the river's edge. There they encountered a black man in wet clothes.

"What are you doing here?" Captain Keys asked, pointing his revolver at the man.

"I's runnin', marse."

"Why are your clothes wet?"

"Jest waded cross dat river, marse."

"Where'd you wade across?"

"I c'n show you, marse."

"Then do that. Just know that I'll shoot you if you try to lead us into a trap."

"No trap, marse, no trap! I's jest tryin' to git away. I wants to fight!"

The contraband slave, as the soldiers referred to the runaways, showed Keys where to cross. The ford was out of sight of the Confederates and the two cavalry companies crossed the river without trouble and moved quietly up a hollow leading to high ground still out of sight of the enemy. Captain Keys and McGee dismounted and crawled to the top of a bluff where they could see the enemy artillery, infantry and cavalry still facing Kelley across the bridge.

"Looks like we haven't been spotted yet," Keys whispered to McGee. "Let's form the men in two lines with the Ringgolds in the front line and the Lancers in the second. At my command we'll charge them, yelling as loudly as we can, fire our revolvers and draw sabers. Our yelling and firing will send the signal to General Kelley to double-quick our infantry and artillery across the bridge."

FRIDAY, OCTOBER 25, 1861, 4:00 PM
ROMNEY, VIRGINIA

Word was passed silently to the men to recap their guns and revolvers, form two mounted lines and quietly draw their sabers. They were told there was no room for any mistakes. All depended on them carrying out their orders to the last detail.

As he moved Shiloh into line, AJ felt outside himself somehow, as if what was happening wasn't real. He pinched the skin on the back of his hand. *It's real, all right.* He took a deep breath, feeling the blood pounding in his ears. He could feel his horse shifting under him, lifting a foot and pawing, sensing his rider's unease.

AJ looked down the line until he spotted Sergeant Harry Hagans. Harry sat tall on Betsy, a slight smile curving the corners of his lips. He appeared to be completely at ease and confident, as though he were standing in the pulpit. *Lord, please don't let me disgrace myself,* AJ prayed. *Let me be like him.*

This time the Lancers were to follow the more experienced Ringgold men, yell when they did, and do what they did. Captains Keys and McGee were composed in their saddles, watching as guidon bearers slowly unfurled their flags. At Captain Keys's hand signal, both mounted lines slowly and quietly rode their horses at a walk to the top of the bluff. AJ could now see the enemy off to their left, several hundreds of yards away, still gazing across the bridge at General Kelley's army. The enemy held a commanding position, AJ thought. Should Kelley charge across the bridge with his infantry or cavalry, the enemy could cut them to pieces with their artillery and capture or kill any remaining soldiers who made it across the bridge.

AJ marveled at the colorful scene before him. He and his fellow cavalrymen were in a position to strike at the left rear of the Confederates. In the surrounding woods, the brilliant leaves shimmered in the gentle breeze. A bright green meadow, perfect for running cavalry horses, lay before him. Near the bridge over the brown winding ribbon of river, full from the recent rains, stood the enemy soldiers, some in grey, some in blue, some in nondescript tan pants and jackets. They were almost mo-tionless. At this distance, they looked like toy soldiers, he thought. He glanced at his watch—4 PM. *The sun is at my back. Good. The enemy will have the sun in their eyes.* A calm descended on him.

Suddenly the tranquil scene changed as Captain Keys bellowed or-ders: "Charge!" All the troopers began to yell as their horses lunged for-ward. Onward they rode, first at a trot and then at a canter, sergeants call-ing, "Hold the line, boys!" Shiloh wanted to run on and arched his neck and pulled against the tight rein. AJ kept a strong hold on him, to keep him in line.

AJ could see that the Confederates were taken completely by surprise by the screaming horsemen descending with flashing sabers and discharg-ing revolvers. Their artillerymen tried to wheel their cannons around to fire at the charging cavalry, but their officers quickly countermanded when they saw Kelley's army coming across the bridge from the other direction at the double-quick. Fear started to spread among the Confed-erates. They could not see how many cavalrymen were charging toward them, or if the oncoming cavalry were followed by infantry and artillery. Already the Union infantry and artillery were on the bridge racing toward them. AJ could see they now thought it was a trap and they would be slaughtered. AJ yelled louder and raised his revolver. He saw the enemy limbering their cannon and starting to fall back.

The Southern troops began to panic and many abandoned their weapons and ran for the woods and the mountains. Some stopped and tried to regroup, firing at their pursuers. AJ heard the "zing" of bullets moving through the air. He didn't know if they were aimed at him or were coming from behind him. His main sense was of noise and confu-sion.

When they reached Romney, the remaining Confederates tried to make a stand. In front of the courthouse they placed a 12-pound howitzer filled with grape and canister shot. AJ reined Shiloh back and decided to watch the Ringgold men, to see how they handled this new obstruction, and imitate them. The Union cavalrymen, as they arrived on the scene, spotted the cannon and simply split right and left to cross streets. AJ followed them. The Confederate artillerymen, fearing they would be flanked and surrounded, limbered up and tried to pull the weapon out. But it was too late. Captain McGee ordered his cavalry to charge.

AJ completely forgot himself, as he and the other cavalrymen swept down upon the retreating enemy as one. All fear of being killed or wounded had evaporated in the sheer energy of the charge. He and the other men managed to take almost everything in sight: bands of prisoners, wagons loaded with goods, discarded weapons and equipment. Captain Keys ordered some of the Ringgolds to chase after those Confederates who were running down the pike toward Winchester. He ordered the rest of the men to assemble in the town center with the confiscated goods and prisoners.

It was all over quickly. In the town, AJ sat in his saddle, feeling trembly and nervous. He'd been assigned to guard a wagon loaded with weapons, hitched to two mules. At least he had now "seen the Elephant" as some of the men called experiencing combat for the first time. He could hardly believe he and Shiloh had come through untouched.

During that first yelling charge on the bridge, he felt sure the Confederates would turn their cannons on them and blast gaping holes in their two lines. Instead, he had witnessed what a surprise attack from two directions can do to a body of soldiers. The enemy panicked, broke ranks and ran. Many enemy soldiers threw down their weapons and threw up their hands rather than be cut down by cavalry sabers or shot by their revolvers. The Confederate cavalry had tried to stop the panic, but when that failed even they turned tail and ran.

But it had not been all one-sided. He had seen some Lancers and Ringgold men fall and some cavalry horses lay dead. But, it appeared to him they had achieved a great victory over the enemy. He felt proud, yet he also felt sympathy for the Confederate soldiers that fell or were taken prisoners. Many were young boys—younger than him—and some had tears of humiliation running down their cheeks.

Later, after he'd been relieved from his guard duty, AJ sought out Harry. He found him overseeing a group of infantry privates loading a wagon with confiscated ammunition. AJ fell to and lent a hand. When they were done, AJ said, "You looked so calm in the line, just before we made that first charge, and it really bucked me up, Harry. I just wanted you to know that."

Harry grinned. "Well, AJ, I sat there, not knowing what would happen to us, when I remembered the words of John the Baptist from Matthew, about being baptized by fire. The feeling came over me that this charge was going to be my baptism by fire, and it calmed me for some reason. I hadn't realized that my thoughts and feelings at that moment might affect others. But that's how God works!"

"I sure hope you realize how much the Lancers—me included—look up to you."

Harry placed a hand on AJ's shoulder. "Thank you, brother. It means a lot to me. I hope, with God's help, I can live up to your high opinion."

Just then they both heard a shout and turned to see the two captains gesturing for the men to assemble. As they gathered the men took off their caps and cheered their commanders, who then thanked them for their bravery and performance that day. The captains went on to explain that all the Confederate artillery, ammunition, camp equipage, and stores had fallen into Union hands.

AJ soaked it all in. Today, he thought, their strategy worked, their military goal was accomplished. It all came down to single brave men, knowing their jobs and doing their duty together, even in the face of danger and possible death.

Kelley's men would stay in Romney for a while and they went to work to make the camp more comfortable, pitching tents and digging new latrines away from the camp. First AJ saw to his horse, fearful of discovering a hidden injury or lameness from the violent charge. So far he seemed fit and healthy. "You turned out to be a brave soldier," he whispered in Shiloh's ear. Shiloh flicked his ear and rubbed his head against AJ's chest.

General Kelley was elated over the victory. The following day he issued a proclamation to the people of Romney assuring them that he came to support and uphold their civil, social and political rights. He wrote in his official report to General Scott, "I must be pardoned, however, in calling the attention of the country to the brilliant charges of the cavalry under Captain Keys and McGee. I venture to say they are unsurpassed by any other in the annals of American Warfare. As a compliment to Captain Keys, the senior officer, for his gallant conduct, I have named my camp at this point Camp Keys."

Kelley gave Captain Keys permission to read this excerpt from his official report to the men of the Ringgold and Kelley Lancers cavalry companies. AJ listened to the formal speeches and was proud of the compliment paid to their captain, but mostly he was relieved that his company performed well under fire—and had survived where some others hadn't. Some of his comrades celebrated with a little too much applejack, AJ thought. But he understood. *We're still green, but after this battle at least we know we can do the job we're sent to do.*

They settled into a camp life routine. When not drilling or in a scouting party, AJ tried to keep busy cleaning and mending his tack, weapons and equipment, and tending to Shiloh. He'd left Red with a young infantryman stationed to guard the B&O Railroad in New Creek. The boy said Red reminded him of one of their barn cats back home. AJ missed the cat; he was good company and was a tangible link to his friend Oliver.

He dreaded the leisure times, when his mind was free to dwell on all he had lost: Sophia, Oliver, and his home. He feared now that he would never see Smithfield again. Already hundreds of Union soldiers were buried at Maple Valley Cemetery in Grafton, some having died from combat wounds but most dying from sicknesses like dysentery, typhoid, measles, and pneumonia. He resolved to do everything he could to return to his family, but he could feel the filth, the terrible food, the drudgery of camp life—and worst of all, the hole in his heart—eating at him, tearing him apart, bit by bit. He'd heard of some men dying from homesickness, but wasn't sure if it was true.

One of AJ's tent mates told him that General Kelley was going to a hospital in Cumberland, Maryland, and the Kelley Lancers were to escort him there. *Good,* AJ thought, *anything is better than staying in this dirty camp.*

MONDAY, NOVEMBER 4, 1861, 6:00 AM
CAMP KEYS, ROMNEY, VIRGINIA

On Monday, a story made the rounds of another bushwhacker attack. A force from the Ringgold Cavalry had been sent to reconnoiter the turnpike toward Winchester, to see if they spotted any Confederates in the area. The bushwhackers had badly injured one of the Ringgold men and killed his horse. The cavalry was put on high alert.

For AJ, it brought back the horrors of the three bushwhackers he had killed, and he had a violent nightmare that night. He awoke Tuesday morning feeling weak, his hands shaking, head aching and his vision blurred. *What's wrong with me?* he wondered. He poured some water from his canteen onto his handkerchief and held it to his eyes. He felt a drip from his nose and touched it. Blood! His nose was bleeding. He held his handkerchief to his nose until it stopped.

Captain McGee announced at morning quarters that the Kelley Lancers would escort General Kelley to the hospital in Cumberland, where he was to have further surgery on his wound. The Lancers would remain on guard duty as long as the General was in the hospital, possibly for several months. AJ hoped the change of duty would bring about a change for the better in him. He was beginning to feel that he had an incurable case of the blues.

FRIDAY, NOVEMBER 15, 1861, 7:00 AM
CUMBERLAND, MARYLAND

AJ slumped on his bunk, head supported by one hand. *I'm sick, but I ain't goin' to sick call.* His body shook from chills. The nosebleeds were more frequent now and his back and head both hurt something terrible. *I seen what happened to Oliver, and I ain't goin' to die in no hospital.* He tried to think what to do.

The monotonous days in this camp had sapped his energy. There wasn't enough for the whole company to do in their role as private guard for General Kelley. Two weeks had passed. Apart from an occasional Confederate raid on the railroad or a scouting run, little occupied them other than drilling, standing watch, and day-to-day camp maintenance and chores. He tried to fill his days with busy work, but he couldn't hide from his aching heart. Sophia was constantly on his mind, his need for her seeming to grow stronger every day. He had to confide in her, tell her how much he cared, especially if death was coming for him. Which he feared it might be.

Then he thought of Shiloh. Who would care for his horse if he died? *I got to find the strength to get home.* He forced himself to stand, to walk out of the tent and find Harry. He needed to find Harry.

Harry as quartermaster sergeant of the company was kept busy with paperwork, ordering supplies and attending meetings most days, but at this early hour he could often be found reading and studying in his tent. Harry looked up as AJ stumbled through the flap, and ran to help his friend sit down on the empty bunk next to him. "AJ! What's wrong?"

"I'm sick, Harry. I'm goin' home."

Harry laid a hand on AJ's forehead. "You're feverish, my friend. You need a doctor! Come on, let me take you over to the hospital."

"No! I swore I wouldn't, after seeing what happened to Oliver. You know what these hospitals are like! I suppose the wards for the officers, like General Kelley, are tolerable, but the ones for privates like me are pigsties, or worse. Crowded, smelly and stinkin' with the men's filth. Harry, I came lookin' for you, to help me."

Harry frowned and stared closely at his friend, a question in his eyes. "What are you going to do, that you need my help?"

"Listen, Harry, I'll die if I stay here. I can't sleep at night. I can't eat much. I'm gettin' weaker. If I can get back to Ma and home, and Sophia—I got to see her one more time at least…" He broke off, his voice choking. "I might make it then. Can you help me get leave to go?"

Harry scratched his head. "It's a long ride—at least two days—from here to Smithfield, AJ. That in itself could kill you! And it's like winter already. Looks like it might even snow tonight. You're not thinking straight. And you can't get a furlough on such short notice. It can take several weeks."

AJ shook his head. His mind was made up and nothing Harry said was going to change it. "I mean it, Harry, I'm goin' home. I'm sick, but I still have some spunk left. If I go now, before I get any worse, I can make it. Or die tryin'. I know I got a much better chance with Ma lookin' after me than in that hospital. But no matter what, I'm takin' Shiloh now and going. If I can't get a furlough, I'm takin' my French leave." He set his jaw and looked Harry in the eye, waiting for an answer.

Harry didn't speak for several seconds, biting his lip, studying his friend, thinking it over. Finally, he nodded.

"All right, AJ. I fear I may come to regret it, but I'll see what I can do. You saved my life once and I'll help you now. Perhaps you do know best what course you need to take. I pray it is so. And I hope you will pray about it as well. Now leave me and go back and pack your blankets and saddlebags. Dress warmly. Pack an extra canteen—you need to keep drinking, with that fever. Can you walk back to your tent, or do I need to help you back?"

"I can make it by myself."

"Good. I need to do some things. Wait there in your tent for me, AJ. I'll have something for you. Don't leave till I get there."

"Thank you, friend. I knew you'd help. If the Lord's willin', I'll come back to the Kelley Lancers just as soon as I get well, I promise. I wouldn't desert you or the Lancers, you know that, don't you, Harry?"

Harry nodded and managed a weak smile. AJ tried to smile back.

Friday, November 15, 1861, 8:30 am
Smithfield, Pennsylvania

"But, how, Harry?" he asked, staring at the pass his friend had just handed him. It stated that Alexander Swaney was granted 20 days furlough. It *looked* official but it was hard to make out the signature.

"Don't ask, AJ. Some things you're better off not knowing. You might be in a little trouble when you get back to the Lancers, but I'll smooth it over as best I can. Don't worry. Just get home safely and get well," Harry said.

Harry also handed him a letter. "When you get to Little Meadows near Grantsville, Maryland, give this to my friend Mrs. Layman at the Tomlinson Stone House Inn. She looks after the inn and she's a kind, Christian woman. She'll make sure you're looked after tonight. The inn sits right by the road and Mrs. Layman will give you some warm tea or broth and let you rest in a bed. Shiloh can get some rest there too. Promise me you'll stop and take some nourishment, and let Mrs. Layman look after you, AJ. Don't try to ride all night in this cold! Besides, there's more danger from bushwhackers at night, for a lone rider. I need your promise, or else I'll call the guards and take you to the hospital."

"All right, Harry, I'll stop to rest and I'll give Mrs. Layman the letter. I promise you." *Harry thinks he might never see me again,* AJ thought.

Together they saddled and bridled Shiloh and loaded AJ's saddlebags with food and shelled corn. Harry had brought two apples and some homemade bread that one of the soldier's wives had made, and tucked them into AJ's bag. "You can share the apples with Shiloh," he said. "I know you will anyway." Harry slid the long rifle into its holster, and held Shiloh while AJ tried to mount. His legs were so weak that he had to ask Harry for a leg up, but once in the saddle he felt a little better. Shiloh turned his head to look at his rider.

"Shiloh's worried about you, too," said Harry, managing a humorless laugh. "Are you absolutely sure you want to do this?"

"It's more what I *need* to do than want to, Harry," he said. AJ patted and stroked his horse's shoulder. "Good boy, you'll take care of me, won't you? Let's go *home*, Shiloh," he said.

The horse lifted his head and pointed his ears toward the west and snorted. "See, he knows the way," AJ said. He turned to look fondly at Harry and raised a hand in farewell. "Thank you, again, my friend. I'll never forget this. God willin', I'll see you back here before long."

* * *

This is where I belong, in the saddle and headin' for home. His spirits seemed lighter already. Or maybe it was the fever… He kept a handker-chief in his hand to wipe away the sweat, and in case his nose started to bleed again. Rocking in the saddle aggravated the pains in his head and back, but Shiloh's gaits were smooth and so far it was tolerable.

The traffic on the National Pike was not heavy. Many of the travelers were Union soldiers on horseback, singles like him, or small groups, probably making their way across the state borders to assignments in Pennsylvania, Maryland and western Virginia. AJ patted his pocket and felt the folded papers there that Harry had given him. He thought he probably wouldn't need to show the pass to anyone until he started back

South, after he got well—*if* he got well. As far as he knew, no border guards had been posted at the Pennsylvania-Maryland border.

The thought of seeing home and Sophia again had focused his energy and during the morning the miles seemed to go quickly. He stopped once to relieve himself. So far whatever this disease was had seemed to constipate him rather than loosen his bowels, and he was grateful for that. He'd seen the horrors of dysentery in the Grafton hospital. But it took all his strength to remount. Shiloh was patient with him, seeming to understand.

They didn't stop at dinnertime. AJ took several long swallows from his canteen and ate part of an apple and a piece of the bread Harry had given him, while still moving. He let Shiloh drink from a brook and grab a few snatches of long grass from the side of the road and gave him the rest of the apple. AJ hoped the food would stay down. His abdomen pained him now.

When they arrived at the Tomlinson Stone House Inn, AJ figured the sun was almost down. He couldn't tell for sure because it had disappeared long ago behind high, dark clouds. The inn was a massive two-story stone building with a thirty-foot-wide chimney at each end. Warm light shone through the windows. A tidy stable stood off to one side.

Light, icy snow whipped AJ's cheeks. He felt chilled and light-headed and knew his fever had gotten worse. He hated to bring sickness into this place. He slowly slid off Shiloh and called to another soldier headed for the door, "Please, could you ask Mrs. Layman to come out here for a minute?"

The soldier looked at him with a frown and continued on his way, but after a few moments a tall, strong-looking woman with steel-gray hair and eyes came out, wiping her hands on an apron. She asked him what he wanted and AJ handed her Harry's letter. She squinted at it in the dim light and then a smile lit her face. "Oh, it's from young Reverend Hagans!"

AJ nodded. It was all he could manage.

Mrs. Layman read on, then looked up and frowned. "Oh, he says you're ill, son! And I'm to care for you and let you rest here till you're ready to go on. And he even sent me some stamps, so I can write to him and let him know you made it here. Well, he knows he didn't have to do that! Such a thoughtful man." She reached out her hand and felt AJ's forehead. "Mm. You're hot! Let's get you into bed."

"Please, ma'am," AJ said, swaying a little, "I need to look after my horse first. We been on the road all day."

"I'll call Caleb to take care of your horse, son. You're Alexander, ain't you? Your animal's a beaut, Alexander. CALEB!" Her shout echoed off the stones like that of an Army sergeant, and Caleb, a strapping boy of about 16, scurried from the adjacent stables. Mrs. Layman turned back to AJ. "Let's take your bags and your rifle with us, Alexander. Caleb will set your saddle on one of the racks. It'll be fine there. He keeps an eye on things. He'll give your mount some water and a little corn and hay. Now how *is* Harry? I haven't seen him in a couple of years!"

"He's doin' well, ma'am. But, say, maybe I could sleep for a little while in the stables? I hate to bring this fever into your nice hotel."

"Tsk. We ain't even half full tonight and I got a clean little room way in the back, on the side next to the stables, so you'll even be near to your horse. I'll take you there. And don't worry, Reverend Hagans sent along enough to cover your bill."

Harry leaned on her arm as she guided him to a side door on the barn side of the massive stone building. She let him into a tiny chamber with a single bed and covered him with a thick quilt. "You must be half froze, Alexander—feels like winter out there. I'll poke up the fire and bring you some soup. My, you are hot. I think I should send for the Doc in the mornin'. What do you say?"

AJ shook his head. He wrapped his arms around himself tightly to stop his shivering, so his teeth wouldn't chatter. "No, ma'am, I'll be fine if I can just rest a little… thank you, ma'am." He could feel sleep overtaking him and his eyes drooped.

He awoke a few hours later, hearing a noise in the hall outside his room. It was still dark but he felt rested and he could tell his fever was down some. He lit the lamp by the bed and saw that someone, Mrs. Layman he presumed, had brought him a mug of beef broth and a slice of bread with butter. His bladder was full and he found the chamber pot under the bed, and a pitcher of water and a bowl. He washed, and then dried his face and hands on the tiny towel left for him and drank the broth. He tried a few bites of the bread but it seemed to stick in his throat.

He decided to leave now, before daylight. *If I stay, Mrs. Layman'll see how bad I look in the daylight and she'll want to call me a doctor.* AJ was grateful for her kindness and he resolved to write her later to tell her so. He had kept his promise to Harry, and now he needed to go. He gathered his things, slipped out, found Shiloh dozing in the stables, and saddled him. He was glad to see the snow hadn't amounted to much, just an inch or two on the ground.

For the first few hours on the Pike, he felt almost himself. The fever seemed to have abated and he was again exhilarated at the thought of home. But then the fever returned. He slumped in the saddle, often dozing briefly. Shiloh kept up a steady pace, alternating between his smooth trot and a canter that ate up the miles, with no urging from AJ. *He seems as eager to get home as I do*, AJ thought.

Once, in the early afternoon, a group of three men on horseback entered the Pike from a side road. In his fever, Harry thought they were the bushwhackers he had killed on the way to Philippi. He yelled and kicked Shiloh into a full gallop, thinking the men were chasing him. But then the vision changed and he thought he saw his ma and sister sitting on the porch of an inn by the road. He tried to wave but was too weak. "Stop, boy," he mumbled. Shiloh flicked his ears back at him, but kept going.

By the time they reached Pennsylvania and Uniontown, late that afternoon, AJ was out of his head and barely had the strength to stay upright. He was riding by rote. During his conscious periods, he mumbled, over and over, "Home, boy, home." The horse trotted on.

The sun was down by the time Shiloh turned into the lane to the Swaney farmhouse. He whinnied and AJ roused, lifted his head, and looked around. He thought he could see his father and John in the stubble of the wheat field, but he wasn't sure whether it was real or one of his fevered visions. The two shadowy figures waved and started toward him. "Good boy," he mumbled as he slipped from the saddle. His legs were rubber.

Half crawling, half stumbling to the steps, he managed to pull himself up onto the porch and pound the door with the heel of his hand. He could feel and smell he had soiled himself and was ashamed to arrive home in such a state. He pounded again and the door opened.

His mother gasped. "AJ! My boy!" He felt her open his jacket and look at his neck and chest. She gasped, then called behind her, "Cynthia! Get your garden gloves on and tie a kerchief 'round your face, then come and help me lift your brother!"

AJ couldn't stand. His mother and sister together lifted him over the threshold into the house.

MONDAY, NOVEMBER 25, 1861, NOON
SMITHFIELD, PENNSYLVANIA

AJ had been dozing and woke to a soft knock at the bedroom door. He supposed it was his mother, bringing his dinner. His stomach told him it was time for the midday meal. His mother had taken charge of her patient immediately, cleaning him up and putting him to bed, on sweet-smelling sheets, in the spare room at the back of the farmhouse. She tended him herself, keeping the rest of the family away. She fed him on broths and herbal teas, apples, and even found an orange for him from somewhere. She bathed his fevers and shushed him when he talked out of his head. He now felt as if he had woken from a horrific nightmare, through which a kind phantom had floated to minister to him in the horrors. Though still weak, he could feel his strength returning. At least the food tasted better now and he was able to keep most of it down. He even looked forward today to seeing the contents of his dinner tray.

"Come in, Ma, I'm decent," he said, sliding to prop himself up on his pillows. The door opened and Sophia entered the room, carrying the tray of food. Her smile, like a ray of sunshine, went straight through his heart. He blinked, not sure what he saw was real.

"Why... it's you! I thought you was Ma," he said, awkward.

"She told me you was past the crisis and it was all right for me to see you a while. She said she thought it might do you some good."

"Seeing you always does me some good, Sophia," he said softly. "Always has."

She colored, which made her even prettier to his eyes. "I didn't know that," she said.

AJ nodded. "I never told you, did I? I've had lots of time to think on all the things I never told you."

They stared at each other.

"You are surely a sight for my sore eyes," AJ said. "If anything can make me well again, it's the sight of you."

"I was so scared you was going to die, AJ! I couldn't bear that!" Her eyes filled and overflowed.

"I'm sorry for being so backward, and so bossy to you, Sophia. I been missing you somethin' terrible."

"I... "

"Shh, let me talk and get this out now before I get clean out 'a breath. Then you can talk. There I go bossin' you again, but I do need to get this all out of me. I've knowed for a long time you was the only girl for me. And I guess I just thought somehow it would all work out that you and

349

me would be together, without me ever havin' to say anything. I guess it's because I'm not used to talking about… deep feelings. I'm not like Harry, you know. I feared you thought I was kind of cold and that I didn't care. But I want you to know I'm not a cold man. I do have those feelings, tender feelings, deep ones. I do love you, Sophia, have for a *long* time.

"When we was off trainin' and fightin', and seein' and doin' things that men shouldn't have to see and do, I realized that you were all that could keep me going. Thoughts of you. When I thought I'd lost you, I couldn't bear it. And I can't imagine being with anyone else for the rest of my life, if I make it back after this dadblame war. So that's what I had to say." He breathed and sighed, catching his breath. "Now yore turn."

Sophia's lips trembled and she blinked back tears. She couldn't speak for a long moment. "When you left here, AJ, I wasn't real sure how I did feel about you. We had got into that bad time of being mad and not talking, mostly over Tip. And Tip, well, I sent him packing when I found out you was right about him. You was right about a lot of things. Comparing you to Tip—well, to me there ain't no comparison! I've had time to think too. And if you'll have me, I want the same as you. To live the rest of my life with you. So you sure better come home from that war safe and sound!"

AJ reached for her hand. The dinner tray was forgotten, as they sat and talked the way they always had, like close friends, laughing, teasing, making their plans, until AJ's mother came in and declared the visit over. "You can come back tomorrow, Sophia. He'll be here yet for awhile."

WEDNESDAY, JULY 1, 1863, 6:00 AM
GETTYSBURG, PENNSYLVANIA

He arose well before dawn to feed, water and care for Shiloh and Grey Eagle. While they ate, he spoke to them as he ran the curry comb and brush over every square inch of horse hide. He could find no bruises or areas of soreness or sensitivity on either horse. He cleaned and checked their feet. He had noticed that one of Shiloh's shoes was slightly loose when he checked them last night, so he left some hay for Grey Eagle to munch and led Shiloh out of the barn to the farriers by the camp wagons. Can't take a chance on losing a shoe today.

"Hey, Mistah AJ." One of the two farriers on duty stood up from the horse he was trimming and raised his hand in greeting. At first AJ was startled, not recognizing the handsome dark man in front of him. Then all at once it came to him—Abraham Blackman.

"Well, if it ain't the horse thief!" he said, grinning.

Abraham's face fell, but AJ laughed and said, "I'm just joshin' you, Abraham. I'm glad to see you here safe. I guess you made it back to your family?"

"Yessuh, I got 'em moved up to Canada, like Preacher Harry tole me. But then I felt like I needed to help with this here fight, 'specially after all y'all done for me. So here I is!"

"Shiloh has a loose shoe. Could you take a look?"

Abraham laughed. "You just bring 'im on over here. Dat Shiloh is still one of the nicest lookin' pieces of horseflesh I ever did see."

The farrier pulled the shoe and replaced it quickly. AJ admired Abraham's efficient, gentle way of handling the horses and the speed at which he worked. "You're surely good at your job," he said, and Abraham beamed.

"Got to get back to the General. Glad you're here, Abraham. It's goin' to be a very... interestin' day," AJ said. "I'll see you around." As he walked back to Buford's headquarters he recalled the incident that had brought them together. It felt as if he were remembering the life of another person. His own point of view on many things had changed so much since those days before he became a cavalryman.

He continued to check over both horses until General Buford made his appearance. "Good morning, AJ. You've got your two charges looking very fit and sleek," said the general as he took the reins and mounted Grey Eagle.

"Thank you, General. Your canteen's full of fresh water. I boiled it last night. Should be cooled off by now," AJ replied.

"AJ, stick close to me today. I'm going to head over and climb up in that cupola in the seminary building so I can keep an eye out for General Reynolds, and another eye out for those damn rebels and our men behind those rail and stone breastworks."

AJ nodded. "Feels like this fine rain has cooled things off a little."

Just then they both heard a single shot coming from the area where Buford had posted their pickets last night. By the time they reached the seminary, they heard more shots. AJ thought, *I hope the rebels think our boys are just militia. If so, they won't take the time to deploy and will try to just push through our lines. Then Gamble and Devin will give them a bloody nose and buy us time for General Reynolds to bring up his infantry… but can our boys hold them back long enough?*

AJ waited for the general, breathing deeply, trying to stay calm so the horses would be calm. He had loaded his long rifle before they left, so he was prepared, just in case, to protect his general, if it came to that. And himself, as he would likely be running orders all over the place today.

AJ pulled out a tintype from his breast pocket and stared, for possibly the ten-thousandth time, at Sophia's likeness smiling back at him. He had written her a letter last night:

Dearest Sophia,

Though we are far apart at present my heart is with you every moment. When we are travelling the lonesome roads at night, I offen

*think of you when you are asleep. The thought of your sweet smile is
all the company I have and all I need. Your
sparkling blue eyes and pink cheeks are what I see when I lie down at
night. I long for the time to come when we shall meet again. I promise to do all in my power to come back to you, as I have much now to
come back for. To make you my wife when I return is my fondest
dream and hope. Remember me always as your friend and your love.
Please write soon. Your letters are the medicine I need to get me
through this vishus war. Pleas pray for me as I do for you, and meet
me in your dreams till I can hold you again in my arms.*

Your future husband, AJ

The End

Epilogue

On October 24, 1861, the day before Kelley captured Romney, the people of western Virginia approved the ordinance, by a vote of 18,408 to 781, to carve a new state out of Virginia. This represented a personal blow to Lee and a political blow to the seceded state of Virginia and the Confederacy. Once the Restored State of Virginia came into being and was seated in the U.S. Congress, the wily northwestern Virginia politicians, especially Carlile and Willey, realized that the chaos of war had given them the opportunity to do what they had wanted to do for decades: secede from Virginia! Virginia lost over a third of her territory when West Virginia was formed—the only state to lose any territory during the Civil War.

The western Virginia leaders proceeded to follow the complicated steps required by the United States Constitution to create a new state from the territory of an old one: first have a Constitutional Convention, draw up a state constitution and let the counties vote on it; put a bill together asking that statehood be approved by both the U.S. Senate and House of Representatives; and finally, have it signed by the President. It was not a smooth process by any means: choosing a name (West Virginia became the popular choice), deciding on the boundaries, convincing the counties to vote for it, and persuading the legal minds of the day in Congress. Fiery debates accompanied each step. Finally, convincing President Lincoln himself to sign proved to be no picnic, as half his Cabinet approved it and half thought the idea unconstitutional and an unwelcome legal precedent. Lincoln sat on the fence right up until he decided to sign.

Here's what he said: "We can scarcely dispense with the aid of West Virginia in this struggle, much less can we afford to have her against us, in Congress and in the field. Her brave and good men regard her admission into the Union as a matter of life and death. They have been true to the Union under many severe trials. The division of a state is dreaded as a precedent. But a measure made expedient by a war, is no precedent for times of peace. It is said the admission of West Virginia is secession, and tolerated only because it is our secession. Well, if we can call it by that name, there is still difference enough between secession against the Constitution, and secession in favor of the Constitution."

West Virginia became a state on June 20, 1863, and legal pundits still debate the process. But she is still a state and that speaks for itself.

Pierpont remained governor of the Restored Government of Virginia, with its five eastern counties and its capital in Alexandria. Arthur Boreman was elected the first governor of the state of West Virginia, but Pierpont's name is the one that remains most associated with the new state.

As for the Confederacy in western Virginia, after the departure of Rosecrans from Sewell Mountain, Lee conferred with Loring and they agreed that Loring's forces would go back to Huntersville, but no further serious offensive was mounted by the Confederates to retake the area of Virginia west of the Allegheny Mountains. Lee withdrew the remaining Confederate forces to Lewisburg, where he received a telegram from President Davis recalling him to Richmond. A dejected Lee finally left the western Virginia mountains on October 30 and returned to Richmond. The Southern press was harsh with him: "outwitted and outgeneralled," "too tender of blood," "preferring rather to dig entrenchments than to fight," "overcautious and too much the theorist." As a final insult, the *Richmond Enquirer* called him "Granny Lee."

President Davis never lost faith in Lee and ordered him to supervise coastal defenses in South Carolina when news reached Richmond that a fleet of Federal warships had been sent to threaten coastal ports in southern states. Nevertheless, Lee's badly tarnished reputation forced Davis to write a letter, before Lee arrived, to the governor of South Carolina explaining Lee's virtues and the severe nature of the problems Lee had faced in western Virginia.

Of all the Confederate leaders, "Stonewall" Jackson was perhaps the only one who had a real strategy to retake western Virginia. It had been his boyhood home and he understood its strategic importance. He wanted a winter offensive during the brutal winter of 1861–1862 and he clashed with Confederate General Loring over it, to the extent that Jackson filed court-martial charges against Loring, which never came to trial. In the end, the winter weather was Jackson's worst enemy. Jackson finally went back across the Alleghenies to Winchester, but the troops who were left behind on the western Virginia mountaintops that winter, both Confederate and Union, suffered terrible deprivation. (Interestingly, the 1860s were at the end of what meteorologists now call "The Little Ice Age.")

Alexander Swaney rejoined his company in Cumberland, Maryland after he recovered from his illness, which was likely typhoid fever, made worse by heart- and homesickness. It was common, especially in the first year of the war, for soldiers to leave camp and make their way home for brief periods due to illness, or pressing family or business matters, or simply because they were homesick and happened to be near enough to home to travel there—"French leave" was their term for intentionally going AWOL. As long as they returned to their unit within a reasonable amount of time, they usually weren't punished severely and it wasn't considered desertion.

New adventures lay in store for the Kelley Lancers in their role as Company A of the First (West) Virginia Cavalry Regiment, fighting the Confederates in the winter under General Lander and attached to a cavalry brigade commanded by the newly appointed cavalry brigadier general, John Buford. Alexander Swaney was selected by General Buford as a permanent orderly and he was with the general at the Battle of Gettysburg. As described in Kautz's *Customs of Service for Non-Commissioned Officers and Soldiers*, a popular army guidebook published in 1864, orderlies were "soldiers selected on account of their intelligence, experience, and soldierly bearing, to attend on generals, commanding officers, officers of the day, and staff officers, to carry orders, mess &c. They may be taken from the guard or put on permanently while the duty lasts: in the latter case they are reported on daily duty and are excused from all other duty that would interfere with their duty as orderlies."

Watch for the second volume in this series covering Alexander Swaney's experiences leading up to Gettysburg and afterwards, coming in 2018.

ABOUT THE AUTHOR

Jack W. Lewis has had a forty-year career as a U.S. Coast Guard officer and a consulting marine engineer. He received his engineering degrees at the United States Coast Guard Academy and MIT. Throughout his adult lifetime, he has maintained a strong interest in Civil War history. His many writings have covered both engineering and historical topics. This is his first novel.

http://jackwlewis.surberstation.com

MILITARY RANKS
AND
TERMINOLOGY

It's often hard for readers living in modern times to understand the complex military terms used in the American Civil War. Today, the United States of America maintains a standing army of professional citizen soldiers who stand ready to defend our country. The wages of these dedicated men and women, and the cost of the weapons they use, are paid for by the taxpayers of our nation.

But it was not like that in 1861. Each state in the Union had its own militia under the control of the governor (the militias are somewhat analogous to today's National Guard). Militias were originally created during colonial times, when each American colony was independent. Those militias were unpaid volunteer citizen soldiers who armed themselves and protected the citizens from outrages by Indians, or pirates, or possibly foreign invaders. At the beginning of the Revolutionary War, the militias played a major role. They were immortalized by Emerson in 1837 in his poem "Concord Hymn":

> *By the rude bridge that arched the flood,*
> *Their flag to April's breeze unfurled,*
> *Here once the embattled farmers stood,*
> *And fired the shot heard round the world.*

The ranks used in the militia in 1861 were similar to the ranks in use today. It's helpful in reading this novel to understand the various ranks of the military. A list of 1861 commissioned officer army ranks arranged from highest to lowest, as well as a shorter list for enlisted men, follows:

Commissioned Officer Ranks: General, Lieutenant General, Major General, Brigadier General, Colonel, Lieutenant Colonel, Major, Captain, First Lieutenant, Second Lieutenant

Enlisted Soldier Ranks: Sergeant, Corporal, Private

The rank of General did not actually exist in the United States Army in 1861, but it did exist in the Confederate States Army. Most of the Army officers that left the United States Army and joined the Confederate forces were given one rank above that which they held in the U.S. Army. Winfield Scott was the highest ranking officer in the United States with the rank of Lieutenant General. Robert E. Lee was one of three officers in the Confederate States with the rank of General.

In the enlisted ranks there were several types of sergeants (quartermaster sergeant, first sergeant, etc.) and they were usually referred to as noncoms or NCOs (noncommissioned officers), because they served without a commission signed by the governor.

It's important to understand that most of the Civil War Army regiments were composed of volunteers. Those regiments were usually named for their states and most had a regional flavor. The commanding officer was often a political appointee by the governor. Many lower ranked officers were also politically appointed.

In addition, the United States had a standing army of professional soldiers called "regulars." Winfield Scott was the head of the regular U.S. Army. Almost all regular Army officers attended the Military Academy at West Point started by George Washington's General Knox. The regular army was small and was paid for by the Federal government. They mostly manned forts such as Fort Sumter and controlled the American Indians and handled other incidents along the frontier as the nation expanded. Commanding and other officers of Federal regiments came up through the ranks and were promoted based on merit. During the Civil War the regular units in the U.S. Army were designated by the suffix "USA" and the volunteers by the suffix "USV."

Yet another term you may come across related to military ranks is "brevet." During the Civil War, a commissioned officer could be "brevetted" to a higher rank. They performed at that rank but the brevet was more like getting a medal for bravery or gallantry than receiving an actual promotion, because the honorary brevet rank usually carried no precedence or higher pay. The brevet system has now been replaced by our military's system of medals.

It is also useful to know the designations and composition of military units. A *company* had 100 men (excluding officers), a *regiment* had ten companies, a *brigade* had from two to six regiments, a *division* had two to six brigades, a *corps* had two or more divisions, and an *army* had two or more corps.

The full number of men in a company or regiment existed only at the time of the formation of that company. Sickness and deaths reduced the numbers and they usually were not replaced by recruits. Near the end of the war, many regiments were reduced by death to the size of a small company, and many just ceased to exist.

By way of background, in late 1860 the state of South Carolina seceded from the Union and was quickly joined in January by the cotton states of South Carolina, Mississippi, Alabama, Florida and Louisiana to form the Southern Confederacy, whose capital was in Montgomery, Alabama. When the state of South Carolina bombarded Fort Sumter on April 12, 1861, *state militia* from the Confederate states forced *Federal regulars* to surrender the fort. President Lincoln reacted to this "rebellion" by calling on all states in the Union to supply state militia for 90 days to put down the rebellion. Lincoln used as the precedent for this action President George Washington's similar call for state militia to put down the "Whiskey Rebellion" in Greene County, Pennsylvania.

Lincoln's call for state militia was sent out to all states in proportion to their population. The state of Virginia did not answer the call. They were holding a convention of all state delegates in Richmond to determine if Virginia would secede from the Union. In spite of great opposition from delegates of the western counties of Virginia, an ordinance of secession was passed and put to a vote of the citizens of Virginia on May 23, 1861. Extreme "secessionists" took this opportunity to attack the Federal arsenal at Harper's Ferry (now spelled Harpers Ferry but the apostrophe was used in the 1860s) and other federal facilities in Virginia. Calls went out to the counties in western Virginia, who were mostly determined to stay with the Union, to capture Federal custom houses, post offices, etc. in the name of Virginia. Mayor Sweeney of Wheeling refused to obey Governor Letcher and offered a commission of colonel to Benjamin Kelley, a previous colonel in the Virginia *militia*, to come home and lead a "loyal" regiment of Virginia infantry militia formed by Mayor Sweeney to defend the western Virginia counties and the B&O Railroad. Virginia *militia* Major General Robert E. Lee was ordered by Virginia's Governor Letcher to take action. He ordered Virginia militia Colonel George Porterfield to capture the key town of Grafton, Virginia, thus starting a civil war between Virginians. "Loyal" western Virginians asked Ohio militia General McClellan to send Ohio militia to help them. He was asked (by Ohio's governor and President Lincoln) not to respond until after May 23, when the results would be known of the Virginia citizens' vote for or against the Ordinance of Secession passed by the delegates. When the vote of the people of Virginia turned out to be for secession, militia forces from Ohio and Indiana crossed over the Ohio River into western Virginia to help the western "unionist" Virginia militiamen defend their part of Virginia against eastern "secessionist" Virginia militia, so western Virginians could stay in the Union.

On June 8, 1861, Governor Letcher, by proclamation, turned over control of secessionist Virginia state militia to the Confederacy and Virginia became part of the Confederate states. Lee was then commissioned as a regular full General in the Confederate Army by President Jeff Davis. Around the same time, McClellan was commissioned a regular Major General in the U.S. Army by President Lincoln.

Now that you're armed with this terminology, you can use the following table to help you understand and remember who's who and why regarding the military officers mentioned in this book. Keep in mind that this table is a time snapshot taken at or near the beginning of the War, and the ranks changed as officers were promoted, resigned, or were killed.

Name	Rank	State	Unionist Secessionist	Federal Confederate	Militia Regular
Scott, W.	Lieutenant General	VA	U	F	R
McClellan	Major General	OH	U	F	M/R
Lee	Major General	VA	S	C	M/R
Morris	Brigadier General	IN	U	F	M
Garnett	Brigadier General	VA	S	C	R
Floyd	Brigadier General	VA	S	C	R
Wise	Brigadier General	VA	S	C	R
Jackson, H.	Brigadier General	GA	S	C	M
Rust	Brigadier General	AR	S	C	M
Rosecrans	Brigadier General	OH	U	F	M/R
Loring, W	Brigadier General	VA	S	C	R
Dumont	Colonel	IN	U	F	M
Jackson, T. J.	Colonel	VA	S	C	M
Kimble	Colonel	IN	U	F	M
Kelley	Colonel	VA	U	F	M
Lander	Colonel	OH	U	F	M
Pegram	Colonel	VA	S	C	M/R
Heck	Colonel	VA	S	C	M/R
Reynolds, J. J.	Colonel	IN	U	F	M
Steedman	Colonel	OH	U	F	M
Porterfield	Colonel	VA	S	C	M/R
Marcy	Colonel	OH	U	F	M/R
Boykin	Major	VA	S	C	M
Benham	Captain	OH	U	F	R
Buford	Captain	KY	U	F	R
Keys	Captain	PA	U	F	M
McGee	Captain	VA	U	F	M
Poe	First Lieutenant	?	U	F	R
Merritt	Second Lieutenant	NY	U	F	R

THE MAKING OF
STORM COMING

During research on my ancestors in the early 1990s, I uncovered information indicating my two paternal great-grandfathers, Alexander James Swaney and Joseph Paul Lewis, fought in the Civil War. Archived military service records indicated they were both in the same Company A of the First (west) Virginia Cavalry. While both enlisted in Company A, I discovered each Company A had a different captain. I didn't think a regiment would have two companies designated A! At the time I had no explanation or theory to explain this finding. Nor did I understand why the Official Record (OR) indicated there were at the time two First Virginia Cavalry regiments.

At the time, I wanted to write a brief story about these two cavalrymen who were my great-grandfathers, because I was a rider and breeder of horses and was intrigued by the notion that my love of horses might be in my genes. I also wanted to write a detailed story about Alexander Swaney because his military records indicated he had been an orderly for Cavalry General John Buford starting in August 1862, until Buford died on 16 December 1863. As it turned out, I first ended up writing a historical article about Joseph Paul Lewis and the First West Virginia Cavalry, covering the period June 1863 to Lee's surrender at Appomattox. I fully intended to write about Swaney also, but it took me twenty years.

When Alexander Swaney enlisted in the cavalry, West Virginia was not a separate state. I had long wondered why a young farmer from Smithfield, Pennsylvania would join a Virginia cavalry regiment. As I delved into the matter, I started to feel that fiction might be the best vehicle for bringing his story to light. At first I intended to focus on his time with Buford, Gettysburg in particular. But during my research, I became fascinated by the story of how West Virginia came to be. I considered myself something of an "expert" on the Civil War, but I discovered I knew next to nothing about the early days of the War in western Virginia. I knew Lee had been there but I had no real understanding of the campaign. The story of West Virginia is well worth all Americans knowing, as it reveals how a true democracy works. The amount of effort put forth and the ingenuity of the western Virginia leaders who made it happen, and the foresight of our forefathers who wrote a method for dividing a state in our Constitution, still amazes me.

Now I understood why Swaney wanted to join a Virginia cavalry company. Morgantown, Virginia was the closest "big city" to his Pennsylvania border town and he, like so many other soldiers from Pennsylvania and Ohio, was a friend and trading partner with western Virginians. The Pennsylvanians and Ohioans wanted to keep that part of western Virginia in the United States of America. If AJ could help northwestern Virginians in their fight to stay in the Union, then he would also be helping (and defending) his own family in Pennsylvania.

I had read several bestselling historical novels by Newt Gingrich and William R. Forsttchen. They use a chronological "diary" format to tell their stories from many different points of view, and I thought that same scheme would work well to tell this story of a young man going off to war amid the tumult and political machinations of 1861.

An amazing thing happened to me when I started writing. I found my characters coming alive and "speaking" to me across the years, helping me to find hidden facts and different ways of seeing things. It was downright spooky. Let me give you an example. In my novel AJ and Reverend Harrison H. Hagans are buddies; they ride together, enlist in the Kelley Lancers cavalry company together, travel to Wheeling to listen to three days of the first Wheeling Convention, etc. I have no idea if any of this happened. All I had to work with was their military service records and the fact that they both were from near Smithfield, Pennsylvania. They did enlist at the same time and place and were in the same company (Hagans soon became promoted to captain of the company), so they undoubtedly knew one another. When I researched AJ's younger brother, John, I found he later married and named his first boy Alexander Harrison Swaney. Did John look on AJ and Harry as his heroes, as described in my novel? Is that why John gave his son that name? Perhaps it's just a coincidence, but it gave me chills.

Many times in writing the novel I ran into events where I had to choose between conflicting viewpoints and actions in the "factual" history books. For example, it was not clear from my research where Colonel Porterfield had his camp at Philippi before the battle started. Was it to the north of town, the south of the town, or in the town? I wanted to include a map of the "battlefield." I found two maps but they didn't agree. Which was right? In such cases I generally placed more weight on books containing maps or information for which the author(s) were alive at, or near, the actual time when the battle took place. I also wanted the map to match up with the preponderance of word descriptions and sketches.

I traveled to most of the places mentioned in the novel. My wife and I live in what is now "western Virginia," about 12 miles as the crow flies from the West Virginia border. Our county didn't quite make the cut! My wife and I traveled the National Road to Wheeling, visited the great museum at Independence Hall, walked along the waterfront and connecting streets and saw the huge suspension bridge still in use. From there we traveled downriver to Parkersburg and found the historical signs that marked the place where the Ohio troops landed. The old railroad terminal is no longer there but we could visualize the troops marching to the terminal and boarding the trains. We traveled to Grafton looking for the place where the old Grafton Hotel was located between the two branches of the B&O Railroad. The hotel is no longer there and the B&O Railroad is gone, having been replaced by CSX. The B&O Railroad was America's first railroad and it suffered during the Civil War. Beautiful structures such as the famous covered railroad bridge at Harper's Ferry were destroyed by "Stonewall" Jackson early in the war. From there we visited Morgantown. More recently we went to the Rich Mountain, Belington and Laurel Hill battle sites. The old turnpikes have changed and it's sometimes hard to find the original roads. For any readers interested in learning more of this fascinating slice of Civil War history, and possibly seeing some of the battlegrounds for yourself, I highly recommend the little book *The First Campaign: A Guide to Civil War in the Mountains of West Virginia, 1861: Three One-Day Driving Tours*, by W. Hunter Lesser. It was a Godsend.

REFERENCES

WEBSITES

West Virginia Sesquicentennial Project, Child of the Rebellion
[http://www.wvculture.org/history/sesquicentennial/timeline.html]
Comment: Authoritative source of detailed information on forming the
State of West Virginia.

Making of America. Cornell University Library.
[http://ebooks.library.cornell.edu/m/moawar/waro.html]
Comment: Online searchable source of the Official Records of the Union
and Confederate Armies (OR).

National Park Service, The American Battlefield Protection Program
(*ABPP*) [https://www.nps.gov/ABPP/battles/wv005.htm]
Comment: Source of map showing route taken and deployment of Con-
federate force in Battle of Cheat Mountain.

BOOKS

BATTLES and LEADERS of the CIVIL WAR, Volume I, THE OPEN-
ING BATTLES, first published in 1887. Available from Castle, a division

of Book Sales, Inc. 114 Northfield Avenue, Post Office Box 7100, Edison, New Jersey 08818-7100.
Comment: This is a truly invaluable source of research information about the Civil War because the leaders of the War wrote the stories. The map of the Battle of Rich Mountain was taken from this volume and is contained in the story titled, *MCCLELLAN IN WEST VIRGINIA* written by Jacob D. Cox, Major-General, U.S.V. who fought in the Kanawha Valley under McClellan and Rosecrans.

HARD TACK AND COFFEE - A Classic Civil War Memoir, John D. Billings, first published in 1887, this edition published in 2014 by Endeavor Press, Kindle and Print Versions.
Comment: Firsthand source of information on the life of a soldier during the Civil War.

A DIARY FROM DIXIE, Mary Boykin Chesnut
Kindle and Print Versions.
Comment: A view of the Civil War from the point of view of a member of the Virginia aristocracy.

ARMS AND EQUIPMENT OF THE CIVIL WAR, Jack Coggins, Broadfoot Publishing Company, Civil War Books, 1907 Buena Vista Circle, Wilmington, North Carolina.
Comment: Detailed descriptions and drawings of equipment and weapons used in the Civil War.

THE CIVIL WAR IN WEST VIRGINIA - A Pictorial History, Stan Cohen, Pictorial Histories Publishing Company, 4103 Virginia Ave. SE, Charleston, West Virginia 25304
Comment: Sterling photo history of the war in West Virginia. This book first alerted me to the little known story of the formation of the State of West Virginia.

THE FIRST VERMONT CAVALRY IN THE CIVIL WAR - A History, Joseph D. Collea, Jr., Published by McFarland & Company, Inc., Box 611, Jefferson, North Carolina 28640

www.mcfarlandpub.com
Kindle and Print Versions available.
Comment: This regiment fought with the First West Virginia Cavalry.
The entire regiment rode Morgan horses.

The 1862 U.S. CAVALRY TACTICS - Instructions, Formations, Maneuvers, Philip St. Geo. Cooke, Originally published: Washington, DC: Government Printing Office, 1862. Published by Stockpile Books, 5067 Ritter Road, Mechanicsburg, Pennsylvania 17055 [www.stackpolebooks.com]
Comment: The book on cavalry tactics that AJ and Harry were looking for before they joined Kelley Lancers.

FREDERICK W. LANDER, The Great Natural American Soldier, Gary L. Ecelbarger, Louisiana State University Press, Baton Rouge.
Comment: Book about a fascinating individual and aggressive general. He arrested Colonel Anisansel of the First West Virginia Cavalry and was disliked by the Ringgold Cavalry.

ELWOOD'S STORIES of the OLD RINGGOLD CAVALRY - 1847–1865 - The First Three Year Cavalry of the Civil War, Sergeant John W. Elwood, Published by Author, Coal Center, Pennsylvania, 1914
Comment: Source of reams of information about the Ringgold Cavalry.

ALL QUIET ON THE BORDER - The Civil War Era in Greene County, Pennsylvania, D. Kent Fonner, Beach Lake, Pennsylvania
Kindle and Print Versions.
Comment: Good book about the politics during the Civil War. Greene County borders Virginia on the west and south and is next door to Fayette County, where Smithfield is located.

SHOWDOWN IN VIRGINIA - The 1861 Convention and the Fate of the Union, Edited by William W. Freehling and Craig M. Simpson, University of Virginia Press, Charlottesville and London, First published in 2010.
Kindle and Print Versions available.

Comment: Good source of speeches made at the Richmond Convention of State Delegates investigating whether or not to secede from the Union.

SKETCH OF THE LIFE OF BRIG. GEN. B. F. KELLEY - U.S. VOLUNTEERS, Major John B. Frothingham, Published by F. Drang & Company, 109 Washington Street, Boston, 1862.
Comment: Brief sketch of Benjamin Kelley who created the plan to capture Philippi and Porterfield's men. Important source of information, as it was written in 1862.

LEE'S INVASION OF NORTHWEST VIRGINIA IN 1861, Granville Davisson Hall, Press of the Mayer & Miller Company, 525 S. Dearborn Street, Chicago, Illinois, 1911
[https://archive.org/details/leesinvasionofno01hall]
Comment: The first detailed and critical review of the western Virginia campaign of 1861.

RETURN TO BULL RUN - The Campaign and Battle of Second Manassas, John J. Hennessy, University of Oklahoma Press, 2800 Venture Drive, Norman Oklahoma 73069
Print Version: www.oupress.com
Kindle and Print Versions available.
Comment: Source of information of role played by Brigadier General Buford and his first cavalry brigade.

LOYAL WEST VIRGINIA FROM 1861 TO 1865, Theodore F. Lang, The Deutsch Publishing Company, Baltimore, MD, 1895
[https://www.forgottenbooks.com/en/books/LoyalWestVirginia_100743
05]
Comment: Excellent source of information on the formation of West Virginia by a military officer who lived through the time and fought in many battles of the war in western Virginia. Contains detailed information on every West Virginia regiment.

THE FIRST CAMPAIGN: A Guide to Civil War in the Mountains of West Virginia, 1861: Three One-Day Driving Tours, W. Hunter Lesser,

Quarrier Press, 2011.
Comment: Essential guidebook if you want to follow in the footsteps of the generals during this first campaign of the War.

REBELS AT THE GATES, W. Hunter Lesser, Sourcebooks, Inc., P.O. Box 4410, Naperville, Illinois
[www.sourcebooks.com]
Comment: A masterful and well-researched account of the western Virginia campaign.

GENERAL JOHN BUFORD, A Military Biography, Edward G. Longacre, Da Capo Press, Perseus Book Group, 11 Cambridge Center, Cambridge, MA 02142
[http://www.dacapopress.com]
Comment: A detailed and well-researched book that explains the many contributions Buford made to the Union cavalry he loved.

THE SOLDIER OF INDIANA IN THE WAR FOR THE UNION, Catharine Merrill, Merrill and Company, 1866
https://archive.org/stream/soldierofindiana01merr#page/n7/mode/2up
Comment: This is the source of the map I use to show the deployment of Union troops and the location of Porterfield's camp just before the battle. Note the date this book was published.

LEE VS. McCLELLAN - The First Campaign, Clayton R. Newell, Regency Publishing, Inc., 422 First Street, SE, Washington, DC 20003
Comment: Another well-written book containing a thoroughly researched account of the western Virginia campaign.

"The Devil's to Pay" GEN. JOHN BUFORD, U.S.A, Michael Phipps & John S. Peterson, Farnsworth Military Impressions, 401 Baltimore Street, Gettysburg, PA 17325, 1995
Comment: A short but memorable book on General Buford's life.

The CIVIL WAR PAPERS of GEORGE B. McCLELLAN - Selected Correspondence 1860–1865, Edited by Stephen W. Sears, Da Capo Press, Perseus Book Group, 11 Cambridge Center, Cambridge, MA 02142
http://www.dacapopress.com
Comment: A glimpse into the brilliant and controversial mind of one of the most famous generals of the Civil War. Fascinating.

THE KILLER ANGELS - The classic novel of the Civil War, Michael Shaara, Ballantine Books Trade Paperback, New York
Kindle and Print Versions.
Comment: What more can be said about this engaging novel, turned into a great movie? As a budding novelist, I read it to learn techniques.

The UNION CAVALRY in the CIVIL WAR - Volume I From Fort Sumter to Gettysburg, Stephen Z. Starr, Louisiana State University Press, Baton Rouge.

The UNION CAVALRY in the CIVIL WAR - Volume II, The War in the East from Gettysburg to Appomattox 1863–1865, Stephen Z. Starr, Louisiana State University Press, Baton Rouge and London
Comment: By far, these two volumes are the best books to gain insight into the changing roles of Union and Confederate cavalry during the Civil War.

THE BALTIMORE and OHIO IN THE CIVIL WAR, Festus P. Summers, Stan Clark Military Books, Gettysburg, Pennsylvania
Comment: The subjects of the B&O Railroad and the Civil War go together. This book, based on Summers's doctoral thesis, explains why.

75385927R00236

Made in the USA
San Bernardino, CA
28 April 2018